ALSO BY ERICA ROSE EBERHART

Tarnished (Book One of the Elder Tree Trilogy)

Diminished (Book Two of the Elder Tree Trilogy)

VANQUISHED

VANQUISHED

THE ELDER TREE TRILOGY
BOOK THREE

ERICA ROSE EBERHART

Published in the United States by Creative James Media.

www.creativejamesmedia.com

978-1-965648-83-4 Trade Paperback

First U.S. Edition 2026

AUTHOR'S NOTE

Vanquished is high fantasy occurring during a war between nations. There is body horror, gore, and blood within these pages. This war shows escalating violence, and depicts a physical and mental battle with ideas of superior race; the action of genocide; imprisonment; physical and mental torture; death, murder, and execution; as well as the burning of people. There is also suicidal ideation, the showing and discussion of scars, PTSD, the grapple of grief and death of a loved one and parent, and mental health crises. If any of these subjects are triggering, please take care. Only you can judge what you are emotionally prepared to consume and your mental health is worth it. If this is not a topic you can handle right now, this book will always be here for when you are ready.

For those who cannot see the light:
may you push forward to bathe in its brightness
and know how important it is you remain.

PRONUNCIATION GUIDE

Many of the names of places and people are influenced from Gaelic, Scandinavian, German, and English pronunciations but some variances from those languages of our world may defer to the world of Visennore.

People
Ailith: *Ay-l-ith*
Caitriona: *Kah-tree-nah*
Greer: *Gh-rear*
Barden: *Bar-den*
Isla: *Eye-lah*
Kayl: *K-ale*
Cearny: *Kear-knee*
Róisín: *Ro-sheen*
Ceenear: *See-near*
Raum: *R-ah-mm*
Niveem: *Nive-ee-m*
Shad: *Ch-add*
Malcolm: *Mm-al-come*
Lachlan: *Lack-lan*
Vanora: *Vah-nore-ah*

Places
Visennore: *V-iss-en-nor*
Wimleigh: *Whim-lee*
Braewick: *Brr-aye-wick*
Ulla Syrmin: *Ooo-la Sear-min*
Invarlwen: *In-varl-when*
Mazgate: *Mah-zz-gate*
Avorkaz: *Ah-vore-kah-zz*
Beaslig: *Bees-ll-ig*
Caermythlin: *Care-myth-lynn*
Umberfend: *Uhm-burr-fend*
Ätbënas: *Hau-t-beh-nah-ss*

N
W
E
S
Ätbënas
NORTHERN WOOD
Mazgate Dominion
Avorkaz
THE BATTLEFIELDS
UMBERFEND
MARSH
BRAEWICK
VALLEY
Wimleigh Kingdom
Elder Tree
Braewick City

VISENNORE
Beaslig
Invarlwen
ENDLESS MOUNTAINS
ULLA SYRMIN
Caermythlin Ruins
Isla's House
Stormhaven
(Gil'dathon)

Within the reeds there is a story.
It wakes daily and shifts to memory as the sun reaches its climax,
to glow overhead and cast light upon the murky existence.
While cattails waver in radiance; their shadows stir remembrance of a
distant face
clouded by desperation, weighed by sorrow, and adorned by love.
The sun's focus drifts with the day and the face clarifies.
Abundant brilliance surrounds it and causes a yearning to touch,
yet it remains just out of reach.
By nightfall, the memory is forgotten as hunger reigns
and directs attendance to the water's edge where the reeds part
and the earth kisses the tawny fluid.
Its desires shift and its focus is to encourage creatures to draw near—close
enough to grasp.

CHAPTER ONE

CAITRIONA

aitriona nearly pulled the door from its hinges before stumbling into Ceenear's guest room, bringing with her a scent of desperation tinged with the honeyed taste of hope. A hand shot forward to grasp her arm and stopped her short from falling. She offered a half smile that didn't reach her eyes. Paul, her guard, nodded and closed the door, letting her proceed forward.

"Caitriona."

Her name was whispered, soft as feather fall, from her fae friend that looked on with wide eyes at a table centered in the room.

"Paul retrieved me as quick as he—" Caitriona stared at the table, the clarity of what was before her struck so hard it took her breath away. Ceenear waved her forward while Raum gripped the table's edge, his back bowed while he studied the familiar face constructed from the pebbles of Ceenear's speaking stone. Caitriona moved like a creature pushing through tide waters, her eyes locked on the table and growing blind to anything else.

She had been trying to cheer Crowley—the poor corvid

wasn't himself since Ailith and Fiana fell into the necklace—when Paul informed her the speaking stone was active. She left Crowley in her room cawing as if the bird knew there was a break in the silence. Two weeks, it was *two weeks* since Ailith and Fiana fell into the jewelry's embrace. Two weeks since Lachlan said the necklace was likely Kayl's holding cell, or something to transport the women far and away. A fortnight since Caitriona returned to Braewick and witnessed Barden's death. Not once did she give up on Ailith. Until Ailith's body was found, there was a chance she lived, and Caitriona clung to hope in all corners of the day and every recess of the night, cultivating it with utmost care so it could take root and grow into substance.

Two weeks gone, now finally, her face and her name on Caitriona's lips like a sigh of relief.

"Ailith."

The culmination of the past days burst in Caitriona's chest and she felt dizzy. Since Barden's murder and the enemy found within the valley, Caitriona was locked in the castle. "For your safety," Greer had said. Caitriona hated it. She wanted to return to the Elder Tree and leave a prayer for Ailith's return and Barden's loss.

Instead, each night, with only Crowley to witness from his perch, she whispered Ailith's name like a wish to stars, begging them to reunite the two. In her sleep, she wandered through dark and twisted woods in search of her. And in privacy, she wept over the final moments they shared on the outcrops of the valley: when Ailith did awful things due to the magic of the necklace's dark influence. Ailith's brown eyes had turned black as pitch, and the momentary recovery of Ailith's mind after they pulled the necklace from her throat was so brief before she vanished that it felt like the universe was taunting Caitriona. The memory tasted bitter now. She gained Ailith back, but only briefly before the guard fell into Kayl's pendant, along with Fiana.

Now she spoke, *alive*, and her voice made Caitriona's head spin.

They *assumed* Ailith and Fiana were with Malcolm. Caitriona asked Greer to retrieve Ailith, but the queen, overwhelmed by grief, refused any movement. For a fortnight, Greer claimed she had to consider how to move forward now that Barden was dead. But Caitriona wanted to move forward as well. She wanted to fly to the fae kingdom with her dragon wings and find Ailith, and Fiana, too. For every day Greer mourned Barden, it was a day Caitriona could have brought Ailith and Fiana home.

"We barely escaped." While the stone accurately depicted the appearance of the sender, it couldn't provide much detail beyond the general appearance. But Ailith's disheveled hair was knotted and hanging in her face, and her voice weak. "We thought Umberfend Marsh was safer than taking roads."

"Ailith," Caitriona repeated. She grasped the table's edge as the strength in her knees disappeared and she sunk to the floor. "You've escaped?"

"Cait?" The stone sighed, the image of Ailith's brow wrinkled. "Cait, I need your help, you need to come."

Ceenear grasped Caitriona, her fingers pressing against the sheen of scales that left Caitriona's shoulders with a permanent golden shimmer. The fae woman leaned forward and spoke softly, "Ailith and Fiana appeared in Invarlwen and were held captive by Malcolm and his followers. They escaped while being relocated to the dungeon. She and Fiana made it beyond the mist with the help of some fae."

"Have you seen Lumia at all?" Raum's voice had a note of desperation in its tone and Caitriona's heart clenched.

Ailith's sandy figure studied Raum for a moment, her face growing placid. "I'm sorry. I haven't."

Caitriona's breath stilled; a pit in her stomach growing heavy. With Invarlwen's King Malcolm declaring war on Wimleigh Queendom, it wasn't entirely odd that all Raum's messages to Lumia went unanswered, but that didn't remove the unease it brought. Even with the strength of the old crow witch, Isla, they were unable to reach the fae woman.

The pebble form of Ailith looked over her shoulder at something they couldn't see and the movement lodged Caitriona to the present.

"Listen, you need to come, but it isn't wise traveling with a large group. The men will spot you. I'm scared, Cait. I'm scared they'll find us and kill us. We're hiding in this broken little town in the swamp. Do you know where that is?"

Raum and Ceenear looked at Caitriona. She nodded. "More or less. I've never been there but I've drawn it onto enough maps—it's abandoned in the center of the marsh."

"We're moving westward. We'll meet you halfway, I hope. Please, please come. Be discreet. I don't want them to find us, Cait. We're injured and I don't know how much more we can—"

Ailith gasped, then screamed. A blood-curdling scream that shoved Caitriona into a memory she wished she could leave in the past.

The same scream that fell from Ailith's throat when Caitriona rained fire upon everything with nonexistent control and broke apart Kayl's home with her massive size. Her dragon was a creature of instinctual behavior back then, and it wanted to escape, so it breathed fire, but Ailith was in its path and was lost to the flame. And Caitriona, thrust into the arms of the curse she was placed under, was helpless and forced to endure Ailith's scream of pain while her body betrayed her for the skies and fire and blood.

Now, with Ailith's scream still ringing loudly in her ears, the speaking stone lost its sandy quality. Ailith's face vanished as the stone collapsed into a pile before gathering into its solid form.

"We have to go," Raum said. "We have to go to the marsh."

"We need to be wise about this," Ceenear cut in, turning toward the princess and looking sincere as her dark hands slipped into Caitriona's quivering grasp.

"Ceenear, Raum's right. We have to go. She said be discreet and I agree. If Malcolm's scouts are in the marsh, they're going to notice an army of guards moving through. It could be seen as a declaration of battle, and Greer's in no way prepared for one." Caitriona stepped back from the table as her hands freed from Ceenear's. She wouldn't admit it, but her stomach turned with unease. The last two weeks were free of attack or movements on Malcolm's behalf, and Caitriona prayed that continued until Greer returned to a better mindset to handle the ebbs and flows of ruling a kingdom. She wasn't there yet; losing Barden was too recent for her to have any semblance of normalcy. Caitriona wondered if she ever would.

Raum grabbed the speaking stone and shoved it into his pocket. "How quickly can we get there? It's barely morning."

Ceenear stepped between them, touching both of their shoulders. "We shouldn't just abscond from the castle. We *must* plan this out. The scouts can be dangerous."

"They haven't met dangerous," Caitriona muttered as fire flickered within her belly. Flame came easily since she accepted her dragon-half. "Ailith's hurt, Ceenear. We don't even know what's happened to Fiana. We need to go *quickly*. We can be there by late afternoon if we ride out immediately.

"Paul? Can you call to get the horses ready? Don't go into detail, just explain we're riding out for the day."

"Caitriona," Ceenear's tone was draped with warning as Paul inched toward the door, ready to obey Caitriona's request.

Caitriona looked at her fae friend whose brow wrinkled with concern. It was a dumb plan, but the only one they had. If Caitriona went to Greer, she'd deny they go, and Caitriona didn't want to put more weight on Greer's shoulders. They would be smart about this trip. Even though they remained within Wimleigh Queendom, there was a risk for enemy arrival. "Would it help if we took Paul with us and another guard as well?"

Ceenear pressed her lips together. "That'd be better. And leave a note too." We can't have the castle in a panic that you've disappeared."

It was clear she felt otherwise, but Caitriona wasn't willing to surpass this opportunity. Flashing a reassuring smile, she turned toward Paul who waited at the door.

"Call Coleene as well. She knows the marsh better than most."

Shortly after midday, they reached the remnants of Trasc, a town that stood before Caitriona's birth and fell not long after. Trasc was a ghost of former dwellings now only serving as places for carrion birds to roost and marsh plants to take hold.

Coleene, a royal guard most often serving within the castle walls, led the party forward with her hand grasping the hilt of her sword, recounting information about the marsh as she moved. "My mother and father were from here. They were courting when my grandparents moved my mother into Braewick City. My father's family remained until they were one of the last inhabitants," she explained. "When King Donal outlawed magic, this was the first town the decree fated to destruction. This is where guards were offered to the drowning dukes during funeral rights. Without the ability to properly give the bodies of our guards to the marsh with ceremony and worship of the dukes, or using gifts to defend ourselves from errant magic creatures, Trasc died out. The magic of the marsh choked it. The balance was off, and it was safer to move to the city. So over decades the town grew smaller, residents died or moved, until no one was left beside the structures we left behind."

"Are we safe here?" Raum asked. "Are the horses?"

They left the horses an hour prior, when the waters of the marsh made it too hard for the horses to proceed. The horses were happy, left by a tree with long leads to graze on marsh grass with a protective circle Ceenear cast keeping them safe, and now the small party moved on foot.

Coleene looked over her shoulder. "The horses are fine within the circle. Plus, most of the creatures here are less interested in animals. They thrive off humans, just like the dukes, and animals are a substitution meal."

"We should get out before sunset," Raum murmured.

The guard smiled. "You and Paul, certainly; the dukes tend to leave women alone. They'll leave you alone, too, so long as you don't touch the water."

Paul and Raum looked at one another and stepped closer to Caitriona and Ceenear.

Caitriona frowned at the sun's position. On foot, time passed fast yet their progress slowed as they cautiously followed old roads into the murky landscape's depths. If they hurried and found Ailith and Fiana without much issue, they could get back to Braewick before the next morning, reserving their travel for most of the night hours. Dangerous, considering the dukes were active at night, but being found by Greer was a type of danger Caitriona wanted to avoid.

She left a note addressed to her mother prior to riding out, knowing full well that her mother often visited Caitriona's room—whether or not she was there—to ensure all was right and tidy.

They slipped from the castle quickly that morning and Caitriona hoped her mother would handle the news of their venture well and delicately tell Greer. Whatever binding Greer used to focus under the weight and expectations as heir—now queen—severed when Barden died. She no longer slept, unless in fitful bursts and often in Caitriona's bed. Hopefully that night Greer wouldn't knock on her door. Hopefully, they'd return to the castle unscathed and successful.

You can never be too safe when there's a war afoot, she thought as she scanned her surroundings.

Caitriona's steady determination kept things afloat. She attended meetings and checked weapon-making progress. She attempted to understand old war logs and better equip herself in knowing what type of decisions she was expected to make. But the fact remained that prior to the curse, she was pushed away from royal information, made to be a ghost in her own home, and now it fell on top of her at such rapid speed she knew little of what to do.

But this was her expectation as heir, and she reserved her own grief for quiet moments in solitude. It was there she wept for Barden, who was like a brother to her, as well as for Ailith and Fiana. But for the two women, there was always hope to finally have them back.

"What else is here besides dukes?" Caitriona asked, looking at a broken signpost along the overgrown, ancient road they walked down.

"Marrow maidens, caroling countesses, sometimes dryads, and occasional will-o-wisps," Coleene ticked off. "Water creatures, mainly."

She drew to a stop and the others paused. Coleene was well-versed in the marshes not only due to her heritage, but because she buried her own husband within its waters.

Dwayne, another royal guard, was the first killed by the Elder Tree sap-dipped arrows the fae archer launched at Greer's party. His death was quicker than Barden's, nearly instantaneous, and it was what Coleene said brought her the most comfort. She and her relatives returned to Trasc for the burial, rather than leaving him to the water's edge closer to the valley as Caitriona and Greer did for Barden, and upon her return she continued working at the castle. She explained her return to duties was what her husband would want, particularly in this time of uncertainty. What was Caitriona to do but agree? She had no right to determine what a grieving person needed, even if she didn't understand what brought comfort.

Caitriona wasn't sure bringing the guard to the marsh so shortly after her husband's funeral was wise, but Coleene jumped at the opportunity. Now, however, there was a quiver to the guard's lip as she studied a larger pond beside the destroyed town. The ground had fresh footprints pressed into the soft soil. Scattered amongst the reeds were bog berries and flowers that seemed to have just fallen. "This is where we carried my husband's body."

"I'm sorry." Caitriona placed her hand on Coleene's shoulder. She straightened her back and swallowed.

"It's where I want to be placed when my time comes. Just so you know. Things can be unpredictable in war."

Caitriona nodded.

Coleene straightened her ponytail, the silver streaks in her otherwise dark hair shone in the sunlight like a metallic pairing to Caitriona's gold. She flashed a smile that didn't reach her eyes and looked at the remnants of the town. "Let's find Ailith, aye?"

The few structures still standing had missing walls, ceilings or both. Water crept to their edges, lapping at the footing of crumbling foundation and empty doorways. The group moved silently as they checked each building, but there was no sight of Fiana or Ailith. All structures were hollow and void of life.

"Are there other villages like this?" Raum stepped out of another building. "Other places they could've meant?"

"The remnants of Trasc extend some way," Coleene replied as she ducked her head into another open doorway and scanned the empty shadow of the home before stepping out. "So, it could be in any of the buildings, but this is the only village within the marsh. There's others along the edges."

"No ..." Caitriona shook her head and continued down the overgrown road. "Ailith indicated they were in the marsh itself, so I don't think it's any of those other towns."

As they moved, the buildings grew less while the marsh water expanded, and Caitriona's hope turned into something different, like a twist in the gut and a flicker of concern heavy like lead. Could they be wrong? Perhaps the women were caught. The memory of Ailith's scream, a sound too easy to bring to mind, echoed in Caitriona's head. She closed her eyes and pressed her fingers to her temple.

"Look," Paul breathed. All turned their attention to the guard. His hand extended toward footsteps in the soft earth leading away from them. Two sets of footsteps that approached from the east and curved along pools of standing water toward a lonely building with a skinny swamp tree growing from its center.

Their feet sunk into ankle-deep mud as they moved forward and exchanged looks. Paul and Coleene drew their blades and disappeared into the dim light of the broken building, the only sound their steps in the patchy water that gathered on the floorboards. They didn't remain within for long before they appeared at the doorway.

"It's empty." Coleene sighed as she and Paul exited with a sour expression on her face. Coleene shrugged and waved toward the building with an air of annoyance. "It's just dust and water. Whoever walked in there must've climbed out a window and continued on."

Caitriona's shoulders dropped. Raum rolled his head to one side and squeezed his eyes shut. But the air was odd, not only filled with the taste of disappointment, but electrified with danger. Caitriona turned on her heel, scanning the landscape and licking her lips when Coleene gasped and fell backward. A shard of ice skimmed along her temple, springing forth red crimson, and nearly struck her eye.

From the shadow of marsh weeds, falling into the light with a gush of air and dust solidifying into flesh, five fae appeared. They spread outward; each gripped knives or pointed arrows at the group. Another dagger-like icicle shot forward from a sixth fae standing the furthest back. They kept their hands up as moist summer air glimmered and shifted into cold frost before hardening to ice. Caitriona rotated her wrist and spread her fingers, calling forth the flames that lived eternal in her core, and shocked the icicle as it came toward them. It shattered and hit as a spray of water.

"They surrounded us!" Paul hissed, following Coleene to Catriona's side. They drew their swords and lifted their shields, ready to protect the heir as if she were helpless.

Caitriona grasped their shoulders and pulled them from further shards of ice with an animal-like cry. Icicles brushed over her skin but melted on impact, and didn't leave a scratch. Dragons barely experienced the cold, and it seemed Caitriona adopted that ability from her dragon self.

Raum and Ceenear's blades flashed as they moved toward the rush of fae.

"*Backstabber*, you betray your kind," a fae with tan skin hissed as his sword greeted Raum's.

"You've sided with Malcolm?" Raum replied. His sword caught the sunlight and the ring of metal kissing metal rippled over the marsh. "You betray the very thing we strive for. We're *peaceful*." He blocked another wide swing from the man. "At least until Malcolm stole the crown."

Beyond, the form of a red-headed fae rippled; his body shimmered before winking from sight. The air vibrated where his body stood—shimmering magic Caitriona saw from another gift from her dragon self. *A gift from a curse,* Caitriona thought with dry humor, as she watched the vibration move toward Ceenear.

Caitriona gathered fire into her hands, the flicker of heat made from her mind, and launched it forward in a stream similar to how she killed the shades that attacked Ailith years prior. But back then it was accidental; an uncontrolled blast of chaos and destruction that left her shaking and crying. Now she was conscious of the effort and directed the blaze to strike the invisible fae, snapping him back into view. He stumbled backward, the fire overwhelming him before he fell into the water. Turning slowly, Caitriona redirected the flames toward the ice-making fae, thrusting her backward and making her a smoking corpse.

In the back of Caitriona's mind, she panicked. She never killed someone before, but she couldn't fall to pieces over this now. The fae wouldn't hesitate to kill her if it was the other way around and there were others who had the same mindset.

"Two down." Caitriona's voice quaked as she looked around with shaking hands. The fae who could vanish from sight still lay in the water unmoving.

Raum and Coleene successfully dispatched another a few yards away—only three remained.

"Don't kill them all!" Caitriona shouted, rushing forward as Ceenear dragged her dagger across the throat of another. Two left. "We need to keep someone alive!"

"Cait!"

Like ice water poured down her spine, Ailith's voice came

suddenly amongst the fray and Caitriona's body grew stiff. She spun on her heel, heart pressing against her ribs and ready to explode. *Where is she?*

Ailith stumbled out of the marshy water. Her wet hair hung against her face as she lurched forward with an arm tight around her torso; her hand held fast to her side, partially obscured by her shirt as if holding back an injury. The sight felt like an icicle pricked Caitriona's heart.

"Ailith!" Caitriona's feet slipped in the mud and her arms swung outward to catch herself.

"Caitriona!"

A part of Caitriona registered Ceenear yelling her name. She shouted over and over—"Caitriona, stop!"—but it was *Ailith*. There and whole and nearly in her arms, nearly *with* her.

Ailith reached with one hand, ready to receive Caitriona's embrace.

"Ailith, finally!" Caitriona's face was hot with her tears, her hands held outward to accept Ailith against her. Two weeks she was gone but now she was just out of reach.

Ailith lurched backward as Caitriona's hands hovered before her, the guard only feet away from the heir. A gasp escaped Ailith's lips, her brown eyes grew wide and she blinked once, twice, before stumbling backwards on uncontrollable feet as an arrow protruded from between her eyes.

Ailith MacCree collapsed into the water and Caitriona screamed.

"Caitriona, it isn't her!" Ceenear's voice grew close. The fae woman came to Caitriona's side, her braids swinging over her shoulder as she dropped her bow and caught Caitriona as her knees went out.

"You shot her?" Caitriona bucked against the fae's hold. Thrashing out of Ceenear's grasp, she hurtled herself forward, her knees sinking into the wet ground as her hands clawed at the tall grass. Tears rushed down her cheeks as she attempted to reach Ailith who lay motionless in the water with the arrow still protruding like a deadly reed.

Ceenear scrambled forward and grasped Caitriona's arm, spinning her to hold Caitriona's face and force her to stare into the depths of Ceenear's gaze.

"It. Isn't. Her."

She let go of Caitriona and stood. Ceenear's lips were flat and her dark eyes held waves of emotion despite her blank features. "See for yourself. It isn't her. I didn't kill Ailith. It was a trick."

She grabbed her bow and turned back to the group, walking away from Caitriona without another word.

Shuddering, Caitriona turned to the water and climbed to her feet with legs that threatened to give out. Her stomach lodged into her throat as she splashed into the shallow pool, uncaring of drowning dukes or caroling countesses. Her ribcage shook as she sobbed. Her hands, covered in mud and bits of grass, took Ailith's arm and pulled her close. But Ailith's angular face didn't appear; her brown, shoulder-length hair didn't fan out in the water. Instead, it was a fae woman. Pale skin like moonlight, black hair as dark as Ceenear's entwined with the reeds, and her thin lips parted with a final breath already passed as her unseeing eyes looked to the sky. The hand Caitriona clutched was limp with a large birthmark covering it.

Caitriona dropped the woman's hand and stumbled back. It wasn't her. It wasn't Ailith.

But it *was*. For a moment it was and Caitriona wasn't certain she would ever be able to recover from that horror.

CHAPTER TWO

"You're going to have to wake, Ailith MacCree."

"I *am* awake." Ailith opened her eyes and stared at the tree limbs overhead. The leaves stirred in the summer breeze and sunlight was dappled through the foliage. "Just resting my eyes, *per your request*. You're the one who said we needed a break, remember? *You* said I've been training too hard."

"This is different. Our break is over."

Ailith rolled to her side and curled her hand under her chin. She was on a rock ledge hanging over the pool the caroling countess had made her home in a few years prior. It was a perfect glade with a pond dotted in lily pads and bordered by cattails. But rather than finding a countess in the center of the water, it was Barden swimming in his pants while the rest of his clothing sat discarded on the shore beside most of Ailith's. She already swam in the chilly waters before climbing onto the rock to doze in the butter-yellow sunlight. They practiced hours every day to train her left arm while her right healed from the burns she received when Caitriona was cursed, and it was Barden's idea to take a break and come to the pool, not hers. He said she needed the break, and he was right; she wasn't about to give it up now.

Yet the edge of her vision wrinkled, and Barden gave her such an intense look she couldn't ignore him anymore. Ailith felt flush with nerves by his look and discomfort leaked through her body. "You're being strange. Did I say something wrong? Sometimes I say things without realizing how they sound."

He tread water and didn't immediately reply. Looking down at him, his auburn hair darkened by the pond, his blue eyes shone bright, and he looked as much a part of the water as a creature born from it. But his face was stern in a way Ailith learned meant he wanted to be understood. Rolling fully onto her belly and placing both hands under her chin, she was all ears.

"The only reason I'm here right now is because it's daytime. I can drift amongst the reeds, I can hear beyond the mist, and I don't believe there's much time."

Ailith pushed upward to rest on her knees. Placing her hands on her hips, she scowled down at the elder guard.

He laid back to float as he looked at the sky. His naked chest sparkled with water and his hair fanned out around his head. "You know, despite the watch towers on the edge of the valley, magic's a fluid thing that can slip in and out. Look at the caroling countess who was caught here. There was that cockatrice a few years ago, too. You and Caitriona even got out of the valley without being seen. We tried our best to prevent anyone from sneaking in, but we had it wrong, because the tower guards were ultimately looking for people, not creatures or magic which can go unseen. But perhaps there's another way in. Maybe magic can just do that, slip in and be everywhere. It's funny; danger can come from tooth and claw, or magic or arrow."

"Have you been drinking? Liquor isn't on your breath.

Did you bring some with you? Will you share?" Ailith twisted, looking amongst the brush and bushes by Barden's discarded boots and shirt. With Barden, things were easy. Ailith could joke and ask questions. She could drop the mask and be herself without ridicule. Barden never seemed upset by her tone or need to understand the specifics of a situation. He never judged her. The only other person she was this relaxed with was Caitriona. "You have a beautiful brain," Barden often commented and Ailith knew he meant it. She adored their relationship more than she was capable of admitting, but this was strange, and it made her nervous. He didn't speak in riddles like this. He didn't try to purposefully confuse her. It made her check herself, her behavior, and worry bloomed in her chest that she offended him.

"Ailith, *listen* to me."

"Shit!" Ailith hissed as she turned to find Barden standing beside her on the rock with dry clothes already on his dry body. He squatted in front of her, inches away, and met her eye-to-eye. Ailith's breathing was heavy, her chest rising and falling from the scare, and she jumped when Barden reached for her right hand. She tensed, expecting discomfort from the burns on her arm, but found none. Her arm was smooth, the burns gone. A dream. This was a dream.

Her stomach dropped as understanding rushed over her and twinged her nerves. This was a dream of the day they spent together at the pool, and yet it was twisting into something else. Unease filled her like rapidly rising water crawling up her throat and threatening to fill her mouth. This was a favorite memory she had with Barden, and she didn't want a dream to discolor it with discomfort and the sense of something else.

"What?" Ailith whispered, looking back at Barden. "What do you have to say?"

"Use your smarts. You'll figure this out. Trust yourself and your gut. But you need to act quickly, alright?" He dropped her hand and stood at his full height as his attention turned to the tree line. "I better not see you until you're old and gray."

Ailith wrinkled her nose, the idea ridiculous and funny, but also confusing. "Okay, Barden." She rolled her eyes and gave a short, forced laugh. She wanted them to return to joking and laughing, not this seriousness that hinted danger.

"And if you see Greer, please tell her to not let it consume her?" He continued staring at the horizon, but something was changing. His skin lost color and grayed to a green hue. A sheen covered his blue eyes, making them dull. The side of his neck split to expose three individual lines like an invisible knife had sliced across his skin, but no blood leaked out. They moved, the flaps of skin rising and falling with a desperation as if seeking something it couldn't obtain. It happened so fast, Ailith gasped and fell backwards.

"Barden, you're—"

He turned his attention back to Ailith and parted his gray lips to expose a mouth filled with rows of fanged teeth. In the sunlight, his skin gleamed damp and slick from pond scum. Black veins spread over his shoulder and up his neck to complete his change to a nightmare in flesh.

"Tell her—" His voice was thick with moisture as if he was drowning as he spoke and his breath smelled of duckweed, a mixture of stagnant pond water, and soil. "I tried to reach her light and I'll wait an eternity for her sun. But for now, Ailith MacCree, snap out of this and wake up."

"What?"

He grimaced, his sharp teeth gnashing and ready to bite as he lunged forward. He grasped Ailith's shoulders as she toppled backwards. His strength could snap bone, his nails lengthened and sharpened as they dug into the flesh of her shoulders but only spread apart just so as webbing formed between each digit. Water dripped from his mouth and hair, his clothing sodden, and he snarled into her face, "I said *wake up.*"

Ailith woke.

The light through the windows was blinding, but after blinking repeatedly, her vision cleared. Lines of stone clarified before she registered the cold from her face pressed to the stone floor. She jolted further into the waking world.

"Ailith?" Caitriona's voice was like spring sunshine and a song of violets as it drifted from beyond the room. It felt like centuries since Caitriona last called for her.

"Cait?" Her tone was nothing sweet. It was like paper, crisp and flat. Her throat felt raw and her mouth dry. Lifting her face, she studied the room. It was a private cell with a chair in the center and iron buckles nailed into the arms. She pushed herself up and tried to get to her feet, but her legs wobbled, and dizziness sent her slumping down. Where was this empty, cold room and how long had she been in it?

A heavy door swung open, sending Ailith inching backwards, and Caitriona stepped in. "Cait," Ailith breathed, immediately undoing her backward progress to pull herself forward as her hands reached for the half-dragon princess.

Caitriona knelt before Ailith, her dress something the fae would wear, her gold hair loose around her torso and what light came through the windows winked on the golden scales on her shoulders. She rested her hands on her knees and one had a dark mark across it that was unusual and new.

Ailith stretched. She was so close to touching her that the space physically hurt. "Why are you here?"

"*Oh,*" Caitriona purred, not making any effort to draw close, "Look at the hope in your eyes."

Caitriona took a deep breath, her lips drawing into a smile, and closed her eyes. Sighing, her skin shivered before the vision fell away and in her place was the pale face of a fae woman with straight, black hair. She opened her eyes, and they were a startling blue while the mark on her hand remained.

Ailith pulled her back as if burned, her mind sluggish to understand what she witnessed. The once-Caitriona brushed her dark hair behind her ear. "Good girl, you've given me what I need."

She left Ailith on the floor with her jaw hanging; nerves tingling across her cheeks and down her neck.

"Cait ..." A whine of desperation leaked out. A small part of Ailith's brain was frustrated by how pathetic her voice was. But she didn't have the energy to fight. She was tired, her body sore and weak, and she couldn't remember how she got there. She couldn't remember much of anything. Only that she felt the loss of Caitriona all over again.

"Enough of that now." The dark-haired woman's thin smile stilled as she looked down her nose at Ailith. "I don't need you anymore. Not for now at least. Guards?"

She backed from the room, holding the door open for the apparent guards to move in.

They don't even fear I'll rush from the room. They know I'm weak. They know I can't get up. How long have I been here?

The woman watched Ailith as another entered with fae men closely following. Ailith tilted her head, trying to see who the newcomer was, but her vision swam.

Her organs rioted and twisted with unease that rapidly grew to ignite her nerves. Her body froze, her skin pricked with sweat, and the maw of terror rose from the center of her being. Terror, the worst she ever experienced. So much more than the fear the day the dragon attacked Braewick. So much more than seeing her hometown smoldering and dust-covered, or the terror when she killed a person for the first time; worse than seeing Caitriona twisting into a dragon and she could do nothing to help.

It was a terror itching up her throat, sinking into her

spine, and flushing through her body with bitter cold that made her gasp. Her back curled, her knees moved toward her chest, and she wrapped her arms around her legs. Burying her face against her knees, Ailith clamped her eyes closed. Every hair on her skin stood on end, her senses rioting with sensitivity, her terror a thing filling the room and spilling forth into halls she didn't know.

Hide, hide, hide; a constant scream in her mind, raw from shouting and broken with sobs; the consuming desire to flee, to run, to escape. But everything was an abundance of terror that locked her body in place as she attempted to become as small as possible. Better to turn into nothing, to seep into the stone floor, than to face this horror.

When hands touched Ailith, her screams renewed. She batted the hands away while attempting to curl further into herself. She didn't know where this terror came from, only that it was there. This beast that swallowed her whole, chewed her senses, and ingested her mind.

The first lessons of guard training were in the moment a threat appeared, you didn't ask how it arrived—you preserved yourself—and that was all Ailith could do. Caitriona was a distant memory as Ailith was lifted, her body weightless, while her tears burned her cheeks. She tried to escape to the protection of her mind and the blissful retreat of unconsciousness. She sought the swimming hole. The place where she relaxed, where she spoke to Barden plainly and the sun was a bright spot to keep her warm and happy. But the pond was empty, and Barden was gone.

CHAPTER THREE

GREER

The world existed in prisms of watery light, cushioned by the underwater muffle of existence, and it was there Greer hoped to find him. It was the only way of knowing she still lived, because despite her attempts, he couldn't be found. Not in the way she hoped. He didn't exist there anymore, not in the physical world or in dreams. Instead, he resided in pools of water in the marsh beyond the valley, and it was a pain with every passing moment that she could not join him. That was how she knew she was alive, because life hurt and death was surely more pleasant.

Time was an odd construct and with grief, it wasn't linear. It jolted her into reality and dragged her along the way as an unwilling guest. She didn't remember the spaces in-between, and moments were either softened around the edge, or sharp and brittle.

Her mother's arrival at her door was hazy at best. Yet the letter in her hand from Caitriona, detailing how she left the castle that morning to seek Ailith in the marsh, was something that shoved Greer into reality and placed the queen of Wimleigh Queendom firmly on the ground. She passed the numerous days prior in a driftless way with nothing to focus on, because nothing gave any true jolt to her nervous system, but this—her sister sneaking away into a dangerous situation —was enough. Caitriona was always enough.

She and what remained of her guard left the castle immediately; it was the quickest action she performed in weeks and one that was so normal it hurt because none of it was normal. She was trailing after her absconding sister, and she didn't have Barden by her side. There still was no clear answer as to who commanded them other than Greer herself. It was a job she despised. The role was Barden's, he was meant to keep the men in line and focused on their task to protect Greer so she could attend her birthright: guiding a queendom, vouching for her sister, preparing for a war, and so on and so on. A task she let slip in recent days.

There were guards eager to replace him, so long as she sat and made the decision as to who received the honor, but she hated it was something she had to do in the first place. So, she simply refused. She hadn't any need for her personal guard if she wasn't going anywhere. At least, not until that day when she left the castle for the first time since Barden's funeral.

"She's certainly taking precautions," Lachlan's voice nestled into her ear and broke through her stubborn thoughts of head guards and unrelenting sisters.

Greer drew her attention to the young half-fae prince riding beside her. She didn't know who told him to go with her, probably her mother, but he was there all the same. She generally avoided him since his arrival. Seeing his pale skin and worldly eyes pushed her back to the day his hands were covered in Barden's blood and his gaze filled with sympathy.

"If she were taking precautions, she wouldn't have left in the first place. She knew this was dangerous, otherwise there wouldn't have been a letter for my mother to find."

They rode from the city, her remaining queen's guards

staying too close, taking her safety too literally or attempting to show off their skills, maybe even both, and Greer closed her eyes wishing for patience. Barden gave her space; these men didn't understand.

At least their insistence to cluster near her flushed Lachlan to the middle of the line and silenced his reasoning.

Once free of Braewick's congestion, they moved through the afternoon as fast as their horses allowed toward what roads remained of the old town of Trasc. As the pathways sunk into the waters and narrowed, they spotted a small camp with horses and one telltale sign that they found who they sought. Caitriona's horns gleamed in the late afternoon light, and the sun reflected off her golden hair as she stood in the center of the group.

After reading Caitriona's letter, Greer was worried for her sister, but now seeing her standing amidst her friends unharmed, there was only room for anger.

"I ask solely because your mother encouraged I do so," Lachlan's voice eased through her red-hot rage with the confirmation Róisín *was* the one who sent Lachlan along. "But what do you intend to do?"

"You're about to find out." Greer slipped from her horse, leaving its reins hanging for someone to grasp. Eyeing her guards, she raised her chin. "Stay here."

She marched straight down the pathway toward the camp. If Greer were honest, she didn't know what she intended to do. She was acting on pure emotion and allowing that to guide her.

Rage was an easy emotion to accompany her sadness. It seemed there was nothing else she was capable of beyond that; joy, excitement, and happiness were emotions meant for another person. Another Greer. The one who died when Barden did. This Greer didn't deserve any of that. This Greer only existed with the expectations placed upon her from birth and the empty gut of someone whose heart was made hollow.

She pushed her hair back as wisps clung to her brow from riding in the late summer heat, and bugs hummed as evening drew close. Ahead, the dukes stirred in the water and the glow of their eyes winked, reflecting the late sunlight as they watched the party standing around a man bound in rope. Her gaze flicked repeatedly at the dukes in the water, her throat clenching as she looked for the curve of a familiar cheek and gaze that once brought comfort, but found none.

Greer's footfall slowed; this was the last place she wanted to be. Her very existence in the marsh was like nails digging into the flesh of her neck, clawing her to stringed bits one swipe after the next as pain swelled with each step.

As she drew close, the group became more distinct. Ceenear and Raum, the two fae who befriended Caitriona and were aligned with Greer's fight to keep Malcolm—the unwanted king of their land—from taking over the entire continent, stood together. But there was also a pair of royal guards, Paul and Coleene. Greer's cheeks grew hot with embarrassment at the sight of Coleene. Her husband, Dwayne, was first to die in the woods beyond the Elder Tree, and Greer barely gave her condolences afterward because she was too focused on Barden. Now she was forced to face his wife. But first, there was her little sister.

Caitriona stared, hands clasped together as she remained motionless and waited for Greer's approach. But Greer pushed past instead and stopped before the bound fae man who sat with a gag in his mouth on the ground.

"Who is he?" she asked the air, expecting someone, *anyone*, to respond.

"A fae guard," Ceenear replied. "He and a group of five fae attacked us. We dispatched the others."

"You're certain this is all who's left?" Greer turned on her heel and stared at the small group. Lachlan frowned as he drew closer, having left his horse with the guards. He exchanged uneasy glances with everyone before pausing on the outer circle of the group and turning his attention back to her. Paul and Coleene kept their eyes lowered, and as Greer's gaze passed over her fae guests, they looked to the grass as well. Caitriona was the only other person who met her eyes as if to challenge her. Despite that her brows were furrowed with concern; Greer couldn't help but interpret Caitriona's stance as calculated.

"There's no one else." Caitriona always spoke quietly, but the softness of her voice this time was greater than usual and with intention. Perhaps it was weighed down with shame, but Greer doubted it. If she was shameful, she would have acted differently and immediately pleaded for forgiveness. At least that's how Caitriona used to be. "We were going to question him."

"First, I want to understand what happened. Mother brought me your letter. Going to the marsh in search of Ailith, doing so without letting the guards know, or my permission—"

"Ree, she encouraged us to be discreet. She didn't want to get caught."

"Why the hell would Ailith encourage you to be discreet? She's your guard, she's always shown an abundance of caution when it comes to your safety. Why would she throw it out the window now? She's made it clear your life comes first over hers."

Caitriona bit her lip, a tell she had since childhood whenever she did something wrong. A rush of pleasure passed over Greer from her sister's reaction, although it was a brief sensation—there and gone—as Caitriona shifted on her feet and Greer nearly tasted her guilt.

"What are you keeping from me?"

Caitriona looked at the ground and Greer squeezed her eyes closed, worried she'd snap if she continued to view her sister. "Someone *answer me*."

"It was a trap," Raum admitted, and a ripple of unease rolled through the group. "There was a fae who appeared like Ailith. She could turn into people and steal their voices."

"Did you know her?"

Everyone flinched at Greer's tone, and she felt no remorse. Ceenear looked up and nodded and her dark eyes met Greer's without hesitating. "I did. We trained together years ago. She had a similar magic to me: she could change her appearance and voice, but the difference was that she only became those she encountered, and she could never remove the birthmark she had on her hand."

Caitriona looked at Ceenear, her brow wrinkled. "That's why you killed her?"

"I saw the mark. She was trying to conceal it, but I saw it."

"So Ailith wasn't even here, hmm?" They turned to Greer, all perfect pictures of failure beside Lachlan who stood amongst them with the same expression of discomfort he wore when she met him in the woods. Witnessing that expression was like a punch to her gut and Greer's hands turned to fists. "You left the castle, traveled to the marshes, did so without sufficient *protection* in these times, all for some fae to pretend to be Ailith—"

"Ree, I'm sorry."

"Ah, there it is." Greer pointed at the gagged fae. "And you were planning to question this one, and then what? Drag him back to the castle so he could endanger me? Mother? What was your plan, Caitriona?"

"We thought he'd provide insight. We found him carrying a talisman to transport from one place to another." Caitriona nodded to Ceenear, who plunged her hand into her pocket and withdrew a small gold disc. She offered it to Greer who waved it away and took a step back. Ceenear's hand dropped as Caitriona continued. "We hoped we'd find out what actually happened to Ailith. If that fae woman was able to turn into Ailith, it means she was with her."

"Can the talisman suck any of you in like that necklace did to Ailith and the hunter? Are we standing here with a magical item that can be used against us at any moment?"

Ceenear shook her head. "These are incredibly rare. Few are made and they're specifically for the person who wields it."

Greer snapped her head in Lachlan's direction and the half-fae's brows rose. His head bobbed up and down. "She's right. I recognize it. They aren't very well known and a lot goes into their creation. But they're made specifically for the person who possesses it and it can't be just given to another. If the owner dies, it stops working."

Ceenear's gaze flicked between Lachlan and Greer as she continued, her tone even and cautious. "We may trace the location to where it last was used. That can give us an indication of where Ailith is, or where these fae came from."

"No." Greer stared at each person before her, her jaw clenched as she looked at their guilty expressions. "We aren't going to do any of that. We know where she's at; she's with Malcolm, that's all but confirmed by Lachlan isn't it? He recognized the necklace Ailith fell into, and Kayl's been reportedly seen within Invarlwen. And finding *one guard* is not our priority right now. We'll destroy it when we return to the castle. It *can* be destroyed, can't it?"

Caitriona's jaw dropped and she blinked rapidly as if Greer slapped her. Her eyes released a slight glow and her hands formed fists as she bit her bottom lip and turned on her heel to look at the water. Greer hadn't meant to hurt her sister's feelings with such bluntness but she was too angry to be considerate. *Good, let her pout.*

Ceenear slowly nodded then returned to looking at the ground.

Greer shifted her attention to the fae man sitting beside her. He glared and maintained eye contact without flinching, and his determination reminded her of the man that killed Barden. At his back was the marsh with dukes gathering close, tempted by the proximity of the male on the shore of their home. She stared at their faces peeking from the water as they shifted back and forth, making slurping sounds in their language. None of the men looked familiar. None had Barden's hair.

Greer's entire core quivered from a quake of rage. It was because of fae who supported Malcolm that Barden was dead. One snuck into the queendom and shot him with those deadly, Elder Tree sap-dipped arrows, and he faded away in her arms. It was a man just like the one bound at her feet who did it, who sentenced Barden to become a drowning duke, and her to being alone.

"All he'll give are lies." Greer's voice was distant, as if it came from someone else's mouth. She watched the dukes shift and their eyes flicking from her to the man. "He'll tell you what you want to hear, or anything to keep himself alive longer, whichever. Malcolm's an idiot, but he's intelligent enough to send people in small parties who are expendable. People he doesn't care to have survive. People he won't miss."

Greer twisted, the motion fluid as her hand grasped the hilt of her sword and cleanly drew it outward. As she moved, the momentum brought her arm back before she thrusted forward and quickly plunged the blade into the fae man's chest. He choked against the gag, his body stuck by the expanse of the sword, and distantly Greer heard Caitriona's gasp.

"We don't need to have any more threats in the queendom." It was a whisper perhaps no one heard, but Greer couldn't stir enough feeling to care. Pressing her foot against the man's chest, she pulled her sword free and stepped back as he slumped into the pool of water. There was a shrill cry from the dukes and water splashed. The man, bound still and bleeding out, made weakened movements to get out of the water but it was pointless.

The dukes had him and Greer watched. *Let them feast.*

"YOU ARE NOT TO LEAVE THE CASTLE," GREER READ from a hastily written paper, "Unless under my expressed permission. You'll attend any meetings I've determined are essential for your presence beginning tomorrow."

She looked up to find Caitriona glowering from her chair like a petulant teenager.

"What about the MacCrees?"

Greer lowered the paper to her desk. "What about them?"

"I visit them every other day."

"They don't live within the castle, so no." Greer lifted her paper, but Caitriona's hands gripped the arms of her chair and there was a distinct crack of wood. Greer raised her eyes and carefully kept her face blank. Caitriona's eyes glimmered with soft, buttery-yellow light and her nails looked longer, like claws.

"I. Promised. Ailith." Each word was emphasized by her barely withheld anger. Caitriona took in a slow breath and let it out, and her eyes lost their glow. "When we were looking for Kayl, before the curse took hold, she was frightened she wouldn't be able to come back to her family. I promised her I would visit them; that I'd make sure her parents were alright."

Greer held Caitriona's gaze; her mind sluggish as she turned over the information. After they returned to the castle late the previous night, she was unable to rest. Her exhaustion caught up to her and weighed down her mind. Was it too much to give her sister this? Was she unfair to keep her from the one tie to Ailith that she had?

"For the rest of this week, you can't visit them. But after that, you may visit twice a week with guard supervision—guards of *my* choosing."

Caitriona slumped into her seat but remained silent.

This brought her attention to Paul and Coleene who stood behind Caitriona. She glanced at the paper again. "For you two, you'll not serve as guards within the castle any longer. I'm stationing you both to the castle walls; your shifts will be there—"

"That's not fair." Caitriona sat upright. "I commanded Paul and Coleene go with me to the marsh. They were listening to my orders."

"They're still being removed. Perhaps it won't be permanent, I'll give them that."

Caitriona sucked in a breath, her jaw setting as she met Greer's blank stare. Her eyes narrowed, the gold hue of her irises more dangerous than before, but Greer didn't back down.

"Ceenear and Raum," Greer continued, looking to the fae who sat at each side of Caitriona. "You're not my staff, nor my subjects, and I cannot do anything to show my displeasure that you went to the marsh. I mean, I *could*, but that isn't the type of rule I'd like to have. But I *will* give you this warning: do anything like this again and I'll send you straight through the mist to become Malcolm's problem."

"*Greer*," Caitriona hissed.

"You're all dismissed."

"Greer." Caitriona didn't move, but the rest did. Shuffling from the room, they kept their gazes down while Caitriona remained seated; a line of sad individuals following each other in silence until a guard posted at Greer's office closed the heavy wooden door. Caitriona's nostrils flared. "This isn't like you."

"Cait, I haven't the energy right now." Greer dropped the paper on the desk and rubbed her eyebrows. Her eyes ached, the lids swollen from all the tears she shed.

"No, I'm not having you brush this off. You're more forgiving than this and you don't punish people who are undeserving."

"I see no one here who is undeserving of punishment."

Caitriona's lips pressed into a thin line. She got to her feet and seemed to chew on her words for a moment. "I've tried to speak with you for the last two weeks, to figure out a plan, and you've barely acknowledged my presence. We have a war that's brewing."

"I know that, Caitriona. I'm *queen*."

They stared at one another like creatures circling each other, waiting for the other to strike. It never was like this between them, they always sided with one another, they always agreed, but Greer wasn't willing to back down. She refused to allow a series of losses under her thumb. Barden was gone because she rashly went to greet Caitriona, why would she allow Caitriona to risk her life to go after Ailith and potentially be lost to the world too? No. Never.

"Greer, I *love* her. I'm scared for her. She could be tortured or killed."

"Ailith's a guard." Greer's hand formed a fist, her frustration swelling. She tapped the desk with it. "She's trained. She knows the risks."

"You'd do the same if it was Barden," Caitriona hissed. Ice crawled over Greer's skin and sunk into her chest. She only stared.

They remained quiet as Caitriona's chest rose and fell, and she rubbed her lips together before attempting to go on. "I thought there was a chance to get Ailith back. If she's trapped by Malcolm—which it seems confirmed she is since the fae know we're looking for her—we'd get her back. If she was with us, she'd provide information from Invarlwen and maybe we'd get an advantage over Malcolm."

Greer sighed. She was glad to shift from the topic of Barden. It was too hard to discuss him and think of all she would have—could have—done if she just had *time* in that moment. "Leave the war plotting to me, Cait. That's not your role."

"Then what *is* my role, Ree?" Her voice rose and she lifted her hands only to drop them with clear frustration. "What is it? I'm the heir, am I not? I'm supposed to take an active role in everything. Who attended meetings and war councils for the last two weeks? Who do you think's shown Lachlan around the court, and brought him comfort after his town was destroyed and he found out he's destined to be a king to a country he doesn't remember? Who took over your role?

"I certainly ask for your guidance, so does mother, and you brush us off each time. I don't blame you for this behavior. You've had a lot on your mind and you need time to process everything. But if you could trust me for the last few weeks, and for the month prior while I searched for Lachlan, you should trust me now. Yet you're locking me in this castle."

Greer's fist came down hard on her desk. Caitriona jumped as Greer's voice lashed out harsh and bitter. "You're *not* locked in the castle. You have expectations and your role, it's just that I can't be worried you'll slip off and go on some hairbrained venture based on information that hasn't been verified and could very well lead to your death!"

Caitriona stepped back as if wounded by Greer's tone, and it only incensed Greer more. "You didn't think it through! That fae who looked like Ailith could've *killed* you! Do you not understand? They had that travel medallion and could've taken you to Malcolm himself. What would you have done then?"

"Become a dragon," Caitriona replied, her voice steadier than Greer managed in that moment. At the beginning of the summer Caitriona was terrified of the dragon that waited beneath her skin. She had refused to acknowledge it and shoved its power away. So much changed in just a few weeks and now she was bursting at the seams to become the creature she was cursed to be. Even now it was there, lurking beneath her skin and flashing from her eyes. "I'd burn the castle to the ground. I'd do *something*. It'd be more than what we've done for a fortnight."

"I don't like this behavior from you," Greer whispered, pressing her hands onto her desk and letting her weight rest on them. She was so tired. "I don't like whatever this is."

"Isn't this what you want, Greer? An heir who'll be involved and try her best?"

Another moment of silence. Another staring match. But Caitriona broke away first, shaking her head and letting her shoulders drop.

"Ree, I've barely seen you in two weeks except when you come to my room to sleep. Even then, you're like one of the undead, meandering in with no words and falling into my bed where you sleep in fits and starts. I know you're grieving; I know you're hurting. What happened to Barden was awful. I miss him and I know how much the loss hurts you. But this bitterness isn't like you. Barden wouldn't want you to act like this."

Greer didn't say anything. Her brain was like a clogged pipe that finally pushed the clog free and rushed forward as she realized what Caitriona said—what she *had* been saying this whole time. Two weeks since his death—nearly half a month with him gone. She moved closer to Caitriona, the air thick from the tension of too many words left unspoken, but Caitriona continued with a steady tone.

"I can't lose you, Greer. I've lost Ailith, we've lost Barden. You need to find your way through all this. It's hard, but I need you."

Greer lifted her gaze. They held their silence as tight as a rope. Caitriona cleared her throat, her hands fidgeting with the tresses of her gold hair. The little girl returned. The little girl Greer had done—would still do—anything to keep safe. Why didn't she understand that was the reason behind these rules? Why couldn't she see that Greer didn't want to lose her either? Caitriona was nearly lost to dragon's fire long ago, nearly lost again when the curse overtook her, and now this?

"I can't lose *you*, Cait. I can't survive another loss. Please understand. Now go. Go to your room. I'll send a schedule of meetings I expect you to attend tomorrow morning."

Caitriona's eyes flickered, their gold catching the candlelight of the room for a moment, or perhaps it wasn't the gold of her eyes but tears.

She turned for the door and left without saying anything, leaving it ajar as she disappeared. Greer was alone, staring at the empty place where her sister was as Caitriona's footsteps slowly dimmed. Greer's heartbeat, her only companion, grew rapid as her breaths lodged in her throat.

She moved forward, closing her door before sinking to the floor as the waves of panic crashed over her. It would pass, whether it took her fainting or enough time to see it to the other side, but as the uncontrolled reaction to her fears and terrors both internal and external took her body, she thought of Barden and could nearly hear his voice. It was like he was there, kneeling beside her, softly saying *breathe, breathe, breathe.*

CHAPTER FOUR

Caitriona wept in her room. Róisín heard her soft sobs from the hall and paused, pressing her hand on Caitriona's door as she considered going in. The guards standing outside busied themselves with studying the floor, pretending they weren't privy to this private moment like so many others they bore witness to. Each day was an exchange of tears from one bedroom to the next; it was nothing new. The Wimleigh line seemed to breed tearful nights. Before her daughters, it had been Róisín who wept at night. Sometimes she still did.

Caitriona held her emotions together for much longer than Róisín expected. Her youngest child put on a brave face in the halls and attended meetings with dutiful diligence for the last few weeks. She joked with Lachlan and eased into a friendship with the fae prince. She attended meals with others and tried to maintain an air of cheerful confidence. Despite the careful mask Caitriona adopted, Róisín knew her daughter well enough that her tense shoulders and moist eyes were noticeable. By sunset, the bedroom breakdowns drew near.

Greer was something else entirely. Caitriona's scheme to

disappear from the castle to retrieve Ailith woke Greer from her listless depression and flushed her with the anger that waited to take center stage. Grief was many things and anger one of them. Róisín was unsurprised by her eldest's rage, but Greer only traded her silent suffering to become a creature with enough energy to snap at anyone within her reach.

Since Cearny's death, Róisín gained her daughters back little by little after a lifetime where their relationship was determined by the moods of their father. She offered them both comfort, but grief was never something a parent could free their child from. It was a silent predator that nestled in the mind. She could only stand aside as they fought free. In the end, only they could see it through and only if they were willing.

Since Caitriona found Lachlan—because Róisín refused to linger over her arrival being the mark of Barden's death—they continued war preparations. Weapons were mass produced, guards trained for grueling hours and only received one day to rest per week, and within the castle walls they learned all they could about the world's magic and the forces behind Malcolm's mist. Lachlan was patient, shy, and incredibly intelligent. He had more power than Isla, but showed it off less. Between Isla and Lachlan, they poured over books of magic, detailed potions that could aid the guards on the field, and began constructing protective barriers for the city as a whole.

Róisín always viewed the outlaw of magic as a right stripped away, but now she saw how truly damaging it was to the queendom. It left its citizens and those who protected them uneducated, which Róisín believed was the greatest weakness of all.

After Greer, Caitriona, and Lachlan returned from the marsh, the castle filled with unease that spread like a thick fog. Greer laid down her punishments and Róisín didn't see either of her daughters until another day passed and she was called to the royal meeting room. Caitriona's solemn expression was unsurprising as she entered.

It was a simple space, yet elegant. Róisín always thought it pretty but rarely enjoyed it while her husband lived; she was never allowed within during those years. Men's work, the king declared before shutting the door, even when Greer was within and privy to discussions.

The room jutted from the side of the castle, allowing three of the walls to have slivered windows cut into the stone. The windows allowed a gentle flow of air during the summer months and dazzling views of sunset through the year. Beside the doorway that aligned the room to the castle's structure sat a large fireplace currently cool and empty. A heavy wooden table was located in the center of the room with a cluster of seats.

As Caitriona moved over the stone floor to the table, Róisín smiled. "You've joined us."

"Per Greer's command." Caitriona sighed. She placed a roll of parchment on the table; one of her maps—she was talented in drawing them and measuring distances over paper —and took a seat across from her mother. Slumping in the chair, she frowned. "I would've come anyway but I'm bitter since it's under her command."

"So, you've spoken to her?"

"Yesterday. She told me I'm to stay within the castle. She won't allow me to visit Ailith's parents for a week."

"Oh." Róisín blinked, momentarily stunned by the admission. This wasn't like Greer. The punishment was crueler than her firstborn tended to be. Róisín worked with Ailith's father to draw out the structure of an orphanage that was near completion in the center of the city. He was a kind man; all Ailith's family was, even the caretaker, Gwen, was a sweet girl who now was dating the royal librarian, Callan.

They weren't a threat and lived within the castle's walls in the guard quarters, and Caitriona's presence was a comfort to them since Ailith's disappearance. "Do they know they won't be seeing you?"

"I went to the library and gave Callan a letter. Hopefully he'll bring it to them when he visits Gwen. I worry they'll be disappointed I'm not keeping my promise."

"Callan will get that letter to them, don't fret. He's good at his word like his father. And if anything, Ailith's parents will miss you. They won't be disappointed in you." Róisín tried to be reassuring but was uncertain how to navigate this issue. "They understand everything's hard right now. But please, what else did your sister decide? Surely that wasn't all of it."

"She said I'm to follow the schedule of meetings she decides I'm to attend. She sent a letter this morning informing me to come to this one, although Lachlan already requested my presence as we rode back from the marsh. Do you know what it's for?"

"The magic of the world," a voice replied as Lachlan stepped through the door. The rightful fae king was young and his age fell somewhere between Caitriona and Greer's. He was a tall fellow, skinny with reddish-gold hair and freckles covering his face, and ever-changing eyes of blues and grays with sparks of green. His entire countenance was one of nervous energy, understandably; he was placed into an unfamiliar position and thrust into a role he only just learned he inherited. She felt for him in a motherly way and while she never knew the fae queen that was his mother, Róisín hoped she did right by the woman in being kind to her son. She could understand why the Invarlwen queen sent Lachlan away to keep him safe; she'd do the same for her girls if she had the power and they wouldn't be found.

When Róisín first met him, his hands were covered in

Barden's blood and the sticky sap of the Elder Tree. His face was pale with a stunned expression that was nearly permanent. It was only a few days since that expression faded to one that appeared often nervous. The rapid blinking of his eyes, his lips constantly parted in seeming surprise, and the pronounced apple in his throat bobbing up and down as he swallowed before he ever spoke. His movements were always quick and his eyes wide as he took note of his surroundings, like a mouse entering a room with cats. He suffered greatly too, witnessing his town attacked by a dragon meant to appear like Caitriona —another fae magicked to destroy the magical village and its inhabitants. Despite the fae queen's efforts to keep Lachlan's existence and location a secret, Malcolm obtained that information and attempted to snuff the young man out. Hopefully he thought the fae prince was killed within the village—there were enough victims as it was—and Lachlan remained Greer's secret weapon. But no one could ever be too sure.

"We've been discussing the magic of the world for the last few meetings," Caitriona commented, not unkindly but with the exhaustion of someone who hadn't slept. Her eyelids were pink and glossy, with a puffiness in the skin, and she seemed unable to fully open them. Róisín reached across the table and touched her hand, hoping Caitriona understood her meaning. *I'm sorry for all the weight you carry.*

"There's a lot to the world, but this is the most important meeting we've had." Lachlan smiled and his energy heightened. He seemed to shine with information and books. "I've found a way to gain the upper hand in the war."

"Besides yourself?"

Lachlan shrugged, his cheeks growing pink. "I think so."

Caitriona offered the man a smile that was genuine despite it not completely reaching her eyes. "I'm only teasing you. You bring an abundance of knowledge here and I'm grateful for it.

I'm in a foul mood, but I'm genuinely interested in what you'll teach us."

Isla stepped into the room without comment and slowly moved toward the table. Ceenear and Raum followed close, appearing bashful as they quietly took their seats. The two fae kept their eyes to the ground and made no motion toward Caitriona who busied herself with the ties around her maps. Whatever Greer said to them hung like a shroud over the three.

Isla, however, greeted all with a smile and sat beside Róisín, patting her hand as she settled into her seat and sipped from a steaming mug.

"How can you handle hot drinks right now?" Róisín gently teased. Her relationship with Isla had grown over many weeks, becoming something more relaxed since her awkward and slow recognition upon Isla's arrival that the old woman was a childhood teacher. When they were last familiar with one another, she was only a child and Isla an elder. Now there was a quiet respect for all they both endured in their lives. "I can't consider hot drinks, not while there's summer still left."

"There isn't too much summer remaining," Isla murmured from behind her mug. "The change is already in the air. The humidity's lifted slightly and shadows hold coolness. Plus, a steaming mug of tea is the only thing keeping me upright for these meetings."

"Is that your map?" Lachlan turned to Caitriona, ignoring Isla. He was the one who initiated the meeting after all.

Caitriona placed her hand on the parchment. "All of Visennore, from what I've learned at least. I haven't filled in all the towns but there's room to add more."

"Why do we need a map?" Greer stepped into the room; her blonde hair a simple braid down her back rather than an elaborate design on her head. She wore training pants and a top often used for the guard yard. It would have been a relaxed look if not for the tension in her face. Róisín studied her eldest; Greer's eyes were bruised from her lack of sleep, her lips dry and cheeks hollow from not caring for herself.

She moved to the queen's chair and collapsed into it, lifting her gaze to meet Lachlan's. Her brows rose with question and a coolness descended upon the room while most of its inhabitants shifted in their seats with clear discomfort.

Lachlan's eyes widened and he stepped forward, gesturing for Caitriona's map which she unrolled with haste. It was beautiful, detailed, and large. The expanse of Visennore and its shores covered the entire sheet. Cliffs were drawn, indicating the drops into the swelling ocean just southwest of Braewick Valley, beaches outside of Stormhaven, and the jagged pools of the Umberfend Marsh, too. The Endless Mountains and its many peaks went from north to south over the eastern half of the map, along with the woods where Isla called home and the remnants of the town Róisín and Kayl grew up in. She hadn't seen Caermythlin in thirty years, but it now was a place on the map that was within reach. Her fingers twitched, desiring to run over the paper, as if she could slip within the map and return. Despite that Caitriona had never been there, she sat with Róisín for hours one evening, noting every detail of the town before artfully placing small, dotted outlines of squares on the map to indicate each building that once stood. The bakery, the orphanage, the fabric store, and so on.

"I wanted to discuss something that might benefit you and the campaign overall," Lachlan stepped from the table and grasped his hands. He looked at Greer and when she nodded, continued. "While the focus of Ätbënas was to train magic makers who had great magic of multiple varieties and could be dangerous without proper training, my town was a place where we kept knowledge. A town of librarians, of sorts. We kept volumes of information on political history for various countries from an outsider's perspective, but particularly to inform ourselves about the treatment of magic and any developments that may have occurred. We kept track of the variety of magic creatures within the world—"

"Yes we've been over this. Wasn't it just a few days ago you reviewed at length the number of magical creatures? I saw the paperwork reporting that meeting just this morning. I've already reviewed it, so there's no need to tell me what I've missed."

Greer leaned back in her seat and rubbed her brow. Róisín frowned and Lachlan paused, his nervous energy lifting off him consistently and spreading through the room to choke them all. After a moment of minor foot shuffling, he licked his lips and nodded.

Greer pressed her lips together, her gaze on the map, yet not. She was somewhere else, perpetually, and barely in the room with them. "Then you're wasting my time by repeating yourself. Is there something new you can bring to the table?"

Lachlan worked his jaw, his cheeks still flush, but he rolled his shoulders and glanced at Róisín who offered a small, encouraging smile. She felt for the young man. He was a half-fae fish out of water, thrust into the world of royalty with no training; she saw herself in him, and there was no way to go about this topic without upsetting Greer.

"Following the invitation from the queen mother, I visited the Elder Tree this week to inspect the damages from the quakes you sustained. As detailed, the great tree split from the roots up during the quake, creating a rather sizable hole. The queen mother wanted me to look over the tree with the arborist, as she was worried the crack is cause for concern."

He glanced at Róisín, and she sat up and offered her own perspective. "Leaves are changing color and dropping. While we're steadily approaching autumn, the Elder Tree's always, consistently, been the last tree to lose its leaves. It's never begun this process so early. I'm worried the tree's dying."

Lachlan took in a slow breath as if bracing himself before a dive into water. His ever-changing eyes passed over the people at the table. "It's important to note that, well, there's high probability it is."

Caitriona looked up; her eyes wide. Greer's dark eyes flicked upward as well and set upon Lachlan as if she would burn a hole through him.

He opened his mouth but nothing came out, then dragged his gaze from Greer and looked at the table. When he spoke, his voice was softer. "The thing is, I don't believe the tree itself will fully die, just this subsect of it."

"What do you mean?" Caitriona asked. Greer continued to sit motionless and staring.

"The Elder Tree's roots run deep and spread across the world. Offshoots develop in different locations, growing into mighty trees elsewhere while there's one central Elder Tree. *This* Elder Tree. There's talk there may be an Elder Tree for each continent, but I'm less certain of that.

"Anyway, the Braewick Elder Tree is the central tree for all of Visennore, but there're offshoots throughout the continent that grow on their own. They're substantially smaller, but if the main tree was to die—the mother tree, your tree—the smaller trees may gain strength from the mother tree's failure. So, the magic and power of the trees will to grow; other offshoots may have enough energy to take shape and grow as well. Another Elder Tree, one that is already strong, will likely take place as the *new* mother tree. But it'll take time, and during that time there's risk as well as opportunity.

"Your tree might not be long for this world. It's good you've begun collecting the sap weeping from it. But I recommend you make plans on how to tell your people. I understand your queendom worships the tree as a form of magic making and it blesses those who give wishes to it.

Although we've never found any evidence that it's capable of doing such—"

"I need to go," Greer growled, pressing her palms onto the table as she pushed to stand. Lachlan stilled and all looked up. Her eyes shone with unshed tears as she refused to look anyone in the eye. "Continue the meeting. Caitriona, come to me with a full report this evening."

"I—" Lachlan began and Greer held up her hand. His voice silenced as she left the room, closing the door behind her. He turned to Róisín.

"I apologize, Lachlan. Discuss the risk and opportunity, please?"

He seemed to hover for a moment, like a bird unable to decide whether it was safe to perch on a limb. With his brow knit and his lips turned downward, he glanced at the map before swallowing.

"Alright. Well," he wiped at his nose and pointed at the map, "As I was saying, with the failure of the mother tree, there's often opportunity. There're offshoots of the Elder Tree here and here."

He produced small carvings of trees from a pocket and placed them across the map. One located in his town and another on the fae mountains. "With the crack that's formed in the Elder Tree, it allows for a one-way passage through its roots to other trees. We could transfer to my town or the mountains. It'd allow us a way into the fae kingdom."

"You're certain the offshoot of the tree's within Invarlwen?"

"There was an offshoot of the Elder Tree in the northern mountains some time ago that died—at times the offshoots do not last. Some of the knowledge keepers of my town traveled through the portal of this dying tree to test this story's credibility. Each one decreed their wish: to visit a different tree. One arrived here, in Braewick—this was before magic was outlawed—while another arrived to our home. A third, to the mountains. Alas, I didn't memorize the exact location, but I know the elders mentioned the mist. I don't know if they were within the mist or on the outside."

"The mist is a protective layer, it won't allow entrance for a war party because they're seeking harm to the king," Raum chimed in. The fae man seemed paler than when he first arrived with word that the fae king declared war on Wimleigh. He still had no word from Lumia, his partner and with each silent day that passed, he seemed to grow more exhausted. His shoulders rose. "If that's what you're getting at."

"True." Lachlan pointed at Raum. "You can't make it through the mist if you're a war party looking to hurt the king, but not if *you're* with the group. You can part the mist couldn't you?"

They looked at each other and Raum's brow furrowed. "Yes, although not enough to let an army through, that would be noticeable if they still have other guards along the mist wall. I've considered returning all this time, just going through the mist by myself to find Lumia, but we'd have to go in a small group and with the knowledge that there's high possibility Malcolm's toyed with the mist to view me as a foe."

Raum wiped at his eyes and looked at Caitriona. "I understand why you wanted to seek Ailith out, I supported that because it's what I've wanted to do with Lumia and maybe Ailith would know where she is. But I've hesitated seeking Lumia out myself and I don't know why. I should've gone to her already."

Caitriona's brows pinched and her lips parted. Lachlan fell silent, deflating slightly.

"Either way, it's good information to have," Róisín said, trying to brighten the mood of the room. "The more we discuss and join our knowledge together, the higher the chance we find a way forward."

Isla lowered her mug and rubbed her fingers along her chin as she studied Lachlan and ignored the display of grief from Raum. "You spoke of a risk. Are you certain that it can't be used for fae to enter this queendom? Perhaps that's how the fae archer reached the woods."

"Only one way, to the best of our knowledge. The earth at the other end of the Elder Trees will spit out the traveler."

"And you're certain that our tree's dying? What of the others?"

"I'm *certain* your tree is dying. The arborist agrees with me. It's already evident; look at the leaves. But I'm uncertain what this means for the other trees. That's the risk. Perhaps they'll fall as well without the support of the mother tree. I'm unsure."

"You said the others should survive," Caitriona whispered, staring at the little tree figurines on her map.

"Our records only speak of subsidiary trees dying in the past, never the mother tree. The death of the mother tree could put her power into flux. It'll likely drift to the other trees and we can hope one takes the place as the new mother tree, but we simply don't know if that's what happens. There's a chance her power will unleash and be uncontrolled, and it may be too much for another tree to handle. We truly don't know."

Would the abundance of its power settle to one of the others? Would it be evenly distributed? The room was silent, the weight of the Elder Tree's magic possibly diminishing from the world hung on their shoulders.

By evening, Róisín gazed out her bedroom window at the well-loved tree. Autumn was still a few weeks away, yet the tree had a glimmer of gold at the top, slowly leaking over the branches. The Elder Tree normally had a vibrant display of color through the entire autumn season and dropped leaves during the first snow while the rest of the landscape lay bare. She wondered if it would sprout leaves next spring, but wasn't very hopeful. In her gut, she knew this was its last summer.

Tired by the day and weight of heavy emotion, she curled into bed at an early hour as daylight still brightened the sky. A dream quickly grasped hold of her brain and led her to the earth beneath the tree. A shower of golden leaves fell around her, covering the grass and roots like citrine, and smothering eyebright flowers that grew in the grass. She squatted, brushing leaves aside to pick a few of the flowers and breathe in their sweet scent. Eyebrights loved the broad shade of the tree—would they die with the Elder Tree gone? She had to collect them when she woke.

"*Róisín*," a voice called. Róisín stilled her hand and slowly turned toward the base of the Elder Tree where the crack stood out against the curving roots and broad base. Kayl waited there, looking whole and like himself. Like the person she knew when he was her friend and the last thirty years never occurred.

"Kayl," Róisín replied as she crossed her arms over her chest. Age fell from her like leaves, her skin plumped and smoothed; her stomach muscles—loosened from her pregnancies with Greer and Caitriona years before—grew taught again; her breasts lifted; and the subtle aches in her joints that grew over time with such tiny progression that she didn't notice were suddenly relieved. She was a girl once more. "Why are you here?"

"I told you to come to the tree, remember?"

Róisín didn't move. "What do you want?"

Kayl's shoulders dropped and he looked sheepish as he

stepped closer. He lifted his hand and rubbed one of the ribbons hanging from the branches between his fingers. "I wasn't sure you'd listen. I've come to the tree repeatedly and you haven't been here."

"A lot's happened and my dreams have been few. Both of my daughters are suffering because of you. Or rather, they *continue* to suffer."

Kayl appeared pained for a moment and Róisín's eyes narrowed. His discomfort leaked from him like water seeping through a hole in a boat and she knew it was true emotion. Just like her daughters, Kayl was always good at schooling his facial expressions but the truth always leaked out. "I admit, I started the whole thing, and I'm sorry. This has been ... awful."

"More than awful, Kayl. What were you thinking? You cursed my daughter when she was *a child*. You started this."

"I may have, but you certainly aren't innocent of crimes yourself."

Róisín glared and Kayl rolled his neck.

"I'm sorry about cursing your daughters—both of them. When I made the curse I wasn't specific of who would become the dragon or kill their father, just that a child of Cearny's would do it." He grimaced as Róisín's expression hardened. "I apologize. Truly. It was a little much to go after a child. I was desperate though—"

"No, just leave it at the apology. Going into detail won't win you any favor from me. Don't explain why, I don't want to hear it, and just because I came to the tree doesn't mean I've forgiven you. Now, why did you want to see *me*?"

"I come with a peace offering: I know where the guard is."

Róisín stilled. "Ailith MacCree?"

"And the hunter she traveled with. They're together in the Endless Mountains. Malcolm has them in a cell."

"That's something we assumed based off your necklace

and the last vision I had, as well as other recent developments. Give me something different, Kayl."

He considered this for a moment, a finger curling over his chin before his eyes brightened. "Your daughter Caitriona doesn't only have the magic of a dragon. She has magic overall. She could direct her mind to Ailith if she tried. Give her the eyebright smoke, let her travel to her guard. And perhaps she can save her, but she'll have to move soon. There're plans afoot. Malcolm's getting desperate. But you, particularly Caitriona, need to be careful. Malcolm wants her. That was the plot in the marsh. He wants to get Caitriona and sup her gifts from her body. He wants the power of a dragon in himself."

"I'll kill him if he touches her," Róisín growled.

"You didn't quite hit the mark with Cearny despite wanting to kill him."

Róisín pressed her lips together. "It wasn't for lack of trying."

"It's hard to fathom but in many ways, Malcolm's worse." Kayl nodded as he moved closer to Róisín but stayed a space away and didn't touch her. *Smart.* He remained quiet, looking over her before speaking. "He killed our entire village, Ro."

He wasn't speaking about Malcolm anymore.

Róisín's stomach dropped and the burn of tears coated her cheeks. "I know. I didn't know then, but I know now."

"I was so angered, I thought I'd hurt him through you all and it would ruin him—"

"It did. You were successful there; I'll give you that. He's a rotting corpse and we're free of him. And we survived, I suppose, although we all have scars from it. I don't regret his death; I only wish it wasn't by my daughter's hand because she has to live with that weight."

"And for that I'm sorry. I'm sorry they suffered." He stepped back and turned to the tree. "Also, Ro? A warning. I have my wits about me in this plain, but beyond this place, be wary of me. I have no body anymore; I'm forced to drift and search for a source of power and my hunger for it is strong. When I'm tethered to a body, I can focus my magic, I can be more clear-headed, but even then when I'm tempted by magic, I struggle to contain it."

"Do you intend to be in my vicinity any time soon?"

"If I can. I must escape Malcolm before he destroys me entirely. He gathers me, not allowing me purchase, but wrings my magic for his own greed. I'm witness to his destruction of people, innocents, just like with Cearny. I'm of better use elsewhere. I can gather what power I still have left and help. I only have to escape."

"But you went to him after the curse was unleashed."

"Because he offered me power to feast upon, because I was hungry and mindless. Like I said, I think more clearly in this plane of existence."

Róisín looked at the Elder Tree's branches. It remained still; there was no breeze in this dream, but another golden leaf fell gently to the forest floor as the edges of the world began to fade and darkened sleep slipped through. "Lachlan said people can only travel one way through a dying Elder Tree. You enter the dying tree and exit one that still lives, but I certainly think there's more to it than that. The roots are all connected, the sap flows both ways, and you aren't much of a corporeal form anymore. When you're ready, travel through the roots and I'll find you here, but not in this plane. I'll find you in reality."

Kayl was blending into the background, the dream coming to an end, but his voice remained clear as he replied, "I'll try."

CHAPTER FIVE

AILITH

"Are you Ailith?"

The terror shut off. The fear disappeared. A room came to focus and Ailith was sitting on the ground of a cell. A different place from before, this wasn't the tiny room, but a corner with two walls made from metal poles that kept them trapped. Ailith ran unbound hands over her torso and the ridges of her ribs; the grumble of her stomach vibrated under her fingers, and her clothing desperately needed changing. She was solid, the world was firm, and she was alive yet empty. A huddled mass shared the floor with her and glaring eyes peeked from the folds of the rumpled, dirty blanket.

Ailith shifted her feet and realized they weren't bound. She was free to move within the cell. Looking beyond its barred walls there was a table with a few chairs and scraps of food left over on plates as if people just dined there. "Where—?"

The mass kicked out their foot and struck Ailith's leg. *"Are you Ailith?"*

Ailith snarled, pulling herself back and rubbing her shin. "Yes, I'm Ailith; what's wrong with you?"

"Just checking." The blanket pulled back, exposing black hair that at first reminded Ailith of the woman who turned into Caitriona, but it was Fiana's dark eyes that met hers with disgruntled energy. "The fae have primarily kept you knocked out for a fortnight but before that, that damn necklace you wore made you ready to slit our throats."

"Knocked out for weeks?" It explained her stiff body and hollow gut. Ailith gingerly got to her feet and stretched. Her movements were shaky and her balance wavered. She studied the cell as she stood, taking note of the single window within—a sliver that brought in a draft of air—and her feet shuffled toward the opening. Pressing her hands against the cool stone wall, she pushed up on her toes to look out. Beyond the window was an outcrop of shining marble like a stage, open to the air but cut from the top—or the edge—of a mountain. Past the ledge the sun shone over distant points of other mountains. "I don't understand."

"Do you even remember the necklace?"

Ailith dropped on her heels and turned to Fiana, frowning. "Unfortunately."

She purchased the necklace after finding Lachlan; it was meant to protect her and her group with magic, but it did the opposite. She recalled her body lurching forward, doing things she would never willingly do. She had the overwhelming urge to protect Caitriona, which in itself wasn't odd. It was that the urge was so strong she would ensure her safety no matter what. No measure was too great.

There were men that threatened to kill Caitriona and now they were dead. She had their blood on her hands and while she didn't recall murdering them in the moment, she had the memory of the event afterward.

When the necklace was ripped from Ailith's throat, it felt

like taking a breath of air after nearly drowning. Her lungs were clear of water, oxygen finally reached her brain, and the world was back and fully around her again. Her body was in her control and not led by impulse.

Then the fae prince Lachlan arrived, and everything rushed forward. Black smoke poured from the necklace. She dove to push Caitriona away from the smoke, from the necklace, from wherever she was now.

"You tried to stop me." Ailith pointed, her mind catching up to the present; at least what brought her to this place. "The necklace was going to take Caitriona. I tried to get her out of the way and you pounced me."

Ailith threw her hand out, swatting Fiana's arm in a playful gesture but jumped backwards when Fiana made a desperate cry.

"My shoulder," she gasped as the blanket fell away. Fiana still wore the same clothing as on the stone outcrop when they fell through the necklace, but her vest filled with potion items was gone, and her shoulder bulged, her arm held oddly.

"What happened?"

"Their sleeping potions didn't work on me. I guess I have immunity from dealing with so many potions on a daily basis. So, they used me as a punching bag. My shoulder's been in so much pain."

"It's dislocated," Ailith murmured as she knelt beside Fiana, her hands alighted over the bulging muscle and bone, and her fingers fell into the divot where the dislocation occurred. "I can fix this. It'll stop the pain."

Fiana glared at Ailith for a moment. "I still don't fully trust you. But it's better than dealing with this."

Ailith positioned Fiana to force the bone back. Her fingers were cold against the warmth of Fiana, and she squeezed Fiana's arm tightly with one hand, the other clamped onto the hunter's shoulder. Ailith sucked in a breath, allowing her fingers to feel out the muscles and joint under the skin rather than studying it with her eyes, before jerking Fiana's arm suddenly and without warning. A sickening pop sounded and Fiana's arm jolted, the odd angle disappearing instantaneously as Fiana let out a cry. Ailith released the air from her lungs and leaned back. "How's it feel?"

Fiana moved her shoulder slowly, tension weeping from her body and relief alight in her face. Her pale face brightened as blood returned to her cheeks. "So much better."

"Good. I never did that before."

"I thought you'd fix it!"

"Well, Barden taught me how, but I never actually did it." Ailith gave a small shrug as Fiana continued glaring. "Now it's fixed. Anyway, you said we've been given potions?"

"*You* have. Daily. They've kept you sleeping and when you'd wake, they'd stuff you up with some food, leaving you in a weird drunk place before giving you more. Some would say you were the best cellmate. Quiet and out of the way."

"Funny," Ailith replied, getting to her feet and drifting to the iron bars. She pressed her face against them to see as much as she could of the room. "Where are we?"

"From the best I can tell, we're in the fae kingdom in the mountains. That table over there is where guards eat dinner while they're on their shifts. Just sitting there with food, tormenting me with the smell."

"Have they done anything with you other than hurt you?" Ailith glanced over her shoulder, noticing Fiana's black eye and bruises on her wrists as she pulled the blanket off.

"Taunted me, starved me, plucked hairs from my head. They're up to something and I don't like it."

"Other than trying to start a war with Wimleigh Queendom?"

"Yes, other than that."

Ailith stepped back from the cage wall to sit with her back

against the bars. "Why did they let me wake up then? If they've kept me drugged for the last—two weeks you said? *Two weeks?*"

"Two weeks. And I don't know. They usually come through to let you eat around noon, but this time they dragged you off. I heard you screaming before they carried you back in. You were fighting them, screaming your head off, then you fainted and they dumped you on the floor. That's been it —the newest development and something they haven't done before."

"I saw Caitriona," Ailith whispered. "I saw her in a room. It was like a cell but without bars. Maybe a holding room? But she was there and then she changed into this black-haired fae."

"The one with the blue eyes?"

Ailith looked at Fiana and nodded.

"She looked you over before they took you out. They call her the Starling. She's some guard for the king that can change her appearance and mimic their voice. Just looking you over was enough for her to turn into you. But she said she couldn't use your voice until she heard it."

"Maybe that's why she took me to that room. She didn't do anything, just made me think she was Cait, before turning into herself. Then—" A shudder rippled over Ailith's skin. "Terror. I was so scared and I don't know why. I don't remember the reason."

Fiana pulled the blanket onto her lap and worked at the fabric. Unfolding it, she offered half to Ailith who covered her legs as she settled beside Fiana. "Every time you've begun to wake, fae came in to check on you and you'd get scared. Like you're hallucinating and frightened of something I can't see, but it's very real to you. It's the type of fear I never want to experience myself. They kept doing this to you, over and over, but they just weren't interested in me."

"Because they don't think they can use you to get

Caitriona or Greer," Ailith murmured as she ran her fingers along the edge of the blanket. It brought minor comfort; the fabric was itchy and dirty. "Greer won't storm a castle for me, but Cait would try."

"You can't let her do that."

Ailith froze, her throat constricting and eyes widening. *Not again.* It was the voice, the same voice as before, the one that filled her mind with the desire to protect at all costs. Fiana stared at her, eyes large as well, and the shock that Fiana was startled was nearly as surprising to Ailith as the voice alone. "You heard that?"

Fiana slowly nodded.

"Malcolm wants her."

Ailith turned, looking over her shoulder toward the door at the end of the room which remained firmly closed. The windows were empty, the room only held her and Fiana. "Who's there?"

"I'm sorry you're here. I can explain it all if you'll let me."

Fiana and Ailith turned to one another.

"I've come with a proposition ... "

Weeping from the crevices between stones, where light was hard to reach, pooled a dark mist that gathered and grew between Fiana and Ailith. They pushed against the confines of where they sat and Fiana's hand was suddenly in Ailith's. Her palm was sweaty and her grip tight and growing tighter as the shadow grew. The substance formed the outline of a man crouched before them and Ailith suddenly understood.

"You." Ailith pulled her knees against her chest and squeezed Fiana's hand in return not for comfort, but rage. "You bastard."

The figure shrunk and Fiana looked between them. "Is this the thing that took us here?"

"The one and only: Kayl." Ailith pushed off the ground. She sneered at the clustered shadow. "How dare you show your face. After all you've done to me, to Cait, you think you can propose something?"

"Just listen. I can help."

"What else are we going to do, Ailith?" Fiana murmured, not moving from the ground but glaring at the shadow. "We're stuck here. Might as well hear him out."

"I'll unlock the door. I can do that, but I need help."

"No." Ailith crossed her arms. "Never. You've used me enough."

"It'll only be temporary. Just something solid, not much."

"Don't you have magic? Can't you just unlock it yourself?"

"My magic's different now. It exists like the swollen edge of a lake; I'm overflowing with it and it's rushing beyond me. I'm too weak, I'm fading, I'm unable to use it as I sit right now. But with a host, I can. Think of it as a dam to contain and direct my magic."

"Because you're becoming unbound."

"I am unbound. This is the result of the curse I created, of looking to harm an innocent, of expelling my magic for destruction while wanting more power to wield. It's the same path Malcolm's on, but he isn't a magic maker by trade. He's stealing magic, taking it from fae who have it, and siphoning it into himself with the aid of the magic he takes from me. He was magicless and often people thought him foolish, but he's quite smart, he's tricky, he's figured out how to use my weakened state to his benefit."

"I'm finding it hard to have any sympathy. I wonder why—"

"Ailith, just let him say what he has to so we can be rid of him." Fiana raised an eyebrow and turned back to the form. "Kayl, why do you want to help us? What's in it for you?"

"If you're able to lend me your body and your energy, you can see what you're dealing with. You may be able to escape. And

I—if I have enough energy—perhaps I can escape as well. Perhaps I can use what's left of me to repair all I've broken."

Neither woman replied. Ailith's anger festered in her heart, becoming a wound that only grew over the last two years. The terror in Caitriona's face, the pain, it was a horror not easily forgotten. It was Kayl who slipped into her mind by the means of the golden necklace and influenced her decisions. It was Kayl who removed her sense of caution and desire for fair justice, and made her into a murderer.

"Why should we trust you?" Ailith whispered. "All you've done is hurt us. We're here because of you. The entire queendom, the entire continent is in danger from all you've set forth."

"Now you're placing unfair blame upon me. I've been in your mind; you're an intelligent woman and you know well enough that this began with Cearny. His hatred, his refusal to understand, his fear of that which was different is what started it all."

"True. I'll give you that." Ailith ran her hands over her face and pulled her hair back. It was knotted, far past greasy, and she desperately wished she had a hair tie to pull it back from her face. Minor comforts in the face of someone who enraged her and a place she couldn't escape. She dropped her hands to her side and tapped her fingers along her thighs. "Even without the curse, Cearny would still exist. He'd probably still be alive. And Malcolm would still be doing whatever he's doing now; however, with significantly less power than he has, due to you."

"There's no point in lingering over what could've been," Fiana pointed out. She was a no-nonsense person and while Ailith typically appreciated that personality, she hated it in that moment. "It's already done. We need to figure out how we go forward; preferably, I'd like to figure out how to get out of here."

Ailith rolled her neck and looked at the ceiling. She'd love to throttle Kayl if she could, but seeing that was impossible, she turned to the only option she had left. "Alright, so you've turned over a new leaf. You want to get away from Malcolm and not be part of what he's doing. You can't even guarantee we can escape with your help. So, what's in it for us?"

The shadowed figure of what remained of Kayl straightened and his life force stretched as he raised his chin.

"Don't you want to save your friends?"

CHAPTER SIX

"Sweet lark, you have to wake."

Róisín rarely came to Caitriona's room at night, at least that's what Caitriona believed, and hearing her mother's voice stirred her to the waking world with a jolt.

"What's wrong?" Caitriona sat up and looked for a threat in the shadows of her room. Crowley wasn't at his perch, and the window was open and empty; he must have taken off after Caitriona went to bed. The fireplace was cold, the room dim, and the moon at its darkest point in its journey. Róisín's hair was a barely visible ember, shimmering as she bent over Caitriona's bed and ran her hands down her daughter's arms with a calm expression that only confused Caitriona all the more. "Mother, what are you doing here?"

"It's time I teach you some magic. Come."

Still brushing aside her sleep, Caitriona pushed her blankets back and placed her bare feet on the floor, listening to her mother even while her mind spun. The chill of night climbed into her skin, but she didn't bother to stand or reach for a cloak. She liked the sensation of the cooler air running over her and since the curse consumed her, cooler temperatures didn't bother her the way they once did. Producing a flickering flame in her palm, she looked at her mother standing before her with a robe wrapped tightly around her body.

The former queen didn't appear surprised by Caitriona's fire. Over the past few weeks, Róisín seemingly accepted Caitriona for all she was. Or perhaps she already had and it was more simply that Caitriona no longer sought judgmental looks from others to fortify her own self-hatred. She did, however, appear impatient.

"What do you mean teach me magic? Mother, it's the middle of the night. You said yourself we have to get as much rest as we can before battle."

"This has to do with that. I've considered it before, but I wasn't sure I wanted to drag you into it. Admittedly, you've been through so much I don't want to put more pressure upon you, but this is the step we have to take. With Greer in the emotional state she's in, we must do more to help, even if it's more than she's allowing you to do. You want to figure out exactly where Ailith is and I know how you can."

The fire grew in Caitriona's hand, pulsating with the increased beat of her heart. "How?"

"I've had visions before through the use of smoke from a flower. With the Elder Tree likely dying, there's a high chance the flowers won't return. They thrive in the shade of great trees. Already we lost a few of the flowers from when the tree broke."

Caitriona cheeks grew hot. *When the tree broke* was a gentle way of mentioning Caitriona falling upon it as a cursed dragon. It broke a substantial limb off and exposed part of the landscape to sunshine that wasn't able to make its way through the canopy beforehand. "I didn't realize any of the plants underneath suffered from that."

"Neither here nor there; now isn't the time to feel shame

over that, Caitriona." She moved to the far corner of the room and gripped one of the animal skins they kept piled there to cover the cold floors in the winter. Róisín unrolled the skin before the empty fireplace. She waved Caitriona over and reached for the small bundle of wood beside the fireplace; nights were cooling off but not rapidly enough to demand a fire just yet. They still had a few weeks before that time came but the wood was already placed in rooms, awaiting the first chilly night.

Pointing to the fireplace, she looked at her daughter and raised an eyebrow. "We need to build a fire, would you mind?"

Caitriona stood a little straighter; at the beginning of summer, she felt like her mother was ashamed by her. The bone horns that sprouted from Caitriona's skull, the spark of scales on her shoulder, and the way she took on a draconic appearance when her emotions were high all caused Róisín to turn away. Crossing the floor, the flame in the palm of her hand grew and encapsulating her fingers. Róisín stepped back and watched silently without any indication of shame or embarrassment.

Caitriona knelt before the lumber while the flames licked her fingers and encouraged her nails to turn to claws and a sheen of scales to ripple over her skin. She was still surprised by the sensation of fire on her skin. It registered as hot, hot enough to burn anyone, but for her the flame was a warm breeze, gentle and passing innocently. Reaching forward, she touched the wood, gripping hard until it caught and a small fire grew.

"Come, sit," Róisín instructed and Caitriona pulled back, the fire winking out on her fingers as she dutifully sat upon the animal skin. Her mother's hand ran over the length of Caitriona's hair as she moved to the fire. "I'm going to place these flowers on the flames and they'll create a thick smoke. You have to breathe it in. Suck it into your lungs and let it stay there, but all the while I need you to think of Ailith. Make your wish clear: you want to see where Ailith is and what's occurring to her. You want insight on what's happening at her location. If this works, you'll transfer there, but only on a plane separate from where we are now with solid bodies. You'll be like a ghost; unable to be seen, unable to interact with your surroundings, and unable to come to harm. Even if you see people, Ailith or others, you'll be invisible to them. When the vision completes, you'll return to your body here."

"Oh, okay. But Mother—"

"It's best we do this now while the castle's quiet. I'll make sure you're safe. You're tied to Ailith in a way I'm not, so you have to be the one to seek these answers. Let's get to it, before I change my mind. I'm not entirely sure this is the right thing to do, but it's active and that's something that's sorely lacking right now within our castle."

Róisín kneeled before Caitriona and opened her hand to show the dried flowers. With her free hand, she ran her fingers down the curve of Caitriona's cheek and smiled, her expression soft and comforting. "I'll be right here. Go. Find your girl. Then let's hatch a plan to get her back."

Caitriona looked at the flowers in her mother's hand; they were tiny, little things with a blush of stars scattered on their petals. Simple little weeds that would be overlooked by anyone; how interesting something so small could hold such power.

"Thank you," Caitriona managed, emotion surprisingly catching her voice in her throat. Her mother was always near, and she grew more open to her daughters after Cearny's death, but this was something else. A secret shared between them and a chance for Caitriona to get ahead, even if it meant doing something behind Greer's back. The idea left her uncomfortable; she never lied to Greer, never went against her, but she was doing it constantly now.

Gripping the flowers, Róisín shifted toward the fire and sprinkled them over the flames. They sizzled, immediately catching and puffing into blue-gray smoke that curled upward as her mother slipped away and positioned herself behind Caitriona.

"Breathe in the smoke, then sit back so you don't fall into the flames." Róisín's hands gently guided Caitriona forward and she followed the directions silently; leaning forward and waving the smoke towards her with cupped hands. It curled over them and drifted toward her mouth. She breathed in and the heat of the smoke coated her throat. She swallowed and coughed.

"Try again."

Caitriona coaxed the smoke forward. It draped over her torso like a shirt and curled into her nostrils before slowly slipping through her sinuses. The world became fuzzy and Caitriona leaned back.

"Good, now remember to think of your request." Róisín said. Her mother's hands rested on her shoulder, guiding her backward to lay on the animal skin, but she was far away now and her bedroom grew distant. Caitriona knew she laid down, but as she pictured Ailith's face and asked to see her, she never met the floor. Instead, she stood in a dimly lit room before a cage in the corner with her feet firmly placed on the ground and the jail a solid fixture around her.

Together, Fiana and Ailith huddled. They were thinner than when she saw them last. A fortnight of barely eating and being imprisoned could do that. Caitriona moved forward, her hands grabbing hold of the metal bars, and pulled. The door didn't budge. She couldn't interact with the world. Right. It was an infuriating and frustrating thing to only witness and provide no help.

Dropping her hands, she squatted to get more level with the two women. Fiana was badly bruised around her face and arms while Ailith didn't sport any obvious marks she didn't already have when she fell into the necklace. Bruises from their travel through the Northern Woods and the still-healing bite mark on her shoulder from an undead—none of it surprised Caitriona to see—but Ailith's hair captured her attention. Streaks of white covered her head that Caitriona never saw before. The color stood out in the darkness of the room against Ailith's brown tresses.

"What's going on?" she whispered. "What's happened to you?"

She reached forward, putting her arm between the bars to touch Ailith, but her hand slipped away and her body followed. The scene shifted and she stood in another room between cots. Ailith and Fiana moved with quiet steps through the room. Ailith went from one cot to the next, cutting straps at the wrists and ankles of fae on the beds. Fiana turned to a table and lifted jars to her nose, smelling the scent of the herbs within before moistening her finger to taste.

Fae were pale and sickly, and bound to each of the cots. She recognized a few, women she met and dined with while in Ulla Syrmin. They welcomed her to their home, and helped heal her body and soul after it was ravaged by the curse. They gave her a place to rest, somewhere away from the scrutiny of a kingdom who hated what she was. These people were kind.

Her stomach lurched and she stepped forward, desperate to help, but the floor began to tilt. Caitriona's arms flung forward, her hands passed through the cot rather than coming in contact and her feet slid out from beneath her. Her stomach upended and she toppled; her feet kicked overhead, and she turned end over end as the room swept by.

She fell through the stone walls and floors, down through rooms with fae speaking and others cleaning, until she collapsed onto the floor of an exterior room where a fae man stood. Scrambling to her feet and clutching the fabric of her night gown to her chest, her breath came fast as she stared before her.

The man's arm wound back and released a goblet, sending it flying through the air and Caitriona herself, before it bounced across the marble floor. She hadn't time to move out of the way but it didn't matter, she remained a ghost.

"I'll make them *kneel*," he snarled, spinning on his foot to look at another man standing behind him. He was a taller, younger version of the one who threw the goblet. They had a similar brow to one another, their scowls reflections, and the energy radiating from them was filled with pride and disgust, even for each other.

"Where's that damned shadow? Where is he?" The snap of the first man's voice was like the snap of a tree branch, sudden and sharp; the result splintered and left Caitriona shrinking back. It was similar to her father yelling in the night, angered by something to do with the kingdom and throwing a fit with plates and cups as his weapons.

"He isn't responding to your summons?" the younger one asked. He appeared annoyed and bored. He shifted from one foot to another and shadows seemed to pool at his feet as if he were perpetually away from a light source. Caitriona's eyes narrowed; the man's body seemed to shed itself and drift behind his movements. "He's been adrift more and more lately, Father. It's time to use him up and let him fall apart. How can we trust him in these moments where he's not with us?"

"I'll be rid of him when I'm ready, Shad. I need him to give me more."

"What is it that he can give you which you cannot obtain from others?"

The man squeezed the bridge of his nose, his annoyance palpable. "How many times do I have to explain this? Kayl ate your mother's magic, and now both her magic *and* his reside within him. Besides that, there's the addition of magic he's consumed from others. While he's fading, that magic still exists. It's been given to me, yes, but the strongest drops still reside within him. It's the life force. While it may not be enough to keep him together, and he's too weak to control it himself, it's enough that if we have it, we'd have every living thing in our possession under our thumb. I can only take a little at a time or he begins to fade too rapidly. If he fades too rapidly, what happens?"

Shad took in a long breath and looked to the ceiling. "He diminishes completely and takes the life force with him."

The older man bowed his head, his point made, but his son bristled. "Also, stop calling her my mother, she never was."

"Queen Onora, then. Fine."

Caitriona backed away, not wanting to see anymore. *Let me go, let me go back to my room,* she whispered in her mind, too frightened to even speak. She squeezed her eyes shut and pictured her mother sitting beside her on the floor. *I don't want to see any more, let me go home.*

She remained without a flicker of change. Magic had its own rules and it was going to ensure she saw all she needed to before she departed. She was trapped in the vision, unable to break free, and she cursed herself for not having asked her mother how to escape.

A brush of cold air hit her skin, the first feeling since her arrival. The sun, the air, the surfaces held no weight, no sensation, but there was a chill. Looking down, a shadow slipped across the floor and over her feet. It paused, gathering itself into the shape of a head, shoulders, and arms that pulled itself across the stone. It paused, looking over its shoulder, and hesitated. Caitriona felt the chill of observant eyes looking her over.

"You shouldn't be here," a voice whispered. She recognized the tone, but couldn't place from where. *"This is dangerous."*

"I can't get back. I'm stuck in this vision," Caitriona murmured.

"I'm sorry, but you have to go. I can feel your power, even through time. It's calling to me and I hunger for it. This is too dangerous, I don't want to take anything from you, and if I did he'd have it with too much ease."

"Kayl!" the man yelled as he relinquished a thin, silver, stringed net and tossed it forward. It passed through Caitriona but fell atop the ghostly smoke, containing it with the glimmering magic knit over the net.

"Leave, leave."

Kayl, that was the voice. A rush of rage passed over Caitriona but she tampered it, quenching the fire brewing in her stomach. This wasn't the time because he saw her when her mother reassured her no one would.

"It's a vision," Caitriona repeated. "I can't just leave."

"Then get back, get back so he doesn't taste you."

The king pulled the net towards him and with it, the shadow that was Kayl. He tightened his grip on it, twisting the magical fabric as he brought it to his mouth as if wringing out liquid from a cloth. A liquid formed, glimmering and bright, and dripped off the netting and into his open maw. He sighed, his body quivering with pleasure. The king seemed to grow larger, more solid, and magic churned under his skin. Caitriona saw it at work, spreading in his veins, and making him glow. Kayl was a caught fish, slippery but contained, his ghostly eyes distant yet looking at Caitriona.

Caitriona stepped backward, looking for a clear exit from the room. The king opened his eyes, the magic rushed through and turned them gold. His gaze locked on Catriona and she felt as if she was forced under the icy surface of a lake.

"Ah." A hungry smile appeared on his face. The vision of his facial features seemed to blend and twist and edge to something different. A flash of something lurking beneath his skin there and gone again. A monster beneath the surface. But his eyes, the gold eyes, continued staring at Caitriona. Not through her, *at* her.

"The Dragon Princess. Here for your girlfriend? Well, I have things planned for her. So, you won't be able to get her. Not yet, at least. But I promise you'll see her soon."

Caitriona gasped; her head jolted back. Her skull crushed the fur of the skin and she opened her eyes. She was on the floor of her bedroom; the ceiling came into focus and Malcolm vanished from sight. She threw herself forward, vomiting remnants of smoke into a bowl Róisín held to her face.

"He saw me," she cried between gags as her body quivered into her mother's waiting arms. "Malcolm saw me."

CHAPTER SEVEN

She tried to find him in her sleep. Greer passed through doors and entered empty halls, she walked amongst tall grasses and swam in deep waters in search of him, but he always eluded her. He was absence itself.

It was her one hope to visit him in dreams, but when each dream became an echo of his absence, Greer avoided sleep entirely. It was enough to be reminded he wasn't there in the waking world where she struggled to keep herself breathing; she didn't need it in her sleep. Like a cruel taunting for something she didn't deserve.

Or did she?

The thought ruminated through her mind over and over, as persistent as the spell that fell upon her repeatedly over the last number of weeks when air sucked from her lungs and her body plunged into panic.

Breathe.

Greer finally found happiness with Barden. After years of trying her best to build her success as the incoming sovereign —even as the world threatened to crumble with this war—she received a gift in his love.

Breathe.

She still recalled his breath stopping—his hands growing cold and stiff.

She recalled seeing the last of him vanish beneath water as his body joined the dukes. His body at first clear beneath the water but growing murkier and murkier as he disappeared into the depths, just as the memory of him was too becoming a cloudier memory.

How could she taste the sweetness of happiness only to have it torn away if it wasn't deserved for all the wrongs she committed? Wronging her sister, wronging her mother, wronging her father, and wronging Barden—after all, she couldn't save him.

Already she was forgetting little things. What did he sound like when he was surprised? He had a specific laugh for those moments, but suddenly it was hard to recall. What about his breath on her neck? She loved it so, but it was a sensation she was desperately trying to hold on to while it slipped away. How, *how* could someone you knew for so long become a memory and slip into the past?

Breathe, just breathe.

Shad's magic that plunged the entire city into impenetrable darkness never ceased in the recesses of Greer's mind; she was lost within it. She drifted, a wandering soul unable to find light, and with no reprieve she hoped it would take her fully sooner than later.

Her father was right, she wasn't fit to rule. Her queendom would soon be attacked by a force stronger than her own; and her sister was making foolish decisions that could easily kill herself and others. Everything her father muttered when she failed a history lesson, lost a duel, or missed a target with her bow and arrow repeated:

"You are not what I had hoped.

I had such big plans for you.

What are we going to do?

The kingdom will die when I do.

Such a disappointment. You are such a disappointment."

Greer rubbed her temples, trying to rid herself of her father's distant voice. He haunted her still, a rotting corpse dragging along floors, the sinews of its flesh catching on errant nails or leaving a streak of wetness glimmering on marble. He followed her with foul breath and lingering stench. Why couldn't Barden haunt her? Of all the dead in her life, she'd rather it be her lover and best friend. At least she wouldn't feel so lonely.

"Murderer."

"Shut up," Greer murmured as she wrapped her cloak around her shoulders. It wasn't her cloak but Barden's. A gift from his mother to the queen, her expression one of sympathy and pity as she handed it into Greer's quivering hands.

Her heart was a frightened rabbit caught in the snare of her chest; quivering, kicking, and desperate to run loose. She squeezed her eyes shut and forced herself to take deep, long inhales of air and slowly release each breath.

Snuggling herself within the cloak she calmed and took in the air around her. She greeted the slow change in season with hatred and eagerness. She wanted to get away from the sticky heat of summer, a season she never enjoyed, but the heat reminded her of the rapidness in which they sent Barden to his watery grave to avoid rot. The moist air reminded her of his clammy skin as he died. She wanted to enter a season where the very sun didn't burn reminders into her mind. Yet leaving summer bid goodbye to the last season he lived. Distance, it was all distance between before and after that filled her with pain. Yet the chill of the late night—or was it the chill of Cearny's spirit following close behind—had her grasping the cloak tightly.

She passed her mother's bedroom and the former queen

whimpered within. She didn't bother to check; her mother was known for having night terrors. She experienced them since the dragon attack when Greer was a child. Róisín would scream into the night, fighting demons she never cared to discuss with Greer or Caitriona. It wasn't a nightly experience, but frequent enough that the castle knew to leave her be. She'd make her way through the nightmares each and every time; they only had to ignore her cries, and hope the creeping sense of old memories and the cast of terror Róisín experienced during the attack passed without lingering.

Maybe this was another curse on their family, one that decreed every woman would suffer the loss of their loves and have nights filled with unease. Generation after generation of women left without their lover, home, or hope, and only the accompaniment of nightmares.

Greer sighed and continued down the hall, chasing shadows and sleep in familiar corners and doorways.

A clink of metal sounded; unusual for the middle of the castle. Greer paused; ears attuned to the sound of blade. The hall was empty of guards; after the royal family retired for the night they would relocate to the doorways of the hall, rather than standing outside rooms, so Greer stood alone.

The clang of metal sounded again, and Greer stepped forward to Caitriona's door. She laid her hand on the handle, her fingers stilling against the metal hinge, and pressed her ear against the heavy wood. Their interactions since returning from the marsh were brief and strained, culminating strictly to business. There was tension Greer didn't like, something that lasted longer than she'd admit she wanted.

"Breathe, just remember to breathe."

Greer closed her eyes and counted to ten with each breath. There was a frustrated sigh within the room followed by clattering, enough to force Greer to lift the door's latch and push it open. She didn't bother to knock, she rarely did when she visited her sister, but she waited in the doorway as was customary.

The princess stood in the center of her room. A fire was lit in the hearth which made the room hotter than it needed to be. They were at that threshold at night where added blankets were needed on a bed but a fire was simply too much. At Caitriona's feet was one of the winter animal skins spread across the floor.

Caitriona looked over her shoulder, her gold hair glittering against the firelight and hanging loose down her back. She wore her nightgown and was barefoot, her brow glistening with sweat that formed beneath the base of her horns and the scales on her shoulders reflected the firelight. She clasped a sword and a training timber sat in the center of the room's open floorspace.

"What are you doing?"

Caitriona's cheeks were pink, either from embarrassment or exertion. She lowered the sword. She began training shortly after returning from the Endless Mountains a year prior. She struggled, weapons didn't come naturally to her, but Barden always encouraged Greer's patience.

"She wasn't trained to wield a sword since she could walk —unlike some people," he had murmured as they watched from the sidelines as Ailith dueled Caitriona, swiftly knocking the princess on her rear before pulling her back onto her feet. "Children learn quickly, but adults take much longer."

Greer reminded herself of this now as she looked at Caitriona's improper stance and the dents in the training timber. She was barefoot no less, a danger in itself of cutting off her toes. What was she going to do with her? She was a mess.

"I wanted to practice."

Greer pressed her lips together at the obvious answer and

stepped further into the room. "How'd you even get the trainer in here?"

Caitriona nodded beyond Greer. "I asked a guard to drag one up here. I couldn't sleep. I figured this is better use of my time because I've looked over maps so much they're sketched behind my eyelids."

"I haven't been able to sleep much either," Greer admitted. Caitriona frowned and sat the sword beside the timber.

"Do you want to sleep in here?"

They shared a bed on and off ever since Caitriona was old enough to sleep outside of her bassinet. Whenever Cearny was in a particularly foul mood, Caitriona slipped into Greer's bed. As they grew older, it switched, and Greer went to Caitriona's bed before traveling or when she came home, exhausted and emotionally weary from the experiences beyond the valley where she witnessed plagues, death, war and poverty. Since Barden's death, she only found sleep when she was in Caitriona's room, but she avoided it in the past few days since they fought.

Greer shook her head, wrapping her arms around herself as she looked at the fireplace. She'd likely find sleep there, but she wouldn't find Barden. The sisters' relationship was too sour for her to accept Caitriona's offer just now. Nodding towards the flames, she flicked her gaze at Caitriona. "Why's that lit? It's not cold."

"A comfort," Caitriona replied too quickly. She was lying. Greer bit the inside of her lip and moved further into the room, casually looking at what Caitriona was up to.

"Actually, Greer, I wanted to speak to you. I was going to wait until morning but since you're here..."

Greer swung her head toward Caitriona. She was exhausted, like her movements were through honey. Cearny's ghost stood behind Caitriona, looking over his youngest daughter with disgust. Half of his face had rotted away, the hollows of his cheek pulsed with maggots and the gold of his hair was a dull, ratted thing filled with mud and worms.

You shouldn't trust her.

Caitriona knit her fingers together and looked at the ground. This was her normal behavior; this was honesty.

She nearly ruined it all by going to the marsh, what's to say she won't do it again?

Greer took a deep breath and focused on Caitriona, determined to ignore Cearny's torment.

"I hoped we could discuss a way to get Ailith. Now, before you say no, I understand what I did at the marsh wasn't well thought out. I apologize for that. I know we can't afford to send troops to find Ailith, I understand the implication to send a fleet of men just to find two people, but could we spare a few to travel to the mountains to find her?"

Greer blinked. "The mountains? How do you know she's there?"

Caitriona stepped back and gripped her hands together. "Mother confirmed the necklace Ailith disappeared into belonged to Kayl and he's in the mountains, isn't he? It seems obvious Malcolm has her just by the trickery of what happened in the swamp. They knew to pose as Ailith escaping, and they knew I was looking for her."

She replied too quickly and Greer bristled.

She's lying to you.

Perhaps not lying, but holding back information.

"Caitriona ..."

Caitriona rushed forward to grab hold of Greer's hands. She pressed them against her chest, her gold eyes shimmering in the firelight. Caitriona's heart beat frantically and her skin was warm from the heat of the room—or was it the dragon lurking beneath? Greer breathed in, suddenly uncomfortable by their proximity when that was never a problem before.

"Ree, please. Please let's just get Ailith back. I—I don't want to lose her. I *already* lost her. I lost her to that possession then I lost her to the necklace. Please, *please* help me get her back. You have the power to do it, I just need you to say yes."

Greer shook her head and stepped back, pulling her hands free from Caitriona's grip. "I can't. I can't just send guards to find her. We need them here—all of them, every last one. We're up against forces of magic and we're magicless ourselves."

"Not entirely! We have guards who've long withheld their magic that can use their gifts now. We have magic users in the city who're willing to step forward to help. You have *me*."

Greer stepped back; her eyes narrowed. Her nerves sparked to life, a crackling ripple of lightning from the back of her skull that spread over her face and down her neck. The instantaneous dislike of Caitriona's offer overwhelmed her. "We don't have you. We're not using you as a weapon, Caitriona."

Caitriona's lips parted; her eyes widened then reflected Greer's as they grew intense. "I'm the heir to the throne. I have as much right to fight in this war as you do. I've been training as much as I can and even without a sword, I have armor and weapons stronger than any you could wield."

She held out her hand and her fingers lengthened, her nails growing sharp, and glittering scales spread over the soft skin.

Greer ground her teeth together. "No, Cait. I told you already and I'll tell you again: I'm not going to lose you. I'll take your help where I need it but not with that. You aren't a weapon. Don't bring it up and don't ask about Ailith. I promise we'll retrieve her, but we have to wait until the war's over or we have a reason to go to the mountains. But right now, we cannot waste the resources to get her."

She turned from Caitriona and headed for the door,

waving her hand, brushing away Caitriona's begging that followed her.

"*Please, please. Save—*"

"I can't, Cait, I can't."

"*But it matters. It matters to me.*"

"Stop asking. I can't."

She left the room and plunged into the darkened hall. With the closure of Caitriona's door echoing off stone walls and bouncing amidst the sleeping castle, it was then Greer realized Caitriona hadn't begged her.

Caitriona remained in the center of her room, her face a picture of heartbreak with tears brimming in her eyes as Greer told her no. She stayed silent and watched Greer disappear. Not once did she ask her to stay, not once did she beg.

No, the pleading hadn't come from Caitriona at all. The begging was from Greer's own mind, spoken from her broken heart and denying her wishes over and over. But there would be no saving Barden. It mattered, his loss mattered, but in the end there was nothing that could be done.

CHAPTER EIGHT

CAITRIONA

The sun was setting when the ringing of hammer on red-hot metal ceased. Sitting beyond the Elder Tree's woods were the extensive blacksmith fields for weapon making. The sounds were so constant it became a backdrop until the blacksmiths paused for their meals and a shift change. Some blacksmiths worked through the night—the preferred shift as the air cooled—and others worked through the day with the summer heat mingling with the fires. But for the moment, there was silence as Caitriona knelt beneath the Elder Tree with Isla and her mother.

Under her mother and Isla's watchful eye, Greer allowed Caitriona to leave the castle walls for this venture to gather starbright flowers for visions. It wasn't without guards scattered along the edge of the tree line, but Caitriona took whatever outings she could obtain. They hoped to dry what flowers they gathered to use as needed, in case the flowers did wilt from the late summer sun that rapidly exposed the tree's undergrowth as leaves continued to drop.

She should be grateful to have the escape, but it only set her mouth into a frown.

"You had a taste of the world and now you want more," Isla pointed out as she knelt beside Caitriona.

Caitriona leaned back on her heels, a basket on her lap half filled with the flowers she already gathered and dirt pressed under her nails. "Not a taste for the world so much as craving to have Ailith returned. I'm restless. Greer doesn't want me in danger but I can do so much more than remain here."

Isla rubbed Caitriona's arm; her eyes sparked with a knowing that always seemed present. What worldly knowledge the old woman had up her sleeve, Caitriona doubted she would ever know. "You've come so far from the frightened woman that dragged Ailith to my home."

That brought a smile to her lips. When Caitriona met Isla, it was after royal hunters tried to take Caitriona to her father and injured Ailith while doing so. With Ailith unconscious, Caitriona had been terrified and unknowingly ignorant as well. She didn't know the extent of her father's cruelty, the genocide he had done, nor the curse that swelled within her body.

Caitriona went through hell from the curse, her body split apart and stitched itself back together to become a dragon. Her human form was completely undone, twisted, grown, and reborn. After she was free from the curse, she battled her mind and fought against her permanent changes. She hated herself and what she had become, and despised that she didn't recognize the person in looking glasses. But she grew to understand the power left behind; she was braver, and understood what she desired in life: to love herself, to love Ailith, and to feel she was doing some good in the world.

"Do you have a role in the war?" Caitriona dropped another flower into the basket. "I know you're training my mother and helping guide her magic, but is there anything you'll specifically do when the battle comes?"

"Whatever your sister tells me to do." Isla's eyes narrowed

as Caitriona raised an eyebrow. "Don't give me that look; it's what's expected of subjects. We look to the sovereign for guidance. We receive that guidance. We *obey* the guidance."

"Something tells me you never listened to my father's guidance."

Isla's home was within the Wimleigh Queendom's borders, but considering the immense power the woman had, there was a high chance she never obeyed the restrictive plans of the former king.

"Well, that was different." The woman had a wry smile that Caitriona loved. She wished she could have met Isla when she was young—she bet the witch was a handful when she was spryer. "Your sister means well and is trying to fix what your father broke, all of that's necessary even without this war. And that fae king, well, Malcolm's fallen victim to the sickness many men face—fae or not."

"And what's that?"

"Greed. Pride." Isla pulled eyebright flowers from the ground with each word. "Envy. All three go so well together and he's experiencing them to the utmost extent. He's so filled with it all, it's made him into a monster without any magic to guide him there. Even if he wasn't focused on fighting Wimleigh, he'd likely destroy his own kingdom. People who're like that, who just want more and refuse failure, are possibly the most dangerous creatures in the world. They'll stop at nothing and spare no one."

Caitriona picked more flowers and allowed herself a short laugh. "You could be describing my father."

"I've said it before, Malcolm and Cearny would've either gotten along well or hated one another if they met. They were very similar. But your father is no longer here, while Malcolm is, and with supporters who have magic too. So yes, I'll do what your sister tells me to, but in reality, my dear, I understand magic more than your sister ever will. I'll use it in any way it will best help her. I wouldn't say you should as well, but, well, how you interpret what I've said is left up to you."

Hours later, after baskets of eyebright flowers were left in Róisín's room to be dealt with in the morning, Caitriona prepared for bed when a rapid knock sounded on her door.

"Come in," she called as she finished braiding her hair and tied it off. The door creaked as it opened and a messenger stepped in. Barely a teenager, the young man's cheeks blushed scarlet as he found Caitriona in her nightgown. Quickly, he directed his gaze to the floor and tucked his hands behind his back. The poor child—the role was usually given to those much older but they were called away to prepare for battle.

"Princess Caitriona, a message from the queen," the boy announced. "She received word of an attack on Greenbriar, north of Umberfend Post. As a show of good faith, she'll ride to the post and offer support to the town and its survivors. She requests you travel with her. You'll leave in a few hours, please be ready."

Caitriona stared, her stomach turning to tar as she processed what the boy said. He slowly lifted his gaze, waiting for her dismissal, but Caitriona only blinked.

Earlier in the summer she visited Greenbriar as she and Ailith traveled to the Mazgate Dominion in search of Lachlan. Greenbriar was a small hamlet near the Avorkaz border where she ate a wonderful meal at Declan and May's home along the edge of the town. She slept in their barn with her friends.

Greenbriar; the hamlet that was attacked.

Clearing her throat, she attempted to pull herself together

and the boy relaxed. "Thank you, please let Her Highness know I'll be ready."

IIT TOOK A DAY OF HORSE TRAVEL TO REACH THE Umberfend Marsh's post. Caitriona was restless overnight, left alone in her room with a guard outside the door. Her room was bookended by Greer and Lachlan in their own rooms. Greer requested Lachlan's attendance as well, much to Caitriona's relief. She was glad to see Greer giving him some attention and even more relieved that the prince was there to lighten the tension between sisters.

Over the fortnight the fae prince stayed with them, it was Caitriona who tried to take him under her wing and guide him through the activities of the royal household. But he was quiet, observant, and their best times were spent at the library while Caitriona worked on maps and Lachlan read. Silent, but together. Coworkers of knowledge.

They rode side by side to the post as Lachlan peppered Caitriona with questions about the marsh. It wasn't until she laid down to sleep that she realized it was all knowledge he already had. He was a scholar after all, someone who grew up in a town with ample literature about the world around him. He knew about the marsh—at least the baseline understanding of its existence. Lachlan hadn't asked her questions to be educated, but to distract her from what lay ahead and she was grateful for that, for him; it made the pain of not knowing Greenbriar's status less choking. Of course, it was awkward to ride along with Greer. They barely spoke. But her fight with Greer wasn't foremost in her mind. It was Greenbriar that overtook her thoughts.

The town became something of a middle ground

between Avorkaz and the Umberfend Post in the last two years. It was always too close to the Avorkaz battles that Cearny waged in his attempt to gain control of the city, but with that threat gone, families torn between the two ruling powers were finally able to come together and the town thrived.

They went through the motions expected with the chill of discontent between Greer and Caitriona a persistent thing. They left the post the following morning and traveled through the day until they had to camp for a night. As the guards set up tents, Caitriona gathered her courage to speak directly to Greer.

"I'll sleep outside, it's fine. I don't need a tent."

Greer didn't bother to look at Caitriona. She stood to the side with her arms crossed over her chest as she watched the tent raise. "You're traveling under the crown and as heir, you'll sleep in the tent."

"I can sleep outside as well." Lachlan stepped beside Caitriona and she silently thanked him. In his gentle way, he persistently tried to mend things while supporting Caitriona with every opportunity he had. Whether he knew it or not, he'd be a good leader.

"There's too much of a risk to have you exposed overnight. This is safer." Greer turned on her heel and walked away, never once looking at either of them.

Lachlan let out a mouthful of air, his cheeks puffing as he did while his shoulders dropped. "I'm surprised Greer wanted me to come."

"I'm surprised she wanted *me* to come," Caitriona said.

Lachlan smiled shyly. His strawberry blond hair fell into his eyes as he looked down and he kicked at the ground with the toe of his boot. "Do you have any idea why she asked us here?"

Caitriona's shoulders dropped and she fidgeted with the

tail of her braid. "Greer wanted me to learn things like this on the field without being in battle."

Caitriona didn't include that Greer had said it with a flat tone that made her displeasure with Caitriona clear. Nor that she started the conversation with "since you feel you haven't been provided proper guidance as heir," but that was beside the point.

She offered Lachlan a gentle smile. "I suspect it's some lesson for you too; or just—I don't know. The Mazgate Dominion seems to have a generally good relationship with Invarlwen. Perhaps it's to see how your kingdom's neighbors are faring?"

"I'm not important enough for the queen to ask me to go with her."

"We need to get that idea out of your head, Lachlan. You're going to be Invarlwen's king soon enough. I mean, you already *are*, technically. It's time you believe yourself to be that level of importance."

The following morning after leaving camp to complete the journey northward, Caitriona shifted with unease. A scout reported massive bloodshed and multiple deaths in Greenbriar. Their scout came upon a crowd during the attack and turned straight around to send a message to Greer. The battle very well could still be waging, and Greenbriar had no army other than from the city of Avorkaz northward; it was likely they would be overtaken quickly.

Caitriona sent Crowley ahead, but he hadn't returned with a message from May or Declan, and the weight of that hung heavy. As they rode through the fields where her father sent guards to fight a few years prior, Caitriona's stomach turned and nausea made her vision swim. It was different passing through this battlefield where the skirmishes between Avorkaz and Braewick occurred while Cearny was alive. The wars fought there already occurred, the scars of the bloodshed and misery left on the land, but whatever happened in Greenbriar was fresh and new. She wasn't ready to experience it.

"Are you alright?" Lachlan asked as Caitriona swallowed. She rode atop Onyx, Ailith's horse. She hadn't claimed a horse for her own but Onyx became Ailith's steadfast steed and was familiar with Caitriona as well. Since Ailith's disappearance, Caitriona claimed everything of the guard's: her family, her horse, her crow. In this instance, where she was nervous and uncertain of what lay before her, having some semblance of Ailith near was necessary. It reminded her that while Greer's faith in Caitriona seemed to ebb and flow, Ailith's had been consistent and steadfast. She was the first to have faith in Caitriona gaining control over her dragon self and she never faltered. She needed Ailith's faith now.

"I've never done this before—facing bloodshed." Caitriona looked at the half-fae prince riding on his borrowed horse. The closer they got to Greenbriar, the paler his already porcelain face became.

"Brace yourself." Lachlan looked forward, his lips turning down and a crease forming between his brows. "It'll be worse than you can imagine."

Caitriona reached for Lachlan's shoulder and gave it a squeeze. His town was lost weeks before and he witnessed that destruction. There was already so much death around them that Caitriona felt dizzy at the idea that more was predicted with the incoming war. It was a dread that sat on her at all moments and left her helpless—how could she stop the inevitable, heartbreaking, bloody future from happening? There was no way. They were just expected to keep moving forward until it happened.

The plan was to visit Greenbriar to provide aid where needed and by showing a good faith effort, the Mazgate Dominion would refuse to join Malcolm and stay apart from the battle. Better yet, maybe they would side with Wimleigh—although the likelihood of that was very small.

Ahead, Greer's horse slowed and her guards continued forward while she waited for Lachlan and Caitriona to reach her. "Here we go," Caitriona said under her breath, earning herself a nervous frown from Lachlan. Greer waited ahead, looking them both over with a serious expression.

"When we arrive, we'll move down Greenbriar's main road. My guards will offer help to any of the injured and if I encounter anyone who appears in charge, I'll offer them aid as well. We'll escort anyone who's lost their home back to Braewick if they have family there, and offer a guard or two to see them to Avorkaz' gates if that's what they prefer."

"Greer," Caitriona's voice softened as the edge of town clarified in the distance, "Our friends are there. Ailith's and mine. Do you remember them? They sent Ailith healing ointments; they were kind and helped us find our way to Lachlan."

Greer nodded. "We'll have enough time that you can stop to see them if you'd like."

"You're sure none of Malcolm's forces are left?" Lachlan asked. They'd drawn close enough that distinct wisps of woodsmoke could be seen rising from buildings. Caitriona's stomach dropped. Not woodsmoke, but burning homes.

"From what our scout said, yes. They came through, demolished the town, and moved on."

"What's the point attacking then?"

"Distraction, more than likely. A use of resources we don't have. I would've guessed it was a chance to pin the blame on us so Avorkaz picks up arms to fight with Invarlwen at the lead. They already are on edge after what happened to your village. But that's not likely."

Lachlan shook his head. "They don't think Wimleigh's behind this attack?"

Greer's expression sobered. "We got lucky. There were representatives for Avorkaz visiting. They barely escaped but they said the forces were magic makers. They're familiar enough with our guards that they knew it wasn't us. Malcolm's a fool."

She flicked her reins and urged her horse forward, picking up speed to join her guards again, and leaving Caitriona and Lachlan following.

It was odd how the scent at first fooled her. Woodsmoke, despite that she knew it wasn't that. The burnt scent was light on the air and just enough to make Caitriona feel everything would be alright, until it changed into something more sinister. If she hadn't known better, she would think she smelt cooking meat, but the town was empty of life and the fires weren't from kitchens.

Lachlan looked green as he shifted uncomfortably on his horse. "This ... this is like my village after the dragon attack. This is what—" He swallowed, pressing his fist against his mouth as if to fight something back. The normal blush on his cheeks noticeably paled. "This is what it smelt like."

They stopped at Greenbriar's entrance. There was silence. No birds, no wandering dogs, no groans of pain from injured people, no cries for help. The silence was wrong.

Down the main thoroughfare, a man in Avorkazian armor walked forward.

"You've come to help?" His voice bounced off the smoldering, broken buildings like a death bringer's song. "You won't find anyone here. They're all dead."

Greer dropped off her horse and handed the reins to a guard. "We come from Braewick. We heard there was a battle and wanted to lend aid to survivors."

"I'm the last one out of Avorkaz. We came through to help as well, but there were few who survived. Even those that did were dying as we gathered them. The town's destroyed. The forces were too strong."

"No," Caitriona whispered. All emotion in her body broke loose; it sunk, lower and lower, and she went with it. Slipping from Onyx she dropped his reins and walked forward as if in a trance. "Declan and May ..."

Greer looked over her shoulder at Caitriona then back at the man. "Is there truly nothing we can do?"

"You're welcome to help with a final check for survivors. Grave diggers are on the way, they'll gather the bodies and handle burial." He pulled a wide brimmed hat off his head and ran his fingers through his sweaty hair. He gave a shrug and seemed uncaring at the sight of a fae beside the two human royals—one who spouted horns and golden eyes. Just like any other Avorkaz citizen—they never were scared off by those touched by magic.

"I—I have to go ..." Caitriona brushed past Greer. Greer attempted to grasp her shoulder but Caitriona left her behind.

"She knows someone I take it?" the man murmured, oblivious to who she was, but just as easily knowing what she came for.

Caitriona passed through streets she had only just visited, following the pathway she recalled toward May and Declan's small farm, past homes that were once sturdy structures with life abundant, now turned to shells of smoldering ruin. The greenery of summer was faded, not due to the encroaching autumn months, but because of the fires set to the buildings. Heat from the flames left trees with rust-colored leaves and the grass was brittle, brown and dead. Buildings were crisps; broken apart and blackened with roofs missing and walls toppled.

Caitriona ran forward, grateful she wore riding pants and boots as she stepped over splintered wood and shattered items. A water pitcher, a toy, crushed underfoot by rushing people, whether the attackers or those fleeing. But there were worse things, broken bodies, fallen in doorways or the middle of the street. Caitriona made a noise, shaking up her throat and out her mouth without her control as she stared at the empty gaze of more dead than she ever saw at one time. These people were trying to leave, trying to escape, and yet the battle raged and there was no sympathy from those who brought this hellscape to their doorstep.

A crow cawed, the first sound of something besides herself, and Caitriona spun. Crowley darted overhead, his cries concerned and frantic. The note she tied to his leg was still there.

Caitriona began to run.

Declan and May's cottage sat on the outskirts of Greenbriar, their barn nothing but cinders, but the cottage—the cottage still stood. Caitriona sped forward, moving all the faster while somewhere in the distance she heard Greer yell her name. Greer followed but was still far off, weaving in and out of the disarray, unknowing of where she was headed.

Caitriona didn't wait for Greer to catch up. She skidded to a stop before the house and looked it over while Crowley continued circling overhead, his cries long and repetitive. The glass windows were broken and the door stood partly open. There was a stillness within that settled into the earth and shot ice into her veins, but still, Caitriona dared to hope.

"May?" she called as she reached the doorway and pulled on its broken frame, barely getting it to widen for her clear entrance with her horns. "Declan?"

She tugged the door again, grumbling as it remained stuck. She had the strength of a dragon; it was worth using it. Gripping the door harder, she focused, braced her feet, and pulled the door one final time to break it free from the remaining hinge. It dropped to the ground and she stepped over the threshold.

When Caitriona first visited this home, the entryway was full of life. The yellow glow of candles, the late afternoon sun warming the windows, painted dishes and bright flowers that hung from the ceiling, as well as colorful blankets and vibrant bottles on shelves; it was a rainbow of life. Now it was dim and filled with lingering smoke. The glass windows, those that weren't shattered, were covered in soot, and the smoke and ash was so thick in the air of the town, that no sunshine shone through.

Caitriona paused in the doorway, listening for sounds of life but only found that sickening silence once more. She flicked her wrist to call fire to engulf her fingers and form into a flaming ball in her palm—hot to all but her.

"Caitriona, wait!" Greer yelled some distance behind, still running to catch up, but Caitriona didn't heed.

She, Ailith, Ceenear and Raum sat at the long table before the door just weeks before. They supped together, laughed over Declan's jokes, and Caitriona had a new chance in life when May produced a potion to make her appear like her former self.

May had looked at her with sympathy not for what she was, but because Caitriona hated herself. *Only when you turn into something other than yourself does it hurt*, she had said as she gave Caitriona and Ailith the potion. She knew, just like Ailith, that Caitriona's worth was more than her appearance; it only took Caitriona longer to reach that same conclusion. May didn't know how far Caitriona had come, would she ever?

The table was now soot-covered. A wooden chair lay on its back on the floor and Caitriona pushed it aside with her foot. It looked like fire was thrown in fits and bursts, burning away areas before winking out without destroying the structure in its entirety. Perhaps there was still hope.

Further in, she paused at the foot of the stairs leading to

the bedroom, and looked at the cooking area and May's workshop whose door stood ajar.

"Declan?" she asked the space. Her breath stirred dust and ash, making it dance in the glow of her fire. "May? It's Caitriona; you're safe."

Greer's voice grew close. Caitriona heard her footsteps pounding on the dust and splashing through liquid of human origin beyond the broken door to the home.

"May?" Caitriona attempted. "Declan?"

Caitriona's foot fell on something that shattered under her boot. She pitched her firelight at the ground to find remains of one of May's vials. But it was what lay beside the vial that made her stumble back.

She was barely seen, partially hidden by the table she prepared meals on. The old woman who was kind to both Caitriona and Ailith lay upon the ground with eyes wide and vacant. She was tucked against the chest of Declan who was motionless, his arms still wound around her body as his face remained turned toward the ceiling, his jaw hanging open.

A feral, broken sound freed itself from Caitriona's throat. Her free hand clutched her chest, the very breath leaving her a painful thing as her stomach churned. She stared at the pair of them—still, lifeless, and dead for some time—as her brain tried to comprehend what was before her. If she was in enough denial, perhaps it wouldn't be true and she could make them rise from the floor right now.

She wanted to cry out her refusal at the sight of them, to yell repetitively *no, no, no,* but Caitriona only continued the dragon-like sounds from her throat as her hand reached out, seeking something solid to pull her back to reality and make her see straight.

"Cait!" Greer gasped from the doorway. Caitriona didn't care that her sister arrived. Shock vibrated through her body and filled her until the overwhelming tide of emotion crested.

When Caitriona first traveled with Ailith, she witnessed Ailith gut a man who tried to kill her. Days ago, Caitriona killed for the first time when Malcolm's fae supporters attacked her friends. Just weeks before, she saw a royal guard lying dead on the ground while life slowly leaked from Barden not far away. But this ... this was different.

Seeing Declan and May's eyes wide with what Caitriona only assumed was fear as they lay in their own blood and excrements repeated in her mind as she stumbled from the dining area. These two people who loved each other with devotion and welcomed them in their homes; people who didn't care that Caitriona was the daughter of the very man who banned them from Braewick Valley long before. They were in their home where they should have been safe. They weren't seeking out a fight or working a job of defense. It was too much, their loss on the heels of losing Barden and watching Ailith vanish from sight. The pain welled within Caitriona, growing into a massive thing greater than any dragon she could be.

It exploded. Her grief rushed forward and out of her, clawing from her throat as she released a desperate cry of frustration, rage, and heartbreak. The world flashed white then amber and crimson. A wink of fire expanded from her and caught what herbs still hung from the ceiling and the combustible items from spells that would never be made. It didn't matter—they were both gone.

Her tears were like lava, her pain like smoke, and as it swelled, it rose to the ceiling and her mind cleared enough to remember Greer arrived at the door, watching, waiting.

"Ree," Caitriona sobbed, turning to her sister with hands clenched to fists, her fingertips lengthened to claws in her fit of grief, and fire still coated her tongue. Greer remained in the doorway but she was frozen like a statue, unmoving beside the rise and fall of her chest. Caitriona expected Greer to be there with compassion, to reach out and comfort her, but the sight of her sister made Caitriona grow still.

The queen's sword was unsheathed. It was half raised, waiting for a threat the queen perceived. The threat that was *her*. Caitriona.

"Greer?" Caitriona whispered, but in saying her name, there was a sense of betrayal and heartbreak in her tone. It was only her name but it held unspoken questions that flitted through her mind since she became a dragon, questions made from fear and worry now seemingly finding a place to fit into her reality:

Do you really think I'm a threat?

That I'd hurt you?

I'd never hurt you, I'm not capable of that. But I'm broken and filled with sorrow, but this—your action as sharp as a blade —is the true dagger in my heart.

"I ..." Greer began. She stepped back from the door. The gleaming point of her sword still directed at Caitriona. Greer looked from side to side, her eyes wide with surprise as Caitriona forced herself toward the doorway. "I just ..."

"Greer!" Caitriona dropped her flames. With each step over broken glass and crisp herbs there was a jolt in her heart. Still, she followed her sister as Greer stumbled backwards with eyes large and lips parted, and the grip on her sword ever present. "Do you really need that right now?"

Greer looked down and blinked rapidly, seemingly surprised her sword found its way into her hand, and quickly sheathed it. "That ... that was dangerous, Caitriona."

"My friends are dead." Caitriona gripped the doorframe, holding herself up as her heartbreak attempted to pull her down. "They killed them. Malcolm's forces murdered my friends and you're raising your sword at *me*?"

"You exploded with fire!" Greer replied through gritted teeth, her eyes bright with her own internal flame.

Caitriona straightened her back as her heart ached in a different way. She looked her sister over; the queen—her queen—and realized she didn't understand her as much as she thought. Caitriona was just a subject, just a person under Greer's rule and little else. She was a danger, something Greer had to keep an eye on. Something that was a threat.

The betrayal reverberated through Caitriona's core and locked her compassion behind a solid wall. Her body emptied of emotion. Distant. Void. Caitriona's voice held no cadence, no quiver as she met Greer's gaze. "I'm sorry my grief frightens you."

Within the grass a lost soul ambles, compelled by a greedy king.
Each step is a drunken swerve to avoid the water's shadowed edge and
there are whispers from the border; commentary undefined yet understood.
Don't come too close, don't look too long, stay on track for safety.
But if you come close, do so soon.
If you look for long, we'll offer our caress.
A smarter fellow avoids temptation, yet the marsh is long and the grass
plays tricks.
They create nets knit amongst themselves to cover pools and appear like
land. The grass desires the same thing the water does; blood is
synonymous to life after all.
The soul falls victim to the moist handholds of creatures beneath brine,
the grass rejoices and drinks the water's offering. Jagged teeth tear into
soft flesh, tongues loll over leaking blood, and down and down they go.
Deeper and deeper, into the depths of the earth
where stone caves greet pockets of air, roots drip sap, and ancient bones
lay. The grass, the water, and everything in between sups on life.
Even the one who gazes at the glow above. Yet there is still a craving
there for something else.
Yearning for something besides blood with the flavor more filling
and lingering on its lips with passion's spiced richness.

CHAPTER NINE

AILITH

"I'll do it."

Ailith's brows knit together. "Why? You saw what he did to me when I had that necklace on."

"I didn't do anything to you when you had the necklace on. I existed in the magic of the necklace. It was a home, but the necklace was magicked before it was given to you. And this isn't the same."

Ailith glared at the sunken figure. "Then why could I hear your voice in my head? You were the one speaking to me, telling me to kill and protect, and everything else. It was *your* voice."

Kayl rolled his shoulders, the substance that made his form rippled down his back from the movement before dispersing. *"The magic of the necklace adopted my voice. I didn't fight it from doing that, I was living off what power I obtained from the blood you spilt. But the necklace is what lowered your fear and patience. It took away what made you hesitant and prevented your bravery from showing. You were given the allowance to protect freely and for all you're capable of to be let out. It would've done the same to anyone."*

"It made me into a killer," Ailith pointed out.

"Anyone can be a killer. If they're lacking enough remorse—if they forget empathy—they can do awful things. We're all capable of it. You had nothing holding you back and as much as you like to think I was in control of you, I wasn't. Granted, the blood—the life force—fed me but it's never enough. When I have a taste, I want more."

"Then why are we going to let you take over one of our bodies?"

"It's different. *You aren't magic and you aren't spilling blood. You aren't being influenced by that stone."*

"And I've done enough training." Fiana lifted her dark gaze to meet Ailith's. "I'm trained to push out possessions and keep them from overtaking me. If either of us is going to do it, it'll be me. You've had your share of possession. Let me help and get us out of here."

Ailith studied Fiana. Her jaw set, eyes steady despite that one was bruised, she still held her arm to her side and her injured shoulder was tense. Ailith didn't know the hunter very well. A week of traveling with her was the length of their experience before Ailith's memories got fuzzy and she couldn't tell if this was a good idea. But Fiana was right; they had very few options and she had a wealth of knowledge at her disposal that could ultimately help. "Only if you're alright with me knocking you out if you act oddly."

"It's a deal." Fiana flashed a half-smile. She looked at the specter between them and kicked off the blanket, nearly blowing Kayl apart entirely with the movement. Getting to her feet with some struggle, she stood at her full height and looked down at Kayl's shrunken, spiritual form. "Let's see how much we can trust your word."

Kayl sighed—his only response before funneling into Fiana's mouth and eyes. She gasped, sucking in the dark smoke of Kayl's essence and blinked. It took only a moment for him to be there and gone.

"Fiana?" Ailith whispered and the hunter turned. A small amount of the bruising on her face faded and the dark brown of her eyes lightened with a hint of gray, but beyond that, there was no difference.

"He's in there, but it's still me. He's already bossing me around." She stepped to the metal door and lifted the hand of her good arm near the lock. Black smoke ebbed from her fingertips, slipping along the metal and into the lock mechanism that relinquished a click. The door swung open and the women looked at each other. Fiana held out her hand. "After you."

Ailith eased from the metal cage with quiet feet. The room was empty, a place set aside and separate from all the rest. Down the room's length stood another door forcing any who passed to squeeze by the cage in the corner, as if the cage was hastily built and never intended to be there in the first place. The door past where the guards ate had a window. Ailith inched toward it, listening for any indication that someone was on the other side, but there was only her and Fiana's breaths, and their soft footsteps. Slowly, she peeked through the window.

"It's another room," she whispered, unable to vocalize the sight before her. A row of cots ran down the room with unmoving fae on each one, similar to a medical wing. Between the cots were barrels and tables with various items and strings leading to each fae. At the foot of the cots was a pathway, and a long table with a collection of herbs and liquids in glass jars. Another door with a similar window was at the opposite end of the room. "What's this place?"

Fiana stepped beside Ailith and went up on her toes, trying to peek into the room as well but with her height being substantially shorter, she struggled. "Are those fae? Oh. *Oh!*"

"What?"

Fiana dropped to her heels and stepped back, staring at the door, her gaze distant as her concentration slipped somewhere else. "Kayl says they're strong fae with a multitude of magics brought here because Malcolm's siphoning their gifts. They're all fae who refused to side with Malcolm and perform magic per his request. He—" Her brow furrowed and she fell silent as she listened. She shook her head and closed her eyes before continuing. "He watched Kayl, how becoming an unbound caused him to siphon magic from others, and he found a way to do it to people. Not to eat the magic for life force like the unbounds do, but take the magic from them, bottle it, then bring it into himself."

"He's making himself as strong as he can."

Fiana nodded; her gaze still distant. "He's given magic to others too. Mainly his son. Kayl says it's partly why he wants to get Caitriona, to take her magic."

"Partly?"

Fiana narrowed her gaze and her lips pierced as she waited for Kayl's response.

"He'd like to convince her to join him, but seeing as we both know that won't happen—even he seems to believe that —he's interested in getting her power."

"Her magic's from the curse. She didn't have magic until it unleashed." Ailith pulled her gaze from the window and forced herself to drop her shoulders and unclench her jaw.

"She can control it. Malcolm had informants in Avorkaz when you were captured. They told him she made fire with her mind. He forced from the minds of some fae they suspected she could become a dragon at will. He wants *that* power. Changing into such a large creature and doing it at will is huge. It's not a gift most magic makers have. Even Kayl was incapable of that. Plus, Cait can be bait for Greer."

Ailith turned back to the door and looked at the fae. They

all were sickly pale, weak, and emaciated. But perhaps they'd have some clue as to how they could escape, if they could wake them.

"Let's go in the room." Ailith pressed her hand onto the door handle and it didn't budge. She pushed again. Locked.

"Let me." Fiana allowed the black essence to drift from her fingers. The door unlocked and slowly swung open.

"Can Kayl unlock every door to get us out of here?" Ailith whispered. Fiana pressed her lips together and listened to his reply.

"He says just this, maybe a door or two more, but to get us out of the castle would be too long in my body. The risk's too great that he'd take too much from me. It's one thing to take a little magic from a person, but since I have none, it'd be my lifeforce. Plus, he's never traveled the castle like a human. He doesn't know the direct way out of it because he's only passed through walls."

Ailith frowned. She hated that it was reasonable. She'd grown accustomed to hating Kayl over the last few years and now this change in his personality, this weakened state that wanted to help, felt odd and frustrating. It meant she would have to consider changing her perspective on him. It was much easier to hate him than deal with the complicated feelings for a once-enemy turned helper.

Moving into the room, Ailith crossed her arms as she looked at the fae. All had their limbs tied to the beds but they appeared too weak to move. Fiana passed her, moving to the collection of magical ingredients on the shelf without a word.

Each step down the row of cots was quiet and slow as Ailith studied the sleeping fae. But perhaps sleep was the incorrect term. Their knit brows, the slight moisture on their faces: they weren't in a restful sleep. This was something else.

"Fiana, are they forced to sleep like I was?"

Fiana turned from the potion's table and stood beside

Ailith. She frowned. "Could be. There's a ton of ingredients on the table, some for sleeping droughts from what I can tell. Nothing's labeled. They're either drugged to sleep or too weak to be awake."

"It's going to make it hard to find out anything from them if that's the case." Ailith turned to the cot where a woman rested. Tall with blonde hair reminiscent of late summer sunsets, her face moved back and forth as she fought the sleep forced on her.

"I feel like the effects of the necklace still linger in me and I can't trust them."

Silence at first, beside the murmurings of the wakeful fae on her cot, then Fiana quietly responded. "What fae would willingly allow someone to suck their magic from them? Kayl says magic's as fluid to these people as blood. They're essentially bleeding out by having their magic taken."

Kayl had said, *He forced from the minds of some fae that they suspected she could become a dragon at will.* Ailith closed her eyes. The only ones that would have known were those who helped care for Caitriona when she recovered in Ulla Syrmin. Fae who helped Caitriona when the mist forced bones for dragon wings to break out her skin, and again after the curse completed and Caitriona recovered. Ailith turned on her heel, scanning the beds for Niveem or Lumia, but didn't see them.

Ailith's mind drifted backward to their travels to find Lachlan. She recalled Caitriona's relief whenever she used her fire gifts; she had been *so* afraid. It was no secret to Ailith that Caitriona feared becoming the dragon and never returning to herself, but Ailith saw how magic coursed through her and sought release. While it was something that could swell and explode from her, it was a part of her, a thing under her thumb if she only allowed it to be. But to have it taken ... wasn't that part of the pain of her transformation? It was something forced on her, as a creature pulled from within her.

The fae woman gasped, her eyes fluttering open, and it unlocked Ailith's frozen state. Falling to her knees beside the woman who looked around frantically and tried to pull the binds off her wrists and ankles. She shuddered and pulled back from Ailith's presence, only to study Ailith for a moment then gasp: "The guard."

Ailith looked over her shoulder, she and Fiana were still the only ones standing and the doorways were closed and quiet.

"Ailith," the woman whispered, drawing her attention back. The woman's blue eyes sparked with recognition. "You don't remember me. I'm not surprised, I look awful, I'm sure."

"I'm—I'm sorry, I don't ..."

"Niveem's my wife. I saw you in passing when you and Caitriona visited, although we never spoke. I arrived from travel while you were leaving, so it was brief. But Caitriona, when she stayed with us, she told me much about you. I feel I know you."

Ailith leaned back, searching her memory and the many letters Caitriona sent while recovering from the curse in the fae queendom. Niveem and her wife. They were married longer than Ailith's parents were alive—fae had a tendency to live much longer than humans. Her wife didn't have a flurry of magic like Niveem, but one specific power of healing. The woman had been on a visit to the mountain she was born when they arrived to Ulla Syrmin with Caitriona sporting bone shards from her back. They just missed each other.

"Vanora," Ailith whispered. "Right? You can heal."

"*Could* heal." She closed her eyes with a look of exhaustion. "Malcolm's taken all my energy. All my magic. I've tried to heal myself, to regain strength, but it's all seeping from me."

"Where's Niveem? We've tried to reach her for weeks and all our messages have been ignored. Is she here with you?" Ailith straightened and looked over the other fae faces. Vanora's fingertips gently touched her arm.

"She was the first taken from our village. She refused to bow to Malcolm and was separated from us all and bound in iron. I've only heard whispers of where she is. Her magic's been taken and she's weak. I fear for her, Ailith. I fear she won't make it." Her blue eyes glistened and she closed them. She took in a deep breath and swallowed, keeping quiet until her composure was regained. Ailith understood the feeling; she hated exposing her feelings to people she didn't know. "But there's one thing I'm certain of, she'll refuse to bow to Malcolm until her dying breath. We aren't a people who seek to harm others. We *accept* the broken, we don't *make* them."

"I know," Ailith whispered, gripping the fae's hand and noting how cold it was. "If I find Niveem, I'll tell her you're here and alive."

"Thank you." A tear leaked down her temple, falling into the shadows of her hair.

"Have you seen any of the other fae from Ulla Syrmin? Lumia, perchance? Raum was with us. He kept trying to reach out to her without success. It's just been nothing. Silence."

Vanora's eyes flew open, growing wide as a small gasp choked her throat. "You don't know? Oh, Ailith—"

A door slammed in the distance and everyone froze.

"We have to go," Fiana whispered. "Kayl says we have to go *now*."

Ailith jumped to her feet, backing from the cots but kept her eyes on Vanora. "I'll get you free, I promise. I'll find a way. And I'll find Niveem, too. Just hold on, okay? Hold on."

Footsteps echoed in the hall like a rabbit's heart, drawing

near the door to their exit. The steps moved rapidly, coming close, and sending Ailith running after Fiana who flew to the door of the room they were celled in. They rushed, spinning on their heels to close their door and the shadow of Kayl's hands reached to place the lock back into position.

"Let's go!" Ailith ran to the other doorway past the cell, grasping the handle and finding it locked. Voices called from beyond that door as well and she slunk back, fear jolting from her heart and spreading to her limbs.

"There isn't enough time, we'll get caught." Fiana stood at their cell, holding the door open. "Come on."

Ailith swallowed, her will fighting against the idea of returning to the cell, but wanting whatever longevity she could obtain to help the fae and escape in her control. The metal door to their cell came next as they collapsed onto the cold, stone floor and pulled the single, itchy blanket they were meant to share over them.

"Close your eyes. Close your eyes and pretend to sleep," Fiana repeated as they curled close together, facing one another with panic. "Don't open them if they speak. Pretend you're still knocked out."

The door swung open. She squeezed her eyes shut and blocked out the world.

CHAPTER TEN

GREER

"It was a moment of emotional expression," Lachlan attempted to reason. "Surely you understand what heartbreak does to a person. Sometimes it's combustible and oftentimes uncontrollable. When you have magic, it can physically explode."

Greer's entire body was sore from riding so stiffly. Gripping the reins, her back straight, her chin jolted forward, and her muscles strained to exhaustion from the statue-esque behavior she adopted as they rode south. She yearned to get to the outpost to rest as soon as possible.

The night they spent in the field was tenser than the previous one. Caitriona said nothing and dutifully went into her tent without comment, but her silence leaked into the following day. Lachlan was the only one willing to talk, whether or not Greer wanted him to.

"I fully understand what it is to grieve, Lachlan," Greer growled.

Lachlan looked panicked; his brows pitched as he rubbed his temples. "Yes, of course. I just mean... the fire. It wasn't meant to harm you. She wasn't trying to hurt you. *She* was hurting; she needed the release."

"She *could* have hurt me. You can admit that, can't you? If I came into the room the fire may have struck me."

Lachlan's silence was the validation Greer needed. She continued riding and Lachlan's horse drifted back. Moments passed as they moved further south with the marshes to her left and fields to her right. Greer was blissfully free of chatter. She rode with her anger and lingering glances towards the marsh. The day was bright and surely chased the dukes into whatever caverns they hid in during daylight hours. The ache that lodged itself in her chest grew.

I'd ask for your advice, you know. And you'd read the situation and tell me exactly what the right thing is to do. You wouldn't hesitate. Even though Lachlan is trying to do that, I suppose, but I don't want to hear any of this from him. I want to hear it from you. I know you wouldn't lie to me. But Barden would never answer her questions or offer advice and that reality was steadily becoming permanent.

Greer looked over her shoulder, the smoke from Greenbriar still colored the atmosphere to the north. Just as the Avorkazian representative said: the town was destroyed and all the people were dead. They traveled all that way to make a good faith effort to help the town, to show Avorkaz they meant no harm and were good neighbors despite their history, only to find it destroyed by magic users who descended from nowhere and hurt just because they could.

It was awful, Greer admitted as much, but the visual of Caitriona remained trapped in Greer's mind. It repeated itself, each time growing more frightening, and making her decision all the easier.

She hadn't expected to witness Caitriona's reaction. Cry, run to her arms as she did when she was a child, that was what Caitriona was meant to do. Greer would receive her and wipe her tears and lead her back to her horse so they could abandon the notion of helping the town entirely. But Caitriona raged. Caitriona exploded. Caitriona was *power*.

The fire enveloped her sister's skin, the pure magic of it not burning away her clothing but licking the surroundings with ease. When Caitriona roared through her grief, Greer saw a dragon in the firelight. Fangs for teeth, smoke billowing from her nose, wings stretched backward that were ready to take flight, and clawed hands that could snap a neck with ease. Even when the fire receded and settled to a flame in Caitriona's hand, she saw the dragon linger. The way her gold eyes flashed in the light, the shimmer of scales on her skin—more than just what remained on her shoulders—and her fingers turned to talons. In the shadows, a dragon lay watching, mirroring her sister's movements, waiting to step forward and take control. Her sister was a creature of rage and power, and Greer understood Caitriona was capable of causing true harm if she saw fit.

Greer hadn't realized she grabbed her sword until Caitriona pointed it out. Her embarrassment at the slight became a thing coating her emotions. A phantom in itself possessing Greer and making her back away as she snapped at her sister. "Get to the horses. We're going home."

"Greer, we need to discuss this," Caitriona attempted but Greer held up her hand.

"Under my order as your queen."

Caitriona didn't speak to her after that. Commanding her as a subject crossed an unspoken line. Caitriona silently mounted the large horse and opted to ride further back in the procession. Lachlan, poor Lachlan, came and went between the two sisters as he attempted to repair what Greer broke. It was in the moments Lachlan retreated to Caitriona that allowed Greer to think.

Turning to her right, a guard pushed his horse forward, answering her subtle movements as he was trained.

"Bring Princess Caitriona to me when we've reached the outpost, please."

"Yes, Your Grace." He receded as the imagery of her sister-dragon and the destroyed town replayed in Greer's mind. Beyond, at last, the outline of the outpost appeared.

"You can't," Caitriona hissed in the outpost meeting room. The guard, as requested, led Caitriona to the room after they stabled their horses. Caitriona came straight away, but kept her gaze lowered until Greer announced her decision. Now she faced her head on and handled it as well as Greer assumed she would. "I'm not doing it."

"You have to." Greer crossed her leg and leaned back into her chair. She raised her gaze to meet Caitriona's and steadied herself. "I command it."

Caitriona's eyes flashed and she ground her teeth together. Her hands tightened into fists and she rolled her shoulders to stand straighter. Caitriona was still shorter than Greer, but with the addition of her horns, they were dangerous reminders eye level to Greer when they stood side by side, but now, with Greer seated, Caitriona nearly towered over her.

Caitriona's gaze lifted and she stared at the wall behind Greer when she spoke. "If it's your command, then I'll do your bidding as my sovereign. But I still ask of you as *my sister* to explain why. Help me understand why you've decided this."

Greer rubbed her lips together as she composed herself. "It's too dangerous—wait, listen to me."

Her sister shifted away and Greer nearly reached for her.

But Caitriona had fire in her eyes and her jaw worked. Greer straightened her back. *Is her mouth filled with fangs? Is she holding back flames in her throat?*

"I'm tired of hearing that reason for things. My whole life you, father, mother—you've all claimed things are too dangerous but in the end *I* was the one who was killed by a dragon, the one cursed, and the one who *became* a dragon. I've faced so much and *I've survived.* So, why do you all keep handing me this excuse that things are too dangerous for me?"

"*Because* of those things!" Greer replied, her voice louder than she intended, but she continued anyway. Her hand fisted as she thumped the table, yet withheld the full strength behind her movement. "Because you've faced all this; why should you face more? Because you're the heir and you're to be protected. We can't have you killed on the battlefield."

Caitriona slapped her thighs with frustration then pointed at her sister. "Why do we keep circling around to this? You've done this. You—as heir—traveled all over the kingdom and fought battles before Father died."

"Because Father didn't care if I died!"

The ring of Greer's yell echoed in the room, growing in volume by memory due to the sheer silence that followed. Caitriona stared; the fight leaving her for the moment. Greer rolled her head back and looked to the ceiling as she attempted to regain her composure.

"I was a failure in Father's eyes as much as you were," Greer admitted. "He haunts me to this day repeating all the things he said about me that are honestly coming true. The kingdom will falter and fail under me, I'll get people killed, and so much more. Here it's all happening. On more than one occasion he hoped I'd get pregnant and have a child that he'd raise himself and make king. A do-over. He planned to marry me off, but the few royals who aren't of fae ancestry had no interest due to all the wars father kept declaring. All these years it's been my savior—that I wasn't forced into some awful, political marriage because so many sovereigns despised Father. But that didn't stop him from encouraged me to sleep with guards with hope one would stick and I'd bear an offspring. Can you fathom that experience? *That's* how little faith he had in me."

"Ree." Caitriona's earlier rage snuffed out and the compassion she was known for filled her expression. "I'm sorry he did that to you. I never knew. I had no idea. You're enough though. You're all the things he feared because he was *weak*. You're compassionate, thoughtful, and understanding. This is so hard because you're trying to do everything right for all the people of our queendom, not just yourself and your self-interests. You're nothing Father said you were, you're so much better than that. But please don't force me to go away. Don't send me off to some cabin. Father locked me away my entire life and I'm done with that. I won't be locked away anymore."

Greer shook her head. "I've told you this before and I'll tell you it again. I can't lose you, Cait. I've lost Barden already. This war is vastly uneven; the likelihood of us failing is great. I refuse to allow others to die while I sit back at a castle, so I'm going to the field. I need to focus and if you're on the field, I won't focus at all. I need to know you're safe so I can do what I'm there for. This gives us a chance. It gives me a chance to survive, and it gives you a chance to live to become queen if I fall."

It gives our queendom a chance to continue when I die in this battle, Greer wanted to say. But she couldn't, *wouldn't*, admit this sinking certainty to Caitriona. She admitted enough as it was. Caitriona could piece it all together.

The possibility was always there when war was afoot, but Caitriona didn't need to know how certain Greer was of her impending failure. In the end they were a kingdom with no understanding of magic and no true advantage against it. In this, her father was right to fear magic makers. The fae had a strategy on their side that many of her guards had never witnessed due to her family's ban on magic. How could they accurately prepare to fight when there was a generational lack of understanding of these powers? Even with the certainty of failure, Greer only wanted to protect Caitriona from the truth of it all.

Caitriona's lip quivered and she swallowed, looking to the window for a moment. "So, you're sending me away."

"To the cottage in the woods north of the fields. The one I sent Ailith's family to when father realized Ailith took you beyond the valley. I'll provide some of your guards to ensure protection, and a few ladies to help you with dressing and food preparation and all the rest. I'll send daily messages with updates about the war so you're still knowledgeable of how things are going."

Caitriona turned her attention to the floor. She looked like a chastised child if it wasn't for the dangerous horns that curled out of her delicate skull. "Could you at least send Raum and Ceenear with me? I know you could use them on the battlefield, but they shouldn't have to fight their own kind and it would be nice to have familiar faces with me."

Greer allowed herself to consider this. She expected more of a fight from her sister but after everything, the least she could do was provide some minor comfort through company. She lost her lover, the friends from Greenbriar, and was being shipped off and away from the war. Ceenear and Raum were both warriors in their own right and would be great defenses should anyone find the cottage as well.

"If they're willing to go with you, I'll allow it."

Caitriona's eyes brightened, but there was still a guarded look to her; something that made Greer's stomach turn. She didn't like the distance between them; would sending her sister away only make it worse? But better to have Caitriona mad at her than dead.

"Thank you," her sister replied and Greer relaxed.

"Once we return tomorrow you're to pack your things and will leave the following day."

CHAPTER ELEVEN

AILITH

The hushed sound of the soles of leather boots crossing the stone floor grew as they approached the cage. The metal door's hinges groaned from the pressure of a hand. Ailith remained motionless with her eyes closed and forced her breathing to slow. Fiana pressed against her, stiff with similarly timed breaths both in and out while Ailith conjured the Elder Tree in her mind for some comfort. She pictured the colorful ribbons above and the large roots along the ground. She thought of the autumn morning she sat there before she met Caitriona. If she were there now, she'd kneel beneath it, her hands touching the thick, familiar roots, and pray to the tree: *May whoever is standing outside our cell truly believe we're asleep and leave us alone.*

"It's a shame we couldn't get the dragon beast, but I suppose her lover will do," a voice murmured. The tone was thick and low, as if he spoke through molasses and spit. It was a voice Ailith imagined matched a face that would specifically bring a scowl to her own and was harsh enough to rip her from her vision of the tree.

"What're you going to do with her?" Another voice questioned.

There wasn't an instant response. Instead, Ailith heard the shuffle of boots, the crinkle of leather, and the metal of the cage continued to groan under the pressure of a hand.

Finally, the low voice responded. "We already took her likeness and a call was made through a speaking stone. The princess and the fae who abandoned us were heading to the marsh like we hoped. We sent the Starling and others to ambush them. Hopefully they'll take the princess."

Ailith's stomach turned.

"Is he going to marry her or just use her for her powers?"

"Depends on his mood. He flip-flops about what conquest he'd like to achieve with her."

"Should we be speaking about this in front of them?" A kick to the metal bars and Ailith tensed, trying not to jump from the sudden noise.

"They aren't going anywhere, it doesn't matter."

Ailith's heartbeat became insistent. The rage she felt when she wore the necklace and heard men in the loft of the Umberfend outpost's barn talking about killing Caitriona flicked back to life. Caitriona was walking into a trap and she was in a cell miles away, unable to warn her. But beyond that, it was the indifferent discussion about her life and power that incensed her. Marry Caitriona? Take her magic? Ailith's breathing picked up and beneath the blanket, Fiana's hand settled over her's, squeezing it to still her.

"It'd go quicker if we found Kayl and used him to force magic into your father," the other voice replied. He sounded small, nasally, and like he had a punchable face.

"He's missing again?"

"More and more. Seems lost to the breeze. But your father isn't ready to let him go yet."

"He's too reliant on him," the man murmured. Ailith

wracked her mind, attempting to recall his name. The son of Malcolm, Shad? A proper bastard if rumors were true, and if there was anything Ailith learned, it was that tales of awful people traveled further than those with favorable characteristics, and she heard nothing but awful things about Shad.

The footsteps shifted, their movement curling around the outer rim of the cage. Shad's hands drifted over the metal; the *thunk, thunk, thunk* of hardened fingers over each bar. The leather boots paused and sighed under his weight. He hit the bar, the clang of the metal loud and making both Ailith and Fiana jump.

There was the breath of a laugh, a taunting thing filled with vile enjoyment from the expense of others.

"That'll wake them," he murmured before his footsteps eased away. A key slipped into place somewhere in the distance, a bolt shifted, and a door swung open, but not to their cell.

Ailith lay still, listening as the footsteps receded and the door closed. At last, the lock sounded. Opening her eyes, she slipped her fingers over the edge of the dirty blanket. The fabric made her nerves bristle and she desperately did not want to touch it any longer. Despite the sensory recoiling, she slowly pulled the edge of the blanket down until she peeked over the moth-eaten fabric. The room was empty beside Fiana and herself.

"Alright, get out," Fiana growled, sitting up and thrusting her hands forward as if pushing something invisible away. Black ink-like shadow funneled from her mouth and wept from her eyes, pooling onto the blanket and leaking over the floor. It gathered, taking all its droplets with it as it congealed and became a more solid figure with dimension and features.

"You have to help Caitriona," Ailith blurted. "She's walking into a trap. You heard him."

"*It's too late and I'm not strong enough.*" Kayl's body curled over itself like a snake, but the shape of his head remained, the wisps of his darkened soul created a forlorn expression.

"What's this about the king still needing you?"

"*We're attached, he and I, at least to some degree. He's used my strength and power so much he can control me. He can will me to do his bidding, at least when I'm nearby. I need distance from him, a way to part from him and tether myself to a magic that isn't in close proximity. Because here, even now, I feel his pull. He's trying to reel me in. He's going to use my power to create things I don't want to. Creatures, beasts, and other magics I regret partaking in.*"

Ailith narrowed her eyes. "Is this what it took to realize what you did to Caitriona was wrong?"

Fiana sighed. "Ailith, not again."

"No." Ailith held up a hand, stilling Fiana. "Let me just get this out and I won't bring it up anymore. I promise."

She turned toward the dark specter and frowned. When she met him, he was a man. Faded, his eyes hollow, and older than he appeared, but he was solid. He lived and breathed. He had a home, a life, and now it was reduced to this. Just a wisp of a ghost, just the darkness of his hatred, and Ailith almost felt sorry for him and likely would if only she released this one thing. "You took an innocent girl and forced her body to turn into something she had no control over. Her body split apart, she was covered in her own blood and gore, and you took pleasure in that. I remember your expression when you froze me into place and watched her double over in pain. You *enjoyed* it. You took pleasure in assaulting her mind and body. She had no say in what she became. She had no say in what she did. Now you understand your role in it all; you were the orchestrator; you understand the pain you caused, correct?"

Ailith expected Kayl to hesitate, but he immediately

replied as his form inched closer and ghostly hands held together as if pleading for understanding.

"For a moment, I felt I won, like I finally achieved my revenge. Then I saw Caitriona's face as she crumbled under the curse. She had such fear, likely as much as the very people I tried to avenge. After becoming an unbound, much of my lingering rage faded and I could no longer ignore my regret. That's something books do not specify, when you become an unbound much of your anger and drive vanishes. My pride, my success, drifted away, and I was left with sorrow, guilt, and knowing there's nothing I can do to change what I did to her. I'd ask forgiveness if I met her, but I don't expect her forgiveness. That would do nothing for her nor change what's already done. It would only be a thing to appease my own guilt."

Ailith found herself silenced. He said it all; perhaps he understood that no apology could erase what he did. Ailith leaned back, comforted by his admission.

"So, what're you hoping to do now, Kayl?" Ailith asked, her voice quieter and less poisonous. "You want to find someone with magic that can help keep you alive but isn't in the proximity of the mountains? How can you do that if you don't have much strength?"

He shook his head and wisps of his essence floated off him. *"Hope I find someone willing to help from within the astral plane. But for now, you need to make a plan. I'll return as quickly as I can to unlock the door but time passes oddly here in this in-between state. I make no promises to time."*

He faded without another word and disappeared like a ghost until there was nothing but the emptiness between her and Fiana. Tension released from Ailith's shoulders, the tight pressure of stress slipped, and she slumped against the wall.

"What're we going to do? We've been here for weeks and don't know what's going on with the queendom. We only know Malcolm hasn't done a formal attack yet and he's growing powerful."

Fiana frowned and sat on the ground. "The room with all the fae has a ton of supplies for potions and spells. I can make some that strengthen us, things to help us heal or keep our energy up. If I'm lucky, there'll be enough supplies to help get us back to the queendom."

"You can do that?" Ailith looked at her, knowing full well Fiana was capable of doing such magic but finding it troubling solely because of Fiana's expression. It was uncertain. Weary. There was something wrong.

"The bottles and vials aren't labeled. There's no detail of what anything is and there are similar herbs and liquids. Whether by color, smell, taste. The differences are so minimal but they can be deadly."

Ailith looked at the door to the fae's room. "Like carrot flowers, they won't kill you, but there are other flowers who have a subtle difference that if you consume them, they'll consume you."

"Exactly. And from my brief look over the table, I don't know what I'd work with. It looks like there's a lot of ingredients to do things that could deeply harm people if used incorrectly."

"It's a risk."

Fiana nodded. "A risk we need to decide if we're willing to take. If anything, we'll have to make some spells for protection and get moving. We might not be able to come back to do more, we might just have to plow forward."

"So, when Kayl returns, we'll go to the other room and make as many potions we can with what they have, then get out, but," Ailith leaned back and checked the doorway, "we have to break the fae's bonds. We need to give them a fighting chance."

"They're fighting your people." Fiana's brows were raised, a silent challenge to Ailith.

"*They* are," Ailith waved towards the window. "Malcolm and those who follow him. But not *them*. Not the vast majority of the fae. Grouping people into one category due to the awful behavior of a few is dangerous work. It's a quick path to becoming like Malcolm or Cearny."

A flicker of a smile appeared on Fiana's lips. "Just checking. I haven't had a chance to talk to the regular Ailith in a few weeks between your being knocked out and possessed by the necklace."

"I suppose that's fair." Ailith crossed her arms over her chest to embrace herself. Her stomach turned as she fought the sense of unease drifting through her body. The memory of fear, the lurking quiver of it, pressed on her insides. Her heartbeat rose and her pulse thundered in her ears upon focusing on the memory of terror. "Fiana, what terrified me so much? I can't remember it; I just remember fear."

Fiana shook her head. "Every time you grew scared, you said nonsensical things or just screamed. It was awful. I couldn't touch you, couldn't draw near you. You kept mentioning a *she*. Some woman. Some fae, I guess. But never anything more than that."

"The fear's still in me, even now."

"I know," Fiana whispered. Her dark eyes took Ailith in, roaming over Ailith's body as her lips turned downward. "Ailith, I haven't mentioned it but, your hair. I can see it in your hair."

Ailith looked at the hunter who, lifting her hand, flicked Ailith's hair forward over Ailith's shoulder. She pinched it between her fingers and held it up for Ailith to see. Her brown hair now had streaks of white.

"Every time you'd have those moments of terror your hair

grew whiter. Like the very terror drew out of your head and sapped your hair of color."

She couldn't help the laugh that escaped her throat. "Cait's hair turned gold in the same way. Not through terror, but streaks like this."

A burst of trumpets exploded from beyond the windows and cut the conversation off as Ailith jumped. The fear curdling in her stomach slipped into her spine like splinters. Fiana let Ailith's hair go as they climbed to their feet. Stepping to the sliver of window overlooking the expansive marble deck beyond, filled with the brightness of the sun that made it painful to look at the white stone, Ailith squinted as she tried to make sense of the scene. The outcrop filled with people; their number reducing the brightness of the white marble, and the trumpets reverberated as a man with dishwater-colored hair stepped out from the crowd. Dressed in fine clothing with his head held high, Ailith narrowed her gaze. She didn't know what Malcolm looked like, but by his stance alone she assumed he was the fae king.

Turning his back to them, he spoke to the crowd. His voice remained only a murmur, but applause and cheers sounded whenever he paused his speech. At last, he shifted toward the cluster of sword-clad guards who parted and allowed two guards to lead a figure forward. The crowd silenced; all watched a tall, thin woman with black hair filled with streaks of gray step forward. Her countenance was one of strength, unbothered by the stares of the fae that filled the area. Niveem.

The woman was the official for the mountain peak of Ulla Syrmin, the very one Ailith stumbled upon when the mist enveloped her and Caitriona two years prior. At the time, they hadn't known Caitriona was cursed. It was Niveem who shared that knowledge in her quiet yet serious way and gently guided Caitriona through learning her draconic powers. After the curse completed, when Caitriona sought refuge in the mountains to heal from the onslaught done upon her body, it was Niveem who attempted to drive the young woman to accept the changes thrust on her.

Ailith always considered Niveem with awe and fascination. She wasn't a queen, but she took care of the people in her town, and she saw the special attributes of all her citizens, whether they had magic or not, despite that Niveem herself had an abundance of high powers. There was no favoritism, she considered the good of all. She was kind and had immediately welcomed Ailith and made her safe in her home during a time where uncertainty and fear was abundant. It was the first time Ailith encountered a person with power who had good intentions.

Powers that likely were now in Malcolm's possession, based on how gaunt Niveem had become and the iron grip the guards surrounding her had on her arms, as if their very presence wasn't to ensure she didn't escape but kept upright and moving. She stumbled and they righted her, leading her through the crowd until she came to stand before Malcolm. He turned to the crowd and spoke again, but Ailith only had eyes for Niveem as she wavered. She thought of Niveem's wife in the next room and desperately wanted to rush there, to tell her Niveem was outside the window, and that she had to hold on and gain her strength to return to her. Perhaps seeing her would empower her and give her more energy to fight. Ailith knew if she saw Caitriona she'd do the same.

And then the blade was produced by a guard. Shining in the sunlight, Ailith leaned back, realizing what it was there for.

"No," Ailith whispered, barely registering Fiana's gasp. Ailith gripped the edge of the window, pulling herself closer. "No, no—"

The blade swung upward, the sun glinted off its curve like a deadly wink, and the guard knocked Niveem to her knees.

She collapsed and caught herself with her hands. She remained on all fours for a moment. Just long enough for the air of the room to choke Ailith from the realization of what she was going to witness.

The blade swung down and Ailith screamed. She pressed her face against the slivered opening in the stone, one hand pressing out with her pale fingers in the daylight reaching, reaching for the fae ruler. Niveem lifted her head, turning to look over her shoulder, in the final moment before the blade struck her neck.

Niveem's head rolled forward, a pool of blood expanding like a carpet, and there was a pause from the group. Ailith was certain they could hear her sobs until Malcolm let out a sound of excitement and his followers fell in line, reacting with applause as Niveem's head stopped its roll and her black hair soaked into the pool of growing blood.

Ailith fell back from the window, eyes hot and tears running down her face. Her body tingled, the world swam, and Ailith found herself grasping her chest with heartbreak.

"How did you know her?" Fiana whispered, turning back from the window.

"She's our friend. She's the one we've been trying to reach," Ailith cried, using the base of her hands to rub the tears from her eyes. "She's the wife of that fae woman I was talking to. She's powerful and kind. She's—"

"*Dead.*"

The glimmer of Kayl stood outside the cage. "*Malcolm's distracted, he's happy with the burst of remaining power from Niveem. Now's our chance and I can't help anymore beyond this. Take this opportunity. Things are moving quickly. There's battles brewing. He's already sent out a group of soldiers, I don't know where, but he's planning to send more. Still, there's more to even that.*"

Kayl rushed to Fiana, siphoning himself into her through

her mouth and eyes. She screamed and fell toward the door of the cage, her hand grasping the handle as black smoke eased from her fingertips to work the lock. The metal door clanked open and swung outward, and Kayl's essence jolted from Fiana's lips, falling to the floor in a heap as she breathed heavily.

"Never do that again," Fiana hissed pointing at Kayl whose form slouched against the wall. Ailith slipped from the cage, staring at the former magic maker.

"I won't, I'm sorry, but for now ..."

Kayl leaned forward, stretching his spectral fingers to their temples and sinking into their brains; cold, cool tendrils that slipped along nerve endings and cells, attaching itself to Ailith like a dastardly virus. Ailith gasped as images filled her mind with detail greater than her most intense dreams. The battlefront, weeks or days away, with the marshes filling with people and creatures. Fire rained from the sky and Ailith's body filled with the sense of dread, terror, and everything she never wanted in the world. The image became a flash of white and it ended as quickly as it began.

Kayl pulled back, extracting himself from connecting with the women, and Ailith swallowed the taste of bile. Kayl's hand slipped over her and Fiana's shoulder, encouraging them forward. *"Now go."*

CHAPTER TWELVE

Róisín

I sla leaned back. A cloak hung from Róisín's canopy bed frame, the color shifting in the low evening light but it wasn't what Róisín focused on. She stood nervously beside the old woman, studying Isla's face for any indication of her thoughts.

"I redid the stitchwork along the right shoulder," Róisín offered; her fingers reached for the stitching. Isla had been silent for so long Róisín was certain the old crow was judging her work. "It was too tight and bunched the fabric and made the thread noticeable. The stitching towards the bottom was loose, too, so I tightened that as well."

Isla held a finger over Róisín's lips, silencing her before stepping backward and crossing her arms over her chest. Tilting her head to the side and narrowing her eyes, she muttered in the same language Róisín recalled from childhood. A language lost to her due to time and lack of interaction. Her mother's language stirred something deep in Róisín's memories, like longing for a woman she barely remembered yet still missed.

The cloak stirred. Although it hadn't moved, the energy

around it twitched. Róisín's stitchwork, done in a green similar to the cloak color itself, brightened and began to glow. A pattern released, covering the expanse of the fabric and detailing the intricate embroidery she did over many weeks. She meant to make two, one for each daughter, but turned her focus entirely to this one because its need became rapidly apparent when Caitriona departed for the marsh to find Ailith.

"This should work." It wasn't praise, necessarily, but Isla's words made Róisín stand a little straighter. The old woman nodded and the brilliance of the stitching disappeared as the cloak returned to being simply a cloak.

"Is there anything else? Should I do more? What about—"

Isla's hand clasped Róisín's and she looked down at the old woman who offered a smile. "You've done well. It's a shame you were so impatient as a child, you would've been a great magic maker if you had the time to take in lessons."

Róisín let out a breath of a laugh that mingled with her own frustration. "Alas, I was too focused on other tasks. I thought you could see the future; could you not have predicted I'd need my magic?"

Isla's expression hardened. "I can only sometimes see the future. But the pain of that ability is that you're left to live with it—knowing what's to come. You can only help guide those you care for to the right path but ultimately, trying to control the outcome takes away their free will, and sends everyone down a dark path with a certain downfall in their future. Anyway, would you have listened if I told you I knew you'd need it?"

"Probably not." Róisín touched the cloak before her. She too had an idea of the future for Greer and Caitriona when they were young. She knew there was a curse and had no idea how to fix it. She was left only with the option to keep a close eye on those around her and protect her daughters as best she could, and now she had to let them go, allow them their free will to leave her for places she couldn't follow in ways she could not protect. At least there was this, the green cloak made with her loving hand.

RÓISÍN FOLDED THE SUMMER CLOAK AND PLACED IT beside Caitriona's bag. When she requested it made, she asked for it to be lightweight for when the sun beat against it, but capable of chasing away the chill of cooler, near-autumn nights. It was the perfect shade for summer foliage and forest floors and would allow the wearer to become part of the background with ease. The embroidery was nearly invisible, not unless you studied the detail of the fabric closely, and that was the point.

Fingering the stitchwork one final time, she turned to the items in Caitriona's bag. Her face was a mask, serious and bordering displeased which didn't reflect how her heart swelled with such love that it was near breaking. The bag was filled with dresses, nightgowns, shirts and pants for many months ahead. Summer through winter; Elder Tree-willing the battle would be over by the following spring. But wars had a funny way of lasting for years and it seemed, despite Caitriona being locked at home for most of her life, her daughter understood that likelihood from the books she read. Books were once the guaranteed route Caitriona took to taste the world and even that was limited since Cearny ordered so many pieces of literature burned or locked away—but also possibly, perhaps more *probably* if Róisín was honest with herself, Caitriona understood due to the many months that passed with Greer away and fighting.

Another bag sat near the bed and Róisín allowed herself to

glance at its contents as well, although she didn't go through it as with the previous. There were scraps of papers, notebooks, quills and jars of ink. A bag of nuts, a knit shawl Róisín recalled the guard Ailith gave Caitriona, and an old wooden horse Caitriona played with as a child and kept straight through adulthood. Róisín knew Caitriona kept it in a drawer. A keepsake, a comfort, and to see it laying in the bag made Róisín's eyes burn with tears. The object came from a time of innocence, a time before there was heartache and injury.

Although that was a lie.

Caitriona had already experienced injury at that point, it was simply that she didn't remember it. She didn't exhibit outward scars of the dragon attack. Some scars rested beneath the skin and found a way of showing much later. Still, time passed and her small children with their sweet voices and worlds filled with possibility were lost to time. Now they knew heartache, sorrow, and pain in ways Róisín was incapable of taking away. She wished she could give them the world and keep them from harm.

She suspected even if her daughters had children of their own, she'd still view them as her babies, but this happened too fast. They were too young to deal with wars and heartbreak to this degree; then again, Caitriona and Greer were both older than Róisín was when she married Cearny. Maybe they weren't as young as she thought, or she actually had been too young for what *she* endured. A child having a child, slipping into a loveless marriage and forced to obey a man who didn't express emotions other than through rage and the stench of drink.

"Mother?" Caitriona called as she stepped into the room, snapping Róisín from her thoughts. "I was just looking for you, we must've passed each other."

Róisín turned from Caitriona's bed and offered a kind

smile. "I was at the tailor; I had a cloak made for you. I also have some other supplies."

Caitriona drew close and Róisín couldn't help but reach out. Her fingers brushed over the curve of her daughter's cheek then pushed the golden hairs back over her shoulder. She missed the red-headed girl Caitriona once was with a familiar ache. It was a version of her that she loved, the form of her that was brought into the world with a swath of hair that mirrored her own. But that form was never to return, yet her love for this version of her daughter was so great it nearly made her dizzy. "How are you feeling?"

Caitriona's shoulders dropped and she looked at her mother. Taking in a deep breath as if filling herself whole, Róisín knew what would come next: a flood of confession.

"I feel betrayed by Greer. I can't believe she's sending me away. I mean, I understand the logic behind her decision. But emotionally? I hate it. I'm hurt and angry I can't fight for others and Greer's too blind by her grief to see my strength."

"You can feel all those things." Róisín stepped behind Caitriona, gathering her hair and braiding it down her back with quick, practiced movements. She learned how to swim through Caitriona's running words of concern years ago and navigating the tumult came easily. "Betrayal, understanding, rage, sorrow. It's all valid and normal. Believe me, I've a lifetime of feeling multiple things at once."

"It hurts. That's the worst of it. I just *hurt* from Greer's behavior and everything that's occurring each day. I can't get my head above water. I can't take in enough air before the next thing hits. I lost Ailith, then I saw Barden die, and now Declan and May are gone. I didn't even get the opportunity to bury them; Greer made me leave. They're probably thrown in a pit somewhere with other people who died. They don't deserve that. No one in that town does."

Róisín tied Caitriona's braid then settled on the edge of

her daughter's bed. She took Caitriona's hands in her own and looked at them, delicate and harmless in appearance with sores on her palm from practicing swords after a lifetime of little work. The hands of a royal. Something Róisín's hands never mirrored, due to scars from slipped knives and the aged skin because she never had the creams royals had until she was an adult. Despite the appearance of lightness Caitriona's fingers portrayed, Róisín knew they could form into deadly weapons.

She held them lightly within her own and made circles with her thumbs over the back of Caitriona's hands as she considered her plans and how the following days, if not weeks or months, would pan out. "When you feel that way, you need to find something to hold onto. That something may change, it may lose its importance and you'll have to find something else, but you must always look for something. Anything that'll make it worth pulling through and existing a little easier."

"That's hard to think of right now," Caitriona whispered, looking at their entwined hands and returning the smallest pressure to Róisín.

"I know. So, you have to get creative. We know where Ailith is now, yes? She's in the mountains and with Malcolm. She's alive. We know the monster hunter you hired is alive as well. That's something to hold onto."

"And Greer isn't allowing anyone to rescue them. She's determined to waste guards to watch me sit in a cottage, but not to spare them to free Ailith."

Róisín nodded. There was no denying it. More guards were going to be stationed at the cottage than were needed to seek Ailith, but Greer was steadfast in this decision to send Caitriona away. Róisín had argued with Greer over it. She attempted to get her eldest daughter to see reason, but Greer was steadfast. In her mind, sparing guards to keep the heir safe was better than sparing guards to save two and possibly be killed in the process. Róisín understood her point, but sometimes making the less logical decision to save a meaningful relationship was the best choice. But who was she to make those calls? She was only the queen mother, and the queen made it abundantly clear she wouldn't accept any advice from her.

"When I arrived at the castle, I thought I'd change the world. I thought your father loved me, and through his love, I'd use him. I'd convince him magic wasn't bad. That it can be a force for good."

"You had this plan in place when you met him?"

"It's why I sought out his attention. But my downfall came through his using me as well. I was a plot point for his story to the masses. In his mind, I was going to be the poor girl that rose to fame and fortune. A good way to convince the lower class to follow him. That he understood the pains they experienced because he loved a lower-class girl. And I didn't see any of it."

"How come?" Caitriona asked, settling upon the edge of the bed as well, but she didn't pull her hands from her mother's grasp. Róisín continued running her thumbs over the skin of her hands. It was amazing they could be covered by slick scales and leather-hard, and then slip back to such softness.

"He spoiled me in those early years with gifts. Trinkets, dresses, soft beds and private baths. All the things I never experienced growing up. He'd listen to me and look so proud when presenting me at court. Then I fell in love with him. Try as I might to only view him as a chess piece on a board, it happened. I loved the attention—maybe that was it, actually. Not so much that I loved him, but the attention he gave me. It filled me up and made me blind. I didn't notice the more subtle behavior." Róisín looked at Caitriona, the way her brows rose and she remained silent and still, taking in each of Róisín's words and digesting them behind those expressive molten eyes. Now that she began to speak, to share her past, words tumbled from her lips and she had little care to stop the flow.

"I failed to see the way his eyes dimmed when I spoke to him, that his smile never quite made the corners of his eyes crease, that he'd shift from me the moment we were alone. I was oblivious to it. When we married, he made no effort to hide his disdain. It was as if, once we were bound beneath the Elder Tree to one another, he no longer had to pretend. He became the man you knew."

Caitriona's lips parted and her shoulders dropped, she pulled her gaze from Róisín's face and looked to the floor. The pink of her tongue ran over the edge of her lips and her voice was soft with compassion. "Mother, why did you stay? Why did you put up with that?"

"There's no place I could've gone that he wouldn't have reached." Róisín looked at her daughter. She kept her voice gentle as she wanted Caitriona to see how impossible leaving could be. "Before I had you and your sister, I foolishly thought I'd still get the upper hand and then later I thought if I stayed, I'd prevent further pain."

"He still caused plenty of pain."

"I know." Róisín's shoulders dropped; her voice came out as a whisper. For decades no matter her choice, it was the wrong one and they would come away harmed, and she knew she'd forever wonder if she made the wrong decision. Would they have found a way to survive if they left? She'd never know.

Caitriona's hand touched her cheek, drawing Róisín's attention upward. Caitriona frowned, her hands finding their way to the length of her golden hair and entwining with the strands at the end of her braid. "Greer said he was disappointed in her as well."

"That's true. Were you happy to leave when Greer helped you escape? Had you ever considered leaving before that?"

Caitriona's brow furrowed. She was silent for a moment, considering her mother's words, then tilted her head to meet her eyes. "I feared disappointing him more. I knew he didn't appreciate me and I felt, foolishly, that if I remained and did as he asked then perhaps one day he'd come around. But also, I was afraid that if I left it would hurt you and Greer. I didn't want to do that."

Róisín nodded. "I didn't leave because I thought the same. That one day, things would change and we'd be better together. That all I tried to do to convince your father to accept magic would sink in and he'd understand. Then I became pregnant with Greer and I couldn't leave because it would put her in danger. Then I became pregnant with you and it was all the same. I was backed into a corner. If I left, it meant leaving both of you to his full control. It meant leaving you to his care or lack thereof. If I took you both with me, I wouldn't get very far."

"He'd have turned the kingdom over to get Greer back," Caitriona murmured.

"Yes, he would have, and killed anyone who tried to help us. Unless he had a bastard child somewhere, but he didn't. I had to take plenty of herbs to get pregnant with Greer and I'm not entirely sure how it happened the second time. He otherwise seemed infertile because I certainly wasn't the only one he laid with."

Caitriona's golden brows shot up; her discomfort obvious. Róisín squeezed her hands, pushing past her comment.

"All to say, I was stuck, the same as you feel stuck now. But I looked to you both, my beautiful daughters, and you were what I held onto. You helped compel me forward. When Greer was taken from me to be primarily raised by your father, with very little influence from me, I focused on you. When you fled the castle, I turned to Greer and I kept an eye on your father. I was certain he was going to do something awful and I wanted to be sure I could try to stop it."

"What would you have done? After all that he did, what could stop Father?"

"At this point, you both were adults. I saw you through your childhood. I would've killed him myself if I had to."

They fell quiet, sitting side by side holding hands as the night bugs beyond the window made their rhythmic songs and the castle held silence as if the very stones of the structure were listening to the discussion with rapt attention. Róisín took in a deep breath and pulled her hands away, pressing her palms to the bedding to push to her feet. She smiled and nudged Caitriona's shoulder.

"I also brought some supplies for you that are of a certain variety. Isla aided me in making them." She turned to the bag she carried in and placed it beside the others. It was smaller in size, more like a purse that could be worn across the breast, but filled to the brim with items. "These are all magical in substance so pay close attention."

Within the bag were vials and pouches. The first row of vials held a dark sap in each. She ran her thumb over the cork stopper of the vial. It was amazing the contents could be a blessing and a curse; that it was strong enough to bring someone back to life, but also take their life away as it had with Barden. "This is sap from the Elder Tree. It has to be ingested to work. Whether through a wound or drained into a mouth. If you touch it with your bare skin, it won't do anything; it must connect within. You've seen what it's capable of already."

Róisín ran her fingers to the next row of vials whose liquids varied in color. "Isla said Ailith had many of these on her when your curse overcame you, so they should be familiar. The blue one will help keep you warm in snowy areas. The green will help you heal from sickness; these from cuts or sores. Oh, and these have energy should you need it."

She pointed to the pouches. "A powder to brush over your hands and feet that'll help silence your footfall so you may sneak about unseen. And more eyebright flowers, should you need to take to visions, although I'd direct the visions to us if needed and stay away from Malcolm's court. They'll end on their own, but I worry since he could see you."

Caitriona touched the bag but didn't inspect the vials. "Mother, this must've been so much work."

"It's to help you." Róisín smiled. "I've attempted visions of what'll happen for you in these coming moments and they're hidden from me. Isla told me that happens at times when a choice is to be made. I want you to be prepared for all you'll face. War's something you can never predict."

Caitriona gripped her mother's hands, squeezing them tightly. "Thank you, Mother."

It hurt Róisín to not tell Caitriona everything. She *did* see the future, just like Isla, and it was grim, but she also saw the bright, vibrance of life; details shared with the smoke of herbs that were not meant to be shared with either of her daughters. Details they'd soon understand through the forward thrust of time.

There was a soft call in the hall; the guards spoke in unison and it brought a moment of stillness between mother and daughter. Róisín looked at the door and frowned. "Your sister's coming. Don't inform her of the measures I've given you, please. Let it be a secret between us. She's suffering greatly, and her morals are teetering due to the hurt she's endured. She loves you, please remember that."

Caitriona frowned, her body rigid as her sister drew close. "I know she loves me deep inside her heart. But she has an awful way of showing it."

Róisín pulled her hand from Caitriona's grip and reached

into the folds of her skirt and withdraw a sheet of paper. She pressed it into Caitriona's palm, closing Caitriona's thin fingers over the paper and tightening her grip.

"Her behavior may worsen before it gets better, I fear. Now listen closely: I want you to read this when you're alone. Let no one see it."

Caitriona stared at her mother as if trying to discern something within her gaze. Her gold eyes glimmered, her pupils dilating, and she nodded. "I promise."

"Caitriona?" Greer called from outside the bedroom door. Róisín dropped Caitriona's hand and moved from the bed, turning her attention to Caitriona's wardrobe where she pulled out additional clothing as if she was doing that all the while.

"Yes?" Caitriona called, looking temporarily confused. She lifted the cloak Róisín made for her and held it to her chest with the fabric covering her hand clutching the letter. She turned toward the doorway and smiled as Greer entered the room.

"I wanted to see how packing's coming along. You should rest, you'll be leaving early tomorrow."

"Nearly done," Caitriona replied with a half-smile. "Mother gave me this beautiful cloak. I think I'll wear it tomorrow."

Greer looked over the fabric briefly, as if just for show. "Alright, well, I'll send attendants to wake you and bring you breakfast. I'll see you then. Mother, Isla requests your presence, can you go to her?"

"Certainly," Róisín replied, smiling at both her girls as if the very air hadn't crackled with discomfort when they ended up in the same room. They would move past this, they had to. "I'll see you tomorrow before you leave, Caitriona."

CHAPTER THIRTEEN

CAITRIONA

The letter from her mother was nothing but ash, burned to a crisp in Caitriona's own hand after her sister left her room the night before. She took the ash and held it out her window, allowing the wind to take it from her fingertips and dance with it through the air. She couldn't risk leaving the burnt remains in the room—not that Greer had magic to revive such broken things, but with Lachlan remaining at the castle, Caitriona wouldn't risk it. Every day she was surprised by another element of Lachlan's seemingly unending power. He pieced together a broken glass just the day before, returning it to perfect condition, with only a wave of his hand. Perhaps he could make a burned letter return to its previous form as well.

Caitriona spent the night tossing and turning. After midnight, Crowley returned from drifting the skies. He followed Caitriona back to Wimleigh after Greenbriar, but he was restless and seemed obsessed with circling over the woods and flying north of Braewick Valley. Caitriona wondered if he was retracing his flight pattern and searching for Ailith once more.

She had the same desire. She wanted to shed her skin and grow scales. She wanted to feel the push of the air beneath her wings and the weightlessness as she lifted from the ground. In her dreams, she searched for Ailith in this matter. But in reality, there were too many eyes to the skies and she couldn't risk the chaos of her dragon form being witnessed in these tumultuous times. At least not yet.

When Crowley landed on the windowsill, clucking and hopping along the ledge until he hummed under Caitriona's gentle pets, she pulled free a few additional nuts and brought the bird to her bed where he snacked before settling into the crook of Caitriona's arm. Finally, still, at rest, and calm. Together, they slept until dawn turned the black sky to gray.

"Fly to the mountains, Crowley." Caitriona carried him to the windowsill. She pet his soft feathers and smiled at the purr-like sound rumbling from his throat. Crows weren't all rough edges and symbols of doom like stories told. They could be sweet, too. With his face pressed against the palm of her hand, she smiled. "Search the peaks; Ailith's there."

Offering another handful of nuts, she continued to run her fingers over his feathers as he ate them whole, tossing each back and down his throat before flapping his wings and hopping to the outer edge of the sill. He looked at her once before launching into the air, flying east toward the rising sun. A knock came to Caitriona's door, pulling her attention back to the room. It was time for her to leave as well.

Caitriona rushed through the morning hours with bites of breakfast while she dressed and her bags were carried from the room to be placed on Onyx's back. She met Ceenear and Raum in the hall, both looking less than thrilled to be sent to a cabin northward and away from the battle.

"Thank you for being willing to travel with me," Caitriona offered. They spoke very little to one another since the disaster in the marsh. All seemed hurt and shy around each other, and the guilt of having dragged them along clung to Caitriona's shoulders. It flared now as she braced herself for the next phase in their journey.

"Perhaps we'll be able to break free," Raum joked, although there wasn't any sign of humor in his face. He looked exhausted and on edge.

"Not with guards surrounding the cottage to keep watch," Ceenear murmured through clenched teeth. She kept her gaze forward, not meeting anyone's eye as she watched the movement of servants and other guards. "But I do thank you for thinking of us, Caitriona. Your sister's found much less use of us since we've returned. This at least feeds my desire to move."

"You'll get your fill, I promise." Caitriona smiled before turning down the hall towards the castle's exit.

"Trust yourself," Róisín whispered as she embraced Caitriona at the castle's gate. "I'll keep things moving along here, I promise."

"Be careful," Caitriona replied, holding her mother tightly. She considered the secrets they shared in the last day; they were so rich that Caitriona held them close to her breast. Her brow wrinkled with worry. "I don't trust him."

"I know. Nor do I, but once I did, and I have to remember that. I hope my judgment's enough to bring you comfort."

Caitriona stepped back and smiled at her mother. She was beautiful and there was a part of her heart fracturing by this parting. They were growing close again, closer in a way she was certain happened to all mothers and daughters who spent time together as adults. The transition from parent and small child, to parent and adult was a shift at first uncomfortable, but now Caitriona found appreciation for it. She enjoyed knowing her mother through honesty and this separation would bring a stop to that.

"Perhaps you can visit if there's little movement with the war?"

"I'll try, sweet lark." Róisín kissed Caitriona's brow before ushering her to Greer. The queen stood straight-backed with her gaze boring ahead. Caitriona licked her lips as she looked at her sister who was seemingly unwilling to meet her eyes.

Caitriona stepped before her. She wanted to hug Greer tightly, slap her, and plead she return to her former self; to cry and beg, but instead she knelt into an awkward curtsy as her cheeks burned.

When she stood, Greer hugged her stiffly; the embrace poured salt into the wound Greer's fear created. "As soon as it's safe, we'll retrieve you," she reassured Caitriona.

"I know." A smile, one that remained only on her lips, was all Caitriona could offer. She turned to Onyx and mounted the giant horse, towering over the others on horseback. She lifted her chin, knowing her arched horns shown in the sunlight as a towering crown, but she was no longer ashamed of them and it made her all the more determined in this moment to show that bravery before her sister.

Greer had argued that Onyx was too much for Caitriona, making her stand out, but Caitriona refused to ride any horse but Ailith's. If Greer was going to control all aspects of her life, the least she could do was allow her to take all remaining pieces of Ailith with her and keep them safe. It was a point that Caitriona assumed Greer expected to hear, because she quickly agreed with a tiredness of expectations being made reality.

They left the castle as sunshine hit the protective walls. Already the sun rose significantly later in the day, the brightness taking longer to slip over the valley's ridge, and the morning held a coolness that reminded Caitriona of the day she met Ailith in the early light of the first day of autumn.

Following the guards, they were a fierce procession that

followed the curve of the castle's outer walls towards the pathway which led to the fields north of the city. The last time Caitriona went down them, she witnessed Barden collapse to the forest floor. She never told Greer she had horrifying nightmares of his face in that moment as the strength of his legs disappeared. That his hand was outstretched toward Greer as his skin turned waxy and pale. His eyes had only been on Greer and no one else. It was a secret Caitriona would keep to her grave; Greer grieved enough as it was.

From that deadly breach of security, Greer had an uptick of guards circulating the woods to ensure their safe passage and that no other fae managed to make their way over their valley ridge. But first, they had to pass the expanse of the Elder Tree.

"May I pause here?" Caitriona called as the great boughs of the tree came into view. She turned to the guards clustered around her, meeting their gazes individually. "I'd like to leave a wish at the tree. And I promised Ceenear and Raum they'd see it while they stayed in our queendom, but they haven't yet."

Paul, granted the opportunity to head the guard for this venture as part of his punishment for the marsh kept him from the war fields, looked doubtfully at Caitriona. The other guards awaited his decision and at last he swallowed. The letter Róisín gave Caitriona stated she spoke to Paul and explained the situation. Caitriona hadn't believed it until she saw his unease.

"Ten minutes." Paul kept his eyes locked on Caitriona's. "We'll fan out to circle the tree and ensure no one can approach."

"Thank you," Caitriona replied. He nodded and turned back to the guards, directing them to spread out. With the tree deemed safe and empty of citizens, Caitriona approached.

"Be good," she whispered to Onyx, petting his nose after tying his reins to a tree. She left her bag of extra clothing and trinkets tied to him, but pulled down the satchel she packed overnight and hoisted it onto her back. Already she donned the side bag her mother brought the day prior and the cloak she gifted her. From Caitriona's waist hung Ailith's sword and dagger. She didn't bring any of her own weapons, but reasoned she wanted Ailith's because she missed the guard so much. It was a way to keep the memory of her close by.

Ceenear and Raum stepped forward, their weapons in hand as added protection for Caitriona. Neither bothered to remove their traveling packs and for that Caitriona was grateful. They followed her silently, oblivious to her plans, as she moved through the hedge toward the open area beneath the tree.

Since the quakes, the tree suffered greatly. A great maw opened at its base, a hole big enough for a man to squeeze through, and the leaves changed into their autumn colors with rapid speed. Branches and limbs dropped, broken off from summer storms, and scattered across the ground with hopes and dreams tied to them covered in dirt.

"So, this is the tree?" Raum asked as he stepped up beside Caitriona. He placed his hands on his waist and looked at the branches. "I have to admit, I'm slightly underwhelmed."

"It's dying. It looked much more impressive when it was healthy."

"What will you all do?" Ceenear asked as she stepped closer to the trunk and placed her hand gently upon it. "With all the dreams and wishes people tied to these trees, I imagine people won't take its death well."

"They aren't, from what I've heard." Caitriona circled the tree and studied the broken half that exposed the brightening blue sky. Her dragon body broke through in that spot, shattering half of the tree as she fell from the sky, and in the two years since, the exposed wood solidified and healed, but the scar remained. "People still visit here, although there've been restrictions placed upon it. Greer wants the tree to last as long as she can make it; losing a symbol of hope and dreams amidst a war is not a great symbol. We'll have to find some alternative. It's encouraging Lachlan said there are other Elder Trees in the world. Maybe another will grow here."

"The tunnels," Raum recalled, stepping to the opening in the center of the tree's trunk. "Do you think it's true? That if you went in you'd end up in another location?"

"Yes," Caitriona replied as she stood beside Raum, gazing down at the hole.

"How come?"

"My mother said it's true, and so I believe it. But just in case she's wrong, well, that's why I brought you two."

Raum turned toward her. She smiled, looking at the tree that still had branches spread overhead and the blinks of blue sky beyond. The breeze stirred the rainbow-colored ribbons still remaining; the coins hanging on strings clinked together and made a chorus of tinkling bell-like sounds.

"Lachlan said there's a tree near the Endless Mountains, even one possibly within the mountains itself. My mother told me there was a tree in her village that they used to worship, similar to the Elder Tree here. They tied ribbons and coins to it with their wishes, but it was much smaller than this. I think that's one of the saplings of the Elder Tree and it's right along the foothills of the Endless Mountains."

"Caermythlin, right?" Ceenear finished circling the tree and stood beside Caitriona.

Caitriona nodded, reaching to touch the edge of the hole before it became the interior wood of the Elder Tree where it split.

"The ruins of the town are near the mist for our kingdom."

"I've seen it," Raum offered. "On various patrols around the mist. It's close."

Caitriona smiled and looked at her friends. "You both can picture it easily enough, yes?"

The fae glanced at each other. "I suppose so..."

"Good, because that's where we're going." Caitriona stepped backward, bowing her head low so her horns cleared the top of the crack in the giant tree. She held a finger to her lips. "Just don't tell anyone."

Caitriona, the heir to Wimleigh Queendom, vanished from sight into the darkness of the Elder Tree's wooded realm.

CHAPTER FOURTEEN

The carts were freshly made, their woody scents still strong, and the iron clasps ensured sturdiness in battle while still gleaming in the sun with fresh grease. Upon the carts were virgin swords, too many to count, that had yet to see blood or kiss skin. The pile was overwhelming and just as dreary as the stacks of fresh arrows Greer and Lachlan passed.

"We still have armor being made, that takes much longer, understandably," the master blacksmith commented as an attendant stepped forward to hoist a chest piece into the air for Greer and Lachlan to look over. It was solid and the queendom's crest—a stylized picture of the Elder Tree—was brightly painted over the metal; a standard chest plate for the men that fought on foot.

Lachlan reached forward to run his finger over the crest, his brow furrowing with concentration that Greer realized was common for the man whenever he was studying something while putting pieces together in his mind. It wasn't just a chest plate he saw, but something else he was calculating.

"I apologize we do not have your kingdom's crest," the

blacksmith began and Lachlan looked up and blinked, as if not at first realizing the blacksmith spoke to him. *He probably doesn't realize they're speaking of Lachlan's kingdom either,* Greer thought as the skin of Lachlan's cheeks grew pink. *Ah, that was it.*

"Oh, don't apologize. It isn't my kingdom, at least not yet. I'm happy to fight beneath Wimleigh's banner."

Predictable response, Greer thought. The poor half-elf seemed so perpetually uncertain of the power they were fighting to hand to him. The blacksmith's chest puffed out and the crowd of guards seemed to straighten their postures. It took Greer a moment to realize the compliment Lachlan paid her. She tried to smile, even though she didn't feel emotion behind the expression.

Expendable, her father whispered into her ear, his spit moistening her skin. *All men who won't be missed. I never expected that lot to return home when they went to battle. Never bothered to learn their names, actually.*

The higher ranks and those from wealthy families had chest pieces designed with the queendom's crest as embossed steel that was thicker and heavier, and protected the wearer more. Greer had such high hopes to provide all guards with equal armor. It was one of the goals she set when she was crowned queen and she was already failing at this. They hadn't enough time nor money to make that provision.

Greer rolled her neck and looked over the gathered people. Lachlan was charming the masses as he looked over swords and additional breastplates. People clustered around him like he was a flame and they were moths. She felt a twist of bitterness in her gut. It all came so easy to him and he didn't even try, he didn't even *want* to be king, while she fought every day for any point of success in ruling.

She pulled her gaze from him and allowed it to drift over the crowd as she fought off a frown. A separate movement drew her attention as a woman from the castle stepped forward. She stood out from the rest—men and women covered in soot and sweat, grease and scars. Her hair was pinned under a cap, her skirts clean and the fabric bright in the sun; she wore the outfit of a castle maid, someone who cleaned rooms or ran errands for those who lived within. This was likely the first time she was ever amongst the blacksmiths and her awkwardness drew looks from those who weren't bent over red metal.

"I understand. It takes time to make armor and you've done a great deal already," Greer replied at last, pulling her attention back to the master blacksmith and offering her a forced smile. "Do you have an estimate of how quickly they'll be complete?"

"If we're attacked this week, your seasoned warriors will be in their armor. All new armor for them is already complete." She nodded to the host who backed away with the sample armor and returned to work. Turning to Greer, the master blacksmith placed her callused hands on her waist and nodded toward the line of blacksmiths who worked diligently. "We're halfway through preparing armor for the new guards. As you know, it takes longer with having to obtain their measurements, and with such an influx over so short a period of time. But we plan to make extra armor as well, in case more join. And in the worst-case scenario, we have old armor they can wear until more's completed."

"Good, thank you." Greer nodded as she stepped away.

"Can we carve into the metal? Will it damage its strength?" Lachlan stepped around Greer and gestured to the chest plate, his finger pointing to the expanse of metal and the queendom's crest. "There's magic in some symbols that can be activated by the hand of a magic maker. We could perhaps press spell work into the metal to provide further support for the guards. Protections that will help their energy or keep their blood from spilling from wounds too quickly. They're small measures, but I feel they're better than nothing."

The blacksmith made a sound of interest but Greer didn't follow what they began to say. Her attention already drifted as she turned to find the maid from the castle pushing through the crowd to a position behind Greer. The girl looked sheepish and Greer sighed, her entire body reacting to her arrival with pinpricks of anxiety and the sensation of her throat tightening. This was never good and whatever it was, she hoped the Elder Tree would grant her the grace to get behind closed doors and into privacy until she spiraled into the depths of her mind. "Can I help you?"

The woman blinked and lowered her gaze. Her hands quivered, and within them was a clutched letter. "My Queen, the Princess Caitriona asked me to give you this."

Greer took it from the woman's hand too roughly based on her slight jump. There was a murmur in the crowd not caused by this interaction but by another newcomer pushing his way through. Paul appeared over the heads of others. His tall, thin body squeezing by, walking forward as the sun glinted off the sweat on his brow. His face was flushed, and his blue eyes showed against his tan skin and the bright day. He shouldn't have returned to the castle already. It took hours by horseback to reach the northern cottage and return. If anything, he should've arrived home in the evening. Not before midday.

When his gaze moved over the crowd and met Greer's, her stomach sank, her throat became restricted as she tried to swallow.

"Your Highness! Queen Greer!"

"Move," Greer hissed to the people before her, ordering the crowd to part and spit Paul out. "What's happened?"

"It's Princess Caitriona."

"*Move*," Greer repeated, this time to Paul as she waved

him forward. "Whatever you're about to say, you'll do so inside." She turned to the crowd and flashed a smile that likely was similar to a grimace. Catching Lachlan's gaze, she gestured for him to stay. Lachlan's brows rose but he nodded, seeming to understand Greer before she announced, "Lachlan will see to the rest of the review. I trust his observances and I urge you all to listen to his recommendations. Thank you."

A guard called out, blades rose into the sky with salute, and the crowd parted to allow Greer's exit. She could never just *leave* a place; it always had to be with so much notice. Luckily this was brief as Lachlan turned back to the master blacksmith while the other blacksmiths returned to their work. Their attendants ran to retrieve items and the working yard was normal once more as Greer hurried to the castle with Paul following. Greer gripped Caitriona's unopened letter in her hand, feeling the paper crinkling in her grip and cutting into the soft skin where her thumb met her palm.

"She's vanished." Paul blurted as they walked through the doorway to the lower halls. A maid looked up from her mop, startled, and Greer waved her away. She grabbed her bucket and fled the hall, only glancing back once. Paul remained silent until she disappeared before rushing forward, his words a string of information with barely any breath. "We stopped at the Elder Tree, she wanted to show it to the fae. She's visited the Elder Tree plenty of times, even after the declaration of war, so we fanned out and ensured there were no threats and yet she took too long. We closed in and they were gone. All three of them. They vanished into thin air."

Greer cursed. "The hole in the damn tree. They took to the tunnels."

Paul blinked. "The ... what?"

"The tree, Paul. There's a hole in the tree, isn't there?" She took off, moving down the hallway to the main stairs with Paul attempting to keep up. Pressure built in her forehead and her breathing hitched. Laughter echoed through the halls that sounded like her father's.

"Yes, where the tree split."

"If you go into the split, apparently it'll spit you out somewhere in the world. They escaped through the damned hole."

"Is there anything you'll have me do?"

Greer stopped before the stairs and turned, her father's amused face appearing in a flash in her peripheral vision. She looked at Paul's young face and the clear panic he wore. She suspected, based on his behavior, he didn't know Caitriona's plans but … "Did you know their intentions?"

He stepped back and his face visibly paled.

"How much did you know, Paul?"

"Only that she'd want to visit the tree," he admitted. "The queen mother spoke to me last night and requested I allow Caitriona to say her peace with the Elder Tree if she asked. I haven't spoken to Caitriona nor the fae other than when Caitriona asked to stop there. That's all she told me too, that she wanted to show them the tree. Nothing about these intentions."

Greer's breathing was constricted in her throat. In the distance her father's laugh continued to bounce against the stone walls of the hall. He lurked in the shadows of her vision. The smell of his rot sat at the back of her nose.

"You're excused, Paul. Shall I find out you're any more involved than this, I'll remove you from your position. No more chances. This will be it." She climbed the winding stone stairs to the royal sleeping quarters, parting attendants who carried bed pans or dirty bedding. Paul remained at the bottom of the stairs, and she could sense his panic following her, but she said nothing else.

"Where's my mother?" She snapped at a woman exiting

the former queen's room. The woman jumped back, clutching bedding to her chest.

She bowed and kept her gaze lowered. "Ah, she's in her room. She just finished her morning meal."

Greer brushed past the woman and without bothering to knock, threw open the bedroom door. Her mother startled at her breakfast table near the window and a shock of pleasure passed over Greer. It wasn't enough to dampen her rage.

"Caitriona's gone."

Róisín stood upright from her chair and smoothed her skirts. She ran her hands through her hair, brushing back the straight, red tresses over her shoulder which placed her delicately pointed ears on display. *The damned fae.* Even within her own home the fae were causing chaos.

"Are you going to say anything?"

"I figured—" Róisín began coolly. While Greer's sudden appearance startled her, it appeared her mother was ready to argue if she saw fit and that only stoked the fire in Greer's belly. Róisín raised her green eyes to meet Greer's and held them steadily. "—I'd let you unload your thoughts first."

Greer stepped back. *She already knew what Caitriona did. She's hiding secrets.* The realization was as hurtful as if Róisín slapped her. Her mouth parted like a damned fish, gaping in the air, and Róisín only continued to look at her. Greer gasped, her breathing an uneasy thing. She inched dangerously close to losing control and spiraling to panic.

Gesturing towards the door and the world beyond the castle walls, she wheezed. "You knew about this."

"Caitriona disappearing? In a sense. I didn't know she achieved it, but I knew it was the plan."

"You didn't tell me? You kept this from me!" She hated that her foot stomped and she was reduced to nothing but a child.

"I do not need to tell you everything, daughter."

"You should tell me when someone's going directly against my order as your queen."

Róisín stared at Greer and slowly crossed her arms over her chest. For all the years Róisín bent to Cearny's will, there were few instances she grew a backbone and it was just in this way, just with that look; her jaw stiff, her emerald eyes glinting. Greer wondered, briefly, if Cearny felt small under Róisín's gaze as Greer did in that moment.

Never, Cearny hissed behind her, the scent of rot now a lob at the back of Greer's throat. She was close to gagging. His ghost had been quiet as of late, weakening by the day, but now he returned with words of poison. *She was beneath me in all areas of life. I was her king. She had to obey me. If she didn't, I made her. Make her obey you.*

"I instructed Caitriona to go to the northern cottage. I told her she was to stay there until the war was over."

Róisín bowed her head. "I know. You recall, I helped her pack. And before I left, I slipped her a note: it instructed her to head to the Elder Tree and move through the crack in it. I told her the pathways were true, they could lead her to Ailith, and she should get her while she could."

A direct refusal to obey her sovereign, Cearny gasped as he circled Róisín, sniffing at her neck and rolling his eyes over her body with clear disdain—or was it hunger? He leaned close to Róisín who shifted on her feet as if holding back discomfort. Could she sense him hunched over her shoulder? Could she smell his stench or feel the waves of disgust radiating from him? *She won't listen to her daughter and she won't listen to her queen.*

Greer's eyelid twitched.

She's choosing Caitriona again; you see that, don't you? She was always her favorite. They share secrets, the two of them, because they're both from the same cloth. They're both magic. And you're nothing. You're magicless, just like me. Look at how they join together and work behind your back. Look at how they threaten your rule by ignoring every expectation you set before them.

"I sent her to the cottage for her safety." The words were forced from between clenched teeth.

Róisín was unmoving. "She has more strength than you give her credit for. You were fine to send her to find Lachlan just a month ago. You celebrated when she returned in her dragon form. But now you've locked her away."

"It was a mistake."

"What was?" Róisín's eyes were unblinking and her jaw rigid. "Sending her to the cottage or giving her the opportunity to taste freedom and responsibility?"

Greer growled. "That freedom and responsibility caused the Mazgate Dominion to believe she laid waste to a town and killed people. It was foolish of me to send her to find Lachlan and support the creature she's become."

If you hadn't coddled her, if you hadn't encouraged her to become that beast, she wouldn't have landed in the field. She wouldn't have led you and Barden to the woods. Barden wouldn't have been struck down. He wouldn't be dead.

Róisín took a step closer. "No, it wasn't. You know this. You aren't in your right mind right now."

It's Caitriona's fault he's dead. She ruined your happiness and your mother doesn't care.

Greer turned on her heel away from her mother. Her father was near now, having moved on from Róisín to stand beside Greer. He was losing his skin. It peeled off, parts falling in chunks where maggots had eaten away at their hold, other parts being reduced to stinking rot, and where muscle and organs should have been was just the squirming, swelling mass of insects. He attempted to smile.

I suppose he isn't dead, not really. A duke now, isn't he? Some murky creature eating fish and catching what vermin come close to the shores. A monster in itself. Imagine if he survived, the force you would be. The threat you would have. You could have been happy. You could have been powerful.

"You've always done this," Greer managed to say, unable to look at her mother. "You've centered your attention and your love on her. You've always loved her *more*. All the while, I've been the forgotten thing. One of your mistakes."

Yes, that's it. She willingly gave up on you and focused on Caitriona. She liked her so much better.

"What are you talking about?" There was ice to Róisín's tone and it was the first time emotion leaked in since Greer's arrival.

Of course. Cearny laughed. *Of course, she'll get sensitive now that you're pointing out the truth.*

"Caitriona's your favorite and always has been. Now she's even more like you since you both have magic. You're proving my point; I can't trust you. I can't trust her either. You both think you know better than me and insist on doing what you want when you want. Our plans, this war, our chance of winning may be ruined due to your decisions."

"What *are* your plans, Greer?" Róisín replied, her voice quiet yet chilled. She moved forward, her skirts a gentle rustle against the floor an odd comparison to the tension building in the room. She stepped before Greer, her eyes boring into her daughter's. "What do you plan to do? Because thus far, ever since Barden died, you've been nothing but bitter and hollow. You've become stagnant. You haven't made any decisions other than placing control on people around you."

"How dare you," Greer hissed, but she had nothing else to say. Her father laughed; flies crawled from his nose and maggots fell from his open mouth to splat onto the floor. She was at a loss for words. "It's barely been a month!"

"My darling girl." Róisín's voice cracked as she wrung her hands together. Her face was filled with an expression that made Greer's stomach twist. It was pity. "You're the queen and your queendom is on the brink of war. I'd understand if you mourn him for an eternity. He was your person and fully a part of you. But you aren't able to fade to nothing right now. It's an awful truth of being a sovereign. Your personal feelings cannot come first."

She couldn't do this; standing still, taking on these verbal hits from a half-fae woman who lied about what she was for decades. She wanted to flip a table, leave the room, yell, *anything*, but was left to pacing instead. Her jaw worked and she glared at her mother with each turn.

Róisín didn't back down. "Well? Tell me, Greer. I know you're suffering; I understand you're mourning, but you haven't made any great decisions for your land. The most you've done was travel to Greenbriar. You've barely encountered your own citizens and they're scared. What are the next steps for this war? What will we do going forward?"

"Like you'd know," Greer continued, trying to turn from Róisín with a growl. She was trapped, as if anywhere she looked her mother would be waiting. She had to leave the room, had to escape and work on plans. Róisín thought Greer hadn't done anything, but she had done so much—she just didn't tell anyone about the plans yet. She had a weapon greater than anything. "Mother, you've always been in Father's shadows wringing your hands, unwilling to do anything to change the course of our lives."

"Because that's where he wanted me and if I tried to shift before his brilliance as king and thrust him into shadow we'd all suffer. Do you not understand that? You were old enough and you're smart, I'm certain you saw how he treated me, and you remember how he treated you. It wasn't with kindness or with love, but with control. He threatened with emotion and destruction, and the understanding he had power while we had none. And now I see you setting forth and beginning to do the same thing as he."

Cearny grew still. He stood with his back to the door, his cheeks torn and hollow with teeth showing through the rips. An eye was loose, drooping from his face as a discolored, graying grape, and his matted hair stuck against his head. The blonde was dulled to dirt and ashen.

She wished Barden could tell her what to do, to lead her forward, to help her figure things out. He would have been a helpful ghost; one who advised her as he did in life. He would have gotten rid of Cearny's haunting and told her if her mother was right.

"We're going to attack the fae. That's what we're going to do," Greer began. A numbness spread over, as if her mind was detaching from the situation. She felt this at times when she had attacks of panic. Those moments after she swore she couldn't breathe; she floated as if someone else controlled her body. The words came from her mouth, but she didn't feel herself saying them. They were automatic, just as her movements.

She stared beyond Róisín, watching her father come apart. But still, she had his attention and she spoke to him as much as to her mother. The plan, her grand plan that would show the fae who they chose to fight. "The sap from the Elder Tree can be boiled. When done so, it turns into steam. That steam still holds the powers of the original sap—it can still take a life if breathed in. We'll allow it to mingle with the mist of the mountains and use magic makers to create a wind that'll direct the mist upward toward where the fae live. Those who breathe it in will die."

Róisín's brows furrowed, her eyes darkening. "How do you know this?"

Greer looked at her mother, whose eyes were flashing, her jaw stern, and her nostrils flared as she breathed. She connected within her body once more and shrunk back, with an inkling of embarrassment. She looked at the floor. "After what happened with Barden, I requested studies on the sap; I wanted to see what it was capable of doing and what happened if it was made into syrup. I discovered that during the process, it became a mist that ... killed. I suppose it'd bring people back as well but—"

"People died doing these experiments."

Greer nodded, looking at the ground. She didn't regret what she did, even if it killed some of her men. She was more regretful that she felt nothing at all.

"And you're going to use this to kill the fae ... but there aren't just enemies in the mountains. There's good fae, too."

"Some good will die to get rid of the bad." Greer lifted her eyes to meet her mother's. Róisín's mouth was hanging. "It's a necessary loss."

"You're sounding an awful lot like past Wimleigh kings. I'd rather you go back to grieving as you were, when you were laying in your bed and unable to correspond with anyone. That was better than planning a genocide of innocents."

Róisín's words were oil and flame, coating Greer and making her burn with such flurry that she could no longer keep her composure. Her hands turned to fists and she ground her teeth before yelling, "I *am* grieving! I grieve every day. I should know, as it is *my* grief to bear."

"*What* of your grief, Greer?"

Greer paced again and turned on her heel, her eyes fierce and filled with rage. Róisín backed up as if she saw Cearny in her gaze, but she kept speaking with unrelenting honesty.

"All experience grief, why is yours so different? Why is yours something that allows you to say and do such things? You think your grief is so unique it allows you to murder innocents?" Róisín's words came like a hiss and carried such strength Greer stumbled back, her eyes wide as if Róisín beat her.

"I *loved* him," she replied, her voice turning into a groan as she further sunk under the weight of her sadness. She clutched her chest, as if her very heart was falling forth and into her waiting palm. "I loved him and I never told him I did."

Róisín stared. Her hand rose, as if ready to reach for Greer, as if she wanted to embrace her, but Greer stepped back. Róisín rolled her lips over her teeth and clenched her hand into a fist.

"Careful, daughter," she warned, her voice shaking slightly. There was compassion there in the root of her vowels and the glistening of her eyes. Did she feel for Greer? Did she sympathize? Róisín continued, her voice soft. "Grief can change a person. It can warp them into something cruel. And the cruelty I see in you reminds me of your father. I see it more and more each day. Is that who you want to become?"

Róisín waited, the hum of the castle remained in the distance, separated from them through the thick stone walls and closed door. Greer's chest heaved, her nerves on fire in her neck and face as she looked at her mother and the ghost of her father. Her mother was distant and removed her entire life, yet when they had moments together, Greer saw the gleam of love in her eyes. Her father was nothing but judgment and hatred. A failure, a disappointment, never his first choice—he said it all so frequently Greer nearly believed it to be true and tried so hard to prove him wrong. Was this how she wanted to show he was wrong? By slipping directly into his footsteps?

Greer swallowed. "No."

Cearny hissed from the corner of the room and attempted to step forward, his hands reaching to grab hold of Greer and her body tensed, ready for the hit that was sure to come as it often did when she was growing up, but his body shuttered from the movement and began to collapse. Falling to the floor, what rotting skin remained tore apart and his bones scattered before sinking into the stones and disappearing from sight. It happened so fast; it didn't allow him to say whatever final words were on his tongue. He was at last silenced.

Greer let out a fresh breath, her skin breaking out in an icy sweat. Was she free from his hauntings? Or was she simply doomed?

"Your sister's off to the Endless Mountains because I saw a vision," Róisín explained. "It was of our future. It was of you fighting and Caitriona fighting as well. You all were at the marshes. Ailith was there and Lachlan, too. The battle was long and bloody, and there was much loss but you were *winning*, Greer. You have to let Caitriona have a part in this, the part she chooses to partake in. She needs you to trust her. *I* need your trust, even though I've given you so little reason to trust me in your life. I'm sorry, but please, give me your trust, if only this time."

Greer looked at her mother with exhausted eyes. She was crying now, the tears leaked continuously and seemed unable to stop. What else could she do? She lost everyone she loved and all she had left was her mother. Perhaps, finally, she could allow her to shoulder the burdens. Even if the burden was just this decision, this choice, that set forth their destiny.

Greer reached forward and Róisín stepped close, taking her daughter's hand into her own and holding it tightly as Greer sighed. "I trust you."

CHAPTER FIFTEEN

The fae hadn't moved since they were last in the room a few days prior. They remained on the cots with lines pulling magic essence from their bodies and potion materials still sat on the table against the wall. Nothing had been disturbed, no fae taken in or out, and relief flooded Ailith as they moved with quiet but quick feet to the table of ingredients. Fiana grabbed vials, pulling off lids and corks to sniff and taste the ingredients. None had labels, a few were marked with obscure lines or symbols foreign to them both, but with Fiana's familiarity they hoped she could put a few potions together for added protections against whatever they faced.

Ailith squatted beside the table to gather empty vials and pouches from a shelf beneath. Most spells were things that needed consumption—whether by drinking, eating, smelling, or through rubbing into the skin—and the containers were normal for such spell casting. Not knowing how to make anything herself, Ailith only grabbed the vials and brought them to Fiana.

"Is there anything else I can help with?" She watched

Fiana go from vial to vial with quick, knowledgeable movements that proved her experience, placing some back and leaving others before her.

Fiana shook her head. She lifted an empty bottle, squinting her eyes at the color, and poured a murky gray liquid into it. She didn't turn her attention to Ailith when she answered. "Go. Do what you need to do. I'll work on this."

Ailith shifted her attention to the weak fae. Between each cot sat small tables with various instruments; tools for whatever was being done to the fae: rocks, herbs, and other oddities, but also sharper instruments Ailith knew would come in handy as weapons. She moved to the first table and smiled. No swords, bows or arrows, but there were knives; small and dainty knives to make tiny cuts. There were larger ones that could saw their way through bone, too, making Ailith grimace at the thought.

Ailith pulled ropes from the medical supplies and made holsters, tying the knives to her dirty clothing and finding a familiar pressure on her thigh where she normally kept her dagger. The press of sharp metal brought a layer of comfort she hadn't expected; maybe she was more the warrior than she thought.

Equipped with enough sharp instruments to feel comfortable, she lifted a knife and returned to Fiana. With cloth scraps, she tied the knife to Fiana as well before offering a rope she found. "You could put the potions into one of the bags?"

Fiana paused her magic-making long enough to finger the rope. Her dark eyes sparked with life and Ailith knew she was pleased. "Thank you."

"How's it going?"

"I'm only certain about the energy potion; those ingredients are easy to spot. Everything else ... well, it could be a healing potion or it could kill us. I'm making some additional supplies, just in case. I should be done soon, then we'll go."

Ailith returned to Vanora who remained motionless and paler than before. Kneeling, her knees cracking with the movement, Ailith touched Vanora's bare arm with her fingertips, frowning at the chill of her skin. Running her hands over the fae woman's arm, she encouraged her to wake. "I'm going to help you."

She reached for the straps holding Vanora's wrists down and slipped the knife from her thigh. Working quickly, she cut through the tie and freed Vanora's wrist, exposing red, raw skin under the leather strap. Lowering the woman's hand to the cot with the gentleness of laying a babe to rest, Ailith moved to Vanora's feet. She cut the ties around her ankles, finding similar raw markings against the woman's pale skin, then back up the other side to Vanora's final tied wrist. A gleaming chain lay at Vanora's throat, pinned in place by a glittering stone. Ailith tapped the stone once with the hilt of the little knife, then touched it with the tip of her finger, pausing each time to see if there was a reaction or obvious magic over the items.

Not feeling any heat or spark, she brushed the stone off Vanora's throat and set it rolling to the floor. Vanora gasped, her blue eyes opening and hands flexing, now free. She rapidly reached for the chain and let it fall to the floor beside the cot where it lay innocently. Ailith leaned back, silent as Vanora looked around wildly until her gaze settled on Ailith, and her blonde eyebrows rose. "You came back."

"I can't do too much," Ailith whispered, slipping a spare, sharp instrument into Vanora's hand. "But I'm going to cut everyone's ties and pull any magic items off. At least the ones I can see."

"Runes," Vanora whispered, her voice cracking. "And any stones or flowers. Chains like what I had on me. They're all different ingredients for the same outcome. Anything beyond clothing on their body, just take it all."

Ailith turned to another fae and cut the straps, brushing a black glittering stone off their chest and letting it fall to the floor as well. It bounced, a part of the stone chipping off, and Ailith smiled.

She moved from fae to fae, freeing them as she worked. Once the magic taps were taken, the fae began to wake. Bit by bit, the cots had more open eyes and the energy in the room shifted with power growing rather than seeping away.

"Ailith," Vanora called, her voice stronger by the minute, as if a leak had been cut off and the well of magic filled and healed her.

Vanora waved her back and Ailith paused, looking between the last few who were tied before returning to Vanora's bedside. Vanora gripped Ailith's hand, though her strength was weakened. "You both need to get away from here as quickly as you can."

"We have to let you free—"

"Don't worry about us. We can free the remaining." She struggled to sit upright and reached for Ailith's other hand which she quickly offered. Sweat broke on her brow and her eyes were bloodshot, showing the blue hue all the more. "In one of my wakeful moments when the guards were here, I heard their plans. You must leave. Malcolm intends to spell all those who refuse to follow him. He'll curse us by transforming us into creatures. Ones forced to obey him and fight under his rule. If you don't leave, you'll be cursed as well."

"What?"

"She's right," Fiana replied, turning from the table. A bag filled with magical items hung from her shoulders and she held two small pouches in her hands. "When Kayl possessed me, he showed me Malcolm's plans. He's been funneling all magic into himself to make a broad spell. He's pushing it into a potion, making it into a curse."

"I thought curses were said, not something you consume." Ailith considered Kayl's curse to Caitriona. It was spoken and created decades before through the magic ties between himself and Caitriona because he recently dumped so much magic into her body to heal her from the dragon attack. But Vanora shook her head.

"Curses are what they are. He's taken from all of us, whether it's blood and emotion from us or magic from them, he's touched us all in a way. He can force that curse work into an object and use it against us. Imagine, he won't just have his supporters fighting for him, but all the people who refuse— whether they like it or not."

Understanding dawned upon Ailith. "An army of magical creatures."

"An entire kingdom. All under Malcolm and Shad's control," Vanora added. Fiana moved between cots and held out one of the small bags.

"Take this," Fiana pushed it into Ailith's hand. It was small, no bigger than a coin, but stuffed with herbs and powder. Hasty stitches were at the top, closing it off with strings ripped at the ends. "Hide it beneath the waist of your pants. Don't put it in your pockets. It's a spell to turn you into a creature just the same as those in the planned attack from Malcolm, but this way you'll keep your wits about you. If we're caught, we need to use this so Malcolm can't gain control over us. You won't be under Malcolm's influence, just a creature to blend into the mix. But—and this is the big issue —I'm not sure if this spell that can be reversed." She lifted another bag. "I have one too."

Ailith stared at the pouch as she replayed Fiana's words in her mind. "You don't know if it's permanent?"

"There are two ingredients that are very similar to one

another. One when mixed with the rest of this makes spells permanent. The other, when mixed, makes spells reversible. It's hard to tell which is which when you're not the one actively foraging the ingredients. I'm not sure what it'll do, but I understand if you don't want to take it."

"It's better to be a creature with my wits than one without," Ailith murmured, slipping the bag along the band of her pants and beneath her undergarments. It sat uncomfortably, nearly tucked between her legs, but it was the safest location on her body.

When Caitriona was forced into the curse, she had no power over her mind. She was at its will and pushed to do what the curse commanded. It wasn't until the curse passed that she controlled the comings and goings of fire. Ailith suspected she had more power over willing the dragon to the surface, but she hadn't convinced Caitriona to try that trick yet. It terrified Caitriona, the idea of being thrust into the draconic form and being unable to control herself. Ailith had been sympathetic before but now faced with the very real possibility of being at the will of Malcolm, her emotions slipped to empathy.

She'd take the powder if she had to and hope she could become herself again. Alas, if she couldn't return to her normal form, at least she'd remember who she was.

"Just throw the bag on the ground. It'll be like a small explosion that'll create smoke. Breathe it in, take it into yourself, and it'll change you. It isn't a great plan, but it's still a plan if we get caught," Fiana continued.

Ailith nodded. "A smart one. Thank you."

The fae stirred in their beds, all gaining enough strength to wake fully. A few wept, others sat upright and appeared enraged, but small noises came from all. Ailith hadn't been listening for oncoming footsteps from the hall beyond. She missed the sound of a key in a lock. She was unaware of the incoming threat until the door to their wing opened.

Fiana and Ailith dropped to the floor and rolled under cots. Vanora collapsed against her bed, going still, but a few of the other fae weren't as lucky.

"What's this?"

The voice made Ailith's eyes go wide. This was too good to be true, this was too much luck, and something in Ailith's gut tightened in forewarning. *Proceed with caution*, it seemed to say, yet Ailith's foolish mind refused to trust the thought because her heart was too loud.

Ailith shimmied against the marble floor toward the edge of the cot and couldn't help but smile. Her brain and gut were at war with themselves. Her stomach recoiled as if finding a threat, surely due to the torment she barely remembered but experienced in the last weeks, but her mind only saw a friend.

Lumia, Raum's partner and one of her fae friends, stood at the end of the room. Her white-blonde hair hung loose down her back, her pale skin was clean of dirt or blemish. She looked put together, well kept, and without any sense of urgency. Lumia looked over the room, her lips turning downward and her brow wrinkling as she took in the fae on their cots.

Ailith inched forward, her lips parting.

Vanora's hand slipped from the bed and touched Ailith's shoulder as she attempted to still her. "No," she whispered, her face turned toward Ailith and she shook her head. "Stay quiet. Don't move."

Ailith paused for a moment, ready to heed Vanora's warning, but she never had the chance as the room plunged into darkness and her body filled with terror.

CHAPTER SIXTEEN

CAITRIONA

She fell as she did in dreams; a sudden thrust of her body into air and the rush of the world passing while she tensed and braced for impact. She could fly, she was a dragon, she knew what it was to float in the sky, but her human brain was more powerful. What could she do as she fell? Turn into a dragon in this tight cavern? Her will was lost to gravity and her body fully in its control. Cold air rich with musk and wet earth rushed up her body like a plunge into an icy stream as it pulled her cloak up and overhead, and flooded her nostrils. She reached into the blackness surrounding her, desperate to press the tunnel's sides, to brush roots, and slow her descent, but still she fell with nothing to grab hold to. As she continued downward, fast at first, time began to change.

With the air rushing past her ears, a flash of Isla came to mind. When Caitriona recovered in Ulla Syrmin, Isla visited once and declared that magic is a creature of little rules, other than those which are iron clad.

Rule one: using power to destroy or take others' magic into yourself will destroy you in return. Kayl was proof of that rule in action.

Rule two: the plane outside of existence, where ghosts and dreams lingered, was a lawless land meant for travel where you weren't meant to interact with the realm of true existence, where people lived and breathed and birthed and died.

Rule three: when magic leaked into time, it stopped being linear and no longer made sense. The further Caitriona fell into the roots of the Elder Tree, down into the earth from which it sprung, the more time loosened and became a feral thing that did as it pleased. Her hair grew longer, her nails needed trimming, and her belly emptied of the breakfast she had that morning.

Her tumbling slowed and the quick jolt of gravity pulling her down and causing her stomach to rise lessened. She floated, or so it seemed, as hands made from roots grasped her to twist their long tendrils around her wrists and run up her horns, before lowering her to the ground with the gentleness of a feather's fall.

At last, her feet pressed into the soft earth of the deepest, healthiest soil, and the Elder Tree's roots retracted. Caitriona studied the subtle glow of magic pulsing along the roof of the cavern. Down here in the dark, the Elder Tree still thrived, but already the energy pumping through its roots redirected to offshoots of other trees. Lifting her hand, she allowed a small flame to develop in her palm. The gentle light illuminated the room and showed its expanse as something three times as large as the Elder Tree's trunk itself; big enough to fill with thirty men if they ever dared to enter the crevice of the tree.

Soil sprinkled down from overhead, drawing Caitriona's attention to the ceiling where darkness gathered. Stepping away from the falling dirt, Caitriona waited and smiled as Raum's boots appeared. A momentary pause of his feet overhead and a shower of further dirt, he emerged with a pop and floated to the floor, gently placed by the tree roots that slipped back into the ceiling. Looking up wildly, the fae man stared at Caitriona with a mixture of confusion and wonder.

"What—what in the hells are we doing?"

"We're forging our own path," Caitriona replied. Her smile broadened when more soil fell. "You may want to move to the side."

Ceenear's feet appeared and Raum stumbled back. The other fae landed gracefully and turned to Caitriona, her lips drawn into a line. "You weren't planning to give us any warning about this, hmm?"

Caitriona's cheeks warmed. "Would you have followed through with this if I had?"

Ceenear rolled her eyes. "Obviously, but I at least would've advised a plan and packed more food."

Caitriona looked at the meager flame in her palm. "Ah, well, I apologize. With how my sister's been, I didn't want to risk anyone else knowing. This felt like my last chance."

"Do you intend to explain what we're doing here?" Raum asked as he circled the room and flicked the hanging roots with the tips of his fingers.

"We're going to use this as a path to get to Ailith, Fiana and Lumia. My mother gave me a letter last night, she said all Lachlan said was true, that she saw the pathways through Kayl—he's better now, don't look at me that way; well, not better, but, *just listen*—we go into the root and think of Ailith, of her being in the Endless Mountains, and we take the tunnel. It should shoot us out at an Elder Tree near the mountains. It's likely it'll be near where my mother's village was. That saves us days in travel and puts us ahead of anyone my sister sends forth and hopefully beyond any movement Malcolm may attempt.

"Once we reach Invarlwen, we try and get Ailith and Fiana. Hopefully we'll gather useful information. You packed the speaking stone, right?"

Ceenear patted her pack. "I always have it near."

"Great, so we'll message Isla and give her any information we obtain from the fae. She can share that with Greer and hopefully we'll be a step ahead of Malcolm."

"This sounds good and all," Raum sighed as he turned casually on one foot. "Beyond the mist perhaps killing me and not knowing for sure where these roots will take us, if we even end up near the mist itself. But how exactly are we going to go through a tunnel? This looks like a giant hole with no way out but up."

Caitriona forced more of her heated power through her hand to expand the fire and allow brightness to cover the space. She couldn't see a difference in the glowing roots either. They were everywhere, covering the expanse of the earthen hole with its glowing pulse, and nowhere seemed particularly different or special. Raum was right, it was nothing but roots and dirt. "Maybe it's covered?"

They pushed forward, hands pressing along the roots and attempting to brush them away without hurting the roots themselves.

"Do you think this is—?" Raum began to ask as he pulled a cluster of thick roots aside and exposed a dark crevice, but his words were cut short as wind blew through the area, snuffing out Caitriona's flame and descending them into darkness. Raum gasped and a hush echoed through the space.

"Raum?" Ceenear called.

Caitriona's hand flailed and fire formed again, exposing only she and Ceenear standing in the room, both with similarly panicked expressions. "I hope he was thinking of the mountains."

They looked at the space where Raum had fallen through.

"Go through first," Ceenear instructed. "Think of Raum. Ask the tunnel to take you to him. I'll follow and think of the mountains. If I end up at a different tree, I can change to something with wings and find you."

Caitriona nodded and stepped forward, looking at the hole and considering Raum. She pictured his height, his olive skin tone and dark hair. She imagined his smile when he joked with Ailith and the way his eyes narrowed when he held his sword to fight. She hoped he was where they planned to go, but they couldn't spare to be separated now. Bending down, her horns scraping along the dirt and roots to shower her with soil, the breeze picked up and the fire in her hand winked out. The air wrapped itself around her like a rope and pulled, taking her off her feet, she fell forward. The gentleness of her descent from before was gone, this being a tumble with pain and bruising. Her horns caught the side of the tunnel, yanking her head to the side and forcing a gasp of pain. Her cloak twisted around her torso, her knees crashed against stone, and then she was blinded by brightness as her stumbling stopped and fresh air filled her lungs.

Blinking, the sky was blue and the sun shone just over the edge of a steep incline, making the flatter land and sea alight in late-summer sun. Even from this distance, the blue-gray of the seawater twinkled as Caitriona sat up and stared before her. Reaching to her head, strands of taproot brushed her fingers and pebbles scattered from her hair.

"Cait!" Raum ran up the hill, taking giant steps that pushed him up the incline, and grasped Caitriona's shoulders. Pulling her up, he brought her forward into an embrace. "We need to have a chat about making plans before setting off on adventures. This is a troublesome behavior."

Caitriona blinked, accepting Raum's hug and gently patting his shoulder until he pulled back. She was covered in roots and dirt, as was Raum, but they were together above ground and somewhere Caitriona didn't recognize. They were on a steep slope with a scattering of bushes and trees. "Where are we?"

Pebbles fell from the slope behind them. Where Caitriona

was spat from the earth, it looked like an overhang where a boulder broke away; roots from the grass and brush hung over the dirty hole and it swelled before spitting Ceenear forth who slid across the ground on her rear until sliding to stop at their feet.

"Glad you could join us." Raum smiled and offered Ceenear his hand. She brushed her pants and Caitriona plucked twigs from her braids.

"At least we ended up in the same location," Ceenear murmured as she straightened.

"Which means we were successful," Caitriona replied. "We made it to where my mother grew up."

But it didn't look like much. The slope was deeply wooded with breaks in the trees showing the distant shores and ocean. They stood on what looked like a game trail with tall grasses parted in the center that exposed a narrow dirt path.

"So where to now?" Raum asked.

Caitriona took a deep breath. It was quiet and the brush lay still. She looked over her dirt-covered friends. It seemed hours had passed, perhaps even days, although it likely was only minutes since they entered the Elder Tree. Her stomach growled and her lips were parched, which further lent the idea that time in the tunnels was odd and it was later in the day than expected. Knowing where her mother's old home was on maps, the slope going upward was also going toward the west where the sun now shone, upward toward Invarlwen and the mist. By the position of the sun, it was late afternoon, and darkness would descend before long. Placing her hands on her hips, she turned back to look at the sea, the puffy clouds over the water already showed summery hues of late day. "Let's find a place to camp for the night and tomorrow we head for the mist."

CHAPTER SEVENTEEN

RÓISÍN

"He saw her."

They sat under the small Elder Tree of Caermythlin. It was half the size of the Braewick Elder Tree—the true Elder Tree—and now Róisín understood why. It was an offshoot, a baby, an attempt to keep living. Kayl's back pressed against the trunk while she settled on the sloping hill, her head nestled amongst wild violets that filled her nostrils with their sweetness and churned to life a memory of times long ago when her mother was still alive and fed her violet jam on toast in the springtime.

Róisín held Kayl's statement against her chest for a space of time, chewing on his words and frowning at the dangerous taste of them. She closed her eyes and took a deep breath, opening them again before she spoke. "I know."

"He wants her," Kayl continued, rubbing the stem of a flower between two fingers and sending it spinning.

"In what way?" Róisín rolled to her side and tucked her hand under her chin. She watched Kayl let the flower fall against his lips and breathe in its scent. His brown hair stirred in the breeze and stubble coated his chin. Here in dreams, he was healthy and himself, the person she once knew and trusted. Here in dreams, it was like the last thirty years never happened.

"To devour her. It's his way of strength. Consume her power into himself, so he controls it all. He could marry her too, make her his draconic bride. It's devouring her all the same."

"The bastard." Róisín was perpetually surprised by the strength of human emotion. She was shocked she could despise someone so much when she never met him. If she could ground her heel into the skull of Malcolm, she wouldn't hesitate.

"He wants to rule in all ways. It isn't a matter of just having a crown, but making people fearful. He wants people to bend to him, and their every movement and decision to be influenced by his own will."

"He must've taken tips from my husband," Róisín mused. "Too bad his son doesn't stab him in the gut like Greer did to Cearny."

Kayl grimaced. "That was my fault. It was part of my curse."

"I understand," Róisín replied. "His death haunts her and if it wasn't for that, I'd say it was the one thing you got right."

She sat upright and brushed bits of grass from her skirts. "Let's move forward. What else do you have to share with me? I've been trying to find you in my dreams for some time now and you haven't been around."

"Malcolm's trying to take the last of my power." Kayl's fingers closed over the flower. "With each drink, his ties to me weaken and soon the last of his bonds will break. I'll be adrift to drink what powers I can until I vanish from this world completely, or until Malcolm swallows me whole."

Róisín didn't respond. When she was a child, she heard of a sickness that plagued magic users on occasion, sucking away their powers until they were weathered things. It was believed the magic user caught an unbound who took root in their body. It left a foul taste in Róisín's mouth to think Kayl would be one of those things soon.

Quiet stretched between them and Róisín looked down the slope to the sea. She always wanted to swim in its waters but never made it far enough from town to do so. When she was younger, she and Kayl endlessly spoke of sneaking away to travel to the sea for the day against Nanny's orders, but they never gathered enough courage to do so. It would've been too far and they certainly would've been caught. Despite Róisín's knack for chaos, she was even more fearful of Nanny's rage than Kayl was, probably because she faced it the most. Instead, she went further inland and to the opposite coast when she agreed to marry Cearny, ensuring she'd never touch the eastern sea's waters. Maybe they could visit it in her dreams and that would satisfy her craving. But she wasn't sure there was enough time for any of that.

Tugging her skirts over her legs, she looked at Kayl. "Is there any news? Any information that may be beneficial?"

"He attacked a village of the Mazgate Dominion. One by the Avorkaz gates and close to your borders."

"We saw the wreckage. What I don't understand is why he did it. He did nothing to hide that it was his people attacking. Doesn't he want the Mazgate Dominion to side with him?"

Kayl opened his hand; the flower was crushed and its petals dropped to his lap. "It was a test. He has an assortment of tricks up his sleeves. He's changed fae who had no powers into creatures under his control. They're becoming the magic beasts your husband tried to make extinct. They're like Caitriona was under the curse: driven by the desires of the beasts they've become and the direction he sets forth for them.

Those who follow him were given magic taken from others and they're allowed to go on the backs of the beasts. He wanted to see how they fought, how good an army of creatures and those given stolen magic would be. It proved successful."

"The entire village was destroyed. All the people killed."

"Exactly. He wants to do that to your people, too. To Greer's army and the land. To truly show his power and ownership, he must destroy all those who bear witness and recall the kingdom beforehand. Surely you're familiar with this, it's what your husband did."

"It sounds like he doesn't want to let anyone live unless they declare loyalty and have something to give."

Kayl looked at her, his eyebrows arched and his dark eyes studying her. "Don't all rulers?"

Róisín shook her head. "Not all. Greer isn't that way."

"Give her time, she'll be like the others."

"You'll be faded from existence before you could see that happen," Róisín replied with ice in her voice. Kayl snorted and crossed his arms over his chest.

"You aren't wrong."

Róisín fell back against the violets. She was tired and sleep was edging in. Her soul was returning to her body. There wouldn't be time to visit the sea after all. "Tell me more before I wake?"

"Malcolm's gathering his forces to move forward. I'm not entirely sure how long you have. I saw them preparing to leave before I faded after he last sipped from me and you know time—"

"It goes by its own rules here, yes."

She smiled and while Kayl didn't return the gesture, his brows softened. He looked young and for a moment, frightened. "I'm not going to last long, Ro."

"Is there anything that can allow you to remain?"

"I need a host if I'm to last any longer. I'm nothing but a

leech. But even that won't be enough. I'll fade either way once my last burst of magic's lost."

"Is it not fading all the time? Wouldn't it fade as you have?"

"Magic's in everything. It's in our blood, our organs, in the air we breathe. Everyone touches it, whether they control magic or not. Those who wield magic control different aspects of it. But in the end, magic's a substance as powerful as what keeps us alive. Do you remember when the cow farmer was dying? We were sent to help his wife as he laid there with breaths that shook and spoke to beings that weren't there. Sometimes he slept so thoroughly we thought he was already dead, and then one morning we arrived and he was up in bed as if he had never been sick. Jovial, discussing a calf that was born, making jokes, doting on his wife."

"He was full of energy," Róisín recalled. "And then he died that night."

"*That*," Kayl pointed, "is the magic. That last force, that return to normalcy before death. That final burst of energy. That's what will be left of me and it'll be a matter of how or when it pushes its way from me. When it does, that's when I'll fade from existence entirely."

"All this for revenge," Róisín whispered. She thought of her husband, of his cruelty to her and their daughters. She thought of his will, his destruction, the death in multitudes under his hand. If her daughters hadn't been involved, Róisín would have kissed Kayl for sending the curse. But that wasn't the case. And yet, she knew the truth of it all. "If I had the power you did, I would've cursed Cearny as well."

It was Kayl's turn to nod. "I know."

Róisín pushed up and stepped forward, enjoying the soft moss underfoot and the scent of violets in the air. Gods she missed this landscape and she didn't realize how badly she did until she returned.

"Kayl," she murmured thoughtfully as she wrapped her arms around her torso and looked to the sea. She wondered if the water was warm there, she always heard it was warmer than the waters off Braewick's shores. "When the tethers break, I want you to sink into the earth and find me. Let your final days not be alone."

CHAPTER EIGHTEEN

GREER

Of course, sleep wouldn't come. Greer expected as much, particularly after the events of the day. Seeing Caitriona off to the northern cottage was upsetting enough but her sister decided to go her own way and the layered feelings of her actions kept hitting Greer in waves.

She wanted to yell at Caitriona and also embrace her. Greer wanted to repeat again and again how desperate she was not to lose her as well, and apologize for how she behaved in recent weeks.

Hours before dark, after the discovery of Caitriona's disappearance, the row with her mother, and witnessing her father's ghost rot to nothing, the tap in Greer's soul opened and she wept.

"Come, my sweet lark," Róisín had said softly, holding out her arms to Greer after sitting on the edge of her bed. Greer crawled onto her mother's lap. She slipped her arms around her mother's waist and wept, catching the scent of her mother's perfume of roses and violets before her nose filled and her tears nearly drowned her. All the while, her mother sat patiently and stroked her hair so gently.

The expressive show of tender care undid Greer all the more. "I miss him," Greer croaked out between sobs. "I miss Caitriona too and how things were. I miss it all. It's as if I'll never be myself again, like I've been altered to someone different."

"I know, darling." Róisín bent to kiss the top of Greer's head. "You're changed and you'll never be the person you were before. You'll be something else. But still a form of yourself."

Her mother remained, not pulling away at all while Greer breathed, with full lungs and a broad throat, for the first time since she killed her father—her father whose ghost was gone, at least for now. It left her both elated and exhausted.

After hours, she returned to her room, giving firm instructions to her guards that she were to be undisturbed, and collapsed on her bed. As the day passed she remained blissfully alone. Everyone had their tasks, even she, but for now the biggest was to gather her mind so she could be a better queen. To do so, she allowed herself to wallow in all the thoughts she constantly fought to not think of too much. She wanted more moments with her mother as they had that day. More moments of honesty and closure were so desperately overdue.

She was a beast left starving and craving for so much. She wanted to complain to Barden about her sister, her mother, the castle, and the staff. Barden would comment with his dry sense of humor that always made her smile despite her worst moods. She wanted to hold him, love him, and weep against his chest. Greer hungered to hear about his day, to watch his eyes brighten, and catch him training some young guard in the yard. Her fingers itched to touch the curve of his lips, feel the grip of his hands, trace the softness of his hair, and savor his musky scent of woodsmoke and herbs.

It was interesting how similar grief was to want. She wanted so many things and the fact she had none compounded that drowning loss.

Being so filled with want left very little room for sleep. By nightfall, Greer wandered as she did numerous other nights. She hadn't even bothered to change into a nightgown. She still wore the pants and shirt from the day and moved through the halls with only a dagger in her belt. She glared at any guard who seemed tempted to follow her as she drifted like the ghost she in many ways wished to become.

It was odd to wish not to live but not want to die. Perhaps it was built on frustration for all the things beyond her control. Either way, what little enjoyment she obtained in her day-to-day came when she felt the furthest from the living.

At night, in late hours, as she passed through halls with her eyes adjusted to the dimness of firelight against cool stone, she saw the castle from a different perspective. The rats ran from approaching footsteps and horses snorted in their stalls; she witnessed mothers standing at windows of guard houses with babes in their arms, humming sweetly to hush their cries; and she watched bakers arrive long before daylight to begin preparation for the day's bread. In darker corners of the castle, she spied maids wrapped in the arms of attendants. There was so much sex to be had in the castle at night, freely in the open, yet cloaked in shadows. Greer could hear the moans and gasps echoing along the empty halls but only twice in her wanderings did Greer catch couples as she passed by. Twice was enough for word to spread and now there were subsequently less trysts to stumble upon as staff found other locations to secret away to.

Beyond the closed doors of rooms, she typically listened to the sounds of her sleeping family and friends. Ceenear's room was always silent while Raum's door nearly shook off its hinges from his snores. Lachlan's often had soft candlelight issuing from beneath his door and the brief turn of pages could be heard. He seemed to stay up late reading more often than not, but tonight it was dark and quiet.

She regretted what little time she spent with the future monarch and that when she was with him, she was terse and straight business. What were they to do with him? He was studious and kind, providing a plethora of information to the household they previously did not have, but she was short with him in her grief. Just the sight of him sent her back to the day they met when his hands were covered in Barden's blood and the sap from the arrow. He was so quick to try everything to bring back Barden despite that it was a lost cause. When she saw those images, her chest tightened and she fought the urge to vomit. How could she ever appear happy to see Lachlan if his presence reminded her of that?

Yet it was the very thought of the poor fae prince that led her to the doorway of the prayer room. It was a place to pray to the Elder Tree, yet long before it was used to worship and call to other deities. To the best of Greer's knowledge, her family never practiced other faiths. They were quite straight forward in believing the Elder Tree provided and would live and die in this world, that perhaps there was an afterlife filled with joy, but who was to know but the dead? But there were other beliefs, those who worshiped the drowning dukes or other creatures. Those who believed in cosmic abundance. It was all something Greer never took much time to learn nor did she have much opportunity since her father removed all texts pertaining to such topics. But the room, despite old images scrubbed from the walls, provided peace and clarity more often than not and it was where her weary feet brought her that night.

Opening the door, she took a moment to view the slender room with the painting of the Elder Tree at the end, bordered by two windows that looked out on the actual Elder Tree. In the painting, there were multiple images of the creatures that spawned from the roots of the tree—all that was dark in the world—and all that was good growing from its limbs and dropping to the earth like nuts. It was hard to view the imagery of people being good in the artwork whilst mothers waited to say goodbye to their children and feared they wouldn't return home. Even now there was the ring from blacksmiths working through the night to prepare weapons to slaughter others. How was that, an action made by people, an act of a good creature?

The room was gently lit with flickering candles maintained to retain their glow, but the gentle weeping from the front pew was something Greer hadn't expected. Moving down the aisle toward the tree, the weeping stopped and a head arose. Strawberry blonde, half pointed ears, just who she didn't want to see.

"Queen Greer!" Lachlan whispered with a mixture of shock and fear. He scrambled to his feet, hastily wiping his face with the back of his hand, and bowed his head. "I apologize, you must want the room, I'll go."

"No, stay," Greer said without thinking. She paused and when Lachlan's multi-colored eyes met hers; he looked as surprised as she.

Rolling her lips together and pressing them between her teeth, Greer looked at the pew across the aisle from Lachlan and took a seat. She waved her hand out, encouraging the man to do the same.

"I can leave ..."

"You can stay." Greer was surprised the words left her mouth. She wanted to be alone, didn't she? She didn't want to see Lachlan because he reminded her of Barden's final moments, right? Then why was she encouraging this man to remain in the same room as her?

Greer studied the prince as he returned to the pew and

settled on the edge of the wooden seat. The tears he cried still showed on his face, glittering in the low light despite his hasty attempt to wipe them clean, and they were too tempting for Greer to ignore. "Are you alright?"

Lachlan's shoulders dipped and he lowered his face. Even in the low light she saw his cheeks turning red. "It's unimportant."

"Important enough you're awake a few hours before sunrise crying in the prayer room. So, I ask again, are you alright?"

Lachlan raised his face and studied Greer long enough that she shifted in her seat but didn't pull her own gaze away. His tongue darted over his lips and he seemed ready to speak but paused as his eyes took in the painting of the Elder Tree, before returning to Greer. "I was weeping over the loss of my mother."

"Oh."

"It seems silly now. I knew her, but I wasn't particularly close to her."

"What do you mean?"

Lachlan withdrew a handkerchief and wiped at his face. "She visited more frequently when I was a child, but as I grew older and my powers became obvious, her visits tapered off before stopping completely. Instead, she spoke to me through sending stones on a monthly basis, the night of the full moon, and at no other point. All our conversations were very straightforward. She asked after my health, if I behaved myself and did well in classes. My mother wanted to ensure I obeyed the elders and asked if I had any friends, if I was seeing anyone and how the weather was.

"I once asked questions in return but she always refused to answer. She never shared herself with me and now never will." His voice cracked and his eyes filled again. "I'm mourning the loss of opportunity with her. I never knew her, and my opportunity to is gone. I'm grieving that her death taught me more about her than I ever learned directly."

"That's something reasonable to cry over," Greer replied, crossing one leg over the other as she looked out the window.

"It's silly. There's a war brewing and my town, my neighbors and friends, are dead. I should weep over them. Not her. And you, you've endured a great loss; I shouldn't burden you with my own."

Greer turned back to Lachlan and for once, pulled herself from the pit she found herself in for the last month. Fresh air floated down, covered her face, and brought her back to reality. Her heart ached for the man before her, for her sister, and all the people she knew. She had been so selfish and blind.

"A loss is a loss. Even if we knew the same person and that person died, our individual losses are unique because no two relationships are the same. Do not simplify the loss of your parent as silly, even if you didn't know her very well. It's still a loss and something only you can experience and that's a very lonely, painful thing."

"It's so interesting." Lachlan looked before them and cleared his throat. "Grief is an experience had by all, and yet when you endure it, it's something that's so singular. I've never felt quite so alone than in this moment, even though I know others experience grief as well."

"It's an emotion that can tear people apart." Greer picked at the edge of her shirt, recalling her mother staring her down hours before. *Careful, daughter. Grief can change a person.* Greer pressed her palms against her legs, reminding herself she was still there, alive and whole. "All the more reason to see it through. I doubt your mother would want you to suffer from her loss, she would want you to live."

Barden would want her to live.

They fell quiet and beyond the windows, somewhere in the brush of the small trees surrounding the Elder Tree, or perhaps in the Elder Tree itself, an owl called while summer bugs hummed.

"I'm sorry I couldn't have done more," Lachlan added and when Greer looked at him, he didn't back down. His jaw was set, his face serious. "I realize that isn't something within my control. The Elder Tree sap's dangerous or a blessing for that very reason, but I still wish I could've provided you the help you sought. I never loved someone, not in that way, but I see how deeply it affected you."

"It's like a wound that won't heal," Greer admitted, surprising even herself. She blinked and frowned, the truth of it all, of all her pain, became rapidly apparent. "As if I had a fist-sized chunk ripped from my chest and it's this gaping, ugly hole that still bleeds. Nothing we do will stop the blood, nothing can stop the pain, it's just been there for the last month and it won't ease. It can't heal."

"May I say something that's likely far and beyond my realm of allowance?"

Greer nodded; certain she wouldn't like what the fae prince said but bracing herself for it anyway. After her behavior since Barden's death, she deserved all that was thrown at her from the people she knew, and this was just the start.

"Your sister praised you openly when I met her. Ailith as well. The fae guards, Ceenear and Raum, spoke warmly of you, kindly. When I met you, your personality wasn't what I expected. But I met you in such extreme circumstances I'm unsurprised you acted differently. Now hearing of your wounded heart, I understand why all the better. But you realize what can happen with wounds that do not heal, do you not?"

Greer stared at Lachlan. She didn't want to say it. His lips turned down. "They fester."

She worried her wounds were already doing just that.

"I have wounds older than Barden's death," Greer admitted. "Wounds my father caused, sores the weight of all this created. I don't believe I've tended to any of these harms, never. I haven't had the time; I haven't had the allowance to focus on myself. There's always, without doubt, been more for me to do, more important things."

"I suspect you wouldn't be the first monarch to feel that way."

Greer smiled grimly and ran her hands down her thighs, pushing her shoulders back and eliciting a delicious crack in her spine. A small comfort. A pop of relief. "For someone who claimed not to understand what ruling a kingdom pertained to, you understand much more than you give yourself credit for."

"Studying books and learning about the intricacies of kingdoms is one thing. Ruling is another."

"Is it?" Greer looked at him. The longer she sat, the more relaxed she felt. Her worries weren't removed, they weren't changed, but there was less weight to it all. She, at last, was able to discuss everything without the burden of expectation; without the role of superior. With Lachlan, she was an equal. Sovereign to sovereign. They were one and the same, even if Lachlan wasn't crowned yet. But he would be, Greer would see to that. At least she hoped to.

Leaning forward, she rested her elbows on her knees and continued. "So much of what I do is a reflection of what's worked in the past. Even war plans, they're considerations of successful campaigns that have happened before, or better yet, looking at the failures and understanding what went wrong so you can prevent that from happening again. Of course, there's the paperwork, so much damned paperwork that comes with caring for a kingdom. But hopefully that's a burden you can share with staff you'll select. You can dole out responsibilities to others and allow them to help you."

"But how do I ensure I'm any good? I worry about that, it's part of the circle of grief I'm in. I think of my mother and how I didn't truly know her—not personally—and yet I did, because I read about her in our texts; her ruling power and decisions, I just never knew my mother and the queen of Invarlwen were one and the same. And then I get to thinking about her rule and how it was peaceful for the entirety of it. If she was still alive, I assume it would be peaceful to this day. How do I know I can do the same as she? How do I ensure my people can thrive and be as happy as they were when she was queen?"

Greer considered this before she asked, "May I tell you a story?"

Lachlan sat up straight, his thin lips curling into the barest smile, but still they reached his eyes. "If you'd like, I'd be happy to hear it."

"Once when I was nearly the same age as Caitriona, my father had an awful cold during the Day of Royal Greeting—it's when citizens lodge complaints. He was so sick, he couldn't attend, and I was picked to be at the helm of it all. It was the first time I ever ran it alone—beforehand it was always with my father—and I was nervous so I requested my mother join me, if only for support.

"This young mother came in with a babe clinging to her chest, crying the whole time. She said she had no family, no one to teach her how to be a mother, and that she couldn't figure out why her babe wept. She said she was at her wits end, she desperately needed sleep, and she wished we provided better resources to help her. These are all poignant things, something I fought to have fixed because my father was deeply against providing any services to 'standard women's work.' He claimed it was something women should understand naturally and that not to was a failure on the mother's part. If my mother could set fire with her mind like Caitriona can, he would've been engulfed in flames for that alone. But I digress...

"Despite all we did after, it was something my mother said in the moment to calm the poor woman's fears that's stuck with me. She looked at her and said, 'a good mother is one who frets that they aren't good enough; a good mother finds motherhood hard.' She told the mother she was doing fine before sending one of the royal nurse maids to help the poor thing. My mother pointed out it's helpful to have the support of others when handed the most delicate of tasks.

"But my point is, the very fact you worry about how you'll take care of your people and be a good ruler is proof enough that you're on the right path."

Lachlan's shoulders relaxed. "That's a comfort, thank you."

"It's the truth and you're welcome."

It was a truth Greer needed to be reminded of. She needed the support of others as well as to focus on the betterment of her people. She couldn't do it all and she had to allow herself the grace to step back and allow others to take charge while she focused on what she knew best.

The pair fell into companionable silence; both studied the painting of the Elder Tree as the candles dripped. The flames were growing low and at sunrise, they would be replaced by the helping hands of attendants with new candles that stood tall and could burn through the day until they diminished the following morning. Beyond the windows, the tree line grew defined, the black sky becoming a dark shade of blue. Sunrise was near and another night of no sleep had come and gone.

Greer couldn't control her sister or that her dreams were absent of Barden. She couldn't control that a mad king sought to usurp her from the throne she had barely the chance to sit upon. But she could allow herself to rest, focus on the battles ahead, and maintain hope of continuing on.

"I think I'll head to bed and get a few hours of sleep before the day truly begins," Greer announced as she pushed to her feet.

"Goodnight, Queen Greer," Lachlan said with a smile. "I think I'll stay here a bit longer."

Greer nodded. "Goodnight, King Lachlan."

As she turned to the door, a pale-faced guard held it open and clutched a letter in his hand. "Queen Greer, King Lachlan, I apologize for the intrusion. The hall guards saw you here. I have a dire message: King Malcolm's forces have left the mist and are advancing to the Umberfend Marsh."

Sleep ... sleep would have to come later.

Within the marsh there is a crime.
Magic to magic, it is necessary to never withhold from what is natural.
Not without a cost.
There are tricks pressed into the dirt,
stretched along roots, and filtered into the waters.
The taste of misdeed is thick in the air;
cunning so foul it coats everything with grime.
It is poison drifting into land. There will be grave consequences for this.
Nightmares are kept at bay seemingly for good, but it is only trickery.
They know—those in the water—they see it for what it is
as they grasp their throats and plunge deeper.
He knows—he who searches for the light—but follows suit and within
the depths he forgets.
They swim down. Down to where caves hold bones that still have
marrow. Down to where old ones sleep. Down to where the world above is
forgotten, the brilliance of light recedes,
and they become something more foreign than their creation ever intended.
The waters are stilled, the grasses starve, the shallows are empty.

CHAPTER NINETEEN

AILITH

Her throat was raw again. She tried to swallow but the movement felt like an iron ball—red hot from a fire—was lodged within. Her tongue tasted ferric as well. Ailith grimaced. Her lashes stuck together as she tried to open her eyes; they were swollen and full of crust, and attempts to lift her hand to rub them was strange. The pull against her wrists forced her eyes open all the way. She sat in a chair, in an empty, white-stoned room with her hands tied by rope.

"Where...?" She looked around. Fiana sat beside her; still unconscious and propped up in a similar chair with her hands tied and the bag of potions gone from her shoulder, weapons taken as well. The room had the same shiny white stone as the outcrop beyond the window of their cage. But this wasn't a cage. There was a large window, glass covered, that overlooked the mountains. The room was too large and perfect to be used as a holding cell. Additional matching chairs to the ones she and Fiana sat in surrounded a table next to the large window. Chairs that were far too well-made for a couple of convicts to be seated in, and yet, that's what they were. There was nothing else. Nothing besides the two of them, the table, and additional chairs.

Ailith felt a chill of concern. She looked over herself. The knife on her leg was gone, as was the other she hung from her waist. She shifted her legs and the bulge of the potion bag wedged into her pants rubbed her thigh. Fiana had handed it to Ailith before Lumia entered the room; she was lucky she was able to hide it well enough.

Lumia—where was Lumia now?

But more peculiar was that they were alone. No guard by the door. No sound of footfall. Even their ties were not very well done. Inching to the edge of her chair, Ailith moved one foot at a time to see if she was tied to the chair itself. Nothing. No rope, no magic, only her hands were tied together and she could get to her feet.

So, she did.

With her hands tied before her, she adjusted the potion bag hidden in her pants then crouched at Fiana's side. "Fiana, you have to wake up."

Similar to Ailith, there were a few streaks of white in Fiana's dark tresses that hadn't been there before. Ailith could only assume the terror she felt caused her own hair to grow whiter with each instance, but now Fiana's was changing too. They had to get out of there before they were scared again— fear could kill people, and she wasn't sure how many more moments of fright she could withstand.

Fiana groaned under Ailith's shaking hand and Ailith reached for the ties at Fiana's wrists. They were tight and the knot something Ailith wasn't familiar with. Cursing under her breath, Ailith looked around the room for anything that could help encourage the knot to loosen.

"What happened?"

Fiana blinked at Ailith; her voice raw from what Ailith

assumed was her screaming as well. "I think we were both frightened again. Magically, I'm sure."

"Gods was this what you went through every time? This is awful." Fiana tilted her head backward and released a breath of air.

With a sympathetic smile, Ailith crossed the glossy floor to the table, checking the sides for drawers or any place a dining knife could possibly be. "It certainly feels like the same thing as what happened before."

"Where are we?"

Ailith straightened, frowning at the useless table as she shook her head. "I woke just before you and haven't seen anyone. This all seems idiotic. They made no effort to keep us from running off other than this damned knot for our hand ties. This isn't something that'd stop anyone from escaping. We have to be missing some provision."

"Maybe there's magic on the door," Fiana murmured as she inspected the binding on her wrists. "I recognize this knot. It's one the fae tend to use. A huge pain to undo, it will take time, but I know how."

"That doesn't comfort me as much as it should," Ailith replied as she returned to Fiana's side and offered her wrists.

Fiana worked at the knot while Ailith looked out the window, trying to pinpoint what mountaintops she viewed. "Why would they sit us in here with just a knot that we can untie?"

"They took our supplies and weapons," Fiana murmured as she pulled Ailith's wrists to her mouth, using her teeth to hold onto part of the rope while tugging at another.

"Do you still have your potion?"

Fiana tilted on the chair, jutting her hip out to the side. Just slightly, beneath the waist of her pants, was the slight bulge from the potion bag. Ailith let out a breath. "At least we have that working for us."

Distantly, a rhythmic sound grew in volume. "Wait." Ailith held out her hand and Fiana stilled. They looked at one another for a moment before Ailith bolted for her seat, throwing herself into it just as the broad, wooden doors swung open.

"Ah, you're both awake," a voice announced as rapid footfall approached. A dark-blond man with fae ears stepped before them, followed by two male fae guards that clutched ropes in their hands with a figure being dragged along from behind.

Vanora flipped her blonde hair over her shoulder and caught her footing to walk upright, lifting her head high and retaining a glare upon the man who Ailith was certain was Malcolm.

"I was waiting for you both to wake, I didn't want you to miss the show." The man turned to them and rubbed his hands together. His skin looked waxy, as if he was sick. It was similar to Kayl's appearance when Ailith met him originally, back when his hatred was already beginning to work upon him and turn him into an unbound. The same was beginning to happen to Malcolm.

He smiled and looked between the two women. "Not very talkative, hmm? You certainly screamed enough. Did you hurt your voice boxes? Was that it?"

He shrugged. He couldn't care less; it was all meaningless chatter. Waving to the guards, they pulled on the ropes tied around Vanora's hands and waist. She didn't move but maintained her regal stance with her chin held high. A guard clicked his tongue and stepped behind her, pressing his hands onto the center of her back and shoving her forward. She tumbled closer to Malcolm, her hair falling over her face, but recoiled before coming into contact with him. He laughed and Ailith tasted his sickly pleasure, like too-bitter liquor.

"Since you both have snuck around like mice, and mice are

prone to discover things they shouldn't be privy to, I felt it time to share a few secrets." He stepped closer to Vanora who mirrored his movement and stepped back. Looking at the guards, Malcom dropped the cheerful act. "Hold her still."

They positioned themselves beside her and gripped her shoulders as Malcolm circled. He switched his smile on again and returned his attention to Ailith and Fiana. "I have plans for you both. If I'm being honest—and I can be because neither of you will remember this for long—it's for the Wimleigh royals. You know them, right? You're the dragon princess's lover and you both tried to help the queen find my wife's bastard son."

Ailith looked at Fiana. She'd have to be tortured to say anything and she knew Fiana would keep their secrets. *How does he know?*

"Here's the plan," Malcolm continued as he ran his finger over Vanora's jaw. He leaned toward her, speaking low but with enough breath to stir her blonde hair. The fae woman remained motionless but a muscle clenched along her jaw. Ailith's hands twitched, she wanted to lunge forward and beat the king. "I'm going to turn you *all* into creatures—don't worry, the Gablaigh sisters will be turned as well if I have the choice—and you all shall be my pets. My army of creatures. But I wanted to show you just how amazing the change is. I want you to see it, enjoy it, so you'll understand what'll happen to you in the future."

He looked over his shoulder and smiled, his teeth yellow and crooked, with a bit of food caught between two. He lifted Vanora's hand to his lips and kissed it. Vanora spat, landing a mouthful of saliva on his brow. The only sign that this bothered him was the tensing of his shoulders. A guard darted forward, dabbing the spit away with a cloth before stepping back.

"Ah, you've reminded me—" His voice was strained, his

anger barely in check, and Vanora didn't flinch—no wonder Niveem married her.

Ailith leaned forward in her seat, tugging the ties around her wrist and trying to loosen them further from what Fiana managed to do.

Malcolm tilted his head to the side, his eyes locked on Vanora as he continued. "I wanted to let you know, before I set this curse upon you, the news about your wife. I wanted to turn her into a creature as well, but too many of her people and the fae of other mountain peaks followed her, so I used her as an example, and now her head hangs from my banner."

Ailith held her breath. Vanora studied his expression which told the truth of it all, but even then, desperately she looked at Ailith and Fiana. Ailith couldn't keep her upset from her face, she couldn't hide the horror she witnessed, and it seemed Vanora understood. Her wife was gone. She breathed out and her shoulders sank, but she still stood straight with her head held high as her eyes filled with tears.

"Hmm." Malcolm dropped her hand. "Not the reaction I hoped for. Well then, guards?"

They stepped aside, the ropes in their hands tightening so Vanora couldn't move. Malcolm pulled a bag from his pocket and threw it against Vanora's bare feet. A purple smoke exploded from the pouch and rushed upward, searching for a source and finding Vanora closest to it. She attempted to push out of the way, but the ropes were too tight. Worse, the smoke was quick. It plunged into her body, pouring in rapidly and disappearing. She stood still, blinking, and for a foolish moment humor filled Ailith whole.

The fool couldn't even perform a curse properly.

Then Vanora gasped and buckled at the waist, taking Ailith's amusement with her movement. The guards dropped the rope and brushed past while Malcolm walked at a considerably slower pace to stand between Fiana and Ailith.

Bending down, he slipped a knife between Ailith's hands and broke the rope. He smelt of fish water, stale and dull, and his breath stunk all the worse.

"You're welcome to try and save her," he whispered against Ailith's neck. "But I doubt you'll get very far."

Ailith lunged, her hands rushing to Malcolm's face where her dirt-lined nails tore into his papery skin and successfully drew blood. It was all she was able to do, the guards were too quick and she was too weak. A blow to the face was all it took to send her crumbling to the ground, and a kick into her ribs took the air from her lungs. Curling on her side with a groan and flakes of Malcolm's skin still under her nails, she glared at the king.

"Little bitch," Malcolm growled while a guard wiped the blood off his face. "I'll save you for last. You deserve to watch everyone suffer."

Vanora collapsed as she screamed, her blonde hair rippled and spread from her head, appearing down her neck and onto her chest. It grew in bursts, changing into a mixture of gold and red feathers as dark blue feathers erupted from her arms. She fell to her side as her feet twisted, the bones breaking and reforming, her toes conjoined and became webbed as they took on a bird-like structure.

Despite her attempt to injure Malcolm, Ailith's nervous system was too sensitive and her terror built as Vanora's screams brought back Caitriona's. She couldn't help Caitriona then; she wouldn't be able to help Vanora now. But Fiana didn't know; she hadn't experienced the horror before and rushed forward after Malcolm freed her hands as well.

A guard pulled Ailith off the floor and threw her back onto her chair. She didn't attack Malcolm again as her face grew wet from blood leaking from her nose.

"It won't work," Ailith whispered to Fiana, even though her voice was lost amongst Vanora's screams. Malcolm patted her shoulder as he passed and Ailith hated that she cringed in her chair. He laughed as he receded, a door closed, and Fiana kept running her hands over Vanora's thrashing form. Fiana wept as she tried to stop the curse from taking hold. Ailith shook her head, her face wet with her own tears mingling with her bloody nose. She thought of Caitriona's hot blood coating her hands and the pain she endured, now happening to the woman before her.

"Fiana, you have to stop. We need to leave before her change is complete. She'll kill us," she raised her voice, trying to be heard over Vanora's cries. "It won't work, nothing will stop the curse."

CHAPTER TWENTY

CAITRIONA

The landscape was so slanted from the Elder Tree tunnel's exit, the only understandable choice was to move down in search of flatter land, and out of reach of the mountain's mist.

"We can camp for the night," Raum determined as they stumbled downward. "And catch up on rest—it feels like days since we left Braewick. We can get our bearings. Then, tomorrow, we follow the paths back to the mist."

"You're certain going downhill now and retracing our steps tomorrow is worthwhile?" Caitriona asked as her heel slipped on a stone and she jolted forward. Ceenear's iron-clad grasp gripped her arm and kept her from tumbling down the hill.

"The mist, at times, has a mind of its own. It also recognizes me. I don't want to rest too close to it and encourage it to draw down the mountain to find me, particularly because we aren't sure if Malcolm's informed the mist to label me as a threat. It's best to rest further from it."

"All this and we may not even be granted entrance through the mist." Caitriona sighed. Between the steep slope and exhaustion from the wavering influx of time her body experienced, she was beginning to second-guess the entire venture. Greer was right, she wasn't thinking things through.

Raum offered his arm. She grasped hold and immediately felt more balanced as he guided her down the slope. He was used to the steep mountainous region and surefooted. Squeezing her hand, he offered a kind smile. "If that's the case, you and Ceenear can fly over the wall of the mist. The mist is meant to keep out ground forces. It doesn't stop entrance through the air."

As the land flattened, they found their way to the dead town. Caermythlin. It was destroyed in a different way from Trasc. While Trasc had fallen away due to time, the destruction of Caermythlin was man-made. What structures remained were due to fire that hadn't taken the entirety of it. The rest was rubble; burned shells of dwellings where age and abandonment was obvious. Signs hung on single hinges outside former shops with the paint faded and wood rotten; some had fallen completely and lay under leaflitter. Windows were broken, doors busted in; moss grew on what roofs hadn't collapsed and those that did sprung forth little trees through the holes. The rest of the structures were burned, the scars of fire clear on the walls and through the holes in roofs. Caitriona paused on the edge of what must have been the main street and stared. Declan and May's town would look like this with time, a shell of a place with the remains of fire still clear. Her chest physically ached, and her eyes burned with tears she couldn't shed because they were still a ball of pain that sat in the back of her throat.

"So, this is it," Caitriona whispered. With Ceenear and Raum on each side, they walked down the broad street. The road cut through the town, moving northward and traveling between the mountains and the sea; that likely explained the attempts that were made to fix a few of the dwellings. Fresh wood that made new walls and entryways cleared, but still none seemed finished. Caitriona recalled few settlements nearby. Travelers probably attempted to make places to sleep while moving between the northern coastal towns and Stormhaven.

But the silence of a town that clearly was once bustling sat heavily on Caitriona. The quiet felt unnatural and visiting the shell of the town brought on a discomfort that crept up her spine. The unease here was different than in Trasc. It was more similar to Greenbriar. She was walking down the path of a murder scene. "My mother grew up here after she came to the orphanage."

"When did her mother pass?"

"I think before she was ten." Caitriona drew to a stop beside a former fountain, now rubble and filled with water that produced cattails and weeds. A frog dove in with a tiny plop and left ripples in its wake. It was hard to fathom that not even that long ago the town was once thriving. Thirty years, that wasn't very long, and yet the remains felt older as the earth rose and took over the land once more.

Caitriona looked past where the last buildings stood and narrowed her eyes at rows of bushes in a field. An old harvesting spot, perhaps?

"Maybe we can pick berries," Raum offered.

The houses dropped off one by one as they walked forward and stepped from the roadway into tall grasses that reached well above their hips. Bugs, hidden within the grasses, sang in the late afternoon light and a bird took flight from within the bushes as they drew closer.

"They're roses." Ceenear stepped ahead to inspect the bushes. "I've never seen roses so dark—"

She looked at her feet and took a hasty step back as Caitriona came to her side. The bushes were thick with blooming roses that made the air rich with their scent, but the flowers were blood red, closer to black, and blended into the deep green of the leaves as if hiding until only those nearby could perceive their beauty. But the flowers weren't as shocking as the mounds of earth before each bush. Long and low, the lumps of soil had softened to gentle ridges that were only a foot above the ground and thick with the tall grasses that surrounded them.

"This is a grave," Ceenear whispered. "These are all graves."

Caitriona looked at the expanse of it all and her stomach turned with nausea. The back of her throat filled with acidic bile.

"These are the townspeople my father killed."

She stared at the rows, because it wasn't a single line but multiple. An entire town's worth of people buried individually and while Caitriona was never privy to her father's meetings, she read enough literature in the last two years to know her father's guards would never have buried any of the bodies themselves, yet here they were. Multiple graves.

She pictured Kayl in Beaslig two years before; he sat alone and spoke to no one when she approached him. He *had* no one. They were all dead. Lifting her hand to her mouth, she no longer held back her gasp. "*He* buried them. He buried everyone in the town. This was Kayl's doing after—after he made the curse."

Her mind lingered in Beaslig; the snow thick on Kayl's house that sat close yet separate from the town. She easily recalled her hope as, at last, she met the very person who saved her life. But he betrayed her—her trust, her health, and her body—all by placing the curse upon her. The stabbing pain of that betrayal still smarted in her chest when she remembered the pride he had when she changed into a dragon. But he was a haunted man as well, his eyes showed as much with the circles beneath them along his gaunt skin. He said he found his town dead and he was the only one to survive the massacre. Who would she be if she experienced the same? Who would anyone? Would they not all be hollow shells?

Caitriona blinked away her burning tears. Somehow sympathy for Kayl curdled in her heart despite her hatred for the man. Perhaps she didn't hate him, not as much anymore. She disliked Kayl for so long after becoming a dragon. The curse left her permanently changed, but looking at the number of graves with planted roses of different heights—indicating it took seasons to finish planting the rose bushes before each grave—made her hatred lessen, and in its place grew understanding. "I would have done it as well, I think."

Ceenear looked at Caitriona, her brows knit. She placed her hand on Caitriona's shoulder. Caitriona met her gaze and released the tension in her spine, exhausted by it all.

Gesturing to the landscape, her voice was soft as she spoke. "I understand why he did it. I wish he didn't, but I understand why. I think I would've done it too, even though it was wrong. To kill this many people, all the people he knew and loved and grew up with, and be able to do something about it? I felt that when I found May and Declan—I can't imagine the flame it would ignite in me if it was everyone I knew."

"Come, let's find somewhere to camp and leave the dead behind." Ceenear slipped her arm around Caitriona's shoulders and gently turned her back into the town proper.

They chose a small field along the town's edge, just where the ridge rose. The destroyed buildings allowed for some protection and blocked the view of the graves, while the ridge-side with the trees not far off allowed a barrier from the breeze so their campfire remained lit long enough to cook fish Raum captured from a nearby stream.

They were plunged into the ridge's shadow rapidly and left to watch the glittering sea far beyond. When at last it winked out and the sky turned gray, the stars brightened and they put out the fire.

"I'll take first watch," Raum offered as Caitriona nestled under her mother's cloak. She thought of Ailith as best as she could—she would find her soon; she was certain of it—but as she fell asleep, she couldn't control her mind returning to the rows of graves and the scent of roses in her nose.

CHAPTER TWENTY-ONE

"Deliver it directly to the queen," Róisín instructed as she studied the rider. Her hand rested upon the edge of the small cart tied behind the large draft horse. "It's important she receive it. Tell her it's from me. Tell her I had it made and it's for her to remember who she is. Tell her …"

Róisín bit her lip. *Tell her I love her*, but Greer would never believe Róisín would send such a message to be spoken by a rider. They were never ones to exchange words of affection, but she hoped Greer understood how she truly felt from the gesture. "Just tell her those things, please. And be quick, she left for the marsh this morning."

It was a day of chaos and heightened tension. The folk in the city were nervous, the swell of discussion and apprehension so thick it hung in the air with the humidity, giving the late summer air a twinge of metal that laid on the tongue and filled nostrils without remorse, causing people to be uneasy and short tempered. There was never a lull in deferring opinions; the city was still adjusting to the idea of magic being welcomed with varying degrees of acceptance, and now with magic threatening their very lives, it created further chaos. Nearly all city guards remained in Braewick City to protect its walls and stop fights amongst neighbors. Had the citizens turned their cheek to their differences, more guards would be on the field preparing for battle, additional to swell their forces and raise the chances, yet here they were, and it irritated Róisín to no end. She'd rather the citizens hide in their homes; instead, they nitpicked one another until fights broke out and guards were called to handle their nonsensical skirmishes. But there was nothing to be done, the vibe was set, and emotions spread.

Comparatively, the guard yard was quiet. Only a skeleton crew of city guards were stationed to keep watch of the castle itself. The numbers were thin and left even Róisín uncomfortable.

This was it, the great battle, the one they waited for.

Typically, wars began with a leak; little disturbances that grew in number, but sometimes they began as an explosive flood. It appeared that was Malcolm's preference. One battle on an innocent town to test the strength of his forces and now this, a straightforward assault. Hopefully meeting them in the middle would prove beneficial and the dukes would rise to fight on behalf of Greer. The landscape wasn't the best for a battle, but it was better than letting them pass the ridge and flood into Braewick City.

Greer packed and left with Lachlan shortly after dawn. For weeks they prepared for the possibility of having to move forces with little warning and now that preparation came into play. They did all they could beforehand, but it was time to move forward.

Róisín remained per Greer's request but she had no doubt she'd follow. She never saw a battlefield, she never wanted to, but she didn't want to be where her family was not. With Caitriona to the Endless Mountains and Greer to the marsh before them, it was necessary for her to follow in their footsteps with due time. If they would fall, she would be there to catch them.

But first, she had things to attend to.

With the key to the garden wall, Róisín slipped out. The northern gates to the farming lands were closed and the area around the Elder Tree blocked from citizens, granting her privacy as she pushed through brambles and bushes to the base of the tree itself. The trunk widened into a gaping hole, dark and deep, the end of it disappearing to nothing, and Róisín couldn't help but smile at the thought of Caitriona bravely descending into the earth. She hoped the cloak, blessed with her and Isla's magic, kept her youngest safe, but time would only tell.

In her hands, she held two scraps of cloth cut from Caitriona and Greer's old gowns. She cherished those gowns, holding onto them as mementos of their childhood as most mothers did, but now there was a churning desperation in her gut. Twisting the cloth together, binding them as one long strip, she kissed the fabric before looking at the tree.

She was scared, and she wouldn't admit this to anyone except the tree.

"Keep them alive?" She asked the Elder Tree as she caught one of its branches in her hand. "Do not have them hurt anymore. Let them live through this battle, let them see happiness. The *both* of them."

She tied the entwined scraps of fabric to the branch and let it go. She remained beneath the tree, her arms wrapped around her torso while she watched the branch lift upward and the sun brighten the cloth. She had hoped making the wish would make her feel better, but it didn't. She felt a certainty of doom. Something was going to happen and the Elder Tree would not answer her call.

Róisín was never one to feast on fear. She was not one for anxiety; reactions, knowings, a sense of certainty for future events she felt here and there but never consistently enough to reliably predict the future. But now? The last few weeks? It was all consuming. Dreams of battles; of Greer falling into the marsh and going under the water; and Caitriona as a dragon slick with blood and fire. The images haunted her and made her heart gallop and vibrate in her chest. She wanted to place herself before them, to block them both from this battle, but she was only a woman. A mother. A former queen. What could she do?

She sighed, but it wasn't her sigh. The sun dimmed behind a cloud, yet the sky was clear. She looked to the hole in the tree with uncertainty and the sigh came again as the darkness of the hole pressed forward and leaked out.

Stumbling backward, Róisín alighted her hand in the brilliance of stars, glowing bright she held them in her palm despite that they stung and burned. When the castle had been attacked by Shad's shadows, it was magic light that chased them away. She'd be damned if the city descended into darkness again under her watch.

But the darkness still came, seeping onto the earth like sluggish water. Róisín held the starlight aloft, digging through her memories to think of a way to direct her energy as Isla taught her. For all her spells and potions, she followed recipes. For the supplies she gave Caitriona, the blessings in the final gifts to both her daughters, and the energy tonic she sent with Greer, they could easily have been created by a nonmagic user because it boiled down to being daring enough to mix ingredients that could come with hefty problems if done incorrectly. But magic made from thought, pushed through will, established through energy was something Róisín was still rusty with. What could she do to stop the incoming darkness? How could she prevent it from spreading?

The starlight brightened but didn't pierce the shadow, although the shadow did hesitate.

"That won't work," it said.

Róisín let the starlight diminish, the brightness of the late summer afternoon startlingly dim in comparison.

"Kayl?" Róisín asked the shadow. It stopped its steady pursuit forward and seemed to gather itself into a tighter mass of impenetrable darkness.

"I told you to meet me at the tree," he said.

"That was two years ago after Caitriona's curse. I've been to the tree many times, but I didn't realize you meant *this* tree."

"What other tree would I speak of?"

Róisín shrugged. "Perhaps the Elder Tree of Caermythlin where we've met in dreams?"

The dark form seemed to shrug as well. *"That would've actually been the perfect place to meet but we both know to get there would've been impossible for you. Anyway, you made the offer to come here, not me."*

"What happened, Kayl?"

"My ties to Malcolm are free. I'm no longer bound to him."

"Which means he has all the power he could consume ..."

The black mass nodded. *"All but the last bit, my final life force. Our binds snapped. He seemed distracted, busy planning something, and I was able to pull away."*

"Then you aren't long for this world."

The mass didn't move. Róisín looked to the branches and sought the scraps of her daughters' old dresses blending with the many coins and ties left by others. The tree appeared at peace, and perhaps it was, knowing it birthed so much life. But it was drained, dying slowly, and knew the terror it brought into the world. Perhaps it wanted to die, to give itself up to the earth, to seek out forgiveness in that way.

"Was it worth it?" Róisín murmured, still staring at the tree but asking Kayl all the same. "In the end, now that you're fading to nothing, your life gone, was it worth casting that curse?"

Kayl was silent for so long that Róisín looked down, wondering if he dispersed entirely but the dark shadow was still there.

"You already know the answer to that."

"So, it was?"

"What I wished my life to be was beyond my control, the pieces to the puzzle weren't in my hands and lost by others. But I still achieved some of my desires—I had Cearny removed and a much better monarch placed on the throne due to those actions. I was also able to speak with you again."

"I'd be careful," Róisín warned. The heaviness of the air and stress of the war left her humorless. "Chatting in dreams is different from face to face. I have yet to forgive you completely and I'm not certain I ever will."

"Honestly, if you forgave me for what I did to your children, then I would think I truly never knew you."

Róisín ran her tongue over her lips and looked at the edge of the wood surrounding the Elder Tree. It was still quiet beside the birds chirping. She'd have to return to the castle soon so as not to raise any alarm once the staff noticed she wasn't within—everyone had a place to be, including her. "We received word this morning he sent his forces beyond the mist. Greer and her guards left to meet them in the marsh."

"This is it. This is the battle he wanted. When I left he was still at the castle but time—"

"Moves differently. Human hosts tie you to time, correct?"

"Yes."

Róisín was at a loss for words now that a cumulation of

dreams led to this moment before her. She told Kayl to find her so he wouldn't be alone and yet she hadn't believed he would. As if reading her mind, he spoke.

"I came to warn you before I disperse. To warn Greer. He has awful plans with any prisoner, with any person who refuses to follow his lead. He's changing them to beasts, he's going to use them as weapons. For those who are caught as prisoners of war, he'll do the same. If he doesn't kill Greer outright, he'll force her to become a creature. He'll rule this land with the fae who follow him and nothing but magical creatures who respond to his call."

"You need to give me something more, Kayl. This is awful but I need something that'll actually help the fight."

"I can try to follow you, perhaps if I see the battle itself I can offer suggestions."

"How do you know I'll go to the battlefield?"

"Because the Róisín I knew wouldn't allow herself to miss out and she certainly wouldn't allow her children to go there without being close by."

Róisín rubbed her brow. She was an idiot, and she surely was going to regret all this, but war was a time for risky behavior, particularly when the odds were deeply stacked against you.

"Tether yourself to me."

"What?"

"Tether yourself to me. You'll last longer, won't you, if you have a life force to hold onto? Tether yourself to me and you can come to the battlefield. We'll figure this out together like we did when we were young."

"You were always the one with the desire to get into mischief and I always the one getting us out of it."

"Exactly. So, let's do this one last time before you're gone forever. But I tell you this, Kayl, if you try and take my magic, Isla will see it. She'll be with me and she'll pull your spectral body from mine and vanquish you on the spot."

"What's your real reason for wanting me to join you?"

She studied the ground where crushed eyebright flowers mingled with the dirt and sporadic grass. Licking her lips, she bolstered herself to admit the truth. "Because if you can give me any advantage to ensure my daughters are safe, I'll take it. Even if you end up killing me in the process." *But I also don't want to do this alone*, Róisín thought but didn't dare to admit. Faced with all that was ahead, she realized she was frightened.

"Now join me before I change my mind." Róisín thrust her hand forward into the shadowed form of Kayl and the wet cold of his essence seeped into her fingers. It was like a shock to the system, a spasm through her veins that froze her body and entered her mind. He was as much a part of her as she was a part of herself. She sighed; her eyes wide as she looked at the tree with double vision that slowly centered itself.

Oh, Kayl breathed in her mind, as natural as her thoughts. *Oh, Róisín, I never knew…*

"Knew what?" she replied out loud, drunk from the mixture of his remaining life-source power interacting with hers. Delighted and tingling, swirling and light. Was this what it felt like to be possessed or was it only him sinking deeply into her very soul?

You've been hiding this all along. You've always had it. No wonder Maeve was so bitter you stopped your magic lessons. You're powerful, *my dear.* He tugged at her magic that wedged itself deep within her ribs, sending a tingling wave that made Róisín moan. *Do you feel it?*

Róisín wavered, her hand reaching out as she stumbled forward. She pressed her palm onto the broken Elder Tree's trunk. Her skin felt hot and alive, thawed from his ice and now crawling with static, sparking with energy, and the spinning plunge as Kayl tasted her power, sucked on it and drained her.

"I will throw you out of me, Kayl," she warned, grasping

her chest. "I will toss you from my body and leave you to die in the brush."

He stopped immediately and Róisín breathed.

I'm sorry, I won't do it again, but Ro, you can do so much with this.

Róisín pushed off the tree, the flush of sensation dying and her body returning to normal. She brushed her hair back and straightened her skirts. "Then let it be used where it's necessary."

CHAPTER TWENTY-TWO

CAITRIONA

Ghosts greeted them in sleep. At first Caitriona didn't realize she had drifted off. Her eyes were still open. Her friends rested beside her, despite that Raum had been awake just beforehand. He was meant to keep watch and yet something stilled Caitriona's hand from jostling him awake. She turned, inspecting their camp, and felt oddly calm —as if this was what she expected all along, for the world to turn strange with daylight and a sun just set—despite that the sun set hours before.

The graveyard of old buildings a few yards away from their camp shuddered under her gaze then began to right themselves with the aid of invisible hands. Burnt timber half rotted in the grass became solid, whole, and lifted to the rafters of hollowed buildings. Sprigs of roof tiles appeared, and faded, chipped bits of paint returned to structures where before it was barely visible. The homes were sturdy again and people filled the streets. In moments, Caermythlin was a bustling town and there weren't any signs of the horrors that happened.

A man passed between two of the closest buildings, leaving the busy street behind as he walked toward the slope

Caitriona sat. She tensed, her back going straight, but he seemed not to see her. His brow was furrowed and waves of dark hair hung into his face. He brushed his hair back and let out a huff of air, clearly frustrated over something. He sat before Caitriona and rested his arms on his knees as he looked toward the town. His hair moved in the breeze and his simple clothes smelt like beeswax and herbs. He seemed familiar, like a ghost of a memory that sat at the tip of her tongue, unplaced but bothersome.

"I'm not going to say goodbye to her." He picked up a stick from the grass and threw it toward the closest house. It spun through the air and bounced in the grass. "I'm not saying anything to her. She made her choice, let her go live it, I don't care."

There was a croaking sound and a crow flapped down, landing in the grass before the man. The crow snapped its beak and clucked, hopping closer to the man and tilting its head to the side as if to study him.

"No, don't give me that. She doesn't deserve my attention. She's made it clear she'd rather be chased after by that stupid prince. Gods, he's awful, isn't he? You have to agree."

The crow ducked its head in a familiar manner. Caitriona leaned closer, studying the corvid in silence.

"The little girls are in a complete tizzy over all this and it's spread to the boys who talk about swords and joining the royal guard. They don't understand King Donal or Cearny would never let them in; he hates magic folk. And the girls! All they speak of is how she's going to be a princess and then a queen, that maybe they can have the same dreams fulfilled. They don't realize that in another ten years they'll still be stuck in this village." He ran his hands over his legs and leaned forward, eyeing the crow as if the bird fully understood everything he said. Something about the way he turned his head and the glint in his eye made Caitriona certain he could. "She'll be married and probably have children with that tattered ass, but they'll still be stuck here. Her fortune will mean nothing for them, but if *I* say anything about it, I'm the one who has to change my attitude, not them. It's infuriating."

Laughter alighted the air and a cluster of girls skipped between buildings. A red-haired young woman followed, smiling shyly down at her feet. Her hair was straight and pooled down her back to her waist, her skin pale and clear, and her ears pointed through her hair. She clutched a soft package to her chest with one hand while the other held the hand of a little girl who skipped beside her. They were laughing, happy, and Caitriona was stunned.

Greer. She thought and blinked, realizing her error. *No, not Greer. That's Mother.* So often Caitriona heard she looked like her mother and Greer like their father, but the teenager on the street smiling broadly had Greer's face. Carefree joy was so rarely displayed from her sister that no one realized their resemblance. But Caitriona saw that expression on her sister's face before. She wore it when they joked together before going to bed. In recent years, Greer's face lightened like that when Barden was nearby. It was an expression vacant from Greer's face as of late. But here it was, worn by her mother.

Her mother from decades before moved along, oblivious of Kayl and the crow watching from their place in the tall grasses.

Kayl sighed and let his body collapse into the grass. He stared at the sky and his eyes shimmered with tears. The crow hopped along the grass and alighted onto Kayl's chest then peered into his eyes.

"I know ... I'm going to miss her." Kayl lazily ran his hand down the crows body, causing it to release the rhythmic, purr-like sound Crowley did when he was happy. "We were going to leave this town together, her and I. I knew it was a stupid promise, that it likely wouldn't come true, and it was one made by us as children, but the fact it won't happen now hurts. I feel abandoned by her and it burns all the more that it's for that dimwit."

Róisín disappeared within a building for a few moments, and when she reappeared, the crow pecked at Kayl's shoulder. He leaned away and sighed. "Fine, fine, I promise I'll talk to her before she goes. Alright, Crowley?"

The scene faded and the town filled with onlookers. People abandoned morning meals to descend to the streets that were decorated with ribbons and dried field flowers. There was a hum of excitement, something was happening, and they were all witness to it, including Caitriona. Beyond the crowd was a carriage, gold edged with dark painted wood. It was helmed by two white horses. A fairytale like no other as a young Cearny stepped out.

Caitriona watched with her jaw hanging. It was amazing how much her parents changed in the thirty years since they married. Her father was thinner back then, his jaw lined with a neatly trimmed blond beard and his equally blond hair ended just below his chin. He seemed broader, taller, and stronger as he descended the steps of the carriage and stood waiting.

In a window facing the slope they sat upon, Róisín and Kayl appeared. Róisín packed her bag, speaking quickly to Kayl as he looked on. The corners of his lips tipped downward, his eyes wide, his pupils watching her every movement and when she turned away, they lingered over her as if memorizing her. Her hands, her arms, her face. When she pushed past Kayl, his hand extended as if to touch her, but he held back.

She turned back and Caitriona saw herself this time. Round cheeks, big eyes, but there was a sternness to Róisín's brow that Caitriona didn't inherit. The way she set her jaw was entirely passed to Greer. She said something before turning and walking from the room, leaving Kayl to cover his face with his hands and remain still for a moment before quickly following.

Outside, Róisín exited the building and the crowd cheered. She radiated joy, even Cearny smiled and Caitriona was surprised—she couldn't recall the last time her father smiled with apparent happiness. Had he ever? Certainly not for her.

He took Róisín's hand and helped her up the steps when a child called out—the little girl who held Róisín's hand as they walked before. She pushed from the crowd and rushed forward, holding aloft a rope knotted into an elaborate design. Caitriona recalled it from her readings, it was a knot made and given to someone you loved in hope they would have joy and luck in their future. Róisín turned, extending her free hand to reach for the rope as she smiled, but Cearny's twitched. For just a split second it faltered.

There was the father Caitriona knew.

Once in the carriage, they wound away from the town, down the road and nearly out of sight. Caitriona watched from her place on the slope as something fell from a gloved hand out the carriage window.

Cearny wore gloves, not Róisín. Caitriona pressed her lips together.

"The knot," Kayl murmured. "She threw the damned knot out the window before she fully left town."

Kayl sat in the grass again and the town was quiet. It was near evening and cold. The crow—surely an ancestor of Crowley by the same name—tilted its head at Kayl and caught a nut the young half-fae man tossed. "She's done with us, I think. She couldn't even be bothered to take that knot with her. Do you know how heartbroken the girls would've been if they knew she tossed it? I burned it so they wouldn't know, but *I* know. And I don't think I'll ever be able to look at

Róisín the same way again—not that I'll ever have the chance."

"No," Caitriona said. "It was my father; he threw the knot out the window."

But visions and dreams didn't listen to simple witnesses and the scene changed rapidly. Kayl disappeared and seasons moved forward. Snow piled then melted, trees bloomed with leaves that grew to deep green then faded to autumn glory, and over and over again as blurs of people and their activities went by. The speed slowed to late summer, just as it was now, and Kayl—a fully grown adult and more similar to the man Caitriona met—embraced an old woman on the steps of the building he and Róisín had argued within.

"Yes, I'll send her your regards, Nanny," he promised. "Of course, she'll remember you. How could she not? You cared for us both."

"Thank her for me too," the woman said; her frizzed hair was stark white and the lines on her face deep.

"For what?" Kayl asked as he pulled a pack onto a horse before mounting it.

"For helping us. I know she will. It's been her plan all along; she'd marry that man and get things to change. Now that she had the girls, and there's an heir and a spare, she can finish him off. She'll do it. She'll save our village. Thank her for me."

Kayl's mouth flattened but he nodded. "I will. Promise. I'll be back in a fortnight, alright?"

"Ride swiftly and be safe," the woman replied. She stood outside the orphanage waving at Kayl until he rode around the curves and disappeared. Even then, she remained for some time looking down the road as if waiting for his return before going inside.

Then time lurched forward, but only so far as a fortnight allowed. The buildings burned, the crops destroyed, and bodies lay scattered on the street. Kayl stood alone in the midst of it and Caitriona didn't look too closely at any of the dead, fearful she'd recognize them from the previous imagery.

Blood covered Kayl's ears and trailed down his neck, staining his shirt to deep red that appeared nearly black, and only his tears seemed persistent enough to clear pathways through the blood down his face. He wailed like an animal and the ache of the sound haunted Caitriona's heart. She heard it from her own sister just a month prior when Barden died, she had felt it herself when she found May and Declan. It was heartbreak, true heartbreak, and Caitriona realized what she witnessed.

"I curse you—" Kayl called to the skies as he stood straight, turning toward the west and holding out his arms. "That your daughter will be the very beast you are most proud of. That your daughter will be your death. That you will suffer knowing those most close to you, those who share your blood, will see to your end."

"Enough," Caitriona whispered, turning away. "Enough, I've seen enough."

She tried to wake but couldn't. She was pinned to the ground, laying in the grass with a scent of rot filling her nose. Kayl was yelling, his curse forming with her witness to it. Would she be cursed again? Would hearing the very thing that made her what she was hit her a second time?

"I want to wake up," Caitriona pleaded, trying to move, to sit up, but felt her body weighed down with a pressure of something not there. "Let me wake up."

She thrashed, but the weight persisted. Then she remembered the very thing Kayl made her into and she allowed fire to swallow her whole. Leaking from her very pores, she became explosive, a blinding light of flame, and at last the weight disappeared. She screamed into the waking world and the receding face of a woman.

The marrow maiden stood some feet from Caitriona, clutching the scraps of her wardrobe over her chest with one hand and a still-smoldering jawbone in the other. Her large, black eyes reflected the flames as they lessened on Caitriona's skin and finally winked out. She flicked the jawbone she held and a puff of smoke rose from what meat remained on it.

Beside Caitriona, Ceenear and Raum braced their weapons and were ready to strike. All were motionless, staring at one another with surprise, and Caitriona rapidly cleared her mind.

"Just wait," Caitriona murmured, keeping her eyes on the maiden as she climbed to her feet. The creature sniffed the air but didn't move. She observed them with soft facial features and quiet interest. "I don't think she means to harm us."

Caitriona had only ever seen a marrow maiden in books. They were cousins to caroling countesses in their lust for mortal blood. Women with pale skin and long, dark hair; their eyes were endearing, innocent, and captivating, but too dark and large. They often, however, wore scraps of clothing gathered from their victims who tended to be humans—particularly men—who drew too close to their lairs and were picked off one by one. It was said the victims would attempt to charm the maiden then follow her, often mistaking her for some helpless prey. She would play the part, knowing her power, and when they surely followed her back to her lair, she'd kill them and suck the marrow from their bones. Their teeth, Caitriona read, were strong enough to snap a grown man's femur in half with just one bite.

But encroaching on sleeping travelers was not their tendency. Sitting upon a sleeping princess with horns, not typical.

"Stopping the dreams," the maiden offered, waving the jawbone at Caitriona. "Dreams devour."

"Like you were going to?" Raum snapped.

"*Raum*," Ceenear hissed.

"What? She's a *marrow maiden*."

Ceenear rolled her eyes and Caitriona clasped Raum's shoulder, noticing how the maiden bristled from his voice and gripped the jawbone harder in her pale, long-fingered grasp. Caitriona raised her free hand to display innocence. "You were trying to help me?"

"Too much death here not by *my* hand," the maiden continued and tapped the jawbone to her chest before waving it toward the village. "The land filled with spilt blood and emotion. It haunts, it *eats*, it traps and tortures. Too much sadness poisons land and land will do tricks."

Caitriona breathed slowly, keeping her eyes on the maiden despite speaking to her friends. "You both fell asleep?"

"I was out before you were," Ceenear said.

"I hadn't intended to, but I must have." Raum admitted.

"Did you dream?"

Raum shuddered under Caitriona's hand. "Lumia. I dreamt of a fight we had before I left. She didn't want me to leave, she wanted us to visit the queen, but Niveem made an order and I was going to listen."

"I dreamt of the Starling and the last time we worked together." Ceenear closed her eyes, her shoulders curved forward. She was hurting. How had Caitriona not noticed it before? "We used to work together regularly. We were close. She was different then."

Ceenear looked at Caitriona; her eyes shone with tears. Caitriona considered the hurt in Ceenear's face when she killed the Starling, and now she knew why it pained the fae guard so much. Less because killing was not a part of their culture—it was something they actively avoided—but because she killed someone she *deeply* cared for. "Ceenear—"

"Did you dream, princess?"

Caitriona stopped and gave the fae woman a nod. There

would be time for comfort later, if that's what Ceenear sought, but for now she would answer. "I dreamt of my mother leaving this town and Kayl sending out the curse. I saw the destruction my father caused and the death of this land."

The maiden nodded and pointed at the ground. "Look."

Where they laid was now scorched from Caitriona's flame, but beyond the smoldering grass, burned vines curled into themselves and shriveled before sinking into the soil. "Trapped and eaten. Land doesn't know. Land just wants to heal."

"Thank you," Caitriona whispered and the maiden nodded. "Do you live here?"

The maiden nodded again. "Travelers come by. Men often linger."

She licked her lips and her razored teeth caught the campfire light as her gaze flicked at Raum.

"Why did you help us?"

The maiden tilted her head to one side, rolling her dark eyes to the heavens and remaining still as if considering. She lifted one hand, a long, thin finger extended and pointed at Caitriona. "Message in the cloak asked me."

Caitriona looked down. She still wore her mother's cloak; she had even slept in it. While it appeared just like any cloth, with only the campfire and the light of stars, a pattern glowed. Pulsing with a steady light, Caitriona gripped the edges of the cloak and lifted the fabric to show the stitching had created different shapes over the fabric. Running her hands over the glowing letters along patterned edge, she attempted to read the words. She frowned. "I don't understand what it says."

"It's a prayer." Ceenear brushed her fingers along the edge. "A prayer of protection for you and yours, as well as a request for aid from creatures."

"Thank you." Caitriona looked up. The marrow maiden waited, still clutching the remnants of clothing to her skin, as well as the jawbone. "Thank you for your help."

"You'll leave?"

"Yes, particularly if the land will eat us."

The marrow maiden's head tilted, her long, slender neck curving. "Going where?"

"Through the mist," Raum replied. The maiden considered this and nodded once.

"Come, I'll show."

She moved forward, her feet bare and footsteps light as a dancer's. In this, Caitriona could see how she roped in less savory men. The maiden's attractive hips swayed with each step and her full breasts nearly spilled from what clothes she wore. Her movements were fluid and would encourage those with little willpower to follow.

Caitriona, however, hesitated. "We don't want to intrude any more than we have."

The maiden stilled, turning on her bare feet that seemed immune to the sharp twigs and rocks beneath, and smiled. It was a beautiful smile if not for her pointed teeth radiating danger. "You are welcome. I won't hurt."

She continued to walk and they scrambled for the few supplies they had before being led up the sloping hill in the dark night that edged ever closer to dawn. As the mist appeared and licked their toes, the sun peeked over the edge of the world, glowing on the sea and eating away the moist haze that gathered there.

"Wait, before you go." Caitriona reached into her bag and pulled free an extra shirt. "Take this, please? It should fit you."

The maiden reached forward; her delicate hands snatched the shirt from Caitriona with little effort. She studied the fabric for a moment and rubbed her thumbs over the material. That terrifying smile appeared again but Caitriona couldn't help but find it sweet.

The maiden nodded and hugged the shirt to her chest as she stepped back, receding down the slope into the trees without another word, all the while looking down at her new shirt. She didn't say goodbye, but Caitriona still watched the woman disappear into the dim light.

Caitriona turned to the mass of shifting white air climbing overhead to make an impenetrable wall. Those who meant harm to the kingdom would be killed by the mist upon entering it. Those who were innocent would be lost, only to be plucked by the fae who worked the border of the mist and could control it—like Raum. The fae would wipe their memories before sending them on their paths beyond the mist again, leaving no one to remember what it held.

Caitriona and Ailith were the only two who didn't belong to the Endless Mountains and passed through the mist with their memories still intact. Now she faced the mist—with intention of usurping the king—but primarily to find Ailith and Fiana.

"Can you part it? Or will it still know our intentions and attack?"

Raum stepped forward, extending his hand as the mist licked his skin, caressed his palm, and pressed itself into him with familiarity. Like a pet. His shoulders relaxed and he smiled. "It recognizes me and doesn't see me as a threat. Malcolm didn't think to have the mist view me as a danger. I can part it, and it should be fine. My worry is that the parting will alert a guard. There aren't many stationed over here. People tend to not come into the mist on this side of the mountain. The slope is too steep and most avoid Caermythlin."

"Well then?" Caitriona looked at Raum and he set his jaw. He turned to the mist and raised his arms. It ran along his body and wrapped its tendrils around his wrists and ankles. Its caresses became more exploratory and Caitriona stepped back. Less like a pet, and more like a lover, the mist brushed over

Raum's lips, sought his nostrils, and after momentary hesitation, plunged into his eyes.

Caitriona gasped but Raum let out a breath, as if the experience was one of pleasure while his eyes grew wide and were blanched of color.

"Go on then." His voice deepened with the weight of the mist pulling his vocal cords. The mist filled Raum's body whole and left a void of space, a pathway for them to pass just a touch bigger than Raum's form himself.

Caitriona turned to Ceenear with her concern clear. The fae woman laughed. "I promise this is normal."

Ceenear went first and Caitriona followed closely, looking at the walls of mist on either side while Raum took the rear. As he passed, the mist exited him, falling from his body to fill the pathway once more. When he joined them, the gaping hole returned to the solid mass of white.

"The king's been wondering when you'd return," a voice said from the other side.

Ceenear's bow was out and an arrow pointed before Caitriona fully turned. Raum's hand fell on the hilt of his sword while fire flared into Caitriona's palm.

On the slope continuing upward toward the first mountain peak stood a pale fae woman with long, dark hair. The shape of her brown eyes reminded Caitriona instantly of Niveem.

She stood with a bow and arrow pointed at Ceenear. At her feet sat a small, dark mop of a dog that watched them with a singular tooth sticking out of its mouth, like a tiny threat of what it was capable of doing if it attacked. Its entire body vibrated and a low growl emanated from its throat.

"Briar," Raum whispered, his eyes flicking down to the dog. "And Berry. You both are usually stationed on the other side of this mountain."

The fae woman, Briar, sneered. "That was before King

Malcolm took the crown. You've been gone for some time, Raum. A lot's changed."

Raum stood straighter but his hand didn't unclasp the sword. "I've heard of the changes. I've heard there's a shift in power and many are following."

Briar's eyes crinkled at the edges, a smile that didn't reach her lips; something amusing that she struggled to keep to herself. Her dog, Berry, looked up at her, waiting for indication to attack. "Then you know the forces you're going to have to endure. There's few of us left, Raum. The mist isn't being guarded as it once was, anyone who's refused to honor the king is plucked away, one by one, to be forced into Malcom's army."

"You've pledged yourself to Malcolm?"

Briar took a long breath and looked at the mist. It curled forward, as if listening to her response. "Only to save myself, but not with my heart. So, how can I help you?"

CHAPTER TWENTY-THREE

The marsh sprawled east of Braewick Valley's ridge. It was a flattened expanse of land, with only the barest indication of the snow-capped Endless Mountains to the east. Dotted with a patchwork of pools of water, aligned with clumps of reeds and tall grasses, it was a haven for birds, bugs, fish, and creatures who hunted flesh. When Greer and her troops arrived at the western edge of the marsh, it lay quiet with only the occasional call of swamp birds darting toward nests in the clusters of reeds, or summer bugs that flitted between shoots of grass. Greer filled her lungs with the scent of the space; grass in the sunshine; the dull, muddy waters; and rich herbs and flowers that grew wild there, spicy and thick in the air. Soon, the air would fill with iron.

To travel the distance from the castle to the marsh took hours, and with the pace slowed under the burden of supplies and marching guards, it took even longer. There were still a few hours of daylight left before they plunged into the realm where dukes ruled and they were sitting ducks. The idea of the dukes waking to speckle the marsh water with their glowing eyes both brought comfort and deep dread to Greer. The dukes were said to rise to aid in battle but no one alive witnessed the event occur. Would they simply take the lives of guards who drew too near their watery home? Or would the stories hold true and they would rise to join her in the fields? That was their hope; that the dukes joined Greer's forces and double their number.

Would Barden, left to eternal rest weeks before, be one of them?

"Do you ever grow used to war?" Lachlan asked; his voice quiet in a manner that seemed normal for him and reminded Greer perpetually of Caitriona. He wasn't one for many words and seemed to consider what he wanted to say over an expanse of time rather than blurting out his first thought. He was silent for the majority of the ride to the marsh and this was the first time he asked something directly to Greer. She shifted on her horse and studied the pale half-fae man.

He sat on a borrowed horse beside her looking over the marshlands. They clothed him in Wimleigh Queendom materials fit for a king, although their banner was not his. While he had proven himself in the guard yard, he still seemed uneasy. No matter how strong one was, no matter how skilled at a sword, the first battle was always terrifying.

"Never," Greer replied, her eyes returning to the pools of water. She looked toward a larger pond, the one where she left Barden's body after he died, and watched the water's surface for any movement beside flitting bugs. "No matter what, I always feel nervous."

Lachlan hummed. "I don't know if that's a comfort or makes me even more uneasy."

Greer offered him a half smile before pushing her horse forward. "We'll set up camp here for the night. It's the largest expanse of space for us all and gives us distance from the dukes. Then, early tomorrow, we'll send units into the swamp. We *can* cross the entire expanse of it without entering the water, but it'll be hard and it's near impossible to travel with any carts or horses. Most travel must be on foot."

Malcolm's army wasn't in sight yet, but they would likely meet in the middle of the marsh within a day or two. The hum of battle preparation rang through the group despite that the threat was not yet there. Everyone was tense and ready to go, but Greer called for caution and to not overdo preparations. They needed rest, as much as possible, before the first blade swung.

After riding in the late summer heat with the bright sun shining down, it didn't take much convincing. Tents were raised and guards settled as best they could. The paths between tents held the heat of the day, preventing the breeze from moving through, and rapidly the scent of sweat grew thick.

Greer left Lachlan at his tent. He looked lost, clutching the handle of his sword as he turned on his heel and took in the sight of the many men and women who settled in, but Greer didn't have the energy to stay with him. She yearned for privacy.

Walking through the pathway of tents, she saw hers at the western edge of the encampment with additional guards nearby for protection. When she was only the heir, her father made her travel with a tent because that was the proper way a royal moved from place to place, but she always preferred to sleep in the open with the fresh air. Now, however, the tent was a sanctuary.

As guards unpacked supplies, there was a hollowness to their discussions and a quiet intensity over the camp. All understood the necessity for rest but there was more to it: there was a good chance this was the final peaceful rest they could endure, and that knowledge was enough to overwhelm. They kept their gazes low and for once Greer was invisible as she moved along the pathways, catching bits of their ongoing conversations as she went.

"Take care of my wife and children if I—"

"I want to be given to the dukes if I go—

"Do you think they'll accept a woman into their ranks?"

Greer stepped into the queen's tent and squeezed her eyes closed, taking slow, even breaths as she tried to quell her building anxiety. In the murmur of voices beyond the flaps of the tent, there was the rhythmic clink of a hammer to a nail as more were set up. She focused on the repetition of the sound, counting each one as it occurred, and breathed in and out as it sounded until, at last, her anxiety calmed. She opened her eyes.

The tent was an expansive, unnecessary thing. The emptiness of the place where Barden would have stood felt like a physical swell similar to a raging sea ready to drown her. He was meant to be there, a solid form making some dry comment about her lodgings, taking away her anxieties, and making her laugh.

"I miss you," Greer told the emptiness. She allowed her eyes to fill with hot, salty tears and didn't prevent them from running down her cheeks. It was a relief to openly mourn, even in the privacy of this temporary dwelling. It was better than trying to maintain her composure. If this was the last night of her life and the last tears she would shed, let them be for him. "I wish you were here."

She filled time with normalcy which felt inappropriate with the reality of things. Going to her wardrobe, she pulled out new clothing that fit under her armor and kept her as cool as possible in the daytime heat while wearing weighty armor over it. She dropped the fabric on her cot before turning to the mirror and stool. Sitting before it, she brushed out her waist-length hair and braided it tightly to pin it to her head. None of this would be comfortable to sleep in, but it was necessary so she could put on her armor in the middle of the night if an attack occurred.

With the last pin in place, she stepped to the large casing

her armor sat in. A solid trunk covered in thin leather with the impression of the Wimleigh crest on it, it was tall and leering, a reminder of how battle loomed as well. Pulling the doors back revealed ... nothing. Her armor wasn't within the box. Her hands dropped and she stared. "Damn it all."

A quick scan of the room produced no sight of the armor —not that it was something that could be easily missed—and she cursed again. Beyond the tent was a yell followed by increased commotion. It wasn't a call to arms at least, but it drew Greer to the doorway where an attendant nearly collided with her.

"Ah, Queen Greer? My apologies." The attendant's eyes were wide as he stumbled backward and Greer's body froze, her back going straight. She still had tears on her face but couldn't wipe them away now. Best to pretend they weren't there.

"Yes?"

"You have a visitor."

The attendant stepped aside, pulling back Greer's curtained door to reveal the pathways before her tent and Róisín standing at its center. Her cheeks were pink from the heat; her spring green eyes bore into Greer's.

"Mother?"

Róisín smiled, a soft thing she only ever gave Greer or Caitriona, and a part of Greer was comforted by that secret smile, despite that she primarily felt panic. This wasn't how things were done. Her mother was meant to remain at the castle, out of harm's way, not *here*.

"Mother, we're about to fight a war. Why are you here?"

"I'm better use in your tent city than within an empty, stone castle. What would you have me do in Wimleigh? Sit and twiddle my thumbs?"

"I may die here; we *all* might."

"And then what? Do you expect me to wait at the castle

for that message? And what would you have me do afterward, go birth another queen? That won't be happening, I promise you. Twice was enough and I'm far too old for it." Róisín brushed past Greer as she stepped into the tent's shadows. Greer glanced at the attendant who stared wide-eyed at the interaction. Letting out a frustrated growl, Greer retreated after her mother and dropped the curtain for privacy.

Greer knew her mother never endured such accommodations since traveling from Caermythlin to marry Cearny, yet Róisín moved through the space with ease as if completely familiar with such arrangements. Greer followed her, each step with a heavy heel and her frustration running high as her mother ran her fingers along the edge of Greer's mirror and checked the under-clothing Greer left out.

"Mother ..." Greer attempted again but didn't know what to say. She watched her mother drift, studying the items within. Róisín paused before the armor trunk and frowned. "Mother, what's wrong?"

"Where's your armor?"

Greer blinked. "I—I was just looking for it. It should've been brought here."

Róisín closed her eyes. Pressing her hands together as if in prayer, she held the tips of her fingers against her lips and took a deep, long breath. "I think the hardest part of being a monarch is that you have to look out for the betterment of *all* your citizens—despite that most are complete idiots. Stay here, please."

She left the tent without another word.

"What?" Greer spun on her heel and followed. Pressure built in her temples as a headache threatened. "Mother—"

Stepping past the curtains and into the aisles between other tents for guard leaders, Lachlan, and medics, Greer spotted her mother marching halfway down a lane while pointing to a young guard with an accusatory finger. Others fled her pathway as her hands gesticulated.

"Mother, what are you doing?" Greer jogged forward. Róisín reached her hand to cup Greer's cheek as if she were a child before continuing to speak to the guard before her.

"He was meant to deliver it to *Greer*. Not to the *camp*, to *her*. The *Queen*."

The guard glanced at Greer desperately, but she was no help, she still didn't understand what was happening. Looking back at Róisín, he lowered his gaze and his shoulders dropped. "I'm so sorry, Queen Mother, I'll speak to him."

"I pray to the Elder Tree he's better at understanding directions on the battlefield than he is from me."

There was a commotion from the small crowd that gathered. A young guard was spat out and nearly fell to the ground had it not been for his fellow guards catching his arms and hoisting him back to his feet. "Queen Mother! Queen Greer! I'm so sorry. Your Highness, your mother sent this with the message that—"

"Heavens, well, it's too late now." Róisín waved the young guard away. He lowered the handle of the wheeled box he dragged behind him and stepped back. Greer slipped her hand onto the handle before her mother took hold of it herself. Róisín continued to glare. "Just be off, get your reprimand from your elders. You've done enough."

"Mother, what's going on?" Greer asked but Róisín brushed her aside and tugged the handle as if she would be the one to drag it up the hill. She was such a force in that moment, Greer was sure her sheer annoyance would power her through lifting it. Unfortunately, Greer wasn't given the chance to witness such extremes as guards tripped over themselves, offering to help with the luggage, and Róisín stepped back and waved them forward.

"Just get the curtain, won't you?"

Greer, queen of the Wimleigh Queendom, took the order from her mother and rushed into her tent to pull back the curtain. Róisín followed the trunk as it was wheeled inside. She crossed her arms and watched silently as it was lifted and placed next to the empty trunk and waited for the curtain to fall back in place before looking at her daughter. Privacy once more.

"Well, the special moment I hoped you'd have is ruined," Róisín muttered as she undid the locks. "This was meant to be here so you could see it as you entered the tent. It's what happens when you assume men will follow directions."

"Mother, while I love that you finally feel free to share your frustrations about the opposite sex, I ask again, what's going on?"

Róisín stepped aside, exposing the open trunk and armor resting within. But it wasn't Greer's armor. Greer's armor had the emblem of the Elder Tree in the center of the chest over the heart, carved with rich detail, and edges of gold over the shoulders, but this armor was something different entirely. The Elder Tree leaves were carved across the expanse of the chest plate as if growing outward to coat the chest and reach to the shoulders, and the shoulders appeared sturdier. Harder. But in particular, rather than smooth edges, the shoulders came to metallic, gold-coated points.

"These look like Caitriona's horns." Greer moved closer, her eyes locked on the armor as her fingertips traced the curve of the horned shoulder pads and etched leaves.

"I modeled them after her horns, yes. Because the queendom is so much more than the Elder Tree now, and you may be queen, but you have the support of your sister, too. Even if you feel she's gone against you." Róisín stepped beside Greer. Her fingertips alighted over the side of Greer's head, tucking in strands of hair that already grew loose from the bun Greer put up. "This battle could be your death; we all know that. But you may survive and it may be the biggest event of your ruling. This will be placed into history books and taught to future generations—something your father worked hard to not do for his own ruling. You realize most written history during his rule are filled with lies, don't you? He had scholars write that he won battles he didn't actually win."

Greer couldn't help the snort that escaped. "I was at a few of the battles he lost."

"He lied to his people over and over again, and for the most part, they were willing to listen. Those who questioned the history and what he said were marked as dangerous fools. They were silenced. But you'll be forthright no matter how this battle goes. You'll not do anything to be ashamed of. If you win, you'll do so fairly, and should you waiver in these thoughts, I hope the design of this armor will aid to remind you."

Her mother's fingertips stilled in her hair. Greer lifted her chin and met her mother's gaze. "I won't make steam from the Elder Tree's sap. I haven't gone through with that plan to kill those people."

"Good. What made you decide not to?"

Greer bit her bottom lip for a moment, her cheeks growing hot with shame. "I realized if Cait is in the mountains, the steam would kill her too, and I—I could never ..."

Róisín nodded but Greer's confession fell from her mouth as if ridding herself of foul food.

"I didn't do it because of her, first and foremost. The good of the people was a secondary reason and I'm guilty of that. I should've thought of their lives and been more concerned about them than I was. It was awful of me."

"But you got there. You reached the realization that their lives do matter," Róisín reminded her. "Let the shame that it took as long as it did for that realization live inside you, because it will prevent you from losing focus and making decisions like that in the future. They matter. The innocents matter."

"This is a lost cause," Greer whispered. She didn't want people outside the tent walls to hear her. An admittance of failure from the sovereign before the war even began would solidify their defeat. "I feel like this is my last night and I wish Barden was with me."

"Oh, sweet lark," Róisín sighed, but not unkindly. She pulled Greer to her chest. Greer allowed her head to drop and her cheek to rest upon her mother's shoulder. "He *will* be with you. He's there in the marsh, is he not? And if tonight is your last night, you'll join him, even if I'm the one to bring you to him. But you don't want that, do you?"

Greer blinked. For weeks since Barden's death, all she wanted was to be with him. To feel him beside her, to touch his wholeness, to make him smile and laugh and grow annoyed and frustrated. She thought she wanted to be buried with him immediately, to sink into the depths of the marshes, and wrap herself in the embrace of water so she remained close to him, but that wasn't what she wanted at all. She wanted a man who was gone to be alive and human once more, and that wasn't possible.

"No. No I don't."

Róisín ended their embrace and placed her hands on her daughter's cheeks. She leveled her gaze with Greer's and raised her slender eyebrows. "Well then, my darling girl, you mustn't die."

CHAPTER TWENTY-FOUR

CAITRIONA

The seat of the fae kingdom wasn't far, but it was a climb up and down steep landscapes. Three days and a bit of magic clearing pathways, quickening their feet, and providing bridges across drop-offs brought the group to the forest dwellings surrounding the castle base with Briar and Berry leading the way.

Raum and Ceenear trusted Briar, but only after she willingly took a truth potion Raum carried, and she repeated that she wasn't a supporter of Malcolm with ease. The numbers of mist walkers had been cut since Malcolm's war declaration and other than waiting until Briar's shift completed, she was free to guide them toward the castle.

Briar was quiet until she wasn't. She observed but chimed into conversations when Caitriona assumed she wasn't listening. But she was a pleasant woman whose bristly behavior toward Raum when they first met immediately evaporated and was replaced by an easy familiarity between the two mist walkers. Upon the final day of their travel, she opened up more freely about the fae kingdom and the shift since Malcolm's claim to the throne.

"Very few fae are in favor of what Malcolm's doing," she explained. "Those that are, well, there aren't enough to do very much."

"That's not surprising." Caitriona ducked beneath a tree branch; if she didn't have horns, she would've cleared the canopy layers of the trees, but instead her horns dragged against the hard bark of limbs and caught in the leaves. She let out a grunt of annoyance. She could feel the scrape, although it didn't hurt. "You've all maintained peace for centuries and this is a stark difference from the norm. Even for good changes, a kingdom doesn't adjust to change in a matter of months. My own struggled for the last year as my sister overturned laws that only applied for two generations. I imagine centuries of peace being forfeited in favor of war is much harder to swallow."

"We don't fight, it's as simple as that." Briar shrugged. "While we're trained, and we defend our border, it's all to maintain peace. We avoid killing. It's in part why the mist defends us—so we don't have blood on our hands. What Malcolm's planning to do is against our very nature."

"What's Malcolm doing with those who haven't joined him?" Raum asked as he tossed a bit of meat from the previous night's meal to Berry. The little dog had been moving along the pathway collecting twigs and bugs with his abundance of hair, and keeping up with them quite well despite his short legs. He jumped and caught the meat, wagging his bushy tail with pleasure and picking up a leaf whilst doing so. It waved back and forth like a little flag as Berry happily chewed his treat. Having an animal companion with them made Caitriona miss Crowley all the more, which in turn left her yearning for Ailith. She glanced to the skies, having lost count of how often she sought the corvid but found nothing.

Briar's clear voice drew her attention back to the ground.

"If we go against his will outright, we're arrested by his followers. They take those arrested to the castle and I've yet to see anyone return. When they're brought to it, they might as well be dead. It didn't take long for many of us to realize it's safer to lie and pretend we support his cause, if only to keep our families safe, and attempt to figure a way to overthrow him in the future. We have a fair number who volunteered to work at the castle, if only to gather information. It's trickled down the mountain; rumors his prisoners are tortured and he's siphoning their magic into himself. Then he's taking the magic to make others follow his lead."

"They're being cursed?" Caitriona asked and Briar's lips formed a flat line.

"Forcing anyone to do something against their will is a curse, don't you think? There's talk of an abundance of creatures appearing at the castle. We have them in the mountains of course; they certainly aren't foreign to the land. But they don't linger in cities or cluster around people, and yet the castle seems to be an epicenter of creatures. They're gathering in wait."

Caitriona frowned and ran her fingers over the edge of her cloak, pulling it over her arms to fight off the slight coolness of the shade. The coolness wasn't a bother, but the feel of being surrounded by fabric was comforting. The change of season was on the wind, the battle between the heat of summer and cooler days of autumn much more pronounced in the mountain where leaves were already beginning to change as the next season gained ground. Or, perhaps, it was the subject that made her skin prickle with chill. "Could he recruit them? The creatures, I mean."

Ceenear and Raum looked at one another but Briar shrugged. "Anything's possible when you have a ruler who's driven solely on greed and his own self-worth. That type of person always tends to do whatever they please, even if it doesn't make sense."

They continued walking, the pathway narrow and a sharp decline just off the edge. The landscape was littered with stones and boulders; ferns, shrubs, and trees with wild roots that clung to the incline. The scent of pine, which grew in abundance, was rich in the air and small birds flitted from their branches as they approached, calling to their brethren in warning. Caitriona studied the path, ensuring her steps were accurate and shying from the edge. She saw so few magical creatures in her life; the majority were witnessed in the Northern Woods which was a place distinctly known for having monsters of every form. But they didn't gather together. Clusters of one type, sure. They were attacked by a pack of shades and a hoard of undead. But the different creatures never blended together.

A thought needled Caitriona like a wedge of skin prying back from her nail. She recollected her experience in the Northern Wood and the constant onslaught of monsters that attacked their party and specifically hunted Ailith who had no magical gifts. "Will creatures seek out my sister's army? Can they sense they're powerless?"

Briar glanced over her shoulder; an eyebrow raised with questioning. Ceenear sighed. "Ailith—our friend who's at the castle—when we were in the Northern Woods, she attracted the creatures and was easily overwhelmed by them."

Caitriona nodded. "She didn't know anything about them, nor did I. We would've been lost without Fiana telling us what to look out for, and Ceenear and Raum fighting back with magic."

"Magic creatures are like any predator. They seek weakness. In this case, it's those with no magic at all. So, seeking out her army does make sense."

"How have you come across this information? All of these

details about everything that Malcolm's doing?" Raum asked as the pathway rose considerably. The intention was to follow the game trails then slip to the outer edge of the castle by means of guards Briar swore begrudgingly worked for the king.

"Like I said, it's rumor," Briar replied as she looked Raum over. "Word's trickling through a network of whispers. We—those of us who've lied about our support—haven't the ability to fight against Malcolm, at least not yet. There've been a few who tried to usurp Malcolm and were cursed to become creatures. Others who tried to leave the mist died."

Raum stopped walking. "The mist killed those exiting it? That's not what the mist does."

Briar nodded. "Malcolm's altered the mist. It only allows people to exit under the king's expressed permission. If anyone tries to exit without it—even those who control the mist—it kills us."

"So, we're trapped here?" Caitriona looked at Briar with wide eyes.

"Only on the ground. If you can fly above the mist you're fine. There are far too few fae with the ability of flight for him to concern himself with making a blockade for those who can take wing."

Caitriona looked at Raum and gripped his hand. This altered things; they had multiple people they wanted to save and while Caitriona could allow riders on her back, she doubted she could fit everyone. They'd have to remain until the king's death or the mist's instruction changed.

Briar continued speaking. "If there's a way to join Queen Greer's war and aid her to success, we're willing to bear arms, despite the wrongness of fighting our brethren. We're safer here in the lower ranks for now. Also, as soon as you enter the castle, you have to proceed with caution. It'll be dangerous. Don't trust anyone. The staff likely doesn't want to be there but anyone else moving freely—I wouldn't trust them."

"Is there any indication of what he's doing with the magic he's taken from the fae? Other than taking it for himself." Caitriona asked.

Briar frowned and turned her attention to the white-stoned castle. "To my understanding, he's broken everyone into groups assigned by the amount of power they have. I don't know what he's done to those without magic or little gifts. But those with greater powers—"

"Do you have any other details of what he's been up to?" Ceenear asked as her footfalls slowed and Briar paused ahead of them at an outcrop. The path continued for some way, but in the distance, on a taller ridge, sat the white castle of Invarlwen.

Briar turned her dark gaze toward the trio and took in a quick breath, her upset evident. "He's vanished in the last few days. I heard the news just before you arrived from the mist. There's a hush about him, something unlike before. His followers were quick to share his status and location before, but now they've grown silent and there's a hum of excitement that draws discomfort from all of us who pretend. He's intentionally missing and some know where he is, but they aren't sharing this information. Whatever it is, it isn't good."

Briar lifted a slim hand and gestured at the castle. "If you continue straight by following this path, there will be a fae waiting for you at a door for castle staff. You can see the angle you want to reach from here—we're facing the back end. That fae will direct you from there."

"Thank you," Caitriona replied, reaching for Briar's hand and giving it a squeeze. Briar used her own speaking stone to inform her coworker of their approach, dutifully leaving Caitriona's presence out of the discussion. She only promised to take them near the castle and no further, which meant this was goodbye. "Thank you so much for your guidance."

Briar returned the squeeze of her hand and smiled. "Stay safe, princess. And for the two of you, remember, don't trust anyone you encounter other than cleaning staff. There are few who are there unwillingly and don't side with Malcolm. Assume you can't trust anyone. Even those you might know."

Raum gripped Briar's shoulder and Ceenear nodded solemnly. Berry's pink tongue shot out, as if he too knew to say goodbye, and licked each of their hands before Ceenear and Raum took the front of the line and pushed forward.

"Take care of them, will you?" Briar drew Caitriona's attention back to her. "It's painful to see people you've loved take a side in war you don't expect them to."

Caitriona squinted and began to ask a question, but Ceenear hissed, "Come quickly before the sun grows any brighter and we're spotted."

A fae appeared to step from the servant's exit and waited. It would still take them an hour, if not more, to reach it. Prior when they were more hidden in the mountains, Briar used magic to form a bridge with fallen trees, but this close to the castle it wasn't possible without being spotted. They would have to make their way on foot down the side of the ridge then up the other to reach the door.

"Thank you again," Caitriona repeated before scrambling down the pathway, gripping stones to ensure she didn't slip and fall. With the castle in sight, they moved quickly, and Caitriona fought back an uncomfortable, dreadful lump that sat in her gut like she swallowed a stone; something she imagined Ailith felt when they arrived in Beaslig to meet Kayl two years before. Something was off, although she couldn't pinpoint what beyond the obvious. She knew they'd find out soon and still, she pushed forward. What else was she to do?

Fly over the mist back home? She came here to find Ailith and hopefully help Greer and she would see to that.

Raum paused before her, staring at the castle with a serious expression.

"We're almost there," Caitriona said, grasping his shoulder as she offered a smile. "We'll get Lumia as well."

Raum frowned in response and Caitriona lingered, her brows raised with question.

"The longer I've gone without seeing her, the odder it's been."

Caitriona dropped her hand. "What do you mean?"

He shook his head and looked to the ground. "I have all these good memories with Lumia but as time passes, I keep thinking of moments where things were off-colored. Like I was in a hazy dream. Moments where I felt like I do now—off centered and uncertain of my feelings for her. It's the oddest thing. She could be in danger, she could be dead, why would I feel this now?"

Caitriona bit her lip, unsure of what to say. Over the few weeks Raum went from being completely distraught over Lumia's silence to these moments where his expression darkened. He spoke more often about arguments with Lumia, something that lacked in their relationship beforehand.

"You're worried," Caitriona began, attempting to find the right words to comfort him while not fully understanding what was happening herself. "Tensions are high and much has happened. You're processing all of that and it's sure to mess with your emotions."

Raum didn't respond right away. He kept his gaze on the ground, his jaw tightly clenched, but he nodded. "You're right. Come, I don't want to hold off our rescue any longer."

THE DOOR TO THE CASTLE WAS AT A SMALL OUTCROP of dirt followed by a steep drop off to the right, opposite from where they climbed. The stench of wastewater rose and Caitriona frowned, attempting not to gag as she gripped the trunks of the trees clinging to the ridge.

"Where are you hoping to go within the castle? Briar sent a message you're looking for someone," the fae guard asked as they pushed themselves over the ledge. He stared at Caitriona but asked no questions, instead keeping his attention on Raum and Ceenear.

"Fiana and Ailith, our friends. They're both human. Do you have any humans here?"

"Likely the very ones you're looking for. Only two have passed their way through here to our knowledge. They've been locked in the guard wing."

"Then that's where we want to go." Raum stepped closer to the door but the fae man put out his arm.

"And Lumia too, if she's here," Caitriona added, looking at the guard with pleading eyes.

He considered her silently before looking back at Raum who he still prevented from passing. "If you go there it's highly probable you'll be caught. I'm not going to have myself threatened, nor Briar. They torture the information from anyone they distrust."

Raum's face darkened, his eyes narrowing as he stood a straighter and clenched his hands into fists.

"What does that mean?" Caitriona asked.

"He wants our memories swept. He doesn't want us to remember this."

Caitriona looked between the two men, not understanding.

"It usually isn't something we do," Ceenear explained. Her brow furrowed as she looked between the fae men. "We don't use our gifts on one another."

"Times are different; we also don't go about starting wars with other kingdoms," the fae man murmured, his eyes unmoving from Raum's. "Let me wipe your memory from interacting with Briar and I. That's all. You'll just remember you entered the mist and found your way to the castle, nothing more. I wouldn't dare to take any memories other than those."

"Can't we take the truth serum? The one Briar took?" Caitriona asked.

"We only had enough for one," Ceenear sighed.

The fae guard sniffed. "I wouldn't choose the serum anyway. It's this or nothing."

Raum shifted his jaw. "Let's make an agreement then; one promised through magic."

"Raum," Ceenear warned but the man only straightened his back and offered his hand.

"I'm fine with it. What should the deal be?"

Caitriona looked at Ceenear who slipped her hand into hers and pulled her a step back. "I still don't understand."

"Raum wants to make a pact. It's a promise that's held together through magic. Should it be broken, there will be consequences."

"He'll forget who he is," Raum replied, keeping his eyes on the man. "That's my request. You can remove our memories, the three of us, of you and Briar, but if you remove anything more than just those memories, you'll lose all of yours. You won't know who you are, who your family is, who you support, what your job is. You'll just exist."

"That's extreme, Raum," Ceenear replied.

"It's fair."

The man frowned for a moment and Caitriona was certain he'd refuse. It seemed like too much. But ultimately, he took Raum's hand in his and gave him a strong shake. "I agree to that."

CHAPTER TWENTY-FIVE

AILITH

Vanora was becoming a cockatrice; tall and dangerous, and filled with venom and rage. Ailith watched the woman change against her will helplessly; she witnessed the splitting of her skin, the shedding of blood; the growth of feathers, talons, and her petite nose growing hard and sharp as it became a beak. Vanora's screams were enough to leave Ailith's ears ringing and yet she sat in her chair, stunned by the repetition of horrors before her. It was a similar assault to Caitriona's and Ailith's mind nearly shut off.

There was nothing Ailith could do. *Nothing, nothing, nothing.* If there was, she would've stopped Caitriona from the change two years prior. But Fiana didn't understand that. Panicked by the change, Fiana tried to stop it and when nothing helped, she attempted to comfort Vanora in her final moments as a human. Ailith saw herself in that, she remembered her own helplessness with Caitriona. But the fear in Vanora's eyes still stuck in Ailith's heart like a thorn.

"I'm sorry." Ailith stared at Vanora's terrified gaze and allowed her tears to fall freely for the woman while her one eye swelled from the hit she endured earlier. "I'm so sorry."

"What do we do?" Fiana wept as she ran her hands over the feathers covering Vanora's back. She repeated the question over and over, but Ailith had no answer until there was a shift in Vanora's gaze. Her once blue eyes turned to a greenish-yellow. The orbs were more circular and their emotion altered. Before, they had a sense of terror. Wide, shifting back and forth, but an emptiness filled them before they became steadily focused.

The fear was gone.

Her eyes were hardened and alert.

"Fiana," Ailith breathed as she pressed her palms on her seat and pushed herself off slowly. She moved to the back of the chair, her ribs aching from the kick she endured after trying to harm Malcolm. Gripping the chair, she held it before her like a shield. "Fiana, you need to move away from her *now*."

The cockatrice's head twitched, jolting to the side and eyeing Fiana who leaned back. Scrambling on her hands and feet, she stumbled backward as the cockatrice rose. With tears still wet on her face, Ailith looked around the room for a weapon, a place to hide—*anything*—despite that her earlier search came up empty.

"The table!"

She thrust her chair toward the cockatrice, distracting the bird as she ran for the one place of safety. Pulling out a chair at the table, she dove. Squatting under, she reached for Fiana as the hunter ran toward her. The cockatrice let out a cry that shook the furniture. Fiana dropped to her knees, sliding over the slick floor to the table and crawled beneath. Ailith pulled the chair back into place to create a makeshift barricade around them as the cockatrice stomped closer.

"How do we stop her?" Ailith looked at Fiana. She was the one who gave instructions when they were in the Northern Woods and being attacked by a cockatrice. Her expertise of creatures was why they hired her, but this wasn't just a creature. It was a fae woman who was forced into the change.

Fiana sat still; her dark eyes wide as she breathed heavily. "Kill her? It?" She looked at Ailith and shook her head. "I—I don't know. It's not her anymore. She's a monster. But she—"

"I know."

The cockatrice's beak came down hard on the tabletop. Her talons scraped the ground, then tried to kick the wooden chairs out of the way. Fiana lunged forward, holding the legs of the chair in place.

"She's going to kill us."

Ailith watched warily, her stomach a pit of misery. "Malcolm won't let that happen."

And she was right. For an hour the cockatrice pecked and clawed at the table, trying to get its bearings while rapidly leaning into its desire to kill. It wasn't until the cockatrice successfully made a substantial crack in the tabletop and emitted its deadly gas from its open beak that the doors to the room opened and Malcolm's guards walked in.

"Be still, creature," Malcolm called and the cockatrice stood up straight, the top of its head brushing against the ceiling as its eyes lost focus. Malcolm chuckled as he patted the cockatrice's shoulder. The guards shuffled by with cloths covering their mouths and unlocked the glass window and pushed it out, leaving air to push the gas away.

Ailith looked at Fiana and placed her hand at her waist where the bag of magic remained tucked away. It was going to be their one chance to survive.

Malcolm cleared his throat. The guards cleared the chairs from the table so Malcolm could bend to smile at the women. He sported scrapes down the side of his cheek that were nearly healed—likely by magic. Ailith wondered if she lunged at him, if she could scrape her nails down the side of his face and reopen the wounds. "That's enough. I don't want you killed yet and our girl here seems hungry for blood. Best to save that energy for your fellow guards."

Ailith worked her jaw. She never had to encounter Cearny's behavior straight on. Not until Caitriona was a dragon did she see him face to face and witnessed the hatred in his eyes. He was a man filled with fear for anything he didn't understand. Someone weakened by those he felt were better than himself. But Malcolm was different, he had a gleefulness in his energy, an enjoyment for what he did. There was a thrill to his control over others. For so long they viewed the two rulers as one and the same, but they weren't the same at all. Cearny was weak and scared. Malcolm was mad with power and enjoyed the taste of dominance.

Alike or different, she hoped Malcolm would see the same end Cearny did.

"Come along now, I have a new place to hold you both until your time is needed. I hear it'll be a few days. Long enough for you to consider what's ahead."

He moved back from the table and Ailith couldn't help but shrink as the guards came close. She had nowhere to go, no weapons, but she refused to go willingly.

"What's the look for?" Malcolm eyed Ailith as the guards dragged her from the table and pulled her to her feet. They worked the ties at her wrist as she stared at the fae king; this despicable man who caused so much chaos and suffering in so short a period of time. There was one village dead and gone already, the destruction caused by Malcolm's distant hand. He was fine to cause death and destruction through those around him, but barely had the ability to do it himself. Weak, all these men in power were weak.

"You're pathetic," she spat. "You're fragile. You can't garner enough support so you're forcing it on people. You're incapable of even getting people to follow you. Without the power you stole, you'd have nothing."

Malcolm stepped closer to Ailith. She caught the scent of his sweat and beneath the salty brine, there was decay. All that stolen power, all that greed was killing him. He was going to become an unbound like Kayl. Even now, after forcing Vanora to change, the curse took something from Malcolm. The creases around his eyes deepened, his skin loosened more, and a spark of pleasure alighted in Ailith to see the twitch to his face that her words brought.

"All the same, I still have power and what do you have, guard? Nothing but the memory of your draconic lover. Nothing but your soul. No weapons, no magic, no hope."

With Ailith's wrists tied and the guards holding her arms, she could only strain against them as Malcolm leaned forward and ran his hand down Ailith's face. His fingers traced the faded scar along her cheek before moving slowly, deliberately, down her neck to her arm where the remnants of burns remained. He let out a short breath of air Ailith struggled to understand. Laughter? Interest?

"Such power in her flame," he whispered, his eyes glinting as he stepped away.

The guards pushed Ailith forward, leading her from the room and down a clean hall. Staff bowed their heads, barely allowing themselves to meet Ailith's eyes. All of them hollow-cheeked and miserable. They continued with their work, sweeping dirt Ailith couldn't see, wiping ledges that had no dust. An act to keep themselves alive as Ailith walked further into the castle and was shoved into a room similar to where she woke to the Starling wearing Caitriona's face. Fiana didn't follow, but a slam of a door nearby indicated she was kept in close proximity.

"What happens next?" Ailith asked the guard, staring as they avoided her gaze. She understood the notion. It took so much to meet their eyes, but she knew the power eye contact wielded. "Tell me. What happens next? What's Malcolm's grand plan now? I thought he was going to turn us into creatures. What happened to that?"

A guard's dark eyes met Ailith's at last and he grimaced. He stepped forward, the sound of his boot a dull thing in the small, empty room, and cut the ties on Ailith's wrists. His large hands came over her shoulders and he pushed, making her stumble further inside the room. Her body was weak from the entrapment and her cheeks burned from the discomfort of that realization. She could have all the spunk in the world and she still wouldn't be able to best these men.

The guard returned to the doorway and sniffed. "You'll stay here until he's ready."

It wasn't much, but apparently enough. The guard reached for the heavy wooden door and slammed it shut, leaving Ailith to spin on her heel and seek the view from the sliver of a window in the center of the stone wall. The view was innocent and unknowing of what lay ahead; the tips of each peak, the gray masses of the Endless Mountains, and far off in the distance, a flattened green—the Umberfend Marsh. At least she could look toward home while she waited.

Pressing her hand to her side, she traced over the small lump hidden in her pants and released a long-held breath. When the time came, she'd have control over herself, and that was all that mattered when faced with so few options.

CHAPTER TWENTY-SIX

War horns declared battle before sunrise. It sent a thrill of terror through Róisín, jolting her to the waking world from her cot in a small tent. Isla shared the cot and continued to snore, unbothered by the blast of horns. Róisín's heart beat rapidly in her breast and she was envious of the woman, blissfully unaware for just a bit longer.

Brace yourself, Kayl murmured in her mind. *They're coming with tricks up their sleeves. This will be relentless. Be prepared for anything.*

Róisín pushed off the cot and inched toward the tent's entrance. Pulling the flap back, the cool morning air and buzz of biting bugs overwhelmed her, and the world shifted under her feet. She gripped the tent frame and blinked heavily as she attempted to chase the dizziness.

"You're weakening me."

I promise I haven't sipped from your magic, Kayl replied. *You would've felt it. You're attuned enough to your body to spot it.*

"Then what is this?"

Kayl was silent for a moment as he seemed to consider his answer. *One could describe it as an overabundance of anxiety, Ro. This is too much for you.*

Róisín sighed. What would she do about that? Nothing.

Since arriving at the battlegrounds, exhaustion pressed on her brow and made her vision foggy. After leaving Greer in her tent the night before, it crashed upon her. The weight of it all felt like the first few months of pregnancy before the quickening when there was no evidence that she grew life, yet every fiber of her body was exhausted.

"Are you alright?" Isla asked, having at last woken. Róisín squeezed her eyes shut; gathering her strength to put on a brave face as she turned on her heel.

"Just tired." Róisín offered a smile, but Isla only frowned.

When they were younger, she never was able to hide anything when the old bat—then called Maeve—came into town, and apparently now was no different. But Róisín knew stubbornness as well as breathing and she refused to admit to anything being off. Even if she was slowly overtaken by worry for her children.

"Sounds like we've a battle to prepare for, hmm?"

"You won't be much help if you're exhausted." Isla kicked her feet off the edge of the cot and slowly pushed herself up.

"I'm not much help to begin with."

Don't say that. You're overwhelmingly strong.

Hush, Róisín replied mentally. *So, what if I have more power than I realized? I don't know how to wield it. I never learned.*

I can help you ... Kayl's voice was soft, his offer hesitant; the weight of it all, *that* made the hesitation. The implied notion Róisín would have to let go of her control and allow Kayl to work within her. To trust him. And she wasn't sure she was quite back to trusting him. Allowing him to tether to her was one thing, a very big thing she was too ashamed to be honest to Isla about. But she could force him out if necessary. Allowing him to toy with her magic? That was something else, particularly when she wasn't clear how much magic she wielded.

Since Kayl poked the magic sitting at her core, she recognized it like realizing she sported a bruise she hadn't perceived beforehand. It pulsed, desperate to be released; hot to the touch, enough that Róisín felt there would be relief to let go of the well of it all after an entire life of keeping it buried. She wondered, as she dressed and prepared to join the morning crowd of the encampment for news, if her mother knew of her magic before she died. Maybe greeting grief at so young an age buried the magic from her knowledge.

The bustle of activity from outside the tent grew and pulled Róisín from her thoughts. Isla stared as if she saw through it all and heard the conversation too.

Can she? Róisín asked.

I don't think so, but she's always had secrets up her sleeves.

A horn sounded, the clang of metal echoed over the field of tents, and a familiar lurch of fear jolted in Róisín once more.

"Isla, I don't know what we should do with ourselves." It took something out of Róisín to admit this; her pride often got in the way of that. She only spoke what she was willing to share and found it hard to admit fear or confusion. But this wasn't a time for pride, at least not in that sense. It was a time for truth and vulnerability. Holding it back, allowing it to weigh her down, could lead to disaster.

"The sovereign typically gives a statement before departing. The biggest thing you need to do, as the Queen Mother, is keep your eyes on whatever task is before you. You can't be distracted by Greer. You may see awful things happen and you mustn't let it affect you."

It took a moment for Isla to fully leave the tent. Her age

caught up finally and the energy she spent in the past few weeks training Róisín daily to expand her magic took its toll. She reached for Róisín's arm and held on tightly as they moved down the aisles of tents toward the gathered masses of guards in their armor with weapons held aloft.

Greer stood on a cart as guards circled, their faces all turned to her like sunflowers to the sun. From the vantage of the hill, Róisín saw her with ease. She wore the dragon-like armor with morning sun alighting her blonde hair from behind to make a growing, celestial crown. It was redone, returned to the tight bun she tended to wear, but the helmet sat at her feet. She grasped the hilt of her sword with one hand from its place on her hip and looked to the crowd, not seeming to notice Róisín and Isla on the hillside as they stuck out against the gray of armored guards.

"You've gathered here this morning not by order, but by desire to protect country." Her voice rang out and silenced the murmuring crowd. "For many, this is not your first battle. You've fought under the banner of our queendom many times and often beside me. I know your passion and drive. I recognize your skill. For those who've just joined, for those who've heard our plea to come to our aid and broaden our ranks, I thank you. Stepping forward to such a task as this, one that's quite frightening, is a heavy thing and yet you've done it all the same. You're all warriors in my eyes; you're all brave and deserve success on this field.

"When I was given the crown of Wimleigh Queendom, magic was outlawed." A murmur rumbled through the crowd and Róisín stood straighter. The law was a sore subject, something many had opinions of and not necessarily in alignment. Within the city itself, it caused fights and disgruntled citizens, but Greer stood steadfast in her decision to allow magic to be practiced and for people to no longer be penalized for their born gifts.

She was silent, watching the crowd as the murmuring swelled but slowly came to a stop as guards recognized her serious gaze. Raising her chin, she continued. "Some of you disagree with that decision, but I stand by its importance. The man who's claimed the crown of Invarlwen plans to take this land and control us all—whether or not we have magic—and that simply will not do. We want freedom to be as we were born. We want freedom to love, live, and die as we desire. We refuse to allow him to take control of this land and ourselves. We refuse to allow him to decide what is right in this world. That is no one's choice but for themselves. Together we stand for those who cannot, we lend our voices for those forced into silence, and we fight for the freedom to be ourselves. Do you agree?"

Cheers, more than Róisín expected, erupted from the crowd. Even those who grumbled and remained silent through her speech with sour expressions loosened their shoulders and grew more passionate.

"Together we'll ensure we keep our land, but not just that, we'll help return Invarlwen to a kingdom of peace as we support the rightful king, Lachlan."

She stepped back on the cart, turning on her heel and waving out her hand to direct attention toward the side. With his strawberry hair a spot in the crowd, Lachlan seemed to visually shrink under the attention of the people around him. Greer waved him forward, bending to speak before offering her hand. He hesitated and Róisín leaned toward them.

"Take her hand," she whispered, letting her little magic burst into her words and take them on the wind down the hillside to slip into his ear. He stood straight and turned his face to the hillside, his attention landing on Róisín. She smiled encouragingly. "Take her hand and accept your fate."

For a moment, Róisín wasn't sure if he would listen. The hesitation remained, Greer's hand still held out, but Lachlan pulled his gaze upward and smiled. He reached and grasped Greer's hand firmly, accepting her aid onto the cart to stand beside her.

The crowd erupted with cheers, their weapons held aloft in the air as they called out Greer and Lachlan's names like thunder vibrating between mountains. Róisín smiled at the sight of her daughter holding Lachlan's hand aloft. A fae man and a mortal woman hand in hand, unified and ready for battle.

"I hope Cearny's rolling in his grave." Róisín crossed her arms over her chest and stepped back. Isla looked up and released a crackling laugh like a crow.

"If he was alive he'd die straight away, that's for certain."

Greer lifted her hand and the cheers fell quiet. "The cavalry is already sent out; they're heading to the northern and southern borders of the marsh to wrangle in Malcolm's forces toward the pools. Because of the water, they cannot go too far into the marsh itself and for us, we'll have to battle primarily on foot, hand-to-hand, with few carted weapons at our disposal other than along these shores. We'll have few field medics in the marsh to tend to the wounded there before bringing them back, but it will be a long, perilous journey to camp. I warn you all to stay away from the puddles and pools —the dukes are said to be in any water you see and while they rest during the day, they come alive near dusk and will take the lives of anyone who steps even in the shallows. There's hope as well that they'll rise before dusk to join our side in battle.

"This is by far not a beneficial place to wage war but it's better than within the city. This allows our families to stay safe; hopefully for good. Remember: we are capable, we know this marsh, and we will win."

The crowd cheered, their fists hitting their armor and shields to create further thunder. Greer grinned and shook

Lachlan's hand. He was similarly eager. Turning, she hopped off the cart and made her way up the hill towards Róisín.

Róisín looked over the marsh that extended for miles. It was so large they couldn't make out Malcolm's men yet due to the expanse. Would she even know if Greer was injured? Would she know if she fell? Would Greer be lost to the marsh? The air lay its strong fingers around her throat, choking her from breathing anymore. Isla squeezed her arm and stepped forward. "We'll provide elixirs immediately. Some to chase off chill from water should they step in the marsh and potions to help fend off infection from injuries. I prepared a cart for the medical tent with the help of other healers. We have all the supplies and can continue to work on items that'll aid them. We'll do all we can to help. Now it's just a matter of finding the tent."

Isla looked over the crowd, a task considering her short stature, and snapped at an attendant who appeared. Letting go of Róisín's arm, she hobbled forward to speak to him and left Róisín staring at her daughter as she stepped before her.

"Mother, listen to Isla, alright?"

"I should be the one mothering here and giving *you* directions," Róisín teased, but it was half-hearted.

There was no hiding it from her firstborn. Greer was always too smart and observant, even as a child. Her daughter smiled. "I'll be alright. I don't fear the dukes."

"Nor do I, but I do fear Malcolm's army."

Greer's smile faded. "The reports from the edge of the mist aren't good. There's fae forces but primarily they're creatures. Monsters, magic makers, things we aren't trained to fight."

Róisín closed her eyes briefly. She recalled when guards were trained in all warfare to fight monsters and men. It faded when Donal ruled because they were breaking the spirits of the magic-laden towns. Those they attacked were more willing to simply give up land, forfeit their magic, and relocate. Once Cearny came to power, he stopped the training entirely. She still recalled him hissing, "We have royal hunters who can take care of these creatures. They're a nuisance anyway and should be extinct."

Decades later and his decision was now the very reason the queendom could crumble.

"Malcolm figured out a way to attack using the very weakness your father created," Róisín said dryly, leading Greer to sigh.

"I can't seem to get away from his mistakes."

"You never will, it's part of being a monarch. You deal with the mistakes of your predecessors and hope to resolve a few before the next monarch steps in."

They fell quiet, a juxtaposition compared to the hectic movements around them. Greer had other guards who could lead groups to battle. Her role would be to seek Malcolm's military leaders and fight them head on. But Greer was also never one to abandon her guards, not entirely. She wanted to be in the thick of the field action, Róisín knew that. This moment would be the last Róisín would see her daughter until the forces fell back.

"Have you heard from Caitriona?" Greer asked and Róisín's heart lurched to see the desperate curve of her brows, the downward tug of her lips, and to know she could only give the least satisfactory answer.

"Nothing," Róisín replied. "But I haven't tried to contact her. She's in a dangerous territory, I don't want to risk anything."

"No news is good news," Greer replied, not at all looking convinced of her own statement. She looked over her shoulder toward the swamp waters and back at her mother with glistening eyes.

"Greer, are you ready?" Lachlan asked as he approached,

having finally freed himself from the crowd of warriors who had been patting his back and shaking his hand. Greer hastily wiped her eyes and stepped aside for Lachlan to join them. He flashed a smile at Róisín and bowed his head. "Róisín, I heard you came to the field."

Róisín nodded. "Better to ensure you all have what you need. Be brave, Lachlan. You'll do your people proud."

Lachlan raised his chin, his expression growing serious. "Defending those who've been lost is an honor. The guidance I've received from your family is tremendously helpful. I hope to make you all proud as well."

More horns sounded and calls rose along the marsh edge.

"Time to go." Lachlan placed his hand on the hilt of his sword. "Thank you again, Róisín, Isla. Greer, I'll see you in the field."

"Stay safe mother, please? I—I need you to." Greer turned back to them with tears still fresh in her eyes.

"I'll stay on solid ground and be here when you return," Róisín promised and she felt it in her bones. She wouldn't go anywhere. "Come back to *me*, sweet lark."

"I'll try," Greer replied and turned away but Róisín saw the swell of tears in her eyes.

THE TROOPS MOVED OUT. THOSE ON SOLID GROUND as additional back up were left to plan, attend the future wounded, and prepare meals and aid. Róisín drifted to the medical tent and set to work making ointments, salves, and potions. She tried her best to ignore the sound of shouts and roars beginning in the distance. The battle had truly begun. As the sun climbed in the sky, causing the scent of marsh grass to fill the air and encouraging more bugs to take flight, she stepped from the tent and looked to the marsh for the first time.

The marshland was relatively flat, yet far beyond the patchwork of pools blending into the horizon, smoke lifted.

"What can cause that?" Róisín asked out loud, uncertain if anyone would hear her.

"Why haven't the dukes risen?" Isla stepped beside her.

Róisín blinked. Isla was right. Everything was too still. The waters unmoving. "It's daytime, they're asleep, aren't they?"

Isla shook her head. "Once the battle begins, they should rise no matter the time of day."

"How do they know when to?"

"How do birds know when it's time to flock and travel to southern lands before winter's first snow? The battle doesn't even have to happen at the marsh but you'd think this would make it easier." Isla crossed her arms. "They should've risen upon the first battle horn. Something isn't right."

"Greer needs the support of the dukes if she has any hope of surviving." Róisín looked over the water more intently as if she would spot something she hadn't noticed before. Stepping from the tent, she moved toward the water's edge. She couldn't recall where Barden was sent to rest, all the water edges looked the same in the daylight, but it could have been here. Surely, if any duke would rise to aid Greer, it would be her head guard.

"Come on, Barden, where are you?" she murmured as she knelt at the water's edge, ignoring Isla's calls from behind. She fell silent as she waited for Kayl to give his input, but he had been quiet since that morning. Not a constant stream of thoughts in her mind, which she appreciated, but his stillness was uncomfortable—was he too weak to speak?

"Róisín, you should back away from the water," Isla warned as she came up from behind.

"There's a reason for this." Róisín ran her fingers over the surface, watching ripples from her movement spread and bump against the grasses and cattails. "You can't tell me Barden wouldn't rise to fight beside Greer. Nothing would stop him. Nothing."

"Dukes aren't their human selves anymore," Isla sighed. "He won't be compelled by the same desires as he was when he was alive."

"No." Róisín pushed to her feet and turned back to the old witch. "Barden's different. I suspect they all are. They may not be human anymore but they once were. They can still recall they wield weapons and fight battles, surely there's more semblance of their past lives beyond bloodshed. He wouldn't leave her on a battlefield without aid."

Isla frowned as she considered and stepped forward. Bending over, she brushed her hand over the water and lifted her fingers to her lips, licking them and frowning.

"You're right, Róisín."

She turned on her heel and moved towards the medical tent without another word, her speed surpassing anything Róisín saw the woman do in years.

"About what?" Róisín called as she hitched her skirts and moved up the slope.

"The dukes. There's a magic over their water; I'm not sure what kind. Come along, we have to break it."

CHAPTER TWENTY-SEVEN

CAITRIONA

They stood within a clean and blissfully empty hall that smelt subtly of mint. The castle, overall, was clear of people as if something forced them away, leaving their footsteps to echo off of the marble walls and floors.

"Movement by Malcolm, perhaps," Caitriona surmised with a certainty she had no explanation for. She didn't understand why she felt he had pushed forward with movements, yet it was the one conclusion her mind kept arriving to.

They continued having similar certainties, a knowing that pushed them down certain halls or through specific doors. Their gut feelings were always right, as if they'd been blessed with prior information. Details came to their minds like remembering someone's name, but uncertain how it was learned. It didn't make sense. Ceenear pointed out that she visited the castle before, yet she hadn't wandered the staff halls, so why was it so familiar?

"Through here," Raum pointed to the door. "This is where Ailith and Fiana are . . . I think?"

He looked at Caitriona who shook her head. "I don't know why, but I agree."

Pushing forward, Raum opened the door to a long room with cots and fae laid out on many, but not all. Toward the end, a tall, white-haired figure closed a door.

"Lumia?" Raum stuttered. As they made their way through the castle, Raum opened up about his experience with Lumia. He admitted his memories were turning strange. There were good moments, happy times, but also those where travel prevented them from seeing one another and when they came together again he felt differently toward her. As if distance brought ill feelings. But sure enough, their romance rekindled the longer he was with her again.

That was why he felt so strange, surely. He was expecting that same experience and didn't actually dislike her. Caitriona believed it based on the brightening of his face when he spotted the woman.

"*Lumia*," he repeated, her name a sigh of relief and longing.

She turned from the door, her light eyes falling on them and widening. Raum moved forward like a moth to a flame.

"Raum?" Her eyes flashed. Something passed beyond them while she kept her expression nothing but delight and happiness while looking at the trio. But the sight of her in the room, her placement in Malcolm's castle in clean clothing, and her entire countenance bright and healthy, sat wrong with Caitriona.

Her stomach lurched and gripped her heart. The taste of flame rose in her mouth as if the dragon woke. The dragon was never separate from her; it was a part of her that she hadn't accepted until recently. It was as much a part of her as her gut feeling, and her gut was certain this wasn't right. Something was wrong. She couldn't—*shouldn't*—trust Lumia. Was that the feeling Raum had been developing all along? *Did I tell him to trust her when he shouldn't?*

"Raum, wait." Caitriona held up her hand as he stepped forward. The glint returned to Lumia's eyes as she turned her attention to Caitriona, her brow wrinkling briefly and her eyes narrowing. It had been months of silence from Lumia and now they stumbled upon her in a room with injured fae and she didn't run straight to Raum's arms. In fact, she seemed annoyed by their arrival.

Lumia blinked and took Caitriona in, then brightened with a smile. "Caitriona, you've been through so much and I'm sure you're worried. I just let Ailith through this door, I'm helping her escape."

"We've been told she was escaping before," Caitriona replied. Her insides grew hot, the constant thought of warning flared with each flickering flame. Lumia's eyes were sharp as knives, too studied, too observant, and still she paused and made no further movement to Raum. Caitriona stepped forward, desperate to push herself before her friends to protect them. "The last time we were told she escaped it was a trap."

"Why would I lie to you? You're my friend."

But are you mine? Caitriona thought yet remained silent as she studied her. It wouldn't make sense for her to attack Lumia, not off a feeling.

Lumia moved forward, returning her attention to Raum as tears filled her eyes. "Raum, I'm so sorry I disappeared. I was brought to the castle with Niveem and when Malcolm requested we follow him, Niveem refused and she ..."

Stepping around Caitriona, Raum continued forward. Lumia choked back her cries, her hand covering her mouth for a moment as a tear slipped down her cheek. A glowing dust lifted from Lumia's hand and drifted over the air. Lumia could control emotions and used it to help the sick and injured. Caitriona herself was subject to her magic two years prior. She calmed Caitriona, kept her levelheaded and away from the grip of panic. But she could impassion people and cause them rage or fear if she tried.

Since the curse completed, Caitriona's own magic was fully formed, and that included being able to see magic at work and for what it was—something that covered all the surfaces and penetrated Raum. A control over emotions that seeped from Lumia's open hand and came slowly toward Caitriona and Ceenear, too.

Lumia was oblivious to what Caitriona saw and kept her eyes on Raum, working him over as she wept. "She died. Malcolm killed her. I've been pretending all along that I follow him just to save myself and help those who are trapped here."

Was this what happened all those times Raum would be away from Lumia? Magic draped over Raum's mind to love and trust Lumia faded, exposing his true feelings when he returned until she worked her magic on him once more?

"Raum," Caitriona warned, barely registering what Lumia said. She didn't have the ability to consider the great loss of Niveem if Lumia was lying about that. Her mind was too foggy. She had a murky memory, something distant that fought to be recalled. It sat like a weight on the tip of her tongue begging to be known. A warning about people she knew. She was told she shouldn't trust anyone at the castle by someone, but she couldn't remember who. "Raum, we can't trust her."

Raum looked at Caitriona, his expression desperate and confused, and it was in the moment his gaze pulled from Lumia's that the pale-haired fae's expression twitched into a frown. The gold light leaked from her mouth, licked at Raum's hands and ran along his arms. It reached toward Caitriona, but she stepped back. "I can see it, Lumia. I see your magic. You're trying to work it on myself and Ceenear. I see it's all over Raum."

"I'm only trying to calm you. You're upset, I see that. You traveled far to get here. It's understandable you're frazzled. Let me help you." Lumia's voice was light as her annoyance drained from her expression. She reached for Raum and turned him back to her. Her hands ran over his chest as the glitter of magic sunk into him.

He stepped from her reach and shook his head hard, making the dust of her magic shake off a little. "No."

"Raum?"

"I said no." He looked at Lumia and the glow lessened from his skin. "We've been apart long enough. I started to realize all that's gone on in our relationship. Every time you'd lose your control on me, you'd slip it around my neck like a noose until I was brainwashed again. It's been too long now and I've realized too much. And just now I felt it, you trying to influence my feelings. You won't use your magic on me."

"Raum." A note of begging in Lumia's voice made her tone higher. Her hands knit together, twisting nervously as she stepped backward. "Raum, I—"

"What in hells are you doing, Lumia? You've been influencing my emotions for you all this time, haven't you."

"Raum, listen. It's so simple."

"It's covering you." Caitriona pointed out. "And it's all over the room, too."

"We don't use our magic on each other," Raum growled. "We had an agreement, you and I as a couple, beyond the understanding of our culture. We don't use magic on each other unless we have permission. And you've been doing this to me for how long?"

Lumia sneered. "Caitriona doesn't know what she's talking about."

"Explain yourself then." Caitriona released flames from her hand and they licked her fingers as she pushed before

Raum and leveled her gaze on Lumia. "What do you have to do with this room?"

Lumia's furrowed brow lessened as she looked amongst the three of them. She dropped her hands and stepped back, bumping into a table with supplies scattered over the surface. "I can explain. I *promise*. Just listen. It's not what you think, none of what's been going on is what you think. Malcolm isn't all that bad. He has good ideas but people run with them and twist them into things that aren't true. They make up these lies of fake ideals. Ones that Malcolm never proclaimed. He's better than that."

Raum let out a bitter, barking laugh. "Really? When Niveem asked Ceenear and I to leave the mountain you had a fit that I was going. You kept pushing for me to go with you to visit the queen. Is this why?"

Lumia looked at the ceiling, blinking rapidly as if she were crying. "Just please listen, okay? Be patient." She licked her lips, the dart of a pink tongue like a cat's. "When Niveem and I traveled here to speak with Onora she was ailing, and we met Malcolm. He asked if Niveem would support his wishes to broaden the empire and gain more land for the fae. It would be a chance for fae to be safe throughout Visennore and we'd depart the mist for good. She refused, Onora was not yet dead and she wouldn't allow Malcolm to discuss plans as if she was.

"But I understood what Malcolm was getting at. We've been trapped here within the mist, stuck on these mountains, cut off from the sea, unable to travel because so much of Wimleigh Queendom surrounds us. We should be able to move freely, to travel and be safe."

"You *are* safe," Caitriona broke in. "Most of Visennore didn't even know fae existed beyond the mist until he declared war! And my sister's trying to make it safer, but Malcolm hasn't given her any opportunity. How can she right my father's wrongs if Malcolm's declaring war upon our queendom when she hasn't held the crown long enough to establish any change?"

Lumia's eyes darkened.

"I thought you knew me; I thought you understood I'd never want you to be hurt," Caitriona continued and the wrinkle between Lumia's brows lessened.

"I know that you didn't want the fae to be hurt any more than they already were. We've spent so much time together. I don't mean *you* when I say all of this. *You* have magic. You have gifts. You're like *us*. But your sister, she's been under your father's guidance all these years. She can't understand, she won't. She'll turn on us *and* she'll turn on you. She'll shutter you away: her magical sister, the embarrassment of the Gablaigh family."

Caitriona took a step back and closed her mouth; the burn of what Greer did after they visited Greenbriar made her cheeks grow hot. Lumia's brows rose and the corner of her lips curled upward. "Ah, she's begun to do that, hasn't she?"

The memory was too recent and alive in her mind; Greer's expression during Caitriona's explosion of grief, the white of her knuckles from her grip on the handle of her sword all still haunted Caitriona. Did her sister hate her for leaving? For going against her requests? She was meant to be in the cottage now, locked away north of the city to wait out the war. Greer loved her and didn't want her hurt, but was there also fear?

There was. Her fear was clear in her eyes and the grip of her sword.

Lumia stepped forward and grasped Caitriona's hand, holding it tightly in her own as she hissed. "Caitriona, you belong with *us*. You belong in a land where you're free to be what you are without judgment, or looks of disgust, or distrust from your own family. That's what Malcolm's searching for, a chance for us all to be free."

"You still haven't answered where Ailith is," Ceenear cut

in. Raum looked lost; his expression was hard as he watched Lumia. Despite what he said, Lumia's magic still pulsed on him. A spell that was realized and slowly losing its power, yet his focus was on Lumia only; as if just seeing her for the first time and not sure he liked what he saw. Ceenear crossed her arms over her chest and kept her face impassive. "You said you're helping her escape. Where is she?"

Lumia remained silent, still gripping Caitriona's hand as her eyes flicked amongst them.

"Where's Ailith?" Raum asked. Lumia's face hardened, her lips turned into a pout, and her expression was of someone ready to flee or fight, but Caitriona wasn't sure which. Caitriona tugged her hand, attempting to free herself from Lumia's grasp but the woman dug her nails into Caitriona's wrist and kept her there as her gaze narrowed.

"She doesn't deserve you. You have fae ancestry; you're part dragon; you'll live for so long and she's only human. Not a lick of magic. She'll age quicker than you and you'll remain youthful. You'll go from appearing her equal to appearing like her granddaughter. And in the end she'll never understand all you've gone through. Her kind is incapable of it. They only see us as threats."

Caitriona yanked her hand, pulling it free despite leaning closer and hissing into Lumia's face. "Where's Ailith?"

Lumia growled. "Taken. Dragged from here and sentenced to become one of Malcolm's creatures. She'll serve in his army, a ruthless fighter, and help bring him success so he'll rule over all this land and *you*." She snatched Caitriona's wrist, grabbing it hard while twisting Caitriona's arm and pulling her to her side. A knife pressed against Caitriona's throat. "You could be a queen. Malcolm would have you by his side. But you're too strong-headed. I think he'd do better consuming your magic."

"Get off me." Caitriona kicked, the knife cutting her neck but not deeply. There was movement around them, too fast for Caitriona to witness as she allowed her dragon's fire to release. It flicked to life on her skin, burning Lumia's fingers while the fae's magic exploded into glittering light and descended upon Caitriona, taking away her anger, her rage, and making her compliant. The fight in her snuffed out, as did her flames. Her hands dropped and she stared at Lumia. Her mind blank, a still pond without a ripple of disturbance, and she was helpless to fight the magician who placed her under this spell.

Raum grasped Caitriona and spun her out of Lumia's reach. Lumia smiled briefly, a look of success, as if she had finally secured her power over them all. But it was short-lived.

Raum turned toward Lumia and everything happened rapidly. A wet, slick gurgle escaped Lumia's throat. Her magic stopped pressing into Caitriona, and Lumia's hands dropped to her chest. Raum pulled back, exposing the knife hilt sticking out from Lumia's chest. Lumia's eyes filled with tears while turning to Raum. Shock and pain passed over her face. "You protected *her*?"

Raum stared, his jaw shifting as it hung open but it seemed his words were caught in the sob that escaped his throat. His hands hovered with uncertainty until they settled on her shoulders. The glittering gold of her magic faded in the room, leaving it bare, and releasing Caitriona and Raum from its hold.

Lumia's knees sagged and Raum held her upright for a moment as she continued to stare, her lips parted, and words that tried to escape only released as bubbles of blood while more spilled from her chest. They sank to the ground together. Raum freely wept as he gathered Lumia in his arms, staring at her as her stomach turned crimson. "How could you, Lumia? How could you?"

She didn't answer. Her skin paled to gray and the sheen of

her white hair grew dim. Ceenear and Caitriona remained still as Raum folded over Lumia's body.

Another groan pulled Caitriona's attention. Sniffing, she hastily wiped at her eyes. The fae in the beds watched.

"You have to go or they'll capture you," a male said. "They come through frequently, taking us one or two at a time."

"Let them try," Caitriona growled, her teeth sharpened against her tongue. She moved forward, pulling Ailith's dagger from her waist and cut the ties for the fae. "We have to get you out of here."

"Don't worry about us," another murmured as Caitriona turned and cut the binds on her wrists. "We'll leave on our own or die trying. They'd feast on your power if they caught you. Get out."

Ceenear moved, swifter than Caitriona's untrained hands and released the others with her own knives. Some remained laying while others gradually sat up. "Were there more of you? Were all these beds full?"

"We've come and gone. You're looking for two humans? They were here with me, trying to free us as well. Lumia caught them and sent them to endure the change on the battlements."

Caitriona stood upright; a chill rushed through her body. "How do we get there?"

"I don't know, but everyone was led through that other door."

"You're no good to Ailith if you're caught," Ceenear cautioned, taking Caitriona's hand in her own and leading her toward it. "Raum, come."

Raum gently laid Lumia onto the floor. His fingers slipped around the handle of his knife and he pulled hard, taking it from her chest and releasing another splatter of blood. He wiped the blade clean on his shirt before returning it to its holder and turning back to Lumia.

Brushing his hands over her, he forced her eyes to close and pulled at her skirts, making sure they covered her legs. "It was all a lie, but she still ... I just ..."

He kissed the tips of his fingers before passing them over her lips and climbed to his feet, pausing before the fae man who spoke to them. He offered his knife handle out. "Take this. Use it to defend yourselves if your magic is too drained."

The fae accepted the knife. "Thank you."

Ceenear pushed open the door they indicated, peeking inside with her sword in hand. "It's clear, let's go."

The room was small with a table for eating and a cage in the corner. Within, there were remnants of someone recently being held. The memory of the room came back to Caitriona from when she traveled by smoke of the eyebright flowers. This was where Ailith and Fiana were caged but now it was a solid, damp place empty of people beside themselves.

Caitriona moved to one of the two windows on the opposing wall and looked out. "There's the marble area they spoke about."

"Then we should exit this door and take any turns that bring us in that direction." Ceenear hurried forward while Raum followed in silence with Lumia's blood covering his clothing and his eyes glossy.

"Wait." Caitriona stepped forward, grasping the shoulders of the bag Raum wore on his back. "Take this off, Raum. Let's fix this as much as we can."

He obeyed as Caitriona dove into his pack, pulling free a new shirt that wasn't covered in blood. She turned to Raum and tugged at the dirty shirt. "Come now, off with that. You don't need this reminder."

She dressed the tall fae man rapidly and left the bloodied shirt within the corner cage. Blood still stained Raum's pants, but it was less noticeable. The new shirt shone white and clean, and while Caitriona recognized it wouldn't cure Raum of the experience he just had, she hoped it would help.

With his pack returned to his shoulders, Caitriona paused and slipped her hand into his, squeezing it tightly as Ceenear listened at another door.

"I'm sorry," she whispered.

Raum's throat bobbed as he stared ahead. "Thank you for what you did."

"You'd do the same for me."

THE CASTLE WAS EMPTY, ALL THE STAFF HIDING, dead or gone. But the outcrop was crowded with those in chains, bowed down from exhaustion and weakened from lack of food or water—perhaps from the loss of magic. Cloaked individuals moved down the line and one by one, blew dust into their faces.

As they passed window after window, they witnessed the group of prisoners in different degrees of transformation. The fae became animals, creatures, with bloodthirst and gifts that nonmagic folk—the very type of people they would fight— didn't possess nor understand.

"The Wimleigh guards will be lost," Caitriona murmured. "Most of the guards who can fight were trained during magic's ban. They aren't going to know how to fight these creatures."

They pushed their way down a mountainside stairwell, their feet splattering chilly water that dripped from the side of the exposed stone surface along the steps. It led to a doorway, another servant's exit to an outdoor walkway along the side of the castle. Voices echoed down the hall and growls from creatures ricocheted off walls from the opening to the outside world and the expanse of the mountains.

"Down there!" Caitriona called, running forward with her heart in her throat. They attempted to keep their footsteps light, their clothes rustling as they reached the mountain wind and glowing sun. Even this far up, the chill of autumn threatened to take over the landscape, but the sun shone hot and blinding in the late-summer sky.

The path kept along the castle until it became the walls of the marble outcrop. As they crept down the path, the calls and cries followed by roars, growls and haunted echoes grew in volume. Steps climbed upward before curving to the right and Caitriona took them two at a time without pause, determined to get to the outcrop. To Ailith. She had enough self-preservation to slow her movement as she came near the top, creeping forward around the corner. She froze.

"It's Ailith," she breathed as Ceenear caught up. The fae's hand came down like a lock on Caitriona's shoulder.

"Wait, we can't have you running out there."

But the fae with their magic powder moved along the line, turning groups into different creatures two at a time. Ailith tilted her face to the side and her lips moved.

"Fiana!" Raum breathed from behind. The two humans were together, bound, and the last in line to become creatures. Ailith wavered, looking dizzy and exhausted, her face bruising, eye swollen, and cheeks hollower than when Caitriona saw her last. Ailith reached to her waist as the cloaked figures moved closer.

"Ailith," Caitriona said more clearly now, taking a step as her body responded to the threat. She wouldn't allow them to turn Ailith into a monster, not like when it was forced on her. She understood the pain Ailith felt now, all the guilt in her gaze after Caitriona returned from the curse's hold. Ailith had promised not to let Caitriona change, but Caitriona did anyway. It was beyond Ailith's control and not something for her to feel guilty over, but still she felt the heavy emotion because she witnessed the transformation and could do nothing to stop it. Just as Caitriona would if she didn't move forward.

The big difference between Caitriona's change and Ailith's was simple: the curse was already within Caitriona and the change would happen no matter what, while Ailith's was clearly avoidable so long as they reached her and Fiana before the robed figures with the powdery substance did. Beforehand, she and Ailith were only human and couldn't fight off the magic. But now, Caitriona was no longer just human. She had magic; she had power.

A growl rippled up Caitriona's throat, rolling over her tonsils and tongue until it fell from her lips like a dangerous kiss. Her teeth sharpened into fanged things that would tear throats apart; her fingers lengthened, her nails grew thick and pointed to better plunge into the chests of those causing pain. The fire was behind her teeth, clutched there with barely held back will as she moved up the steps and paused on the final one.

Fiana pressed her hand to her mouth and then began screaming. Her body twisted and bent over as she was thrust into the change. The men in cloaks hadn't reached her yet, but it was already beginning.

Too late, much too late.

Ailith moved as well, throwing something to the ground that created a cloud of smoke and took her from Caitriona's sight. She stared, searching for the pair, but only heard the chaos within. Caitriona's heart beat in her throat, pulsing with fire and panic, until Ailith stumbled through the wall of smoke, eyes locking on her as she ran forward and directly into Caitriona's waiting arms.

CHAPTER TWENTY-EIGHT

"Cait, oh gods, Cait!" Ailith cried, running into Caitriona's arms and savoring the embrace with eyes shuttering closed.

"Ailith," Caitriona clasped her hard against her chest. Her hands were slick with scales and cold through Ailith's shirt as they moved over Ailith. She pulled Ailith back, gripping her shoulders as her golden eyes took her in. After so much time had passed with little hope of reuniting, the well of Ailith's emotions spilled forward and relief came in the form of tears. She was alive, she had her memory, she had control and she was *herself*.

Ailith reached a shaking hand to brush Caitriona's shimmering hair behind her shoulder, savoring its softness as it tangled with her fingers. Their noses bumped. Ailith looked into Caitriona's eyes, the only gaze she held without the persistent urge to turn away. "Hello, my love."

Caitriona's sharp teeth appeared as she smiled, her eyes glowed golden with barely withheld magic, and her breath steamed like magma ready to escape the earth, but the taste of her kiss was the sweetest heat Ailith ever beheld.

"I thought I lost you," Caitriona whispered, pressing her forehead against Ailith's.

"You nearly did." She moved her hands down Caitriona's arms, savoring the softness of her skin and the familiarity of her. Gripping Caitriona's hands hard, the draconic attributes slowly receded and the soft plumpness of Caitriona's palms returned. "A few times, actually. But I can tell you about that later, we have to go. The guards were turning prisoners into beasts. Fiana made us our own potion and took hers so she still has control of her body. She managed to get the real potion to fall on guards."

"How did you avoid it? I don't understand what I just saw." Caitriona ran her hands down Ailith's arms as if reminding herself Ailith was truly there while Ailith shifted towards the stairs.

"She gave me a spell too, but something must have gone wrong. I saw you through the smoke and tried to make my way to you. We have to go before it clears."

"What about Fiana?" Caitriona looked over Ailith's shoulder, drawing her attention back to the expansive space. The smoke was lifting but chaos remained. Creatures were in a tizzy, thrashing against their ropes and leaving the remaining fae guards to try and control them all. Wyverns, shades, cockatrice, and more were filling the expanse. High above them, a black spot in the sky began to spiral downward. Ailith laughed.

"Crowley!" she called softly as he took a quick dive toward a guard and scratched at their head. With satisfaction, Ailith saw the second spellcaster doubled over, the bowl of his powder at his feet and the dark essence of the spell work wrapping the spellcaster whole. He too was falling to his curses, one of the few who were deserving.

Amongst them stood Fiana who outgrew the length of her clothing. It still looked like Fiana in some way; the curve of her cheeks and the angle of her brow remained, as well as her brown eyes and long, glossy, dark hair. But feathers were knit through her tresses now and her lips pushed forward as fangs erupted from her once human mouth. Her legs were clawed, similar to the cockatrice, but she walked like a human as she stepped to the bowl of magic and kicked it in the direction of another guard while dark wings spread wide from her back.

"This is her doing," Ailith whispered. "She made this spell. She's herself."

As if hearing them, Fiana flashed a smile of daggers.

"Go!" Fiana yelled, but her voice wasn't her own anymore. It was like a croak of a crow, strange coming from her changed face.

"She had this planned all along." Ailith nodded toward Fiana. A fae guard fell over as the powder attacked him and another yelled, running toward her with a lance. Fiana twisted, her elongated fingers snatching at the lance as if it were a toothpick and snapping it with ease. Ailith gripped Caitriona's arm and stepped back. "Now's our chance."

Caitriona and Ailith moved down the marble steps and beyond the wall where Raum and Ceenear waited. They retreated via the path Ailith had been led out from hours before. It was a marbled pathway along the wall of the castle to a door, but they passed it and followed an even narrower, dirt path that hugged the walls with a steep drop off the side.

Crowley followed overhead, keeping his distance but mirroring their movements and letting out a caw when the coast was clear. As they inched toward a curve, the corvid screeched. A door opened onto an outcrop and a guard stepped out, appearing unsuspecting and just as surprised to see them.

For a second, they stared at the man before he spoke under his breath, his eyes growing wide and black.

"*No.*" Caitriona's voice was soft as she lifted her hands.

Ailith couldn't see what he was casting, but there was likely no good intention behind his creation. He continued muttering but Caitriona was fast, using her magic without speaking any incantation and creating an expanse of heat that left Ailith stepping back and closing her eyes.

There was a sound of his leather shoes sliding on the ground and a rush of air. Ailith opened her eyes just as his body fell from sight over the ledge. She stepped forward and peered down, witnessing him slide down the sharp slope, and hitting boulders and trees. The scent of his burning hair and flesh remained as the fire Caitriona held winked out.

Caitriona gasped, stepping back as she looked at her hands. They appeared human, yet wisps of smoke lifted from her fingers where fire dissipated. A shaking breath filled her chest and her eyes glimmered with tears. Ailith reached forward and touched her shoulder. Caitriona jumped under her touch and Ailith braced herself as Caitriona's hands clenched into fists. No fire appeared and Ailith pulled Caitriona backward and against her chest.

"Let's use this area to switch spots. You go behind me, okay?" She kept her voice soft and hoped it brought comfort.

Caitriona shook her head. "No, you're weak from everything. Let us lead."

"We should take this as a chance for a break," Ceenear pointed, her gaze focused on the spot where the fae man had fallen. "There's more space here due to the door, let's make sure no one's coming and take a moment to breathe. Ailith needs medicine and food, and we can figure out our next steps. We're going to have to get far away from here and somehow get over the mist safely, but we can't do all that here nor while weak."

Caitriona lifted her face from against Ailith's chest and sniffed. "Are you certain that's a good idea? We're still against the castle, we could be caught."

"We have to make it to the back where that game trail is, which will take time, and then through the slopes without being seen." Ceenear pulled her pack from her back and turned to the formerly-kidnapped guard. "Ailith, I'm sorry but you look awful. We need to get you strong enough to make the trip without stopping. At least in this moment the castle's too focused on the chaos with the creatures being changed."

"They may notice Ailith's gone." Caitriona quivered underneath Ailith's hand.

"How will they?" Ailith asked, touching Caitriona's cheek to gain her attention. "I'm supposed to be a creature now. They're gathering hold of all they've made and sending them off. Ceenear's right, as much as I hate to admit it, I'm weak."

"I need the break," Raum spoke. He had been relatively silent since Ailith joined them and barely regarded her. Avoiding their gazes, he stepped to the door the guard came from and pulled it open before disappearing into the castle.

Ailith looked at Caitriona with confusion. Caitriona's lips parted, as if to explain, but Raum returned. He held a pole and forced it through the handle to secure the door from opening from within.

Ailith looked at the outcrop and snorted. Giant drums of soapy water and lengths of rope connecting to trees where fabric flapped in the breeze sat along the edge. "This is the drying area for the palace laundry."

"Let's settle in so we can get moving soon." Ceenear waved for Ailith and Caitriona to take a seat. Raum stepped away and sat without another word, swinging his legs off the edge as he pulled out an apple. He cut pieces off with a knife and popped them into his mouth in silence. Ceenear sat closer to the castle wall and dug through her bag, pulling out food and placing a selection onto cloth. She held it toward Ailith. "Eat something and we'll go."

CHAPTER TWENTY-NINE

CAITRIONA

Caitriona touched Ailith's hand, her movements clunky and shaken as she tried to brush her emotions aside and focus on who was before her. Ailith. After weeks, Ailith. Was this how the guard felt when she tracked Caitriona's movements after the curse? The desperation followed by quivering relief? When Ailith turned her attention to Caitriona, the tension in her shoulders lessened.

She nodded to the outcrop along the wall where they could sit together. Ailith's cheeks were hollow, her clothing loose on her already thin form, and her hair was a greasy mess. Amongst her brunette tresses were the streaks of white Caitriona saw in her vision.

"Oh, Ailith," she murmured, as they settled with their backs against the wall. Taking her bag from her back, Caitriona pulled out the satchel of medicines and potions her mother gave her while Ailith ate the food Ceenear offered.

Pushing the Elder Tree sap aside and pulling forth a vial marked for energy and another for health, Caitriona worked on the corks then held them out. "Take these, maybe they can help give you a boost until we return to Braewick."

Ailith accepted the vials, her hands thin and nails thick with dirt in the creases. "Where'd you get these from?"

"My mother made them." Caitriona smiled at the flick of surprise that passed over Ailith's face. "It's an assortment of medicines and life-saving measures. She's quite the magic maker now."

As Ailith drank the vials, Caitriona couldn't help running her fingertips down Ailith's hair. Her nails still glinted gold from her half-change and Caitriona made no effort to hide it.

Ailith's free hand snaked up and entwined with hers before she pulled them to her lips.

Caitriona's heart bloomed. Blood rushed through her limbs and to her cheeks, and she smiled, but couldn't help but ask what brewed in her mind. "What was done to you?"

Ailith's lips thinned as her brows met. She looked to Raum then back at Caitriona, shifting as she sat and her lips tugging downward. "I—"

She shook her head and swallowed as if fighting off the urge to vomit. She began to explain the past few weeks, what she could remember, and Caitriona found her grip tightening over Ailith's. Her resolve to never let Ailith be far from her again solidified.

"I was overwhelmed with terror," Ailith continued. "Like my nightmares from thunderstorms. They completely consumed me, but it didn't matter the time of day or the weather. All I knew was fear." She glanced at Raum. "Have you come across anyone else we know?"

Caitriona lowered her gaze.

"Lumia," she said softly. "But ..."

She shook her head, unable to admit what transpired and Ailith's brows rose, her hand tightening around Caitriona's. "I understand. It's tied to her—what happened to me."

"Ah ..."

They fell silent as Ailith ate. The potions began their work. The pallor of her skin brightened, her lips pinked up, and the swelling around her one eye lessened and turned into dull bruising. Caitriona dug through her bag to pull out more food to share. She had been driven by the desire to find Ailith from the moment Ailith slipped into the necklace, but now that she accomplished the goal, she was at a loss for words and the exhaustion of weeks caught up to her.

Plus, there was all that was left unsaid. The moments before Ailith disappeared were moments of mistrust. Ailith was possessed, driven to do things without guilt, and they weren't certain if she was trustworthy. But in her final moments, she protected Caitriona—or at least that was what Caitriona thought—before she vanished into the necklace along with Fiana. She looked at Ailith who met her eye.

"I was trying—"

"You helped—"

A laugh, simple yet filled with nerves. Caitriona wanted nothing more than to fall into the roots of the Elder Tree and return home with Ailith. To bring her to that northern cottage and remind herself of who Ailith was all over again. But the war was present as were its horrors. She couldn't escape the reality of it. It waited for her in Braewick and it lingered in the mountains.

"I left Braewick to look for you against Greer's orders. Twice," she admitted and the look of surprise on Ailith's face was a rock in her gut. Was she disappointed in her for doing that? Probably. Ailith was a lawful person who sought justice and followed rules—for the most part. Her own heart was what made up the majority of right from wrong, and Caitriona was certain listening to Greer's orders was a part of that. Ailith studied Caitriona yet smiled.

"I bet Greer didn't handle that very well."

Caitriona let her shoulders drop with relief. "No, no she didn't. She was very much not pleased with me."

"How long have you been traveling? Do you know what's happening in Wimleigh?"

"The battle was about to begin, or it already has. Greer wanted to send me away to keep me safe while I wanted to rescue you and find more information. We came here to get you. The mist's been altered, it attacks anyone who tries to leave. Then we discovered all those awful plans with the creatures."

"It's a sure way for Malcolm to win. The guard isn't ready for magical creatures to attack," Ailith admitted. "Hopefully, Fiana can do damage. The potions she made were supposed to change us both into creatures but ones that kept our wits about us. What's happening to the others, they're losing their will as they're changed. I don't know what happened to my spell, it must have gotten messed up because it just made smoke, but Fiana seemed happy to send us away and fight on her own."

"At least we'll have one magical force on our side here."

"That's true. Maybe she can stop some of the creatures from leaving the mountainside. But what now?"

"We'll go to Braewick and fight. Or cause chaos here if we can't get through the mist." Caitriona flashed a smile, but she didn't feel particularly hopeful. Knitting her hands with Ailith's she looked at her lap and realized she still wore Ailith's dagger and sword. "Oh, Ailith."

The weight of Barden's death came out of nowhere. She had forgotten it; how could she forget so soon that she lost him? That Greer was heartbroken without him? That Ailith didn't know. Perhaps it was as simple as growing used to his loss, but that hurt even more. Familiarity in death felt too heavy, particularly so soon. She had to tell her, but they needed to get away from the mountain first. She didn't want to weigh Ailith down by the news when she was already weakened.

"My sword; you brought it all this way?" Ailith gasped. She touched the handle as Caitriona pulled it free. Her hands hesitated over the blade before receding. "I understand if you don't want me to have it. The last time we saw each other it wasn't good. What I did—"

"Oh gods, Ailith, no," Caitriona gasped, stilling Ailith's hand. "No, I brought these because you need weapons. *Your* weapons. I'm useless with a sword, you know that. I'm better with my flames."

A crooked smile on Ailith's face emphasized the silver of the scar on her cheek. "You're using your flames without issue then?"

Caitriona couldn't stop her smile, a genuine one. Oh, she had so much to tell Ailith. "After you fell through the necklace, I—"

Wind spung up from the valley floor and hit them hard with a gust appearing out of nowhere, drawing up the changing leaves of the trees. The air took the words from Caitriona's mouth and sent them flying upward.

Caitriona covered her face, turning from the assault of tree branches, leaves, and drying fabrics pulled free. A familiar sound rumbled over the wind. She looked up, her eyes meeting Ailith's which had gone wide.

The vibrating hum of a dragon's roar crested the slope with the rhythmic flap of heavy, leather wings. The wind came, waves flowing over the mountainside and becoming a torrent on the ledge before sucking away. Raum was up, rushing to the castle wall and pulling Ceenear with him. The foursome clung against the wall, the cloths with food blowing off the edge, and their hair whipping in the wind.

Caitriona looked into the valley where they would have been traveling had they not paused, squinting through the bits of leaves and dirt in the air, and the flapping sheets of the clothing lines that tore from their clips and escaped to the skies, but there was no way to miss the moving creature lifting from the valley floor. Its scales were black with white highlights, its eyes white with small pupils, and its nose and head were aligned in small spikes that were dwarfed compared to Caitriona's crown of horns.

The dragon was large, so much larger than Caitriona in her dragon form, and its long tail ended with spikes that made up for the lack on its head. The beast took to the skies, flapping its wings repeatedly as it got momentum and lifted further up.

"Malcolm," Ailith whispered, her eyes wide and frozen on the beast.

"That's Malcolm?" Ceenear shouted over the wind.

Ailith pressed her hand against her chest, her fingers shaking. "I saw him days ago and then he disappeared. It didn't seem anything was being done at the castle. We were all sitting ducks. I assumed he was planning something or mixing magic, stealing it from the fae, or his other hijinks. He said he wanted all the powers and Caitriona, too. He seemed interested in her ability to become a dragon. I bet you, I swear, it *has* to be him."

Ailith's hand slipped into Caitriona's and held it tightly as the dragon took to the sky and released a large roar. Flames licked its lips, steaming the cool mountain air, and Ailith vibrated against her. The dragon arched its neck and spat flame, setting trees in the mountain valley on fire in a rush. Satisfied, it began to glide and with one, two, three pumps of its massive wings it sailed toward the west. Toward the Umberfend Marsh.

"Oh, Elder Tree, it's going for my sister," Caitriona whispered, drawing her friends' attention. Caitriona scrambled to her feet, watching the dragon drift from sight.

"We have to go back to the outcrop and see what the other creatures are doing. We have to get intel, and find a way to get back to the marsh, we have to—"

She didn't wait for their replies as the rest of her thoughts died upon her lips. She said nothing to her companions but ran, retracing their steps down the path as her lungs burned from the altitude. There was fire within there as well, swelling in her chest from the panic of it all. The black dragon was gone, rapidly becoming a dark spot in the air, and in the distance her fears were confirmed as figures leapt from the outcrop. One by one, the creatures took to the air. Those with wings held creatures without, all ascending from the marble floor in favor of the air and sped toward their destination. The guards were gone, the powdered curse being tossed to the ground forced them to become creatures as well. The entire outcrop was nothing but monsters ready to fight in a war as their king had called for aid as he flew past.

Caitriona skidded to a stop at the steps where she first saw Ailith and watched the figures disappear. She didn't spot Fiana but prayed she was causing hell amongst the rush. The war had begun and she was there, trapped on the mountain, and unable to help her sister.

At least, the Caitriona of times before couldn't help her sister. The Caitriona who was filled with self-disgust and hadn't found her own power would have cowered and cried and been useless. But that wasn't who she was anymore. She had changed, grown, and she had faith in herself which was an abundance of power in itself.

"Cait, wait," Ailith called, her footsteps pounding against the path. The exhaustion that coated her face before was gone and the bruising was turning to healed skin. Her cheeks had even gained a healthier color. The vials continued to work their magic and Caitriona felt a rush of gratitude for her mother. Seeing that her mother had put in the work and was successful only bolstered Caitriona all the more. She was ready.

Ailith stepped back, her brows rising. "Cait, what are you going to do?"

"Oh, Ailith," Caitriona laughed, taking Ailith's hands and still thrilled to know she was there. "You've missed *so* much and I was so eager to tell you, but we've run out of time. You need to know you were right all along. I can be both dragon and human. One doesn't take away from the other—I'm still *me*. I learned that due to you. And now I'm going to be Greer's secret weapon."

She let herself go and it was freeing. The change wasn't painful as it rippled across her skin. The small, blonde hairs on her arms stood up and solidified into a sheen of golden scales. Her teeth lengthened, her tongue sharpened and grew long as it ran over the points in her mouth. Her nose shifted forward, her nostrils turning into slits. She loosened the knot of her mother's cloak with ease and it fell to the ground at her feet. Her shoulder blades pressed outward and she scrambled to pull off her pack. Her wings were about to sprout and spread, to gather the warmth of the sun and kiss the breeze.

Ailith reached for Caitriona's pack. She clutched it in her hands and watched open mouthed, the corners of her lips turning upward, and tears in her eyes. They weren't sad tears; Ailith seemed to glow with pride and Caitriona knew it was for her.

In the final moments before she shed her human form completely, Caitriona cupped Ailith's cheeks in her hands. Her touch light and intentionally delicate as her fingers lengthened and her nails became claws. The pads of her hands thickened and became rough. There was only the gentlest impression of her nails against Ailith's cheek and the scar that covered the one side. As her lips hardened into serpentine creases and her mouth became crowded with her fangs, she spoke the one request she dreamt of since she took to the skies after Ailith fell into the necklace. "Darling, will you fly with me? Will you join me in the skies?"

Ailith leaned forward, her brown eyes wide and sparkling. The sun glinted off the streaks of white in her hair. She was beautiful and *here* and Caitriona hoped they wouldn't have to part so soon. Her lips met Caitriona's, so soft and warm and human. She smiled as she pulled back and her hand pressed over Caitriona's shifting paw.

"Cait," Ailith breathed. "Always."

CHAPTER THIRTY

GREER

"To your left!" Lachlan yelled, drawing Greer's attention and blocking the swing of a sword too close for comfort. Greer twisted her blade and pushed forward with a cry, her teeth clamping down as she grimaced and threw the fae fighter off balance. His death was swift and she pulled her sword from his chest as she tried to catch her breath. The first wave of battle was lessening, but the opposing forces were centering their attention on the two sovereigns.

"They're drawn to me; I need to move away from you."

Greer turned back to Lachlan who was breathing heavily, his reddish hair plastered to his forehead beneath his helmet and his sword shown slick with different colored blood from the various creatures he fought. A new wave of creatures with talons and beaks, wings and slithering tails were moving over the marsh in their direction but for the moment they no longer had anyone to fight. A moment to breathe and consider the truth of the matter.

He wasn't wrong. Through the entire battle they adopted a strategy of fighting toward one another before becoming separated again. Greer took down a fae who rushed forward, and he brought down a shade that bit at her heels. The various guards helped, but they moved as if tied. Together and apart and determined to reach the other's side. But now it was clear how much the creatures wanted Lachlan and Lachlan specifically.

"Move to the north and I'll go to the south. If you need me, call my name. Doesn't matter how loud or soft, I'll hear it." Lachlan turned to Greer. He pulled his glove free and reached for her face, his thin fingers brushing over her cheek and sending a tingling warmth over her skin. Magic. "Stay safe."

He pulled his glove back on as he turned and marched forward. Beneath his feet, dirt rose to kiss his soles and marsh plants sprouted, leaving behind a trail of footsteps through pools of water that he did not touch. Greer stared, realizing the quiet, meek man who said so little at the castle had just directed *her*, and she didn't mind. She turned toward the north as he instructed.

After another hour, the dead were scattered through the marshland. Blood soaked the waters, turning them to a murky brown with the gloss of red across the top like an oil unwilling to mix with the pureness of the ponds. It was even in the air, the bitter iron scent so thick it filled nostrils and coated tongues with its wrongness.

Greer bled from her arm and lip, her helmet was lost to a pond some time before, and her hair came loose from her bun. Her body screamed with exhaustion that she could not answer until the battle was done. Lachlan was a spot further into the field—they were separated from one another rapidly during the fight—but he still moved and breathed which was all that mattered. In the field, Lachlan's power was at last apparent. Lightning and fire, ice and stone shot from his hands through creation of simple determination and power. The fae with magic and creatures that endured such hits like cockatrices. Undead were attracted to him and he disposed of them one after another.

It empowered Greer; she wasn't made of magic but she had strength and skill with a blade. She was never that leader who abandoned her men and women to get out of harm's way, and she wouldn't begin doing that now.

They had fought through the morning, encountering the first round of fae guards and a few creatures that came before midday. Deathbringers—birds that ate souls—flit through the air and dove toward fallen bodies to gobble their souls like worms pulled from the ground, ending any opportunity for the guards to become dukes or see the afterlife. It had been hours, but at last, it seemed the first battle finished. A break from it all, a reprieve to bat away the damned birds trying to take souls.

She had a retinue of protection but she urged her guards to back off and give her space so she could recover. The first round of fae were dead; she was relatively safe and finally alone. Yet the silence from human life was haunting as there were still so many bodies around her. Guards who died defending her from a wyvern were silenced while the expressions on their face were anything but.

She never fought a wyvern before and it was a terrifying experience. The creature snapped its mouth lined with teeth toward her face while its dangerous tail flailed across the ground, sweeping out the feet of guards from beneath them. They couldn't hold back their gasps as they went airborne. It spat blasts of acid, a hideous orange and yellow stream of liquid from its mouth, that splattered onto the body of one guard. He screamed with agony, falling backward as the acid melted his skin and exposed his skull. He died quickly, but his mouth remained held open in horror. It was plain luck they were able to decapitate the wyvern, but the experience left

Greer shaken and the remaining guards were happy to step aside and catch their breaths.

Greer pulled swords from dirt and creature alike, and forced them into the limp hands of dead guards. She dragged their bodies to pools of water and rolled them in so perhaps the guards would be given a proper rest amongst the protective dukes. She couldn't go into the marsh to gather marshberries floating on the surface, nor did she have dried flowers to decorate their bodies, she didn't cover their corpses in honey, and no song of heartache rose from her. Still, she hoped it was enough in the skirmish of war, and the dukes would understand.

Hope was all she had, because the dukes hadn't come, they didn't rise, they didn't even ripple the water. All the stories Barden had told said they would rise for battle, yet they abandoned her.

Barden abandoned her.

Greer hoped offering dead guards would stir them and she stepped back, looking at the corpses left in the water. Each body floated for a moment before sinking and there were no hands to take them, no duke's attention was drawn.

Her frustration spiked, festering into a ball of rage that exploded, igniting her nerves with a pulse of energy. She kicked the water's edge. "Just *take* them. Take their bodies, they served me well. Let them live out their days with you. Accept them into your ranks. Don't let their souls be swallowed by these damned birds!"

Nothing. The dukes remained silent and the fight left Greer as quickly as it appeared. The water remained undisturbed, the dead floated along the surface or sank from sight and she sank as well, drawing dangerously close to the mental hole she was trapped in for the last month.

"Not now. There's time to mourn later." Greer's voice shook with unshed emotion that she swallowed back.

"Greer?" Lachlan drew close, his hair remained plastered to his brow as he pulled his helmet off, and a sheen of sweat covering his cheeks. He paused a few yards away, seeming uncertain if he could proceed. "Are you alright?"

The other guards kept their distance—busied with the wounded and dead—they already got an earful from Greer that she needed a moment alone, but Lachlan consistently pushed past those boundaries and Greer didn't have it in her to be annoyed. Her shoulders dropped. "The dukes didn't come."

Lachlan's lips turned down and he looked at the closest pond. "I know. There's something wrong with it, something off—like poison in the water."

"Are the dukes dead?"

Lachlan shook his head. "There's still life below the surface; it's just deep. I'm not sure. Are you coming back to the base? We have some time to rest; you should do the same."

Greer stared before her and shook her head. "I'll make my way over there; I need a moment."

He drifted from her without another word but she caught him glancing over his shoulder as he walked away. Other guards remained, scattered but keeping a protective eye over their sovereign.

The day pushed forward with annoying insistence, the skies grew dark as clouds increased and moved to the east, toward the mountains, and the heat of summer at last diminished. Early autumn grasped the landscape with the scent of death inescapable in the air as she turned west and picked her way over the marshland eberward the encampment.

The medic tent was a blaze of white. Even from the marsh she spotted the red of her mother's hair outside it. It was a comfort to know her mother was close yet safe. She still, however, worried over Caitriona, who she chased away with her stubborn behavior and her unwillingness to see her as more than someone to protect. How much of what was going on, what threats they endured and the harm that came, was her fault? Barden took an arrow for her, Caitriona snuck away because Greer refused to let her go, and her mother arrived at the marsh after Greer said she could not.

Pausing, unable to push away the dread and emptiness, her knees met the ground. Greer tilted her head up, allowing the cool breeze to dry the sweat on her neck and brow. She would rest here, if only for a moment, before returning to camp. She needed to get her head on straight before encountering more of her citizens. They needed a leader who was certain and of sound mind, not whatever she was. Just a little rest and then, hopefully, she would secure her royal mask in place for those on shore. Surely there was time before the next wave of creatures and fae attacked.

But the first rule she learned when training for the guard was that war is never a thing of fairness.

A horn echoed across the expanse from camp and Greer opened her eyes. Dark figures appeared on the battlefield in places where no one previously stood. They magically winked into the space while to the east creatures swarmed the sky. Further out, in the distance where the mountains were, a darker shape took form. Flapping its wings, it pushed forward through the air, moving quicker than Greer could comprehend. With each pump of its wings, it grew in size. With the land so flat and only a few short trees, the sight preceded the pulse of death in the air of what was to come.

A large, black dragon pushed forward and from Greer's distance the glow of flame held in its mouth flickered, ready to spread across the land.

"Elder Tree," Greer whispered, uncertain if such wishes could be made so far from a dying tree. "Elder Tree, help us. Please help us."

"What good will a tree do?" A voice asked.

Shock rippled up her spine and spread over her skull, her hand clasped the hilt of her sword as she pushed to her feet in a fluid motion.

"It served its purpose by killing that damned guard of yours. You aren't much on your own. I've seen that in the halls of your castle and my hands have craved to squeeze your neck again."

"Shad." Greer sighed as she slipped into stance with her sword raised. She met Shad only once and it was when he was nothing but darkness, but he was solid now, taller than her in this form; broader, and more defined. Yet shadows drifted from him and Greer wondered how whole he actually was. Maybe he was still part shadow after all. "And what of you? I know your secret; you're as human as I am, not a wink of magic save for your pointed ears."

"Not anymore," Shad hissed; the shadows rose from his skin. "You think I only have one trick? My father gifted me with power and this is what I chose."

Greer tilted her head to one side. The benefit of growing under her father's thumb was a lifetime of taunts thrown at her. She liked to think she was quite skilled at it herself. If she learned anything, it was that men were particularly sensitive to any comment about their weaknesses, and she suspected Shad had many. "Shadow magic? How talented are you during the day? Cloud cover tends to wipe away shadow and blend light with dark. So, I doubt your performance will be memorable. Probably like your performances in all other aspects of your life."

Her grin broadened as she watched Shad's face grow red.

"I'm going to celebrate having your blood on my hands," Shad hissed. His sword swung forward.

It was an easy block, but the weight of the blade and Shad's strength behind it was a surprise. She moved backward, pressing her feet into the soft earth by the murky waterway. She pushed his blade back, leaving him stumbling.

Quickly she shuffled to the side, seeking a broader expanse of space between the waters where hopefully the ground was more solid. Shad advanced, uncaring that the ground was soft where he stood and with each step the sweep of shadow lifted off his feet.

Greer darted forward, bringing her sword toward his side but shadows leapt and tugged at her blade where there should have been an easy hit. He twisted, reflecting her move and Greer stepped aside, narrowly missing a cut to her stomach.

Swinging her blade in a circular motion, she swept toward his arm but missed completely. He took a wide step forward, equal to two of Greer's, and swung his blade again. She was steadily pushed backwards toward the pools of water as he swung repeatedly to drive her further and further. Her energy, already spent from the first battle, was burning out quickly, but this would not be her final battle. She wouldn't allow it.

Stabbing forward, she missed his move. His sword found a spot where her rerebrace slipped and cut into her arm below her pauldron, its sharpness burning as it sliced through her skin with ease. She gasped and felt hot with twisting embarrassment and anger as Shad laughed.

The wind pulsed, sucking forward and moving back as Greer tried to catch her breath and brace for her fight to continue. A roar shook the earth, vibrating the water of the marsh and making Greer cower from the volume. Shad stood all the straighter and smiled.

"Greer, you haven't met my father. This is Malcolm, future ruler of Wimleigh Kingdom and soon, conqueror of all of Visennore." His blade swung and Greer blocked it.

"I'm going to tell you our plans since you won't be alive long enough to see them through." His blade sung through the air toward her. Greer blocked it. "My father's going to set fire to all your reserves on the edge of the marsh and then he'll strike your city."

Another swing, another block.

"He'll kill as many as possible and force the rest to become pets. This way we can begin with a clean slate."

A swipe towards her feet and Greer jumped away. Shad snarled but kept talking. "He wanted to keep you alive and turn you into a creature, but he allowed me my request: that I play with you and kill you however *I* please."

Another roar vibrated through the sky, the sound coming from a closer distance, and different—the tone higher—and Greer looked to the heavens, her eyes widening. Beyond the incoming surge of Malcolm was another flying creature; smaller in comparison but still large and *gold*. A half-laugh escaped Greer's lips and drew Shad's attention to the skies as Caitriona pushed forward, flying as quickly as she could toward Malcolm himself.

Seeing the opening, Greer rushed forward and raised her sword, to stab forward and pierce Shad. He twisted, hearing her movements and the mark missed, instead going into his shoulder under his gardbrace. His scream made it clear Greer injured him at least somewhat. A shoulder wound for a shoulder wound, but hers was substantially worse.

His arm sagged as he shifted the longsword in his hands, gripping it more intensely with his unwounded arm, but it was off balance. The blade was meant to be held with two hands, not one. He grimaced at Greer before spitting at the ground and smiling, "Let's play."

CHAPTER THIRTY-ONE

The wind would have been numbing if it wasn't for the warmth radiating off Caitriona's body. Golden and sleek, Caitriona flew with as much grace as a swan gliding over waters. After Caitriona fully turned into her draconic form—an experience that appeared as easy as taking off one's clothes compared to the blood and gore of her first change—Ailith climbed upon her broad back. She straddled her shoulders and wrapped her arms around Caitriona's elongated, draconic neck. Stuffing Caitriona's cloak into her pack, Ailith secured it on her back and ensured her dagger and sword were set. Caitriona lunged off the side of the mountain. Ailith's stomach thrust into her throat as Caitriona dove, the earth rushing toward them before her broad wings caught the air and pushed them upward.

They were flying, gliding over the mountains and quickly rushing toward flatter lands. The speed left Ailith clutching Caitriona with her eyes squeezed shut until the motion and wind became something less frightening. The movements grew repetitive and Ailith squinted at the world rushing by.

She assumed the sky would be empty, but it wasn't. It was

filled with figures flying toward the marshlands; wyverns and cockatrice that carried other creatures and people alike. Ahead was the black dragon. Caitriona continuously pumped her wings as she attempted to catch up. Other creatures were just as determined to bring them down.

A wyvern snaked through the sky, attempting to reach Caitriona with quick speed. Its teeth gnashed in the air and nipped at her heels. Caitriona kicked her powerful legs, her body jolting and Ailith tightened her hold on Caitriona's neck. The talons of her clawed feet caught the wyvern's side and sent it spiraling toward the ground.

"*Hold on,*" Caitriona's voice slipped into Ailith's mind, making her jump and nearly lose her hold.

"You can talk?" Ailith yelled over the wind and a rumble sounded from Caitriona's throat. Laughing, she was *laughing* at her.

"*Apparently,*" she replied like the memory of a voice being brought forth in Ailith's head, clear as a bell except not a memory at all.

Ailith couldn't help but laugh too. "I really did miss a lot."

She leaned forward and pressed her cheek along the slick, warm scales as Caitriona dove downward and caught an updraft that lifted her body once more. It brought her speeding forward in an uptick. They drew closer to the black dragon and with it, the air became warmer. He radiated heat and Ailith's unease grew with its size.

"Do you think he knows who he is?" Ailith yelled. "Or is he lost and still in a haze like you were."

"*I don't know,*" Caitriona said in Ailith's mind. *"He may be driven to destroy like I was."*

"Could you get near his wings?" Ailith pushed her torso upward but still gripped the jagged horn-like points along Caitriona's neck. Her spikes, similar in shape to her horns but thicker and shorter, traveled down Caitriona's spine and grew in length over her back, but provided enough space for Ailith to sit between them. "I can try to cut into them."

"Don't fall, Ailith."

She angled her wings, tilting them to the side, and Ailith clenched her thighs. Regaining her balance, she pulled her sword from her waist and held it at the ready. They positioned themselves beneath Malcolm and waited for the flap of his wings. The powerful gust of wind they created nearly flattened Ailith against Caitriona. She adjusted her seat, and gritted her teeth as the wing bent down. She swung her sword outward. The blade cut through the leather-like skin of his wing with a sickening, dry ripping sound and a spurt of blood.

He immediately tilted in the sky, a roar exploding from his throat that left Ailith quivering as she tried to cover her ears without dropping her weapon. Her body immediately reacted from a lifetime of fear for such sounds, her muscles growing tight and her breathing stopping.

While he was large and threatening, and Caitriona dwarfed in comparison, her size allowed her quicker movement. Curling to the left, she darted away but Malcolm urged himself after her. The one wing struggled and the tear left blood falling rapidly toward the earth in a burning rain as a more terrifying sound began; something that haunted Ailith's nightmares even to this day, despite how young she was when she first heard such a noise.

The sound of fire churned up a pipe, crackling and hollow as it rushed forward, and the precursor of sulfur drafting on the breeze made Ailith press down.

"Go, Cait! Go!" Ailith cried, scrambling to return her sword to her scabbard and hold Cait's neck with both hands. They spun downward, then veered to the right at the last moment as fire released in a stream over the marsh, catching creatures that still traveled toward the battlefield and set what marsh plants existed on fire.

Malcolm pushed forward and snapped at Caitriona's tail with long, crooked fangs. She whipped it back and forth, and Malcolm repeatedly attempted to catch it with his sharp teeth. He was too close, and his fangs caught the side of her tail and ripped at the scales. Caitriona roared, the vibration of her cry going through her throat and outward, shaking Ailith violently as Caitriona's human voice screamed in Ailith's head.

"*I need—*" she breathed in Ailith's mind as she pumped her wings to try and veer Malcolm further off track. "*—to get you off me.*"

"No, I'm not leaving you again!" Ailith yelled. "Absolutely not. I'm staying here."

"*I can't have you fall!*" Caitriona twisted her neck and laid her glittering gold eyes on Ailith for a moment. They were *her* eyes—Caitriona's—human in appearance with her golden lashes, but so large Ailith could see the entirety of her body reflecting in the orbs. The stubborn frustration and terror was clear on Ailith's face as her dark hair moved in the air. A sob brought on by too much emotion escaped Ailith's mouth as she looked at Caitriona.

"*It's too dangerous.*"

"Then drop me on him!" Ailith yelled. "One last try. Get above him and let me drop down. Let me try to cut him and catch me before I fall. You're smaller than him and you're so quick, Cait. You can make it if you dart around him. Then drop me to the ground, okay?"

"*I don't want you hurt! I couldn't stand it if I let that happen!*"

"I knew you were capable of being a dragon and holding onto yourself. I believed in you, I trusted you, now please do the same for me." Ailith leaned forward, touching further up Caitriona's neck, just behind where Caitriona's human ear would have been in her true form. "I know I can do hard things. But it's all for nothing if I don't have you supporting me. I have to do this and so do you. I'll meet you in the air or on the ground. We just need to survive this and then, I swear, I want to spend every day with you for the rest of our lives."

Caitriona continued flying, silent as she dodged Malcolm's advances and blasts of sulfurous fire. She circled over the swamp before pushing southward. Ailith leaned back with defeat as Caitriona arched her neck and directed her powerful wings to bring her higher into the air.

"*I'll do a quick cutback*," Caitriona's voice was stern in Ailith's mind. She wasn't pleased with this idea, but she was doing it. "*Hold tight, it'll be sudden, and if you can't make the jump, don't.*"

"I'll stay here if it looks dangerous, Cait. I promise."

A single nod from her golden head and up they went higher into the sky. Ailith checked Barden's sword on her waist and tightened the straps of Caitriona's bag on her back. Malcolm tried to keep up with them, but the sudden climb was too much for his heavy body and it took longer for him to gain height, allowing them the chance to fly all the higher. Ailith lowered herself against Caitriona, keeping her eyes locked ahead. When Caitriona pitched backward, twisting in the sky and dropping from the turn dozens of feet, she barely flinched. They sped toward Malcolm now and Ailith gripped her dagger and pressed her foot against Caitriona's shoulder, ready to push herself off.

Three, two, one ... she let herself fall off Caitriona, gasping at the sudden loss of Caitriona's warmth and the rush of air over her ears. Twisting her body, she gripped her dagger, angling it to cut, while her other hand reached with hope to catch onto something. Malcolm was void of sharp horns on his back, but had plenty of bumpy scales that were large enough to grip.

Ailith spread her limbs and readied herself as her body descended and at last, hit Malcolm's neck. Her body slammed against it, her bruised ribs shocking her with pain as the wind pushed out her lungs. Ailith gasped and fought to find hold as she slipped and scrambled for purchase. Malcolm was flying erratically, aiming for Caitriona as she flew overhead then turned downward. He released flame and the heat washed over Ailith as her foothold against his scales continued to slip. She wouldn't be able to make it onto his back or do much damage, but before she fell—to her death if Caitriona didn't fly fast enough—she would cause as much harm as she could.

She threw back her hand holding the dagger and stabbed it forward, finding its mark between two of the tough scales and cutting into the meat at the base of Malcolm's neck. Blood leaked and scalded what it touched. It burned Ailith's sleeve and ran over her right hand that sported scars from Caitriona's flames. The nerves were nearly dead in that hand and she didn't feel pain in the usual sense, but she smelt her burnt flesh and knew it was worse than she could feel. She had to get away before his blood burned her more.

There wasn't much choice in the matter; the dagger cut further down and broke off a scale that flew toward the earth. But without the scale holding the dagger back, it slid against the meat of Malcolm and slipped, and with it came Ailith, tumbling backward to dangle briefly, her legs swinging in the air as she clung to the handle of her knife before it pulled free from the meat of his neck. Caitriona was a blur of gold as Ailith turned end over end and the earth came rushing upward toward her. She couldn't help it; her bravery had run out.

Ailith screamed.

Caitriona's teeth caught hold of Ailith's shirt, nearly missing her entirely. It was a split second, long enough to cut the speed of her fall with the earth not far now before the fabric ripped from the thrust of Ailith's movement and Ailith fell again. Caitriona roared in the air as it mingled with her human scream in Ailith's mind. Wind pumped from Caitriona's wings, lashing Ailith as she pivoted to catch her.

Don't let Caitriona's cries be the last thing I hear, Ailith thought. *I don't want to die; I don't want to—*

The marsh waters grew wide and Ailith fought the wind to right herself; Barden's sword broke free, tumbling to the ground away from her while the waters below rushed upward. Crossing her legs, folding her arms over her chest, Ailith straightened her body as much as possible before she hit the water.

Her body shot to the bottom of the marsh. The rush of cold water pressed around her and the impact pulled air from her throat. She was disoriented; her body stung and her ribs throbbed. Her feet hit the bottom of the marshy waterbed and sunk deep in the muck, bringing her body to complete stillness for the first time since she and Caitriona left the mountains. She moved her arms out and pulled at her boots, relinquishing them from the hold of the silty floor. Nothing seemed broken from what she could tell. She was able to move and she was alive. Pushing off, she forced herself upward. Above, through the murky water, was a brilliance of flame rippled through the watery surface and she swam up and up, toward the fire, as if it were a beacon to home.

CHAPTER THIRTY-TWO

"It's a curse on the land," Isla hissed, slamming the book she read closed and hitting it with her fist. Stormhaven sent copies of magic books just after the declaration of war and Isla dragged them to the battlefield, insisting they could come in handy. She was right—they did. They spent most of the morning reading through the books, hoping to find answers for what was occurring with the dukes, and it seemed they found what they sought, but there was little information to help fix the issue. "Malcolm placed a curse on the marsh. It's forcing the dukes to remain in the water. Even if they want to fight, they can't break free. They're trapped there."

"Do you think there's more to the curse than that?" Róisín asked, abandoning her book to join Isla by her side. She flipped over the cover and turned its pages, attempting to find the spot Isla had read. "You can't stop a curse, can you? It has to run its course."

"Yes, unless the person making the curse is willing to stop it or ..." Isla frowned and sat back in her seat, staring at the pages of the paper as if they offended her.

"What?" Róisín waited. Letting out a huff of air, she gripped the edge of the table and leaned closer to the old woman. "Isla, when Caitriona succumbed to the curse, there was no way we could've stopped it. Everything I've learned, it all says it had to run its course. Was that incorrect? Could I have saved Caitriona from that experience?"

Isla rubbed her brow and shook her head. "Regarding Caitriona, no, we couldn't stop her curse. A curse applied to one or two people has more consistent rules. But something this large? A curse knit into the earth? This type of curse can be broken, there's a way, but it involves a great deal of power as well as sacrifice."

Róisín turned to the entrance of the medic tent. The battle had gone on for hours and finally came to a pause. People were returning, injured or otherwise, but Greer was still in the field. By the state of those returning, it seemed they already lost a fair number of people and would likely lose more if there was another wave of fighting. "Without the aid of the dukes, Greer will lose."

"She will." Isla pushed herself onto her feet. She wrung her hands together, looking at the provisions on the tables. "I have to return to our tent and gather my resources. We *can* end the curse on the dukes; it never does well to stop an entire fleet of creatures from doing what they're created for. Wait here."

She shuffled away, leaving Róisín overlooking the field. A figure weaved their way through the watered land and Róisín breathed a sigh of relief. Her blond hair and the sheen of her armor paired with the points on her shoulder plates made Greer easy to spot. Her daughter was alive. Well, the eldest was. Róisín still wasn't sure what was occurring with Caitriona and considered the starbright flowers she had in her belongings.

"No news is good news," she repeated Greer's words from

earlier and secured them to her heart. "Now to figure out what sacrifice is needed."

I suspect the old witch is going to sacrifice herself. Kayl roused from within her. He had been quiet as of late as his strength waned.

"Herself?" Róisín asked, turning back to the tent. Those injured were drugged to sleep and the medics had gone to wait along the edge of the marsh to tend to more wounded as they came in. Róisín was as alone as she'd get beside Kayl's internal company. She stepped to the table and returned her attention to the book Isla left behind. Taking Isla's seat, she turned its pages. "A sacrifice of a soul or one of magic?"

With this type of magic, it could be either, it could be both. Giving up a life or an abundance of power to break through the curse on the land are both mighty things. She already said it would take a great deal of magic and a sacrifice, so my assumption is it requires both. Magic and life. Land curses that affect both the soil and its creatures often align with sacrifices tied to nature itself.

"This is different from curses placed on living creatures?"

The curse I placed on Caitriona played out entirely; therefore, it ended. Cearny had a dragon in his home and was killed by his daughter. I hadn't specified which child was to do this, but the curse took to Caitriona due to my magical proximity to her. Since Greer performed the final part of the curse, it ended, returning Caitriona to her human form. That curse had to play out or the curse would return to the bearer. But for land … it isn't a substance you interact with like a living soul. There are different rules.

"Hmm …" Róisín ran her fingers down a page as she reread the information. Turning the onion skin sheet, she took in the details on the back. "It says if an Elder Tree is near, it has the power to break a curse. The tree's a blessing on the land, but not necessarily the people. I wonder, if the Elder

Trees' roots go throughout Visennore, perhaps they reach through the swamp as well?"

But its roots are dying. The life's ebbing from the tree in the valley and traveling to others in the land. It's drifting away rather than constantly circulating as it once did. You'd likely need an Elder Tree to physically be here. A tree itself, growing from the swamp.

Róisín leaned back, a flicker of memory capturing her attention like the flash of light on water, and it became something far more formed than it had been in years. "If a tree was here, it would bless the land, correct? It'll unlock the dukes?"

Perhaps... Róisín, what are you getting at?

"When the girls were little, I told them a story about the Elder Tree. It was a story I barely remembered, one my mother used to tell me, and I had to fill in the spots but, well ...""

Kayl was silent as Róisín looked over the table of books for a scrap of paper. She had a jolt of energy that was missing before, a thrill in her body that sent her moving with haste. "It was Greer's favorite story when she was younger and Caitriona was forced to listen to it over and over. In it, the Elder Tree was quite small, nothing miraculous, when it first rooted itself to the land."

She found a piece of paper and smiled. Searching for a quill and ink, she turned over books and dumped bags of supplies. It was something not readily available in a tent filled with wounded individuals. The map tent, she'd find what she needed there. As she walked toward it, she continued telling Kayl the story.

"The tree was lonesome and wanted more from the world, more with life. For years it sat by itself, but now there was more it could do. It wanted to see other things *grow* and so it worked with all its might to birth creatures. From its roots came the darkness of the world; all the dangerous things. From its branches dropped the brightness and the good. Together they mingled, the good and bad blending to become a mixture of both. Not all humans are good, not all magical creatures are bad, and while the Elder Tree did not seek to create such opposing opinions, which in turn birthed chaos into the world, it was no longer lonely."

A roar drew her attention skyward. A black dragon flew towards them; beyond it was a glimmering form, small and growing in size quickly.

Caitriona.

She grinned and moved quickly despite that her mind swirled, running to the tent with maps and her piece of paper clutched in her hand. "The tree was able to witness the world grow. It saw what it birthed thrive. And when its creatures were broken and weeping, it lent what power it had to bring its creatures happiness and peace."

She entered the tent and paused before the abandoned mess of maps and darted forward to snatch a quill from a table. "I thought of the story when Barden died—when we learned the sap can bring death but also life. It reminded me of myself. I birthed my daughters and I'm abundantly glad to see them grow, but I've killed in order to try and dampen the hatred around me. First Donal, and then multiple failed attempts on Cearny. Perhaps that's in part why the sap can do both. The Elder Tree said enough to all the fighting."

Róisín what are you getting at?

She didn't answer, focusing on the scrap of paper as she quickly wrote a message.

Oh, Róisín, no, Kayl replied, reading the letter through her eyes.

She stepped back from the paper, watching the gloss of the wet ink slowly fade as it dried. A letter to her daughters, should they survive; it was the least she could do.

"Kayl, I won't have you argue with me about this. We

both are to blame. You made the curse, I had the arrogance, and now we must fix it. Let me end the chaos."

Róisín ...

She left the map tent and looked over the landscape once more. Caitriona was closer now, her golden wings a brightness against the gray skies, and Greer was further along in the marsh. But forms appeared over the landscape, winking into existence or coming from the skies, and floating down on wings. The next phase of battle was upon them.

They needed the dukes. Greer and Caitriona both.

"It has to be done, Kayl."

He was silent in response.

Róisín glanced over her shoulder at the hills of Braewick Valley's ridge, savoring the sight of it before moving down the hillside and toward the swamp edge. Each step brought her closer to her children. She closed her eyes briefly, thinking over all that she wanted to do in life. She was settled. Happy. At the very least, she saw her daughters survive Cearny. She also found even ground between herself and Kayl. There were other things, but they were smaller. Only one regret moistened her brow.

She'd never swim the eastern sea, but she would taste the water.

"Róisín?" Isla called.

She paused, turning to the old crow woman who looked down the slow at her from the entrance of the medic tent.

Róisín smiled. "Isla."

Róisín, don't ...

Isla brows rose briefly before she shook her head. Her shoulders slumped. "You've figured it out, haven't you?"

"I'm going to step away from the tents. Over there, I think. By that one pool of water with the slope of the rising land beyond it. It seems like a restful spot, doesn't it?"

Isla's grip on the papers and vials in her arms lessened. "Róisín, you don't have to do this."

"I have to save my girls," she replied and returned her attention to the marsh. Caitriona's powerful wings pushed her higher into the sky, her gold scales glorious and her crown of horns a danger. She was beautiful, so beautiful. "Let me make this choice so my daughters have a fighting chance."

The papers Isla held fell softly, a hush to kiss the tall grasses that were half-pressed by so many footsteps in the last day, and the shatter of glass as the vials burst on impact. With her hands now empty, Isla reached for Róisín.

Swallowing her tears, Róisín held Isla's hand tightly as they turned back to the marsh and moved together toward the opening.

This would be as good a place as any. A soft place like laying in tall grasses in the summer with your dearest friend. A quiet place like autumn nights with little ones sleeping nearby. A peaceful place a few yards from the roadway to the Umberfend Post, in sight of the hills of the valleys and with the mountains far in the distance. Close to all she loved, but not too close. The marsh waters were within reach to touch, to drink. Yes, it was a good place to take root.

At the water's edge, Róisín embraced Isla, squeezing her tight and savoring the rich scents of herbs that always followed the witch around. She kissed her cheek and stepped back, holding Isla outward at arm's length. "Thank you for all you've done in my life and theirs."

Isla nodded, her eyes glistening. She gripped Róisín's hand. "Let me guide you one final time. Look *within* yourself. It's in a different place for all, located where their love rests. For some it's their chest, others it's their mind. Look at what you're giving. And with the well of energy in the depths of your soul, in that place you locate, seek the roots threading through the earth. Their power will bleed into yours and guide you forward to destroying this curse."

Róisín nodded and stepped back. She turned toward the swamp where Greer was on the ground, struggling to get to her feet as a looming darkness stood before her. Caitriona was in the skies, being swept aside by the black dragon.

Oh, they could die, they could die right then and there. But she was their mother, and like many before her, she was willing to give her life in exchange for theirs.

It was there at the base of her gut like Isla said. There where each of her babies had grown. Greer who moved constantly in the womb and burst forth into the world screaming far too early and eager to get on with living. Caitriona who stayed the longest and needed to be coaxed out by the breaking of Róisín's waters, who entered the world silently with wide eyes until a nursemaid forced her to cry. It was in that place where life grew that Róisín's power rose. But she was more than someone to birth children. She was a queen, a baker, a trickster, a daughter, an orphan. The power was through her. It was in her hands, in her mind, in her eyes. She was sarcastic, stubborn, cunning and calculated. And she was loved. She also loved; she loved with such intensity that this was the only answer.

But it will kill us, Kayl whispered, the last remnants of his form curling around Róisín's soul like a vine; twisting throughout, penetrating her essence so it could hold onto what life it still had.

Róisín continued studying the marsh where her daughter who was at one time cursed—now bigger than life and more dangerous than she could ever imagine—tumbled through the sky towards the ground before trying to adjust herself. She witnessed Greer—her strong-headed queen that would rule well and true if given the chance—fall backwards and sink in the water as she fought to regain her footing.

Róisín *loved*. She loved them *so greatly*.

"You don't know me as well as I thought you did, Kayl, if you'd ever think I'd save my life or yours over theirs. They love me, and I love them."

To Róisín's surprise, Kayl laughed. *How stupid of me to think all these years that you were different than the girl I grew up with. You know, I loved you too.*

"And I you, Kayl," Róisín said out loud, drawing Isla's attention. Róisín's green eyes glanced down at the old woman and she smiled softly. "Tell my girls I love them, will you?"

"Róisín ..." Isla sighed, reaching forward to grasp Róisín's hand again. "Are you certain?"

"It has to be this way. Let me do this one final thing. Let me prove that I've *always* been on their side."

"You don't need to prove—"

"*Maeve.*"

Isla's lips stilled. It had been so long since Róisín called the old witch by her former name.

"I'll tell them."

"Good." Something relaxed within Róisín despite the chaos around her and the distant call of war horns unfamiliar to her. Another fleet? More warriors? It didn't matter. She had to stop this slow death upon the land, and their impending demise.

She closed her eyes and whispered in her mind: *Not for long, sweet larks. Not for long.*

She pulled at her core, at the life-creating magic, at the death awaiting her, and she pushed outward. Through her hands, her feet, her hair. Through her body and into the world, to twist into the air and seek the coolness of the earth. Down and down it spread, rooting itself to the ground, seeking the refreshment of the marsh's waters, spreading until it took what energy the dying Elder Tree was willing to give. Her body shuddered and pain made her moan. It wasn't enough power to make the change and Róisín bent, gasping as her lungs filled with sap and her veins with splinters.

Her skin pricked; energy turned her blood to fire. Kayl sighed; his last bits of energy encapsulated her. *I'll give you what I can, that final explosion of it all for your girls, and for you.*

"Thank you," she whispered, her tears hot on her face. She forced herself to stand upright despite that her movements were rigid as she grew solid; she held her chin high, and her eyes opened on the beautiful, wild, chaotic world before her.

I'm sorry I didn't help before. But I will now.

His power filled Róisín and entwined with hers. With a final breath, her mind on her daughters, Róisín Gablaigh grew. Years ago, she told Kayl that she would become a great something, and she was right. Her arms spread as her love and heartbreak mingled together to create a canopy over bloodshed.

This was the sacrifice needed for the marsh: that she would be tethered to the ground for eternity. The heartbreak to lose, to not be present for her loved ones, and yet to always witness them, to always be near, unable to interact, unable to embrace, a presence that could not touch while watching them and the generations that sprung from their love. She would be a silent viewer and grateful because even with all that was lost, she could still lend her energy to love.

Within the marsh there is love.
Tucked deep and hidden for safety, it is a creature of its own,
fed in private to keep it alive, but nearly starved from years of denial.
It caused the world to quake and fire to rain down,
it caused loss of the corporeal and free thought;
it caused death and it caused life.
Love guides loss and therefore, creation, immortality, and chance.
Thrust into the world or flesh, with splinters through eyes and roots
spread through veins,
love expands, it reaches to the light,
it brings shadow, it creates bitter endings when held back.
It exposes all that is hidden.

The marsh opens. The spell is broken. The dukes rise.
At last, at last, they march to battle.

CHAPTER THIRTY-THREE

GREER

S had's sword swung forward and crashed with Greer's shoulder armor. The pauldron vibrated hard, creating a ringing pain as it shook through to her core. The weight of the collision made her stance crumble; she stumbled back and felt her boot chill with water as she stepped into the marsh water. Fire filled the sky and turned the world red, setting a demonic background to Shad as he stepped forward and grinned.

Yet her attention slipped past him, her eyes broadened as she saw the gold of Caitriona fighting as hard as anyone, her wings pumping as she dove toward the black dragon and attempted to brush it off target. The sound of battle overwhelmed the fight in the air, the clash of swords against shields constant amidst the cries of pain and success.

Greer was too aware of her surroundings, too focused on her forces under the pressure of the opposing party. Because it wasn't just her forces—it was her *people* fighting, it was her family, and those who followed her guidance and strove toward what she declared good. All fighting and dying, all because of her word.

Shad saw her distraction and drove her back, further and further into the marsh waters where her feet slipped along the muddy shores and slippery rocks. She pushed upward, her breath coming fast and heavy as she gritted her teeth and glared at the man. Swinging outward, their blades kissed and she allowed herself a growl of frustration. Their fighting was dragging out; he was too large, too strong and powerful, and all around her there was death. More and more death as her people fell.

This is the end, isn't it? She took in the landscape and felt the cool waters soaking through the leather of her boots. There was a sound on the wind, buried underneath roars of dragons and crackle of flame, tucked aside by the wails of injured and the splash of corpses falling into the ponds of the marsh; something shifted. A sound that grew in volume.

Shad glanced towards the north and blinked, his footfall going backwards as he hesitated. Greer scrambled to her feet and darted her sword to find his flesh along the side of his armor, and through the thinner placard covering his side.

He snarled, stumbling backward and away from her blade, and the pause in fighting was enough for Greer to hear the oncoming sound with clarity.

Cries, cheers, and battle horns carried over the field as new soldiers ran forward from the baseline of the marsh. With distance between herself and Shad, Greer looked and let out a wild laugh.

"All that work to get the Mazgate Dominion to join you," Greer taunted, turning back to Shad and pointing at the crowd of men and women flooding the field with her northern neighbor's banners. "And here they joined us to fight against you!"

Greer sent one last desperate letter to the Mazgate Dominion and Avorkaz City before leaving for the marsh. She shed her professionalism and begged for their help, apologized for all the harm her kingdom brought to theirs—sometimes under her own hand, and made an abundance of promises to help aid the dominion in rebuilding Greenbriar and all the damage Wimleigh brought to the land. All they had to do was give Wimleigh aid.

They were doing just that. Greer had fought some of their very guards when her father set sights on Avorkaz, but now they stood beside Wimleigh banners and struck down the creatures of Malcolm's forces. The marshland flooded with warriors with their different colors and banners. A mixture of nonmagics and magics alike came forward to help her very own people. Greer could have wept if it wasn't for what was at hand.

Shad's lip curled with disgust and he raised his sword, running forward with speed and the rush of the shadow-work he exhibited weeks before. Greer braced her feet for his strike but it was still too strong, making her totter on her feet and fall back. Again and again, after he knocked her to her knees, she rose and continued fighting with all her heart. For every strike, every cut, there was little celebration that could remain. Malcolm's men fought those of Wimleigh and Mazgate, but a circle formed where all guards seemed to know this battle was just for the two and it would be to the death. All but Lachlan, who Greer saw amongst the crowd, attempted to push forward to aid Greer. This was his fight too, after all.

Her blade kissed Shad's skin more than once but the shadows always slipped from him to knit the wound closed, healing him quicker than any tonic she could have provided.

Swinging outward, his sword knocked against Greer's chest, sending another vibrating shock through her body as the armor shook. Her chest ached and she felt nauseated as exhaustion gained the upper hand and her balance remained unstable. People rarely spoke of how tiring battle was, but her body throbbed with strain, her muscles screamed, and she wasn't sure how much longer she could keep up with one-on-one combat without a break.

"Just accept your fate, queen," Shad taunted, lifting his foot to kick Greer. She tried to move out of the way and shift her sword upward, but her lack of sleep and the exhaustion of battle slowed her moves. His foot connected with ease, sending her into a nearby pool of water.

Her hands reached out but the momentum was too much and her body splashed into the murky water. She dropped, the weight of her armor pulling her down, and the water overtook her. Light from dragon fire and the gray clouds dimmed. She pushed upward toward the surface but was frozen. Despite her kicking and attempts to push ever upward, she was trapped, as if the very weight of the air forced her to remain under water. Her hands greeted what should have been the breaking of the surface and it was a wall. Pounding against it, the pressure of the world pushed her back.

The light dimmed as air burned in her chest, its time spent and her lungs desperate to expand, but she had to hold on and hold back until she could reach the surface.

I won't die in this war from drowning. I won't abandon my men and women because I fell into a puddle. She was stubborn like her mother and she refused to let this be it.

Lachlan, help me. He was the only one making his way toward her; surely he had the magic to break this invisible force. She remembered what he said—that he would hear her no matter where he was—she only had to call.

"Lachlan!" she yelled into the water, his name floating to the surface through large bubbles but not popping.

Greer's fists collided with the edge of the water, still not breaking through the surface despite her best efforts. Her surroundings grew dark—no, not her surroundings, it was her vision fading. Then the pool quaked.

There was a shift, a quiver of movement as if giants shook

the pool itself. A pressure passed, a roll of thunder crawling over land and vibrating the water, and Greer was thrusted upward. Her hands broke the surface as water filled her nostrils. She faltered, her body dipping beneath the assault of the marsh again.

Hands reached from the dim and murky water, and ran along her armor. They felt her brow, touched her hair, and passed over her lips. It was dark, she couldn't see who it was and she wanted to fight—an instinctual reaction to rear back from the phantom hands—but they were kind and gentle. They were curious and loving. They lifted her and guided her to the water's surface. Greer gasped as her face broke through and the dizziness overtaking her receded. She coughed and breathed the cool air. Free from the clutch of the water, she pushed forward.

"Still not dead?" Shad taunted from the banks. "Still not drowned?"

"What did I say?" Greer spit up water as she sat upright and her knees sunk in the muck. "Poor performance."

Her breath came as wet wheezes while her vision sparked. Despite remaining on her knees, she couldn't help but smile viciously. "You're relying on water to do your job. You can't even kill me yourself."

Shad's eyes narrowed. He shifted the edge of his sword slowly and positioned it against Greer's neck. She could attempt to strike, but her sword was gone, lost to the reeds. Pressing her lips together and raising her eyes she met Shad's. *So, this is it. Decapitation in the marsh.*

Perhaps the helping hands in the water would catch her and bring her down to her final resting place. She would finally be near Barden, wherever he was, and sleep.

The skies were empty of creatures and the dark clouds parted to expose blue that dimmed with a hue of gray— evening was drawing near.

"Goodbye, queen. It's been fun," Shad whispered, lifting his sword to prepare for the swing.

Lachlan yelled her name; he heard her after all. He ran through the marsh and flicked out of sight as he became a golden eagle, flying faster than his feet could carry; he still wouldn't reach her in time. She was alone in this and she wouldn't allow herself to show fear. She swallowed and raised her chin, keeping her eyes on Shad's and refusing to look away in her final moments. She wouldn't give him the satisfaction of any emotion beyond cocky bravery.

But he froze, a choke crawling up his throat and out his lips as his eyes grew wide.

His arms dropped. The sword splashed into the muddy edge of the water. His head lolled downward, losing strength as he looked at his chest, and Greer followed his gaze to a blade sticking through its center. It slowly eased back, slipping out with a slick, wet sound, before Shad dropped to his knees and face planted into the mud.

Greer stared, her jaw working as her eyes filled with tears. He was everything she hoped for, but still not enough. He never would be because he wasn't alive, but she didn't care because he finally found her. Barden, *her* Barden, risen from the marsh at last.

He stood on solid land in the armor she chose for his funeral. His sword that she placed upon his dead body was clutched in his hand and coated in Shad's blood. His pale skin was covered in algae and duckweed, and his eyes lost their vibrant blue and were diluted with a filament that blinked over them. Along his throat were gills, pressed flat as he stared at Greer. Their gazes met and Greer's heart lurched back to life, as if thawing after a winter's freeze.

"... Barden?" Her voice was bedroom soft from withheld emotions finding their way to the surface after the passing weeks since his death.

The membrane over his eyes flicked, the pupils focusing on her, but he didn't speak. He stared with an inquisitive expression; head tilting to the side as his gills expanded then closed. Greer fought the urge to throw herself at him; she wanted to, desperately. She wanted to hold him, embrace him, love him, but she remained on her knees in the water with Shad's body between them.

"Barden," she repeated. "*My love.*"

He blinked, the filament crossing over his eyes from side to side again, and something was made up in his mind. His head straightened and he stepped around Shad's body. His feet were sturdy on the soft earth and unbothered by the slippery mud as he held his hand to her.

"Greer!" Lachlan's voice came, this time closer and returned to his human form. He pushed his way through the fighting bodies but Greer didn't turn toward the fae king.

She reached forward, not moving her eyes from Barden, and accepted his offer. His hand was cold and slimy, as if she could easily lose her grasp from it, but he clutched her hand, strong in its hold, and it was still his own. The shape of it was ingrained in her mind, the lack of it for weeks painful, but this ignited her. Tightening her grip in his, he pulled her to her feet. He let go of her hand and she let hers drop to his chest. They stood whisper close, inspecting one another as she breathed, but his chest remained still while he continued to silently study her. His hand lifted and his fingertips hovered over her cheek.

"*My love,*" she whispered again. Her hand traveled along his chest to his arm, feeling the solidness of him under her fingers as if he were alive, but the cold chill of his skin persisted and there was no rhythm of heartbeat beneath, no breath of air from his lungs. Still, she begged him to remember her, to come back to her. They were the last words he spoke in his mortal life, surely they were enough to trigger some memory. "Please ..."

Footsteps sounded and over Barden's shoulder Lachlan came into sight. He was bloodied and wet, his sword coated in grime, but he didn't draw near. He knew they needed their space and Greer silently thanked him.

Flicking her attention back to Barden she smiled at the knowledge in his eyes while he studied her. She could see his understanding; she swore it. His gaze moved over her face, traveling to her lips and back to her eyes. His eyes dilated, blue-tinged lips parting and his teeth were all sharp, deadly things. She'd still kiss him; she didn't care.

The tips of his fingers brushed over her cheek and she held her breath, certain he would speak, but he only blinked. His hand slipped into hers as he stepped back, pulling her with him to move out of the water.

He let go and turned away. His movements paused as he took in Lachlan who still had feathers receding into his hair and an avian look to him. Barden's body stilled in an unnatural way, a predator spotting prey. Greer watched, as if witnessing a still pond and determining what lay beneath the water.

"It's nice to meet you," Lachlan stated, standing straighter and giving a bow of his head. "We've been waiting for you."

Barden swung his sword in a circular motion, a fanciful, playful movement he did while alive, and gripped the handle again as he stepped onto firmer ground.

Greer and Lachlan followed his attention to the marsh where men stood upright along the shores, one by one with weed-thick swords and algae covered shields. They stood still despite the chaos around them, their membrane-covered eyes on Greer alone, and she could no longer hold back her tears. They were waiting for her command, all of them.

The dukes had finally risen for war.

CHAPTER THIRTY-FOUR

A shudder coursed over the landscape. The waters of the marsh rippled, and faces appeared, leading to the solid bodies of dukes climbing from pool beds to join the living once more. Ailith was thrust from the surface of the marsh and deposited on the shore by dukes she did not recognize. They stood amongst her, looking toward a specific spot, and Ailith could just make out the blonde head of Greer through the throng of bodies. There were others near her, but they weren't clearly visible from where she stood. Close and protective. Good.

But more was happening beside the dukes rising to fight; the creatures Malcolm made bent at their waists; their arms, talons, wings, and claws clutched at their sides before their forms split, and the transformations reversed.

Ailith rose, her body quivering from cold. Caitriona's pack was soaked and heavy on her back, leaving a waterfall as it drained of the marsh water. Her sword was in the cattails sticking from the mud, the metal reflecting in the dull light and encouraging her to draw near. She stumbled forward past dukes that were moving further onto the land and lifting their blades to fight. Her sword had survived the fall, but her dagger was gone, at least she had something to use for protection. She stared at the moving forces and wrapped her arm around her chest; her ribs throbbed with each breath she took.

The dukes' bodies were similar to how Barden appeared in Ailith's dream. Creatures made of bog water, duckweed, and covered with the red berries that grew near the water's edge and clung to their clothes. Their eyes bore no recognition to their earthly domain, but alighted with the presence of battle. A cry rose from Greer's guards, a revival of energy that pushed them forward. Ailith turned on her heel, taking in the sight of the marshland filling with dukes and familiar guards alike. Paul and Coleene were nearby, their swords glinting as they fought. City guards who she once worked with at the gates were there as well.

The sight of Greer was lost to the mixture of fighting bodies when a scream pulled Ailith's attention back to the skies. Her nerves ignited to fire and shook her revelry away.

Overhead was the twisting fight of dragon against dragon. The darkness of the black dragon overtook the brightness of gold. Malcolm's large mouth clasped over Caitriona's shoulder and blood exploded into the sky like fireworks. The droplets fell to the ground, catching fire to what they hit as Malcolm let go with a laugh fresh in his serpentine throat. Ailith's chest tightened; pressure built and the ground shuddered. It was like when the dragon attacked the city when she was a child; her fear was so great and entwined with the creature's presence to make her body twist with sickness. Her ears popped and Malcolm grew rigid in the air, his body twitched and locked, still and floating, before he began tumbling, plummeting toward the ground.

His massive form shrunk in size as his fall sped up, turning him to a dark star coming down to the earth where he crashed ahead of Ailith with a plume of water from the pond he fell into.

Caitriona was a flash of gold; her wings attempting to straighten and keep herself aloft but failing. Her head lolled and her body went limp in the air as she lost consciousness. She fell, her draconic form not lessening as she rushed toward the earth and Ailith was able to move again.

No, no, no.

Ailith splashed through pools, pushing toward the golden dragon as her ribs screamed with pain. Past where Malcolm fell, Caitriona's large draconic body hit the earth with a crushing sound and mud flung upward. Ailith's hand still clutched her sword as she raised it upward, ready to strike anyone who got in her way.

"Ailith!"

Amongst the fallen bodies and pools of waters, fighting dukes and fae alike, a strawberry haired man ran toward her. The sight made Ailith stumble to a stop, her chest burning from her rushed breaths and pounding heart. She was dizzy, the potions she took earlier that day had worn off and she was still weak and overstimulated by everything. She bent over and attempted to catch her breath. "Lachlan?"

"How did you get back?"

Ailith stared at the blood splashed over his body and cuts to his arms and face. He was in the midst of the fight; he had truly joined them and Ailith hadn't known. He stood before her in armor that was not his with a confidence Ailith had not seen of him. He looked like a king.

"Caitriona!" Ailith pointed in the direction of the dragon in the marsh before resting upon her knee. Her skin stung on her arm as blisters formed along where Caitriona's fire from years before hadn't already scarred her—specks like tear drops made from droplets of Malcolm's draconic blood. "I need to go to her. She's hurt."

Lachlan looked forward, his gaze trailing over the landscape. He licked his lips, his expression turning somber. Someone cried nearby, a wretched sound of pain and anger, and Lachlan's eyes darkened as he looked toward the sound. "Malcolm."

"He's the black dragon," Ailith pointed out, a ripple of embarrassment immediately passing over her as it did when she spoke too quickly and without thinking. Of course, he was the damned dragon; it seemed so obvious.

Lachlan didn't respond. He ran toward Malcolm and Caitriona. His long legs carried him over the marsh water where he jumped over creeks between pools and rocks that jutted from the tall grassy surface. Ailith followed him with much less grace. "Lachlan, where's your sword?"

"A fae took it when I stabbed him."

They crossed the marsh, growing closer to Caitriona as they passed creatures shedding themselves to reveal the fae they were behind the curse. Ailith spotted fae she had tried to free and others from the outcrop with her and Fiana.

"Ailith!"

She looked wildly and found Vanora a few feet away, crying with relief, yet naked in knee-deep marsh water. The feathers of her cockatrice form floated on top of the pool.

"Vanora!"

"I've got her—" Another familiar voice. Coleene, a guard Ailith knew from the castle guard, ran forward as she unclipped the cloak from her armor. "Happy to see you aren't attacking us."

Ailith slowed, confused. "I—yes. Me too."

Coleene offered Vanora her hand and pulled the woman from the marsh before wrapping her in the cloak. Other fae climbed unsteadily to their feet as they were freed from the curse. For all the power Malcolm consumed, it wasn't enough to keep his army of creatures in permanent entrapment. His power was as temporary as any man's.

Ailith left Coleene and Vanora. Looking over the marsh, she continued forward but couldn't spot Fiana. Hopefully the hunter made it off the mountain and was returning to her human form as well.

Ahead, Lachlan slowed as he approached a naked man standing on shaking feet. His hair was faded, his skin pale and gray-like, as if he were part dead. He was a shadow of himself, his body falling into the possession of the sickness that overcame magic users too selfish in their quests; those who fell into the avaricious embrace of becoming unbound. His shoulder was the only bright spot as blood ran from the injuries both Ailith and Caitriona left; muck from the marsh coated his chest and legs.

He was terrifying in the castle. Large and threatening and with so much power. But now Ailith was reminded of what he always was, even beneath the show of power: weak.

Ailith caught up to Lachlan who looked uncertain as he observed the naked man before him.

"That's Malcolm," Ailith explained. Malcolm turned on his feet and took in the surrounding. "That's the man who killed your mother. Lachlan, he's the one who took the throne that belongs to you."

Lachlan didn't move. All this way Malcolm flew with the power of a dragon, but changing into such a form for the first time was exhausting, and turning back to a human, as well as falling from such a great height was enough to kill a person. Caitriona had slept for weeks after she returned to herself, but that was the result of a curse. For Malcolm, becoming a dragon was his choice.

"We met briefly, you and I. We know each other little. But you need to take this blade. You have to take the throne. This is one way to guarantee no one will claim the throne over you.

I know it's hard but ..." Her voice drifted off. There was never a justified reason to kill someone, not really, and it wasn't what the fae of Invarlwen were taught to do. Not until Malcolm rose in rank.

Other guards drew close, Paul to the left, Coleene helping Vanora to the right, and so many more that Ailith recognized as friends. They called outward, urging Lachlan forward, with accents Ailith recognized. They were enough to witness it all.

Lachlan held out his hand, his eyes not moving from Malcolm, and Ailith offered her sword handle first. Lachlan lifted the blade.

"Malcolm." His voice was steady and drew the fae king's attention upward. The old man's eyes narrowed.

"You look just like her," Malcolm growled. "Do you have her magic? Will you kill me with it?"

"You'd like that, wouldn't you?" Lachlan's voice was hushed. He wasn't putting on a speech for those around him. This was personal and private. "So empty of it you stole from others. I wouldn't give you the pleasure of tasting magic as the last feeling in your life."

Ailith stepped back and Malcolm flailed—unable to even face his own death bravely. When Lachlan swung her sword, she didn't flinch, nor did she turn when Malcolm's head rolled to rest at her feet.

Shouts erupted from the guards. The rush of footfall over mud and through shallow water became applause. The summer had been wasted worrying over this man who could not accept his faults. Over this man who stole his place as king; all for it to be finished with the precise swing of the blade directed to a man sniveling for forgiveness. The battle was done. Malcolm lost and Lachlan would be king.

"Go," Lachlan sighed, turning to Ailith and holding out her sword.

Ailith wiped it clean on her still-dripping pants. She

secured it to her side and pushed past the encroaching guards until she was in the rapidly emptying fields as the group surrounding Lachlan grew dense. Her eyes passed over the field to the mass of the dragon that lay in the mud. It still hadn't moved, still hadn't returned to Caitriona's form, and Ailith's heart rose into her throat and lodged itself there. How could no one go to the golden dragon? How could she be left alone in the marsh?

"Cait!"

Ailith ran. She rushed through the crowd, tripping over roots and avoiding pools, and pushed herself despite her wounded ribs and weakened state. She ran as fast as she could to the girl who had traveled all that way to save her.

The dragon was motionless as blood leaked from her tail and shoulder. Her chest didn't move and her eyes were partly closed. "Cait?"

Ailith slipped in the mud, falling beside Caitriona's draconic face. The heat of the blood from her shoulder rose off her body, setting fire to the grass and steaming the water. The bite was deep and the red flesh of muscle and white bone shown through, but it was just a shoulder wound. Not enough to leave her so still.

"Cait, wake up. This isn't enough to kill you." Ailith clasped the dragon's face. The sliver of her golden eyes were waxy, dim, and faded. Ailith looked Caitriona over, her chest filled with pressure again, like she was swelling up to burst. Caitriona's head lay in the grass in a twisted, unnatural way for a dragon, despite their long, flexible necks. There was a bulge beneath the scales, a place where it seemed something wasn't sitting correctly. Ailith took in a shaking breath and returned her attention to the dragon's face, slapping the cheek to attempt to get a reaction.

"Nothing," Ailith whispered, the swelling in her chest

reached a crescendo as hot tears pushed from her eyes. "*Nothing.*"

"Ailith!" The scream shook Ailith from her panic. Over the tall grasses, Greer ran toward them. Blood and muck covered her face, her hair half held back in her bun. "What's wrong? Why isn't Cait turning back?"

"She's hurt," Ailith cried. The words ripped from her chest and the pressure was released in sobs, completing its process to undo her. Her legs felt weak and she allowed herself to sink to the muddy grass beside Caitriona's head. There was something wrong about her stillness, and the empty, dull coloring of her eyes wasn't right. "Look at her neck. She's not —she's not waking, Greer. She's not waking up."

Greer dropped beside Ailith and ran her gloved hands over the golden scales before pushing back Caitriona's eyelids to expose her unseeing eyes. "Cait, Cait, wake up, dammit. I demand you to wake up, *now.*"

Ailith crawled backward, looking over the dragon, and pushed onto her feet. She stumbled toward Caitriona's chest. Two years ago, Ailith overcame her terror to press her ear against the golden dragon's chest, embracing her as she tried to make the recently-turned dragon remember that she was human. Now she did it again as she prayed out loud that she would hear the rhythmic thumping of Caitriona's heart in return. This time only silence greeted her. "I don't hear anything. I don't hear her heart."

The panic welled in Ailith and her vision spun down to pinpricks. Her breathing was uneven, her heart thudded in her head, and her fingers tingled with terror. She fell back from Caitriona and looked to Greer for guidance. "What do we do, Greer?"

Greer's lips parted with horror. The queen shook her head, her hand darting forward as she slapped the dragon hard, jolting Caitriona's face despite its hefty size. "*No.* You hear me? No! I lost Barden; I'm not losing you too, dammit!"

"Lost Barden?" Ailith repeated, staring at Greer who shook Caitriona. The queen paused and gave Ailith a quick glance filled with a million heartaches that weren't vocalized. *You've missed so much,* Caitriona said at the castle with the saddest expression. Ailith looked around. They were alone when usually Barden would be there. Greer's very shadow never followed her as studiously as Barden did. "No ..."

"I can't lose her too," Greer wept, pressing her face to Caitriona's.

Ailith turned, the world kept shaking and she realized she was near fainting. The lack of food, the terror, the fighting, the heartbreak was all proving to be too much. She stared at the marsh, seeing the naked fae freed from spell work and the shining metal of Wimleigh soldiers. Lachlan's strawberry blond hair shone in the distance, growing redder with the late day sunshine coming through thinning clouds in the west. Her mind swept outward, rushing backward with hurried steps as she recalled the moment before she lost contact with Caitriona and fell from the sky. Before they flew together, and before even that to when she took Caitriona's bag and put it on her back.

"Wait." Ailith wept, turning on her heel and stumbling to Greer's side. She pulled Caitriona's bag from her shoulders, dripping wet and pouring water as she dumped the contents on the ground. "Your mother gave Cait medicine, all sorts of medicine. Maybe something—"

She pulled free a collection of vials with black sap, holding one aloft as she dug through the bag for healing vials like what she took in the mountains. Greer lifted her face. Her brown eyes taking in what Ailith held and her body froze.

CHAPTER THIRTY-FIVE

Caitriona lay dead before her for the second time in her life. Her little sister, her pride and heartbreak, broken on the ground. And the damned sap found its way back to her hand.

"The sap, I need the sap." She held her hand out while simultaneously lunging toward Ailith and snatching the dark vials, not giving the guard the opportunity to pass it over.

Ailith handed Greer the sap without a fight, but studied the vials as they passed hands, her brow wrinkled in confusion. "What is that?"

"It's life and death in a jar." Pulling the cork from the vial with her teeth, Greer crept to Caitriona's still form.

She had just moments of a familiar, dizzying dance with Barden as they fought together. Moments to cherish seeing him again while they slaughtered Malcolm's men and defended Lachlan's right. Her forces went from the fringe of loss to gain so rapidly as the dukes and Avorkazian guards came to their aid. She felt alive for the first time in weeks as her blood rushed through her veins and sweat spread over her brow. She relished as her back met Barden's while they fought together, grinned as he helped her push forward, and felt almost, so close, to normal.

He was there, solid, whole, and a force of strength Greer had assumed she imagined in the weeks since she lost him. He was there to help her. He had survived the change. He lived.

Then she turned on her heel and Barden was gone, somewhere in the marsh waters again. The rest of the dukes too. The battle was done and they simply ... left. Departed the earth for their watery home without another word. *He* left her without a wave, without a touch, not even a goodbye. He could have pulled her heart from her chest and it would have hurt all the same. Now Caitriona lay unmoving, causing Greer to realize that there was such a thing as worse pain, and she wouldn't be fearful of the sap any longer.

"I won't lose you, too." Greer plunged the vial into the dragon's large, open mouth.

Ailith stood beside her, wearily watching the fallen dragon as the black sap drained over Caitriona's tongue. The guard was vibrating with energy. Shifting from foot to foot, rocking, and twisting her hands together with worry as she watched Greer pour the sap. It coated the creases between Caitriona's fanged teeth and her pale gums; it sunk into the flesh and brought back a pinker tone to Caitriona's mouth. The blood from her shoulder wound slowed; the bone that showed through disappeared over rapidly returning muscle and flesh.

Caitriona's body slumped and settled further into the earth. Her head rolled, her long neck straightened, and the dangerous bump of broken bone lessened. Gradually she shrank in size. Smaller and smaller as the shoulder wound clotted, scales on her body fell, and the draconic features melted away to expose human skin and golden hair.

Caitriona lay naked in the weeds, the bite to her shoulder a healed wound, and her chest motionless. Ailith lifted a soaked cloak from Caitriona's bag. Together they draped the wet fabric over her.

"Cait," Ailith called, kneeling to brush Caitriona's blond hair back from her pale face. "Cait, please, just breathe. Do something."

They waited, holding their breaths as they stared at Caitriona's body. How long had it taken for the sap to kill Barden? It felt like an eternity but in reality it wasn't that long. Longer than it could have been, as it took time to travel through Barden's body from his shoulder to his heart.

"Give it a moment," Greer cautioned as she circled Caitriona to squat behind her and place her hand on her sister's uninjured shoulder. "Just let it take its time."

The sun pushed further through the cloud cover as night drew near. The clouds overhead flushed a fiery red as their blanket slowly pulled back and slipped to the east. The color of her mother's hair and what Caitriona's used to be cast down upon them. The sunlight burned away clouds bit by bit and slowly filled the marsh with light. As it coated their skin in red, Caitriona twitched. Her eyes fluttered and finally opened wide.

"Oh, thank the Elder Tree," Ailith gasped, lunging forward and grasping Caitriona to her chest. Cautiously, slowly, Caitriona lifted her hands and wrapped her arms around the guard's back.

"What—"

"We nearly lost you." Greer stroked Caitriona's hair as the lovers parted. Her sister sat upright, holding the cloak to her naked body as she looked at Greer.

"Oh." Her eyes grew wide. "Ree, it's you."

Greer threw her arms around Caitriona, hugging her as best she could despite her armor. "I'm sorry, I'm so sorry. How

I acted towards you was wrong. I trust you the most, Cait, and I was so wrong with how I treated you."

"I'm sorry I left," Caitriona began but Greer quickly hushed her.

"It doesn't matter, you don't have to apologize, you aren't in trouble." Greer pulled back smiling.

"Not with her, but you are with me." Ailith grabbed hold of Caitriona to embrace her again, her thin arms tight around Caitriona's shoulders as she wept against Caitriona's chest. "You scared me so badly. Never do that again, you hear?"

Greer smiled, genuine and true, if only for Ailith and Caitriona's happiness.

"Don't do that to me again either," Greer said. "Don't die."

"Ever? That seems unfair," Caitriona replied as she parted from Ailith and wiped her eyes. Their hands still roamed over each other's shoulders. With a twang in her chest, Greer realized they were as drawn to each other as she was to Barden. "Living forever sounds awfully exhausting."

"At the very least, promise me you'll let me die first."

Caitriona smiled. "I'll try my best."

Greer leaned back on her heels and sighed with relief. She pushed off the ground and offered her hand. "Come, the both of you, let's get back to the shore and tend to your wounds."

They held onto one another, all three battle-weary women, as they crossed the marshlands and circled pools of water where ripples stilled. There was no knowing who was worse for wear; each sported unique injuries and moved with aching steps.

Greer nearly didn't search the surface of the water for Barden's face. Nearly. After a few wayward glances and the well of disappointment still placed firmly in her gut, Greer opted to look ahead instead, focusing on the white medical tent as their guide toward safety. It sat on the hillside with crowds before it—those who remained at the encampment cheered for the war being won. Greer searched the crowd for the familiar blaze of her mother's hair as they approached but couldn't pinpoint it.

The sun shining over the Braewick Valley ridge was too bright and blinding, leaving Greer squinting toward the side of the tents where, a few yards away, something glowed.

A trick of the eye, certainly. Nothing truly there beyond the cluster of tents for the guards. But the sun slipped behind the valley ridge, plunging the marshland into shadow while the sky overhead still appeared bright.

And yet, fire remained in the marsh, but it wasn't burning. This fire was soft, gentle, and appeared like it was always there; a broad tree, its black trunk wide and its canopy broad with the brightest red leaves; a tree that previously was not there, now firmly planted with its roots expanding over the earth.

Greer's steps slowed and it drew Caitriona and Ailith to hesitate.

"What's wrong?" Cait asked. Ailith's hand fell to her waist where her sword hung, prepared to jump toward danger despite that she looked like a strong wind could knock her down.

Greer blinked. "There's something different."

Their gazes followed Greer's and the trio stood, staring at the large, red-leafed tree. They inched on, growing closer to firmer land that started a slow rise toward the valley ridge. A small, frazzled-haired form could be seen pushing apart from the crowd and picking her way over the marshland with a bundle in her arms.

"There you all are," Isla sighed, but there was a quiver in her voice she couldn't hide. Ailith and Caitriona looked at Greer. A twinge of discomfort lodged itself in her spine. Isla unfurled the bundle, producing a large robe with sleeves and a tie. "Put this on, child, before you catch your death."

"I already did that," Caitriona said softly, the joke falling flat. She accepted the robe from Isla as Ailith helped Caitriona dress.

"Malcolm hurt Caitriona and the fall killed her," Ailith murmured, avoiding eye contact with Isla as she spoke. "There was some sap in Caitriona's bag. Greer gave it to her."

Isla looked at Greer with gentle surprise and something like pride. Her emotions welled in her throat and Greer attempted to swallow them. "It was sap my mother packed."

Isla shifted on her feet and looked to the ground; her discomfort clear as Greer narrowed her gaze.

"Isla," Greer's voice was hard and void of emotion. "Where's our mother?"

Isla's movements stilled and she didn't raise her gaze. "There was a curse on the land, it prevented the dukes from rising."

"Where's my mother, Isla," Greer repeated.

"To break the curse, a sacrifice had to be made. Your mother ..." Isla's voice drifted. Ailith stared at the old woman while Caitriona's attention shifted to the large, red-leafed tree. Her body inched closer to Greer's. Greer reached for her little sister's hand and held it tightly, just as she did when they were young and their parents argued. She felt like a child waking from a nightmare and unable to shake her fright. This wasn't good.

"Kayl came here," Isla continued, drawing the gaze of all three women.

"What?" Greer hissed.

Ailith's shoulders slumped. "He said he was going to get away from the mountains so Malcolm couldn't use the last of his powers."

"He *said*?" Greer repeated, turning towards Ailith.

"The dukes were unable to fight due to the curse on the land and the battle was vastly uneven," Isla continued.

"Without their aid, your forces would have failed. To release them, a sacrifice was necessary, and it was done by Róisín, but she didn't act alone. Kayl was with her. He was in her body."

"He made her do this?" Greer asked.

Isla shook her head. "No, she welcomed him to take nest in her soul and remain alive through her energy. When it came time to sacrifice herself, she struggled at first as her body became that tree. She had power but not enough to push herself through the change. It was the last bit of Kayl's power that allowed it to happen. He guided her through the final stages to push her over the edge to obtain her desire. Without him, you all would likely be dead."

Greer stared at the tree as her mind untethered from the earth again by the staggering loss. "Just as Mother began to regain power and autonomy she let it all go."

"But not really," Caitriona replied, and her grasp pulled Greer back to the earth. The heat of her hand radiated through Greer's gloves and returned her to her senses. "Because this was her decision. Her choice. She wanted to do this and so she did."

Isla inched forward, her hands out to clasp both Gablaigh daughters on their shoulders. "She wanted to save you both. Her children were her life and what life would she have without either of you? She had the makings of this power from before you were born, but she was always meandering, her soul couldn't find focus until she had you. Her power was exhibited when the dragon attacked and killed Caitriona the first time. And it was exhibited again with Malcolm harming you once more. Twice killed by a dragon, twice saved by the passion of your mother, and the love Kayl had for her. Now they're forever entwined."

Caitriona moved forward, tugging Greer's hand to encourage her to draw closer to the shore and the massive tree. The drifting branches and its hanging leaves stirred in the low breeze as if the tree itself wanted to reach forward and wipe their tears. Greer took in a shaking breath, her hand clutching Caitriona's all the while as she caught the scent of the tree bark and its leaves. Beneath the tree, in the grass, violets and eyebright flowers bloomed.

EPILOGUE

CAITRIONA

Two Months Later

The carriage slowed to a stop and thrust Caitriona forward. She laid a hand on Ailith's shoulder, keeping her from falling off the seat beside her. Caitriona stroked the guard's hair reassuringly as the guard's eyes fluttered open to the waking world. She turned her face from where it rested upon Caitriona's lap and looked at her. "We're here?"

Caitriona's fingers drifted down Ailith's brown hair, tracing the lines of white streaks that were a permanent mark from her time in Invarlwen underneath Lumia's terror. "It seems so."

Ailith sat up and Caitriona begrudgingly allowed it. She'd rather stay here just as they were, in peace together in the carriage, entwined as they often were since the Marsh Battle ended. Through the horrors endured, they found one another to be a presence of comfort, a stationary thing to remind them the war was over and they were okay.

More or less.

"Are you ready to go?" Ailith pulled back the curtain and peeked out before looking over her shoulder at Caitriona. She frowned. "I know this is a lot. We can stay in here for a bit if you'd like. There's no schedule of what we're to do here."

Even following a war there were still expectations, appearances to keep, traditions to follow, and activities to attend: vigils, visiting families of those lost, overseeing funeral after funeral. It all left Caitriona exhausted in a type of bone-weary way that sleep did not allow recovery from. They were stuck in a series of expectations and while following a schedule was almost nice—it took away thinking—it also made this visit odd. This was the first time she was free to do what she wanted, although within the confines of the two hours they had to be in this place. It was strange. The freedom from the confines of details allowed the weight of grief to slip in. She reminded herself regularly that it had only been two months since she woke in the marsh. That wasn't much time to recover from all she lost, nor process what happened.

While the fae forced to become creatures were released from the spells thanks to Róisín's sacrifice, Fiana—who survived the battle—did not return to her human form until Lachlan lent his aid. Fiana still had lasting attributes from her concoction that even Lachlan struggled to get rid of. Her hair was filled with black feathers, her eyes too large and owl-like. She was frightening to behold for those who were inexperienced with magical creatures.

"Honestly," Fiana said with a laugh as she studied herself in a looking glass following another session of Lachlan unsuccessfully attempting to force the magical changes off her. "This should be a benefit in the Northern Wood."

"You're still going back to that then?" Ailith had asked.

"I miss my home," Fiana explained. "I miss my fellow hunters; they're family. But I think I'll adjust my work methods. I'll escort helpless travelers like yourselves. I won't hunt the creatures anymore. After being one, it feels wrong to hunt them."

She left shortly after, barely recovering in Braewick for a week but accepting potions from Lachlan all the same. From the mountains, they received word from Raum and Ceenear that they survived as well. The battle raged there too, but with more hand-to-hand combat that quickly completed. The castle staff rose to fight Malcolm's remaining supporters. Guards of the mist, led by Briar and her little dog Berry—who both seemed oddly familiar to Caitriona in a way she could not put her finger on—joined as well, and Malcolm's followers and those cursed were quickly overwhelmed.

The moment Malcolm was dead and Lachlan made king, the mist of Invarlwen changed and no longer attacked those who left. Ceenear was rapidly named the keeper of Ulla Syrmin's peak. After recovering in the valley, Lachlan departed for his kingdom with the fae who once worked alongside his mother and Niveem. Letters tied to Crowley's ankle detailed that Lachlan was getting his bearings and planned to have his crowning the following year. The priority for the moment was to settle his kingdom and return it to normal, something Greer said she understood poignantly and wrote to Lachlan regularly about.

It was hard, Caitriona knew as she worked beside Greer. Her position as heir felt true as she attended meetings with Greer and even welcomed Jace Hergrew, steward of Avorkaz, to the castle's doors after battle. She orchestrated a peace treaty between the Mazgate Dominion and Wimleigh Queendom; her first official act as heir beyond the disastrous Day of Grievances earlier that summer. But peace prevailed after Jace led his forces to the marsh and fought alongside Greer's own.

Had they not arrived to fight, Wimleigh would have lost so many more lives.

All in all, things were calming and a new normal formed.

"Come along, girls," Isla's rough voice called from outside the carriage. She hit the door with her cane, a solid *wack-wack-wack* that jolted Caitriona from her thoughts.

Ailith looked at Caitriona, sleepy eyes still present. "I suppose it's time."

Breathing deeply, Caitriona sought Ailith's hand and squeezed it tight. "Alright. Let's go."

Beyond the carriage were the russet tones of deep autumn. The tall grasses were gold and stiff. Shades of brown grew more forceful in the land and the water of the marsh took a darker hue as the occasional colored leaf found its way from the sloping hill of the valley to its surface.

Few purple and gold flowers bloomed, lending brightness in a world that rushed toward the burnt embers of the dying season, and what bees remained greedily gathered the last of the pollen before winter descended. It was a beautiful tapestry of richness paired against the blue sky.

The dukes, since their battle, were silent. They returned to their nightly watch with glowing eyes but no longer screamed cries of future battles, and they had no reason to rise.

Arriving as the sun warmed Caitriona's skin, she looked at the expanse of the marshland. Two times in her life she was killed in an event tied to a dragon. How much luck did she have left? When would it run out? She thought of Lumia; the fae woman was certain Caitriona would outlive everyone in her life, in particular Ailith, and be alone forever. After her most recent encounter with death, she was certain that even if she did live longer, even if she was separated from Ailith, she'd find her again.

She didn't tell anyone that it wasn't a simple blank space after she fell to the ground. When she died, she felt as if she lived. She had flown upward and greeted the blinding light of the sun above the clouds. She had soared through the air, her body free from pain and discomfort, until she heard her mother's voice.

"Caitriona, little lark, go home," she called on the wind. *"Return to them. It isn't time yet. Go home; you have so much more life left in you."*

She had paused in the air, looked for her mother in the sky, and when she blinked she was reborn in the field; waking and covered in her own blood and little else. She still saw that glorious light above the clouds in her dreams, but she was abundantly glad to be on the ground for the time being.

Now returned to the marsh, Ailith pulled her hand and nuzzled her nose against Caitriona's cheek as her other hand ran through Caitriona's hair.

Other things changed since the battle as well. Her personal acceptance of her dragon half opened a fountain of power. Caitriona changed at will, partially or fully, and without pain. But more than that, she could remove the horns from her head and return to having the rounded skull she was used to.

Not always, because she grew to love them as well. Sometimes she allowed their release, but they were a bit of a pain in a carriage and tended to scratch the ceiling. No, today she appeared the most like herself. Human-like—beside golden hair and eyes, and the glint of scales on her shoulders.

"Do you have your ribbons?" Ailith asked as she dug into her pocket and withdrew her own. Ailith's ribbon was simple and understated, and would blend into the tree more. A deep red ribbon Ailith picked from her mother's collection before they left that morning.

"Yes." Caitriona slipped her hand into her skirt to pull free a yellow ribbon with stitchwork in golden thread. She looked at the carriage ahead of them where Isla waited as Greer stepped out.

Her sister looked older now, lines etched between her brow from her constant frown and concentration. She was not yet thirty, but the weight of the war and loss held firm to her, aging her in the span of a summer as it did to the best of leaders.

While Barden rose with the dukes and fought alongside her, his disappearance into the marsh hadn't fully healed Greer's missing for him, but it did help. She finally slept, true and restful sleep, and a little bit of herself returned.

Caitriona remembered her promise to stick around as long as she could, and she'd do just that, because that was what her sister deserved. They both lost so much, the pain was relentless, but Greer lost most of all.

"I wish I could make this easier for her," Ailith sighed.

"Just being here is enough."

They moved forward, joining Greer who gave a half smile. "Do you have your ribbons?"

They held theirs up and Greer opened her fist to expose a mossy green ribbon of her own. She lowered her gaze and rubbed her thumb over the softness of it before reaching for Caitriona.

Ailith let Caitriona go and stepped back, giving space for the sisters to walk hand in hand through the tall grasses that swayed in the gentle drifting air as if bowing to the royalty before them.

"I'll stay back here," Isla proclaimed as they passed her by. "Give you both time together."

"No Isla, you should come with us," Greer said as they paused their forward movement. "You have a right to be there."

The old woman shook her head and smiled. "Take your moment. Ailith and I will follow."

A rustle of feathers drew Caitriona's gaze upward as

Crowley flew to the tree and disappeared into its branches. The new Elder Tree, birthed the day of the Marsh Battle, stood between the roadway to the outpost and Umberfend Marsh. The base of the tree was a tangle of wild roots, spreading like an uneven carpet amidst the grasses with eyebright flowers growing in the dirt. Its bark was black and brown, the darkest Caitriona ever saw, but the canopy of leaves overhead was vibrantly red. The tree's canopy was so large, it shaded both the roadway and a pool of the marsh, and they were already beneath its shade while still having yards to reach the tree base.

It was bigger than the Braewick Elder Tree, and just as important. For the last few weeks, it stood guarded from worshippers by Greer's decree. She didn't want anyone to draw too near because she wasn't sure what to make of it herself. She worked with Caitriona and they determined it was best to accept its presence and allow worship—once they visited.

"Do you think she's happy here?" Caitriona asked as she gazed into the canopy while Crowley hopped from branch to branch.

"It was a sacrifice; are any sacrifices happy?" Greer stopped before the trunk.

This close, the wood wasn't as dark. Lighter veins were covered in light green moss which entwined with the dark wood like a braid, twisting over each other as the tree grew up and out.

"Maybe not for us, but she got what she wanted in the end." Caitriona pressed her hands against the trunk where light and dark wood twisted. She missed her mother; she missed the woman she was beginning to know. She had so many questions that were left unanswered, so much of Róisín's life that she never learned about. She witnessed the winks of what Róisín once was through the dreams at

Caermythlin, and it was painful to think the queen mother was able to finally become that again but for so short awhile.

"I wanted to learn from you," Caitriona whispered. "I wanted to know you all the better."

"I wanted to love you." Greer said as she touched the bark of the tree. "Your loss made me realize I always did; I just didn't realize how deeply until you were gone. I wish I could express that to you now, and show you just how much you meant to me."

"You both were destined to miss out," Isla said as she came up. "Greer, you're most like your mother: being unable to express your emotions for the betterment of others. It's all an act, these positions of power. She acted unbothered and removed to protect you, to allow you the best chance to succeed. But she loved you deeply."

"I understand now." Greer ran her hand up the bark and looked into the red leafed branches. "I've learned it too late."

"That didn't bother her." Isla settled amidst one of the roots jutting from the ground. "Your life was all that mattered. Your survival. Don't regret what can't be undone. Appreciate what you had. Love what she gave you."

A bird called from somewhere in the marsh, a hushed sound that was sweet on the autumn air. The sisters circled the tree, inspecting the roots and nooks, discussing the health of the limbs, and that when a red leaf fell, a new one appeared ready to birth from the branches shortly after.

"Do you really think we can leave wishes?" Ailith asked as she sat beside Isla on a bulging root. "Would that offend Róisín?"

"She was a woman made of wishes. Her core was created by the intention of the future," Isla murmured. "From the first time I met her, she desired to change things. If nothing else, besides the happiness of her daughters, granting wishes would be her pleasure."

"Then we should start." Caitriona clutched her golden ribbon. "The first wishes of the tree. Greer, you go first."

Greer shook her head and stepped away. "No, not me. Isla, you were with her in the end. You offered to be the one to sacrifice. You should do it."

"Greer—" Isla began but paused when the queen held up her hand. "Alright, but someone fetch me a branch. I surely can't reach any of them."

She tied her ribbon—black like Crowley's feathers—to a branch Ailith pulled down. All stood still while Ailith released the branch and it rose back to its place.

"Ailith, your turn," Greer decreed.

Hesitation was clear in Ailith's eyes, but she nodded and sought a spot. Rubbing her thumbs over her ribbon, she licked her lips as she jumped to grab hold of a branch. In silence, she knotted the ribbon. When she let go of the branch, the red ribbon immediately blended into the canopy overhead, seemingly vanishing entirely.

"Caitriona, can we tie our ribbons at the same time?" Greer requested. Caitriona turned toward her sister and paused. Greer's brown eyes were awash with tears and in her hands, she clutched the moss-green ribbon with shaking fingers.

"Of course," Caitriona embraced Greer first. Pressing her lips against Greer's ears, she whispered, "Are you okay?"

Greer sighed, but there was a catch in the sound of the weariness the last year had given her. "I just wish things were different and this wasn't such a lonesome affair."

"I know." Caitriona kissed her sister's cheek. "Do you have your wish ready?"

Greer nodded, wiping tears with her hand and catching them with the ends of the ribbon. The tears bled into it, making the moss green darken in spots.

"Together then?"

"Together," Greer replied.

They sought a perfect branch that split in two. A place for each of their ribbons, each of their wishes, to be given to their mother. Was it too much to ask for wishes after their mother already gave herself in body and soul? Róisín grew them in her belly, birthed them to the world, fought for them, cared for them, loved and died for them. Was it too much to demand more?

Caitriona had to agree, her mother always had her eyes on the future and making wishes—if she was capable of doing such in her immortal, natural form—it made sense she would continue. But she still hesitated before tying the ribbon.

What could she wish for that she didn't already have? She had Ailith who was healing from battle trauma and discussing taking a new role of teaching upcoming guards about magical creatures. She had Isla who just that week agreed to take a room in Braewick's castle where she could spend the winter months teaching Caitriona about magic. She had her own magic, a thing she never thought she would possess, and it grew in power as she learned how to properly wield it. She had her sister who was alive, if a little broken. Her sister who lost so much, who stood alone, and was due her own happiness.

Caitriona studied Greer who worked to tie her ribbon on the branch, her bottom lip bit between her teeth, then turned back to her own. Caitriona lifted the ribbon to her mouth and gave it a kiss.

Let Greer find happiness, she wished. *Let her find joy again. Let her find love and receive all she deserves. I wish she's allowed a chance to rest with contentment. She's lost so much; she deserves more in return.*

Tying the ribbon to the tree as a bow and freeing it, she watched it lift upward with Greer's green ribbon beside it. They were silent, even marsh birds were silent, and all remained with their wishes as the breeze moved the ribbons overhead.

Slowly the marsh's chorus of sounds returned; the lapping of water along the bank and twitter of birds and buzz of bees. Greer stepped closer to Caitriona and slipped her arm around Caitriona's waist before burying her face into her shoulder where she wept. Caitriona held her sister, running her fingers through Greer's long hair as she released all she carried.

The marsh water nearby rippled audibly against the shore and there was an intake of breath as Ailith stood in a flash of rapid movement. Caitriona raised an eyebrow with question as Ailith gazed at the water of the marsh, her eyes locked on something.

"Well, I'll be," Isla breathed and placed her hand against her chest.

Caitriona followed their line of vision and gasped. "Greer, Greer look up."

She pushed Greer toward the water, not allowing her sister the opportunity to actually look on her own. Greer wiped her eyes and froze.

In the water were faces in the sun. Green, gray, blue, and brown-skinned dukes watched from their watery home despite the daytime hours. Their wet hair lay plastered to their heads as they remained silent observers, withholding their slurps and clicks that often accompanied their movements. Feet away, on the edge of the marsh, a figure stood in the mud and weeds. A body with skin no longer covered in the web of Elder Tree sap, lips pink with the flush of life and eyes that shown blue—as blue as the sky.

"Barden?" Greer's voice croaked. The figure looked around himself, his brow wrinkled with confusion and his lips parted with disbelief. He lifted his gaze, his eyes clear of muck and death as they fell upon Greer.

His lip curved, a shadow of a smile as he stepped onto the

shore. His footstep unlocked Greer, sending her into motion. She rushed forward, leaping over the web of roots to collide with Barden, her arms wrapping tightly around him as they nearly lost their footing. He stumbled backward, catching her against his chest as his feet splashed in to the water's edge. He laughed and the sound bounced across the heavy canopy of the red-leafed tree.

"Greer?" His voice was whole and strong and his. He held her face in his hands, grinning as he pressed his nose against hers. "I've been trying to get to you. I've searched for you, my sun."

He lifted her off her feet as she wept, spinning on the edge of the marsh with her in his arms and releasing sparkling drops of marsh water from the tips of her boots. His laughter cut off by Greer's lips as she held his face still with both hands to his jaw. They stilled, kissing each other with the hunger of long-lost lovers as her feet slowly returned to the ground.

Ailith stumbled over the tree's roots and caught Caitriona's hand, pulling her close and wrapping her arms around Caitriona's waist. Her lips found the curve of Caitriona's jaw, a quick peck, and she grinned. "I guess your mother *is* interested in granting wishes."

Caitriona relaxed in Ailith's embrace. "You too? You wished for this?"

"I suspect we all did," Isla replied and stepped beside the pair with a toothy grin.

Sacrifice in the name of love, for love, pushed them into the rush of life. Love for themselves, love for one another, all left to live on forever under the boughs of the crimson-leafed Elder Tree.

Within the marsh a final gift is offered.
Bequeathed in faded memories of both tree and creature;
there is a wish in the air that desires time better spent.
It is caught on the ears of the leaves,
stilling their dance from phantom wind to listen intently.
Sap rushes through the heart of the tree,
where red and black concentric rings loop,
and past where once was muscle,
where bark was supple flesh, and where two souls entwined.
Is it too much to request more from that who gave all?
Never.
Never when for love.

ACKNOWLEDGMENTS

Vanquished is a novel of love and grief, and the persistent bond the two share. When I sat down to write *Vanquished*, I didn't think it would be a story like this, but that's what it became. Through writing, I met many griefs head on and realized how deeply love persists and expands within that place.

I'm not unfamiliar with grief and have lost many friends and family who I love with all my heart even as they're gone. Grief's such a substantial thing that we experience, yet it's so often brushed aside and spoken of in hushed tones. I feel this often makes us wonder how normal we are to hurt so deeply when we lose someone, and I hope this book will be a comfort to those who are hurting. But there is not grief unless there was first and foremost, love, which persists and transcends. What a powerful thing it is to love and be loved.

First and foremost, I want to thank my grandma and grandpa (Barbara and Anthony) who taught me love and grief with time. You showed me that love is a choice and were my first true grief. I also want to take this space to remember Jasmine and Cathy, two girls who died far too young and I carry their memory with me.

I want to thank Jean and Staci who wanted this book sight unseen. They had faith in me and the story before it was even close to being readable. I'm also thankful to my creative team as always: Michelle and Dewi for their detailed interior artwork; Diana for the wonderful third cover design; and

Luxury Banshee, who's drawn all of my characters since before *The Elder Tree Trilogy* was a reality.

My beta readers of this final book, who were willing to read despite the emotional trauma-I did to them with book two, I thank you. Ali, Meredith, Christine, Taylor and Josie. You've been such champions this entire time.

For my elementals who sat with me as I wrote and rewrote the first chapter of this book while at our writing retreat: thank you for encouraging me and leading me through this heavy book. The secret "beak" club for the laughter and bright spot of community while so far apart. And the 2025 small press sluts for hijinks and togetherness.

Lastly, I want to thank my amazing family who have supported me from the start of my writing, straight through publication and beyond. My parents, the very first fans I had. My spouse, Bruce, who is my best friend (you had me at Huzzah). And last but never the least: to my baby boy, my love for you knows no bounds, whether I am here on this earth or part of the stars, you fill my heart with the light of a thousand suns. I would definitely turn into a tree for you.

ABOUT THE AUTHOR

Erica Rose Eberhart grew up in the Catskills and spent many formative years in both Eastern Pennsylvania and Northern Virginia. She now resides with her family and cat in the Finger Lakes region of New York. A technical editor by trade, she has a master's degree in English and Creative Writing. Erica has written stories since she was able to write sentences and has found comfort in fantasy her entire life, whether by consuming fantastical stories or creating her own. Beside the comfort of books, Erica adores nature walks, crocheting, embroidery, cats, baking and autumn. Her debut novel, *Tarnished*, released in 2025. The Elder Tree Triology is her first published series.

Visit us online:
creativejamesmedia.com

@creativejamesmedia   @creativejamesm1   @creativejamesmedia   @creativejamesmedia